WORLD SERPENT ARCANIST

FRITH CHRONICLES #5

SHAMI STOVALL

CONTENTS

Published by
CS BOOKS, LLC

This is a work of fiction. Names, characters, places, and incidents either are the product of author imagination or are used fictitiously, and any resemblance to actual persons, living or dead, business establishments, events, or locales, is entirely fictional.

Cover Design: Darko Paganus

Editors:

IF YOU WANT TO BE NOTIFIED WHEN SHAMI STOVALL'S NEXT BOOK RELEASES, PLEASE VISIT HER WEBSITE OR CONTACT HER DIRECTLY AT s.adelle.s@gmail.com

ISBN: 978-1-7334428-3-1

ACKNOWLEDGMENTS

To John, who never stopped believing.
To Beka, my sister.
To Gail and Big John, my family.
To Ann, my friend through thick and thin.
To Brian Wiggins, for giving a voice to the characters.
To Tiffany, Mary, & Dana, for all the jokes and input.
To my Facebook group, for naming the world serpent.
To Steven Carlton, for the many creative thinking sessions.
And finally, to everyone unnamed, thank you for everything.

ATTEMPTING TO SLEEP

The creaking of the airship kept me awake.

That wasn't entirely true. I never would've been able to sleep, even if I had been wrapped in perfect silence. Yesterday, I had been fighting for my life. It almost felt surreal to be back on the *Sun Chaser*, an airship I considered to be a second home. If someone had told me I was dreaming, I would have probably believed them.

The fighting yesterday had been so *real*.

I could see the Excavation Site clearly in my mind's eye. Tucked away in the woods beyond the Lightning Straits, where the trees had white trunks and gray leaves, there had been a pit filled with black bones. That location had been the heart of operations for our greatest enemies—the Second Ascension—and the bones they had been gathering belonged to an apocalyptic dragon.

Somehow, despite all odds, I had made it out alive.

I tossed in my hammock, chuckling to myself.

"My arcanist?" came a voice from the shadows.

My magic allowed me to see through the thickest of darkness, and although it was the middle of the night, I had no trouble glancing around my tiny room. My hammock hung in the corner, and barrels with iron rings filled the rest of the space. A single porthole allowed me to peer outside. Clouds whipped by, preventing me from seeing the land and sea below.

Although I didn't spot anyone else in the room, I knew I wasn't alone. Luthair, a knightmare, was capable of hiding in the shadows. He blended with the darkness so perfectly, he might as well have been invisible.

"Luthair?" I asked.

"You seem preoccupied." He spoke from the shadows under me, and his voice had the low rumble of a grizzled veteran. While it spooked some, I had come to enjoy it.

"I'm just thinking about yesterday," I muttered. "The Second Ascension, the apoch dragon—our fight. It's almost too much to take in."

"Do you regret fighting?"

"No," I said without hesitation. "I just haven't had a lot of time to reflect on it all."

"I believe that's why Master Zelfree insisted you have a room to yourself." The shadows in the room shook for a moment, but then they settled into their natural places, only disturbed for half a second. "You should stay here as long as you need to recover."

"I'm no longer injured." Despite my many previous injuries, I felt fine. Arcanists had the ability to recover, as long as a wound wasn't fatal. "I don't think I *need* a room all to myself."

"Mental exhaustion is still a form of exhaustion."

My thoughts jumped to something important, and I sat up straight, my heart hammering against my chest. "Luthair. We need to tell Master Zelfree about the bones of the apoch dragon. I... well, *we* smashed the Excavation Site, but that doesn't mean the Second Ascension won't return and dig it all up again."

"Be calm, my arcanist," Luthair said. "Master Zelfree is aware. He said he would make arrangements with associates. Now isn't the time to fret about future problems—we must keep our eyes on the present."

Luthair's words had a soothing effect. He spoke reason, even when my mind was searching for a million problems to fret about. I rested back on the hammock, forcing myself to take deep breaths. Our enemies were still out in the world, but they hadn't achieved their goals yet. We still had time to thwart them, and that fact alone allowed me to let go of my anxiety.

The creaking of the airship returned to the forefront of my thoughts.

"You still can't sleep," Luthair said.

I exhaled, my gaze locked on the oak wood of the ceiling. "Are Adelgis, Fain, and Karna okay?" They had been the three with me when I had fought the Second Ascension. I had told them to escape while I stayed behind, prepared to die in order to defend them. "I know they're on the airship, but are they *fine*?"

"None of them were injured."

"Can you check on them for me?"

"As you wish, my arcanist."

Luthair slithered from the room, moving as a shadow would. As a knightmare, he was a masters of darkness. Anywhere a sliver of shadow could go, he could go.

Once alone, I closed my eyes and attempted to force myself into slumber. I needed to rest because we had bigger problems to deal with. The Second Ascension had summoned god-creatures into the world, and now we had to stop them from bonding with them—especially with the world serpent. That one creature was powerful beyond measure, and our enemies had already-cowed rulers lined up to relinquish their countries the moment the world serpent arcanist appeared.

If the Second Ascension had the strength of six nations—including the Argo Empire, the largest one around the Shard Sea—what hope would a single arcanist guild have? We would never be able to defeat them.

I gripped my shirt, my breathing shallow.

Luthair was right. Now wasn't the time to dwell on future problems. I shook my head to dispel the thoughts, and focused instead on the immediate. I was tired. It had been a long couple of weeks, and I needed my rest. What could I do to help that along?

For whatever reason, I thought about the others in the Frith Guild. A month ago, I figured I would never see them again. Now they were on the *Sun Chaser*, just a short jog away. That fact comforted me. Illia, Zaxis, Hexa, Atty, and Adelgis—all my fellow apprentices—it felt like forever since we had last seen each other.

I couldn't help but smile.

And before I knew it, I was fast asleep.

When I awoke, it was to pounding on the door. I flew out of my hammock, ice flooding my veins. Standing straight and tense, I tried to remember where I was and how I had gotten here. Once I recalled everything—about the *Sun Chaser*, about being plague-ridden—I ran a shaky hand through my black, disheveled hair.

"Volke?" someone said from beyond the door. "Are you alive? Just say something if you are!"

I glanced to the porthole. Sunlight shone through, brilliant and bright. How long had I been asleep?

"I'm here," I said, my voice rusty. I coughed and rubbed at my throat. It felt like I hadn't spoken aloud in years. "Is everything okay?"

"Yes," the person replied. The feminine tone was familiar, but I couldn't place it while I remained groggy.

"I'll be out in a minute."

"That's good. We have food ready for you. We made you breakfast, lunch, and dinner for the past two days, just in case you woke up, and we've saved what we could from all of that. Hopefully you're hungry!"

Two days? I had been sleeping for two days?

My back *did* feel sore. I had to twist and rotate just to loosen up.

"Master Zelfree wants to speak with you," the woman said. "So, once you've eaten, you should go see him."

"Okay," I replied as I straightened my shirt and grabbed my belt off the floor.

For years, I had worn the clothes of a sailor—coat, trousers, high boots, button-up shirt—and the moment I was fully dressed, I felt whole again. My weapon, a long sword in its scabbard, sat on top of a nearby barrel. I secured it to my leather belt and exhaled. While my clothing made me feel complete, the sword brought with it a sense of security.

I touched the hilt. On the blade was the word RETRIBUTION. It was the name of my weapon, one forged by my father.

"My arcanist," Luthair said from the darkness in the corner of the tiny room. "Adelgis, Fain, and Karna have never been better. They anxiously await to see you again."

I pinched the bridge of my nose. "Have you been waiting two days to give me that message?" I asked.

"Knightmares don't sleep," Luthair said. "I had plenty of time to observe them, question them, and even mingle with them before returning to you."

At least he hadn't just been sitting around.

Once my boots were laced, I headed for the door. "Let's go, Luthair. I can't wait any longer to see the others."

2

JOURNEYMAN ARCANIST

Wind whipped across the deck of the *Sun Chaser*. Black storm clouds hung in the distance, perhaps a mile away. They swirled around the Surgestone Mountains that made up either side of the Lightning Straits, creating a perpetual storm. Thunder rolled across the sky, filling the area with a low rumble.

I ate my biscuit and jerky as I headed for the quarterdeck. Master Zelfree stood at the stern of the ship, conversing with Captain Devlin, the roc arcanist who owned the *Sun Chaser*.

Where were the others?

I glanced around, hoping to spot someone from the Frith Guild, but all I saw was the crew of the airship. Unlike most ships I had been on, the deckhands for the *Sun Chaser* were mostly women. Karna, the quartermaster, had gone out of her way to help those who had nowhere to go, especially people who had come from terrible situations. They all seemed happy to work on the airship—and even happier to see me. Each crewmember waved when I glanced over. I hesitantly waved back.

Once finished with my food, I clapped my hands together to clear the crumbs and then ascended the stairs of the quarterdeck.

"That's not how I normally operate," Captain Devlin said, obviously in the middle of a conversation.

He had a stern and gruff voice that matched his hard expression. Although I didn't know the man well, from what I had seen of Captain Devlin, he wasn't an angry man. On the contrary—he had always been quite reasonable. What were they arguing about?

"The Frith Guild could use a man of your talents," Master Zelfree said. "Your whole crew, actually."

"No one here likes workin' for the guilds. They have harsh rules, and some of our crew members don't fit into a rigid hierarchy."

"Did you not hear a word I said?" Master Zelfree crossed his arms. "This isn't a normal proposition to join a guild. The whole damn world is about to change. God-creatures are among us. If the wrong people get their hands on them, you might not be able to sail the skies anymore, don't you understand? We need your help."

Their conversation was iced over by an uncomfortable silence.

Standing next to each other, Captain Devlin and Zelfree seemed similar. They were both men of the seas—or the skies, in Devlin's case. They wore loose shirts, sailing trousers, high boots, and thick coats. Zelfree wore black, whereas Devlin had bright reds and vibrant browns, but it was clear the style was the same.

They looked as though they could be friends, had their discussion not turned sour.

"I'll think about it," Captain Devlin finally said. He stroked his chinstrap beard, his eyes narrowed. "But I'll have to speak with my officers before I come to a decision."

Zelfree replied with a short exhale. "Fine."

With that, Captain Devlin turned on his heel. When he spotted me, his eyes went wide—and then immediately to the arcanist mark on my forehead. Devlin's mark was a seven-point star with a large bird behind it —a roc, his bonded mystical creature, his eldrin.

I rubbed at my own forehead. My star was interwoven with a sword and a cape, as I had bonded with a knightmare. And unlike most arcanists, whose mark was nothing more than an etching in the skin, my mark glowed a soft white, indicating my eldrin had achieved its *true form*.

Not many arcanists had a true form of their eldrin.

"You're awake," Captain Devlin said to me. "Nice to see you in the land of the living, lad."

"Thank you," I replied.

He walked by and patted me on the shoulder with a firm strike. "Karna and Jozé would've been mighty upset if something had happened to you. Keep that in mind for me, will ya? If they're upset, *I'm* upset."

The captain kept his curly hair shoulder-length, despite the winds, but he kept most of it tamed with a bandana and a tricorn hat. He reminded me of classic swashbucklers, which I had always admired. A small part of me liked the man just because of those details.

"I'll try not to get myself into trouble," I said.

"Good. Because Karna told me all about your little *adventure* on the ground. Fighting plague-ridden arcanists? Are you touched in the head?"

"Someone has to do it," I said, no hesitation in my voice. "Or else everyone will suffer that terrible curse."

My words hung between us. Captain Devlin had no response, his expression hardening right back to the same cold look he had given Zelfree. He grumbled something as he headed down the stairs of the quarterdeck, his footsteps heavy. I hoped he would consider Master Zelfree's offer to join the Frith Guild. We really would need all the help we could get to fight the Second Ascension.

"Volke," Zelfree said as I approached. "I'm glad you've come."

"Is everything okay?"

"Depends on what you mean by *okay*. I want to know what happened at the Excavation Site. Karna, Fain, and Adelgis told me their side of things, but you were in the thick of it."

"I destroyed the Excavation Site," I said as I rubbed the back of my neck. "Because they were digging up the bones of the apoch dragon. But burying the site won't stop them. If they want to get that dragon again, they can."

Master Zelfree, my mentor for the last two years, always had a clever intelligence to his gaze. He mulled over my comments before forcing a smirk. "There're always a million problems, aren't there?"

In an attempt to be positive, I replied, "There wouldn't be adventures without problems, right? We just need to make sure we're ready to handle them."

"Yeah, well, let's hope that your ability to pull victory out of thin air inspires everyone else. Word of your true form eldrin has everyone impressed and working a lot harder." Zelfree half-chuckled. "Even me. I've only known a handful of people who have achieved what you have—and most of them didn't have the obstacles you started with. You were second-bonded to Luthair... I figured you'd never reach the peak of your magic."

The words cut, but I pushed away the doubt. Second-bonded arcanists always had a harder time with their magic—of course Zelfree had figured I'd have problems.

"I'm sorry I doubted you," Zelfree said. "I knew you were talented. I just didn't realize how much."

When I had met Master Zelfree years ago, I had thought he was a drunkard past his prime. Now he reminded me of all those stories I had read about him—he was a cunning arcanist, someone unpredictable, someone who managed to get the upper hand in even the direst of situations. He had taken down hundreds of pirates and fought off dragons in the oceans. He had taken on the Second Ascension long before anyone else had.

Zelfree thought *I* was talented? I almost couldn't believe it.

Wind rushed over the *Sun Chaser* as we neared the Surgestone Mountains. Zelfree's black hair was no longer long and out of control—he had cut it short and shaved the sides, giving him a clean look, even if he still had stubble on his chin.

His arcanist mark was unique, even if it wasn't glowing like mine. He had a star, like all arcanists, but instead of having a picture of his eldrin wrapped around it, he had nothing. That was because he had bonded to a mimic—a strange creature that could shift its shape and resemble almost any other mystical creature in the nearby vicinity.

And that reminded me of something...

"Master Zelfree," I said. "I met the Mother of Shapeshifters."

He lifted an eyebrow. "Is that right?"

"Yes. At the Excavation Site. Theasin Venrover was going to kill it and use its body for trinkets and artifacts. I saved it—but I don't know where it went."

"You needn't worry," Zelfree said. "I'm not sure how Theasin captured it to begin with, but the Mother of Shapeshifters is quite enigmatic. I'm certain the same tricks won't work on it twice."

I nodded along with his words, thankful he thought Theasin wouldn't get his hands on the creature again. After everything I had learned about Adelgis's father, I knew nothing good could come from Theasin tearing apart the Mother of Shapeshifters.

"So," I said as I glanced over the side of the airship. "Where're we headed? What's our plan?" We had so many things to do—a sense of overwhelming urgency gripped at my chest, making it difficult to breathe.

"Guildmaster Eventide is out searching for someone to bond with the world serpent," Master Zelfree said matter-of-factly.

"How will she know when she's found the right person?" I asked. "The world serpent is so powerful and significant... It can't just be someone random."

"Have you heard of Fini Isle?"

The question seemed like a non-sequitur, but I decided to humor him. "I know of it. The arcanists there bond with sibyls—mystical creatures capable of glimpsing into the future."

The island was famous for its prophetic statues and paintings. Gregory Ruma had been gifted with three statues that told his future, but each was vague and difficult to interpret. A sibyl's future sight was limited and often blurry—yet disturbingly accurate. Not always perfect, but damn close.

"Is Guildmaster Eventide heading to Fini Isle so she can ask the sibyl arcanists who will bond with the world serpent?" I asked.

Zelfree nodded.

"That's a great idea," I said. "I never would've thought of that, but it'll eliminate some of the guesswork. I can't wait to hear what she brings back."

After a long exhale, Zelfree said, "I'm not so certain of this plan. What if the sibyl arcanists foresee someone from the Second Ascension bonding with the serpent? What good will future-sight do us then? The whole point is to stop them. Eventide wants us to wait in Fortuna until she returns with the name of the individual who will bond with the serpent, but that just gives our enemies breathing room. And trust me—in a fight, you never want to let your opponent recover."

"But we *need* someone to bond with the world serpent," I said. "It can't just be *anyone*."

All of history would be changed by whoever wielded such power. We couldn't hand that over to the wrong person. That was why trials of worth existed, but the god-creature's trials had already been tampered with when Queen Velleta gathered all the runestones and hoarded them. The trial wasn't fair anymore, so we had to compromise. We had to find someone worthy.

"I tried to convince Guildmaster Eventide that killing the beast was still an option," Zelfree said, his tone neutral, his gaze on the thunderclouds.

"Why would you say that?" I asked. "Those god-creatures are meant to help clear away the arcane plague. They're here to help."

"If someone from the Second Ascension bonds with the world serpent we might be forced to kill it anyway."

I didn't want to consider that. It seemed terrible to come all this way, only to kill the world serpent just because it had bonded with a madman.

Perhaps the world serpent would refuse anyone with a black heart? I hoped so.

Zelfree returned his attention to me. "Listen—our plan of action is to head back to Fortuna and wait for Guildmaster Eventide. Until then, you should focus on recovering. You've been through a lot."

"What about Akiva, the king basilisk arcanist? He's on an assassination mission to kill the guildmaster."

"She can handle herself. And it won't be long until we meet up with her again. You just have to trust that she'll make it back."

Although I hated the thought of *sitting and waiting*, I knew it couldn't be helped. Guildmaster Eventide *was* a talented arcanist. She was the only other one in the Frith Guild with a true form of her eldrin, and she was one of the few who had thwarted the plans of the Second Ascension since they had formed years ago.

I had to believe she would be okay.

"Where is everyone else?" I asked. "Are they relaxing?"

"They're in the hold of the airship. Training."

"Really?"

Zelfree shrugged. "The moment they realized you had obtained a true form of your eldrin, they all decided they had been slacking. They've been working ten times as hard."

I turned to leave, but Zelfree grabbed my shoulder and held me back.

"Wait," he said. "I have something for you." He dug around in his coat pocket and produced a copper guild pendant. Normally they had a person's name, rank, and eldrin stamped into the metal, but this one was blank on one side. The other side had the Frith Guild symbol—a sword and shield.

I took the pendant.

"Congratulations," Zelfree said. "You're now a journeyman arcanist."

I couldn't help but smile as I slipped the pendant over my head. "Are you sure? I thought there was a test to pass first..."

"Yeah, well, you ran off, cured yourself of the arcane plague, and then gained a true form eldrin. Test passed."

"I don't know what to say." I fidgeted with the metal. "Thank you." There had been a point in my life when I had figured I would never see the Frith Guild again. It felt like a terrible burden had been lifted from my shoulders now that I was back with them all.

"The others took their tests and passed," Zelfree said. "And it seems fitting that you should join them. Plus, journeymen arcanists can help train apprentices, under the right circumstances."

"You want me to help with training?"

"Yes." Zelfree dismissively waved his hand at the comment. "But we can talk about that later. For right now, you should go see everyone. Go on."

Still smiling, I stepped into the shadows and shifted down the stairs and onto the deck, moving through the darkness as a sliver of shade. It felt amazing now that my magic didn't hurt anymore. I emerged from the shadows and headed for the stairs below deck.

Journeyman Knightmare Arcanist Volke Savan.

It had a nice ring to it.

3

TOGETHER AGAIN

I entered the hold of the *Sun Chaser* with my breath held. The others were between the crates and barrels, chatting or practicing their magic. They didn't notice me as I quietly descended the steps.

Zaxis leaned against the bulkhead of the ship, the most distinguishable member of the group. He wore crimson scale armor—from a salamander, I suspected—and his pants were a dark brick red, held up by his belt of phoenix tail feathers woven into a vibrant cord. If I had to guess, they were all magical trinkets that resisted fire so he wouldn't burn his clothes when he used his phoenix magic.

Zaxis lit flames in the palms of his hands and then extinguished them a moment later. He had an intense focus—he always had, ever since we had been kids—and he seemed obsessed with lighting the fire faster than the time before.

I caught my breath when I saw Illia standing next to him. She had been my sister since we had been adopted by Gravekeeper William, and I had so much to discuss with her, it almost hurt my chest to keep it all in.

Illia leaned closer to Zaxis. She evoked white flames in her hands, but unlike Zaxis's phoenix fire, her flames didn't burn—they teleported bits of things away, piece by piece.

She wore an eye patch over her right eye. Most eye patches weren't much to look at, but hers had a rizzel stitched across—a cute ferret creature with white-and-silver fur—a gift from Gravekeeper William. The eye patch matched the arcanist mark on her forehead and also resembled the rizzel on her shoulder, Nicholin.

"You don't need to rush your magic," Illia said to Zaxis. "I don't think you're evoking it right."

Zaxis slowed his evocation and allowed the flames to build in his hands before snuffing them out. "I want to improve my reaction time," he muttered. "It still feels slow."

It amused me to see them standing side by side.

Illia was lithe and lean, whereas Zaxis was bulky with muscle. Zaxis had red hair that grew long enough to get into his eyes, but Illia kept her wavy, brown hair tied back in a tight ponytail, held in place by her tricorn cap. Although distinctly different, they moved closer together, comfortable with each other's presence.

Zaxis's eldrin, a phoenix with peacock-like tail feathers, hopped around near his feet. "My arcanist," the phoenix said, his voice regal. "Perhaps you should try manipulating the flames into shapes."

"I'll try that next, Forsythe," Zaxis replied.

I wanted to approach them, to blurt out my whole story and hear what they had been doing for the last few months, but I stopped myself and instead panned my gaze across the rest of the hold.

Hexa and her hydra eldrin, Raisen, stood on the opposite side of the hold. Hydras didn't normally travel far from their homes since their bodies were so rotund and heavy. Raisen captured that stereotype perfectly. He had the fat body of an alligator, complete with stubby legs. His four heads, on the other hand, had snake-like necks and pointed dragon faces. Each head hissed at Hexa the moment she turned her gaze to the porthole overlooking the passing clouds.

"Don't give me that," Hexa said. "We've been workin' all day. It's break time."

"We should practice our poison on the deck of the ship," one head said.

Another head added, "Or maybe we should toss things in the air and shoot them—to better your aim."

Hexa patted the many heads of her hydra, her attention still on the weather. "We'll go up to the deck in a bit."

She wore clothing that was uncommon for island life. Hexa had grown up on the mainland, after all, but it still surprised me whenever I saw her on ships. She wore a coat and shirt with no sleeves, exposing her arms—and the many scars she carried—as though they were points of pride. Her curly, cinnamon hair bounced freely whenever she tilted her head. Most sailors who kept long hair preferred to tie back their locks, but Hexa seemed to dislike that habit.

I spotted Atty and Fain near the back of the hold. They leaned against a stack of crates tied to the floor, their conversation so engrossing that they never glanced in my direction.

Atty swished back her blonde hair, and I was instantly aware of her elegant beauty and poise. I had never truly forgotten, but seeing her now was both a relief and a reminder. I had wasted too much time—I needed to tell her how I felt.

I stared, probably for way too long, if I was being honest, but I couldn't help myself. Atty seemed older—and prettier—and I wondered if I was just imagining things.

"I finally discovered what I can manipulate with my magic," Fain said to Atty, his arms crossed. "Volke and I tried most days we were traveling on the *Sun Chaser*."

I had almost forgotten Fain was in the hold of the airship.

He was taller than Atty by a few inches, though he still wasn't as tall as I was. And while Atty wore a bright white tunic and a pair of white puffy desert pants, Fain wore the outfit of a classic pirate, complete with a heavy coat and tall boots. Fain's most striking features, though, were his frostbitten fingers and the tips of his ears. They stood out, even in the dim lantern light of the hold.

"I want to master every aspect of phoenix magic," Atty said to Fain as she tapped the tips of her fingers together. "And healing has always been my weakest point. If you manipulate flesh and injure someone, perhaps I can stitch it back together?"

Fain laughed once. "There aren't many people who wanna watch their skin get torn apart and then pieced back together. Maybe *Moonbeam* can handle it, but most others can't."

"Uh, I'm sorry. Who... is Moonbeam?" Atty asked, her eyebrows knitted.

"Oh, well, I meant *Adelgis*. Sorry."

"Hm? I wasn't aware he had such a nickname. It's very... unique?"

Atty glanced to the crate next to her and gave her phoenix eldrin, Titania, an odd look. The phoenix shook her head, scattering soot onto the crate and floor. The bodies of the phoenixes burned bright, and whenever the phoenix feathers flared out, I enjoyed catching sight of the flames underneath.

But where was Moonbeam?

Er, *Adelgis*.

Where was Adelgis?

When I spotted him, I almost called out, just to make sure he was okay. He stood in the very back corner, his attention focused solely on the odd creature in his arms. It was Felicity, his eldrin, an ethereal whelk. She was no larger than a human head, but her sea snail body glittered in the lantern light, demanding attention. Tiny tentacles hung from the snail-portion of Felicity's body, and the iridescent sheen across her spiral shell gave her a mystical quality.

Adelgis didn't speak to his eldrin. He just stared, his dark eyes unblinking.

For a long while now, since we had left Thronehold, after the Sovereign Dragon Tournament, Adelgis's behavior had seemed off to me, but this was a new low. He could speak telepathically, and I had no doubt that was what he was doing, but why did he have to practice that in a room filled with people? Surely, he must've known it made him seem odd in comparison.

Despite his deep concentration, Adelgis was the first to look up from his training and notice me.

He could hear thoughts—perhaps he had heard me thinking about him?

Adelgis's shiny black hair, which hung loose to his shoulders, matched his black shirt and dark leather trousers. It seemed he was taking after Master Zelfree when it came to appearances—or perhaps he wanted to blend into the corner of every room he entered, I didn't know.

"Volke," Adelgis said, loud enough for everyone to hear. "You're awake."

All at once, everything went silent, like the calm before a storm.

Hexa was the first to dash over. She collided with me—we both hit the bulkhead—and she wrapped her arms around my neck. She was stronger than I remembered, and when we were up close, I noticed the scars on her arms appeared to be claw markings that had healed in fine fashion.

"Volke! Thank all the good stars!"

I patted her on the back. "Hexa—you saw me board the *Sun Chaser* a couple of days ago. You knew I was okay."

"You've been sleeping *way* too long," she said as she held me at arm's length. She had an intensity to her expression that I hadn't seen before, and I wondered if I had angered her. With narrowed eyes, she continued, "Who does that, huh? Are you okay? Are you sure you don't have any lingering effects of the arcane plague?"

"I don't think so," I said as I rubbed my glowing arcanist mark on my forehead. "Having a true form eldrin protects me from any ill effects of—"

Raisen bounded over, each hop-step creating a loud *slam* on the oak wood of the airship. I probably could've gotten out of the way had I been paying attention. Instead, I was thrown to the floor by the many heads of Hexa's hydra. Raisen's curled and prickly scales stung as he rolled around on top of me, but I gritted my teeth and endured. Why did he always have to knock me over?

"Hey," I said through a chuckle. "Stop that!"

Raisen's four heads hissed as I pushed him off my body and got to my feet. Atty helped me the last of the way, her touch delicate, but strong enough to help. She turned her blue eyes to the scrapes from the hydra scales on the back of my hand. With a simple touch of her fingertips, she used her phoenix magic to heal my minor injuries.

It wasn't necessary, though I did enjoy the warmth of her magic seeping through my skin and deep into my muscles.

"I'm so glad you're feeling better," Atty said. "I worried you might've been sleeping that long because of the medicine from the Grand Apothecary."

I shrugged. "I'm fine. And I'm much better now that we're all together."

Zaxis, Illia, and Adelgis stood close, each hovering around, waiting for me to step away from the bulkhead and join the group. No one else felt the need to tackle me to the floor, for which I was thankful. The two phoenixes created trails of soot as they flapped over to the group, and a smile escaped me. I had always admired phoenixes.

"You need to tell us about your adventure," Atty said. She grabbed my hand and held it close. "Adelgis told us a few things, and Fain elaborated, but no one knows *how* you gained your true form knightmare." She tightened her grip on me and laughed to herself. "I almost couldn't contain my curiosity. I wanted to wake you, just so you could tell us."

"Uh," I said as I glanced between everyone.

It seemed the whole room held its breath. No one looked away or blinked. Even the airship creaked less, like it *also* wanted to hear the tale.

"Well, I was fighting the Second Ascension," I said.

Raisen's four heads all lifted and held still, the eight golden eyes locked on me.

I had never experienced such rapt attention, and although it made me nervous, I knew I couldn't back out of the story now. They wanted to hear the details, and I didn't blame them. I'd be the same way if I were in their shoes.

"They were digging up the bones of the apoch dragon," I said.

Zaxis waved away the comment. "We heard that part already. Get to your true form. What happened in that moment?"

"Uh, okay. Let's see... I was fighting with plague-ridden arcanists. I was outnumbered, and I knew they were stronger." I closed my eyes to visualize the scene better. I could still smell the smoke and blood from the Excavation Site. "But I had to keep fighting. I didn't want the enemy arcanists to catch Adelgis, Fain, or Karna—and I also couldn't allow them to keep digging up the bones. Somehow, in my gut, I knew I wouldn't be able to do it, but I had to try and do it anyway."

I knew that didn't make much sense. Why hadn't I concocted a brilliant strategy? Or retreated and then attacked from the darkness? In the moment, I hadn't thought of anything other than what *needed* to be done.

"My magic was slipping," I said, my voice growing quieter as I remembered the feeling of death clawing at my soul. "I was trapped, and I couldn't think of a way out, but I just... I just kept doing what I had to do. And then—out of nowhere—I felt this spark of power. Wait, *no*, not power. It was like a spark of *possibility*. Like I could achieve anything, or be anything, or create anything. When the feeling went away, it was as if I had woken from a long rest."

Once Luthair had become true form, I had felt *good*. No, better than good. Everything felt *right*.

I opened my eyes, done with the memories. "That's it," I said. "Then Luthair and I defeated the plague-ridden arcanists and smashed up the Excavation Site. Afterward, I met Illia in the woods, and that's how I got here."

"But what triggered it?" Zaxis asked. He stepped closer, his muscled arms crossed. "Was it the fact that you were dying?"

His curiosity and need to know didn't bother me. So little was known about what made a mystical creature *true form*. From what I had read, a creature changed—and grew in power—the moment its arcanist displayed the virtues of its kind. Sovereign dragons required arcanists who were ambitious and authoritative to become true form. Wendigoes required arcanists who were hermit cannibals. And now *I* had gained a true form with a knightmare, the virtues and requirements vastly different from the others. But what were they *exactly*? It was difficult to articulate.

"I don't think it was because I was dying," I said.

"Was it because you were fighting the Second Ascension?"

"I don't think that was it, either."

"Then *what*?" he snapped. "Tell us."

At first, I thought he was being pushy, but when I caught sight of the others, I knew he was just voicing their inner thoughts. Each of them—except for Adelgis, who had turned his gaze to the floor—stared at me with knitted eyebrows.

Especially Atty, and I knew why. For years, she had been interested in discovering the key to having a true form phoenix. But each mystical creature was different—what I had done wouldn't apply to her. Why was she so obsessed with hearing my story?

I shook my head, realization dawning on me. Sometimes it was inspiration enough knowing that someone else had achieved something once thought impossible.

"I think it was the moment I realized that I would die fighting," I muttered. "A weight had lifted off of me then. And... I accepted my fate. If I had to die to stop the Second Ascension, I would do so."

Although I wasn't *certain* that was the moment I had gained my true form, it had felt the closest. Something about that sacrifice and choice resonated with me, even now.

Perhaps that was what it meant to be a knightmare arcanist—what it meant to embody the virtues of a knightmare.

The others didn't say anything. They exhaled and exchanged glances, but no one else asked any questions. Even the ship resumed its normal creaking.

Illia stepped forward, and the others moved aside so she could get close.

"Volke," she said, her voice hushed. "Do you mind if we talk for a bit? In private? I think we need to discuss something before any more time passes."

I nodded, and she motioned to the stairs.

"Let's speak topside, on the deck."

4

BETROTHED

The winds whipped harder across the *Sun Chaser* the closer we got to the Surgestone Mountains. The storms above the mountains came and went on a fixed schedule. As soon as the thunderstorms waned, we'd be able to fly through the Lighting Straits and continue on our way to New Norra.

Illia stood by my side, her one eye set on the horizon. I was content to observe the majesty of our surroundings. Whenever Illia felt like speaking, I was certain she would do so.

Her eldrin, Nicholin, swished his little ferret-like tail as he glanced between me and her.

"It's too quiet," he said, his voice proper, but his tone laced with whimsy. "My arcanist, remember all the things you said you wanted to discuss with Volke? We don't have time for quietness! It'll take the whole trip back to New Norra for you to finish your thoughts."

Nicholin squeaked and poked his nose into Illia's ear. She giggled and flinched, finally turning her attention to me.

"Volke," she said. "I really *did* have a lot to say to you before... Well, before we found you. But I can't remember half of it, to be honest."

I smiled and crossed my arms. "I feel the same way. I couldn't wait to see everyone from the Frith Guild, and I thought I'd have a million things to say, but now that we're together, it almost feels like we were never apart."

And the one thing I wanted to tell them all—about how Luthair had gained his true form—I had already explained. What more was there to talk about? I was ready for life to resume course and move on from my time with the arcane plague.

Illia met my gaze, her expression betraying none of her inner emotions. Unable to read her, I just waited.

"You were emotional when we reunited," she finally said.

"*Very* emotional," Nicholin chimed in.

I gave him a sideways glance. "You weren't there when Illia and I finally reunited."

"But she told me all about it, mister. I'm her eldrin. We have no secrets."

"Enough," Illia said as she held up her hands. "I just wanted to point it out and make sure everything was okay."

At first, I wanted to deny everything. I hadn't been emotional—right? —but the more I thought about it, the more I realized Illia was correct. Now it seemed silly, yet at the time all I could do was express my feelings for her and everyone around me.

"It had been so long since I last saw you," I said, grasping at words to explain, though struggling to find the perfect phrases. "All I could think was that I wouldn't get another chance to tell you all the things I felt— and all the things I wanted to thank you for."

Illia lifted an eyebrow. "Thank me?"

The chilly winds rushed between us, so I stepped closer. It almost felt like we were kids again, and I was trying to explain some weird habit that had bothered her. It made me smile.

"If it weren't for you, I never would've bonded with Luthair," I said, my voice quiet. "I never would've made it this far. I never would've taken part in any of these adventures. I just..." I closed my eyes, trying to piece together the last parts of my thoughts. "I wanted to say that you've influenced a lot of my life. You're my family. I love you. And I mean that in its purest form. I'm sorry if I came across as *overly emotional* back at the Excavation Site, but in my defense, I thought I was dying at the time."

Illia laughed once and then stifled the rest with the back of her hand. "Volke," she said, smiling. "I should've known. It's always the noblest of answers with you, isn't it?"

Nicholin frowned. "What about me?"

"Hm?" I asked.

Nicholin disappeared from Illia's shoulder in a puff of white and glitter. A moment later, he appeared on mine, his soft fur brushing against the side of my neck. The silver stripes on his ferret-size body glittered in the last of the light pouring through the storm clouds.

"You should be thanking me as well," Nicholin said. He nuzzled my jaw. "I'm the one who first told you about Luthair! Clearly, I'm as much a hero and family as Illia." He poked his nose in my ear and whispered, "I want to be your kooky uncle."

"No one is becoming my *kooky uncle*," I said as I scooped him off my shoulder. I held him in my arms, and he looked up at me with bright blue eyes, his pupils growing larger as though pleading through cuteness.

I sighed. "Fine. I take it back. You can be my kooky uncle."

Nicholin teleported out of my arms and right back onto my shoulder. He poked me in the ear again. "I knew it! You're soft and unable to resist my charms!" He followed his statement with an evil snicker.

I lifted him off my shoulder a second time and gave him straight to Illia.

Although Nicholin continued to chortle, Illia didn't seem to notice. She placed her eldrin on her shoulder and patted his head.

"Are you okay?" I asked. "You seem a little standoffish."

She half-smiled. "I'm fine. I just... I wanted to make sure everything was right between us. There's still one thing we need to discuss." She looked up at me, her expression brighter than before. "Remember how you were upset when I ran off to fight the Dread Pirate Calisto without anyone's help?"

I could already hear the *I told you so* and *you're such a hypocrite* in her tone.

With a sigh, I said, "Yes, I remember." In order to cut this lecture short, I added, "And I'm sorry. I didn't want to risk infecting you or the others, but I probably could've done something different than running off on my own. I acted on impulse. The situation was dire, and—"

Illia placed a hand on my shoulder. I swallowed my words, confused by her contact.

"You don't have to explain," she said. "I understand. Obviously, because I did the same damn thing, just... stupider. But as your sister, I need to point out what you did and why it's ironic. You *also* made everyone worry, especially Master Zelfree."

"Okay, okay," I said. "I really do get it."

Illia jabbed me in the ribs, and I flinched.

"You need to promise me you're never going to leave like that again," Illia said, more serious than I had heard her in years. "I don't care what happens. We handle it together."

"I understand."

This time, when she smiled, so did I.

It wouldn't be long until we crossed over the storm-covered mountains. Electricity hung in the air, and the sounds of distant plague-ridden monsters echoed through the clouds alongside thunder.

I hadn't realized how hungry I was until I was done speaking with Illia. Although I'd had food when I had woken up, I needed more, as though my stomach was trying to make up for the many days I had been sleeping.

The crew of the *Sun Chaser* didn't mind when I entered the galley and asked for seconds. Most ships had to ration their food for long treks, so asking for seconds usually caused a problem. Either the *Sun Chaser* had plenty of supplies or the cooks were giving me special treatment, because I left with a pile of jerky, a hard biscuit, and a small tin cup of ale. I wasn't a fan of the stale flavor of barrel-preserved alcohol, but something to drink was better than *nothing* to drink.

Instead of eating at one of the tables in the galley, I took my food and headed for my quarters. I wanted to relax, avoid any questions, and spend the next few hours practicing my magic. According to the books I read, true form creatures were more powerful than their standard counterparts. Would I be able to feel the difference when I evoked terrors or manipulated shadows? I wanted to find out.

My quarters were nothing more than a storage space between two of the officers' cabins. Seeing the nameplates of the officers made me want to speak with Vethica, the airship's boatswain, and my father, Jozé, the ship's blacksmith, but that could wait until the evening.

Thinking of the officers reminded me of Karna. I was certain she would visit me whenever she felt the urge, even if I were sleeping. As a doppelgänger arcanist, she could be anywhere—hiding in plain sight— so tracking her down was a futile effort.

Balancing my food on one arm, I opened the door to my tiny quarters and entered.

"There you are," someone said.

I snapped my attention to a girl standing next to my hammock.

"Evianna," I said. "What're you doing here?"

As a former princess of the Argo Empire, she held herself with a haughty, and somewhat stiff, posture. She wore an outfit of expensive leather that reminded me of thigh garments meant for horseback riding. Everything had been tailored and fit just right—it wasn't the clothing suited for a long trip, but she wore it anyway. The dark brown of her pants matched her waistcoat, which accentuated her white tunic.

And while Evianna's clothes marked her as *different*, they paled in comparison to her long, white hair and bluish-purple eyes.

Evianna held her head a little higher, displaying the guild pendant she wore around her neck. It was bronze, which denoted her status as an *apprentice*. She looked young—she was smaller than most—and I wondered if she was old enough to even join a guild. The age someone became an adult was fifteen, and if I had to guess, I would've said she was younger.

"I'm training under Master Zelfree," Evianna said, pride in her tone.

I sarcastically glanced around the small room. There was a hammock, three barrels, and a crate. Nothing else.

"Is Master Zelfree here?" I asked.

Evianna frowned. "Of course not."

"Then... what're you doing?"

"Master Zelfree said, given your expertise on knightmare magic, that you'd be helping with my training." She crossed her arms and glared at me with her distinct eyes. "Aren't you happy to see me? You should be elated."

The shadows around Evianna's feet shifted with subtle movement. "My arcanist," came a feminine voice from the darkness. "There is a time for acknowledgment and a time for patience. Journeyman Savan has yet to fully recover from his ordeal."

I knew the haunting tone of a knightmare like I knew my own voice.

Evianna was a knightmare arcanist. Her eldrin, Layshl, circled her feet, moving as a shadow.

Luthair used to be the same way before he had become true form. Now I couldn't detect his presence. It was probably for the better—an enemy couldn't detect his presence, either—but I did miss catching glimpses of him as I walked.

"Do you still need time to recover?" Evianna asked as she examined me with narrowed eyes.

I walked over to my hammock and took a seat. "I'm much better now," I said. "But I would like to eat. You can, um, stay if you want, but I don't think I'm going to start training you until Master Zelfree is around. He's a master arcanist—I'm still just a journeyman, even if my knightmare has achieved its true form."

The ranks of arcanist were meant to indicate a level of formal training and explain the extent of someone's demonstrable power. I hadn't yet mastered all the magics of a knightmare.

Evianna stood next to me, her gaze on my food. "Well, I also came here for another reason."

I took a bite of my jerky and then motioned to the crate.

She shook her head. "Sitting isn't appropriate for this conversation."

I lifted an eyebrow as I chewed, confusion slowly taking over my thoughts. What possible conversation could she be meaning to have with me?

"I didn't realize it when we first met," Evianna began, "but you remind me of... of my sister. Of Lyvia." With haste in her words, she added, "And I'll have you know there's no higher compliment! My sister was beautiful and special and wonderful, and anyone who compares to her is in a category all their own."

Evianna was practically yelling the information, like this was an argument.

After I swallowed, I nodded. "Listen, I understand. Lyvia was talented, and it's a shame she's no longer—"

"*Don't say it.*" Evianna huffed afterward, her arms tightening across her chest. "And don't interrupt me. I'm not finished."

"Uh, okay?"

I took another bite of jerky and listened, still unsure where all this was heading.

"I've spoken to all the other apprentices of the Frith Guild, and even to several crewmembers of the *Sun Chaser*," Evianna said. "Everyone has told me the same thing—you're terrible at wooing women, and you have no love life."

Although I hadn't finished chewing, I forced a hard gulp and half-coughed afterward. With a raspy voice I asked, "Wait, *what*? Who said that?"

"Literally everyone," Evianna said, matter-of-factly.

"Why would you even ask them that?"

"Because."

I motioned with my hand for her to continue. "Because what?"

Evianna's cheeks reddened, but she maintained her *matter-of-fact* tone. "*Because* not only do you remind me of my extraordinary sister, but you also saved me the night Thronehold was attacked by the Second Ascension." Evianna ran her fingers through her ivory hair as she glanced to the wall, breaking eye contact. "You've proven yourself to be a valiant knight. And..."

"Is everything okay?" I asked.

She pursed her lips and brought her bluish-purple eyes back to meet my gaze. "I came here because I wanted to bestow upon you a great honor. I will allow you to save yourself for me. When I am ready, we will be wed."

We stared at each other for a long moment, and no matter how many times I mulled over her statements, I couldn't accept them as reality. Was she proposing that we *marry*? That was what she had said—but it couldn't be real. It couldn't be.

"How old are you?" I finally asked, more gauche than I had wanted.

"I'm nearly of age," Evianna snapped. She returned to crossing her arms. "In a few months, I will be an adult."

"Four months," Layshl said from the darkness.

"*Hush*, Layshl. Four months is soon enough."

I shook my head. "That's too young."

"You're only seventeen," Evianna said. "We aren't far apart in age."

"Yes, but—"

"We'll be traveling," she interjected. "The time will fly by before you know it. Is four months really so long to wait for a princess? Besides, we were obviously meant to be together." Evianna motioned to the shadows at her feet and then swished her hair over her shoulder. "I'm a beautiful maiden and a knightmare arcanist. You're a chaste and pure hero of the ages, waiting for true love. We're the perfect candidates for a fairy tale, and your sister said you enjoyed those old stories, just like Lyvia did."

I ran a hand through my disheveled hair, too flabbergasted to speak.

This couldn't be happening. Could it? No. It was too bizarre. People didn't just *declare* someone would be their spouse. This wasn't normal.

I set my food on a nearby barrel and then stood from my hammock. Evianna had to be a foot shorter than me—she was five feet, compared to my six feet and a few inches—and it made it awkward glancing down at her, but I felt too restless to sit.

"Evianna," I said. "This is, uh, unexpected to say the least, but Atty and I have said in the past that we'd be together, and—"

"No," Evianna stated.

"What?"

"No," she repeated. "You lost the privilege of choosing a woman to court when you dithered around for so long. Now I have chosen for you, and I say you *won't* be courting Atty. I am a princess, and my words carry more authority."

"You can't pull that card on me," I said, done with playing around. "You're not really a princess. It was more of a ceremonial title due to your relation to the late queen. Your brother holds the throne now, and we both know he'd never give you authority in the Argo Empire. Plus, we're not even *in* the empire."

Evianna stared at me, unblinking, her eyes becoming more glazed with tears after every word I spoke. I stopped, my concern for her growing.

"Are you okay?" I asked.

"How dare you bring up my murderous, traitorous, *monstrous* brother," Evianna said, her voice low and shaky. "That's cruel. I can't believe you, my betrothed, would do that to me."

Before I could respond, she turned on her heel and flounced out the door of my tiny room, slamming the door on the way out. Her brother, Rishan, had killed her sister, and I should've known it would be a raw subject, but I hadn't expected such an outburst.

"Luthair?" I asked.

"Yes, my arcanist," he said from the darkness in the corner.

"You saw all of that, right?"

"Indeed."

"Do you... have any advice? I feel like I don't know what to say or whom to go to."

"All I can say is—you are most certainly different from my first arcanist. He never got himself in such predicaments." Luthair said every word with dry sarcasm, like the whole event was both comical and foolish.

"Thanks," I said with a sigh, equally sarcastic. "I guess I'll just figure this out on my own."

5

THUNDERBIRDS

I had been an arcanist for more than two years, but my magic had never felt like *this* before.

Mist from the nearby clouds rushed over the deck of the *Sun Chaser*, and while I wanted to enjoy it, all I could do was stare at my hands in disbelief. Nothing hurt. That fact was a relief, one that I almost celebrated right there on the deck. I wanted to turn to a random crewmember and tell them the good news—my second-bonded magic no longer burned my veins!

"My arcanist?" Luthair asked.

I hadn't yet grown accustomed to his effective invisibility. "Yes?" I replied.

"Why have you stopped practicing?"

"I was just thinking."

After taking in a deep breath, I shook my head and refocused on the task at hand. I wanted to manipulate the shadows in controlled bursts. Normally, I used the darkness as a net or a tentacle that held things, but if I could master a finer manipulation, perhaps I could use the shadows as tools. Lock picks, a doorstop, a needle—anything I needed.

I lifted my hand and moved the shadows across the deck. The storm clouds above provided plenty of darkness, and the low light of the area made everything easier. In the day—or under harsh lights—my sorcery wasn't as effective.

With narrowed focus, I stared at a sliver of shadow by the railing. I tried to imagine the darkness coalescing into something small, something button-sized. Although shadows didn't normally have substance, my knightmare magic gave it form. I condensed the void-like substance, creating something solid, and then held my hand out, trying to guide the shadows into the shape I wanted by imagining that I was holding it.

Despite the fact that my magic came easily—and without pain—it still slipped away from me, like water running between my fingers. I lost hold of the tiny glob of darkness before it became a "button," and it all melted away.

I lowered my hand and sighed. "What am I doing wrong?" I whispered.

"You should think of your abilities like muscles," Luthair said from the shadows near the railing. "Stretching and working them every day will add to the results. You shouldn't expect to master everything immediately."

I chuckled. "I dunno. I figured now that you were true form, everything would be a lot easier."

"It might be—but that doesn't mean it's *easy*. There is a distinction there."

"Yeah, I understand. I just... I want to fight the Second Ascension without having to worry about my abilities."

Although I had created a perfect eclipse aura once, I still hadn't mastered it. I could face them in a fight with a broken aura, like I had done several times before, but it wasn't efficient. And now that we were heading to the lair of the world serpent, there wasn't much time left to master all the essentials.

"Look alive!"

Captain Devlin walked to the railing of the quarterdeck and motioned to the deckhands scrambling about. His eldrin, a roc the size of a small boat, lifted out of the nearby clouds, a mere twenty feet from the airship. Her golden feathers caught the flash of distant lightning, and her sharp beak cut through the sky as she glided alongside us. Rocs always impressed me—their gigantic majesty was a sight to behold. They truly were the dragons of birds, and when she flapped her wings, it practically changed the weather in the nearby area.

"*Mesos*," the captain called out to her. "Lead the way over the mountains, ol' girl."

Mesos screeched in acknowledgment, her cry loud enough to echo on the rocks below.

"Keep an eye peeled for thunderbirds! They're plague-ridden in this area. We've got too many arcanists aboard to risk gettin' into a tussle with them."

Another screech pierced the sky as Mesos flapped her wings and dove ahead.

The Surgestone Mountains stretched on for miles in two directions, creating a natural barrier between the Shard Sea and the lands to the south. I walked to the railing and glanced over, fascinated by the dark speckled boulders that made up the mountains, each with a bluish-black coloration. The surgestones created electricity, but they could also burst with power at random times, making them dangerous to hold, even for a few seconds.

"You should probably return to practicing," someone said, pulling me from my thoughts.

Adelgis stood next to me. I didn't know when or how he had gotten to my side—but there he was.

"Hey," I muttered. "How long have you been there?"

"Only a few moments," Adelgis said with a shrug. "You stopped training, so I came up on deck to encourage you to continue."

"How did you know I had stopped?"

"I heard your thoughts. The button-sized shadow was intriguing."

Ah, right.

Adelgis's mind-reading was more powerful than I had ever heard of. Even the old tales of swashbuckling arcanists never involved someone who *constantly* heard the thoughts of everyone around them—even through wood or steel, even hundreds of feet away. It was a gift, and likely a curse. Knowing the thoughts of everyone around would probably drive me insane.

"It's not *that* bad," Adelgis said, answering my inner musings. "Some people do have dark and disturbing imaginations, but it's made up for when there are lots of people around who have pleasant or amusing daydreams. Take your training, for example. I've learned quite a bit about knightmare magic through your constant focus."

"Uh, thanks," I said. "Is that why you're always around? You could be with the others, you know."

Adelgis's long, black hair tangled in the wind, his expression unchanged from a hard neutral. "I find that your random thoughts are the most upbeat—and the most earnest. I like that about you, Volke."

I wasn't sure how to respond, but a small piece of me knew it didn't matter. Adelgis could sense how I felt. Did I even need to use words with him anymore?

"Not really," he muttered. Then he tilted his head to one side, as though listening to something different. "Actually, you should probably use more of your words with Atty. She's very curious to see you and Luthair merged together."

"Why?"

"She wants to know about your true form."

I nodded and cursed under my breath. I should've guessed—Atty had wanted a true form phoenix since we had left the Isle of Ruma together more than two years ago. Was she jealous or upset that Luthair and I had managed such a rare feat? I shook the thought from my mind. Atty was more reasonable than that. I doubted she would be upset over our accomplishments.

"You can speak to people telepathically, right?" I asked Adelgis.

He nodded.

"Why don't you invite Atty to the deck? We should be spending more time together, regardless. She can help me train."

Lightning and thunder rumbled in the distance. It made for a fascinating backdrop, even if it wasn't the most romantic. It didn't matter, though. I didn't want to waste any more time—I could die fighting the Second Ascension, and I didn't want to *dither around* anymore, as Evianna had so lovingly put it.

"Atty is on her way," Adelgis said, once again breaking me free from my thoughts. "She and her phoenix are delighted to train with you."

Although I had thought it would be beneficial to have Atty training with me, it turned out to be the exact opposite. Not because she wasn't proficient with her magic—on the contrary, she was quite capable—but because I couldn't stop thinking about what I wanted to say to her. Atty had a natural beauty that was only heightened by the flames she evoked from the palms of her hands, and that made it difficult to concentrate.

Her red embers burst into the sky, clearing away patches of clouds. The storms wouldn't be deterred with simple magic, however. They stretched on for miles, and the small bits that Atty destroyed were quickly replaced with even more clouds, some thicker than before. The air smelled of water, and I suspected it would rain soon.

Atty's white tunic and loose pants jostled in the bluster of the winds, giving her a mystical appearance, as though magic was perpetually swirling around her.

I was supposed to be moving the shadows and making small objects, but I had stopped to ponder my words. Should I tell her she looked beautiful? Would she appreciate that or think me rude for focusing on something other than training?

Atty's eldrin, Titania, flew around the *Sun Chaser*, her flame body flashing through the gaps in her feathers. The long, peacock-like tail fluttered behind her. Titania was smaller than Mesos, but she had the same amount of majesty as she soared through the sky.

"Volke?" Atty asked. "Is everything okay?"

I returned my attention to her and nodded. "Of course. Why wouldn't it be?"

"You've been distracted this whole time."

"Was it that obvious?" I said with a forced chuckle. "I'm sorry. I was just... thinking that your eldrin is quite striking."

Atty patted the sleeves of her shirt. The cuffs were singed—a problem Zaxis often had when he unleashed too much fire. "Titania is very beautiful," Atty said.

"More than beautiful." I hesitated before continuing, "She's the most beautiful eldrin on this whole airship."

Atty stopped fiddling with her shirt and hesitantly met my stare. The look she gave me said she knew what I had meant and that realization frightened me more than I had thought it would. Atty had already voiced her desire for us to be together, yet I still felt hesitant—fearful my affections would somehow bother her.

A blush crossed Atty's cheeks as she rolled up the remainder of her sleeves and brushed back her long, golden hair. "You should tell Titania how you feel about her more often," Atty said with a coy smile. "I'm certain she would enjoy hearing it."

"I will," I said, caught a little off guard by her acceptance, but delighted nonetheless.

The feeling didn't last long, however. A hot breeze chased away the promise of rain, followed by a pulse of bone-tingling power. I shuddered as I turned on my heel, the hair on my arms and the back of my neck on end. Something *ominous* was close—I swear I could feel a heartbeat contrasting with my own.

Yet when I glanced around, I saw nothing. Just the clouds, the *Sun Chaser*, and her crew.

"Volke?" Atty asked, concern in her tone.

I withdrew my sword, Retribution, from its nullstone scabbard. Although I had only owned the black blade for a short while, it had never failed me. If something *was* nearby, I would strike it down before it harmed anyone.

"Volke?" Atty repeated as she jogged over to my side. "What's going on?"

"Don't you feel it?" I asked. The odd heartbeat of the distant creature grew frantic. The heat in the air irritated my senses—something was terribly wrong. "It's close," I muttered.

"What's close?" Atty evoked a bit of flame in her palm as she panned her gaze over the deck. "I don't feel or see anything. Are you sure?"

"I don't know what it is... but it's here. Stand back."

"You needn't worry about me," Atty said as she took her place by my side. "I've fought villains and monsters alike."

I nodded, though I couldn't help but be concerned. Since my eldrin was true form, my magic ran pure and incorruptible. It meant I couldn't be affected by the arcane plague—at least, not again. But Atty... the same couldn't be said about her. What if this *creature* I felt was actually carrying the plague? I wouldn't want to risk her safety. *I would be the one to handle the beast in that situation. It was the only way.*

Lightning crackled in the clouds overhead.

The deckhands gasped and pointed, and someone rang a warning bell. They rushed around, everyone heading for the stairs to get below deck.

"*Thunderbird,*" a deckhand shouted. "Get the capt'n! It's a thunderbird!"

I craned my head back, trying to spot the creature. The clouds remained thick. I couldn't see anything, though I could taste the electricity in the air. Static made everything cling and move, even my hair.

Atty had the same problem—her blonde hair frizzed at the ends, but she didn't pay it much mind. Instead, she undid her belt and threw it to the side.

"What're you doing?" I asked.

"Thunderbird magic is attracted to metal," she said. "Their thunderclap aura specifically targets it."

"A mystical creature can't create an aura without an arcanist."

Atty shot me an odd look. "Who said this thunderbird didn't have an arcanist? We need to be prepared—the Second Ascension has been spreading the plague wherever they can."

Retribution was made of both bone *and* steel.

I sheathed it, but I didn't get rid of it. The nullstone of my scabbard would prevent it from attracting magical lightning. Following Atty's lead, I also rid myself of my belt. The metal clasp wasn't large, but I didn't want to risk getting struck with enemy magic.

The foreign heartbeat became so prominent I almost couldn't focus on anything else. It was coming from above. Louder. Faster. Desperate.

It was the thunderbird. Somehow... I knew it was plague-ridden.

And it was diving for the *Sun Chaser.*

6

BATTLE IN THE TEMPEST SKY

"L uthair," I shouted.

The shadows across the entire deck of the airship answered my call. In an instant, they rushed to my feet and slithered up my body, coating me in icy magic that seeped down to my bones. My focus sharpened, my senses heightened, and when I took a breath, it seemed as though I drew in power rather than air.

Shadow plate armor formed around my body, covering me completely. The helmet wrapped around my head and blanketed my face, but the darkness was forever my ally—I could see through the helmet as though it weren't there at all. And unlike normal full plate armor, Luthair's shadow armor appeared near liquid—a cascade of inky darkness that shifted as it needed.

Luthair and I finished merging right as the thunderbird broke through the clouds.

I hadn't anticipated the massive size of the beast. The thunderbird had to be half the size of the entire *Sun Chaser*, large enough to capsize a standard merchant ship on the seas. And the monster ripped through the storm with an intensity that matched its gargantuan size. Laughter followed its arrival—insane, unchecked laughter.

The plague-ridden monster slammed onto the deck with its giant talons first. Planks across the whole airship cracked and splintered.

Thunderbirds typically glowed dark amber, their feathers crackling with each twitch and slight movement as electricity burst from inside their bodies at random intervals. In all the books I had read, they had reminded me of phoenixes—thunderbirds were fierce elemental beasts that could both harm with lightning and heal the land with gentle rains.

But *this* thunderbird...

There was nothing regal about it.

The lower portion of its long beak was missing, allowing its eel-like tongue to dangle. Instead of saliva, blood poured from its mouth, splattering across the deck of the *Sun Chaser*. Its eyes were gone—only empty eye sockets remained—and its body had three growths protruding from it. At first, I thought the growths were extra wings, but once I had a better look, I realized they were human arms, each complete with half-formed fingers. They reached and grasped, as though looking for something without eyes to guide them.

The monster thunderbird didn't screech like a normal bird—it screamed as if dying, followed by a long string of unhinged giggling.

"You're here..." it said, its voice and cadence so unnatural that it sent shivers down my spine. It didn't even matter that it was missing its lower beak—it spoke as though its mouth were somewhere deep in its throat, its voice echoing up and out. "You're *finally* here!"

The beating of an erratic heart rang in my ears. I didn't know why or how, but I could sense every movement of the tainted blood coursing through its veins.

Three smaller thunderbirds plunged out of the sky, their amber feathers falling out at a disturbing rate, as though they were molting away into nothing. Lightning snapped off their bodies with their movement, and they swirled around the airship, their chuckling creating a creepy chorus for the giant mother thunderbird.

Mystical creatures only grew when they were bonded to an arcanist. The smaller thunderbirds were probably unbonded, but the giant one—it had to have an arcanist *somewhere* nearby. Or perhaps its arcanist had died? Either way, it had only gotten this large through bonding, I was sure of it.

Atty lifted a hand and unleashed a torrent of red flames into the air. The smaller thunderbird caught in the heat chuckled as its remaining feathers smoked and caught fire.

I also raised a hand, but unlike most arcanists, who evoked something visible, I evoked sheer terror. I willed my magic to target only the four thunderbirds—avoiding Atty and the crew of the *Sun Chaser*. The monsters affected by my magic screamed and thrashed their heads. The three little birds fell away from the ship. My terrors created visions in their minds' eyes of their greatest fears. It took someone with a strong will to shake them off, but in the meantime, the thunderbirds weren't as devastating.

Unfortunately, the large monster wasn't caught for long.

The thunderbird burst lightning from its body in all directions, flashing outward so fast, I didn't have time to dodge. The lightning struck randomly. Two crates exploded from the force, part of the railing blackened and smoked. One bolt caught me across my left arm, the shock and intense pain almost too much to handle.

End this quickly, Luthair spoke to me telepathically.

Shuddering from the pain of the attack, I stood straight and gritted my teeth.

The three smaller thunderbirds—each about the size of a large dog —returned to the fray, all of them bursting lightning from their bodies. Their bolts wrecked more of the ship, but they weren't strong enough to reach me or Atty before dissipating.

"Get below deck!" someone yelled.

Captain Devlin leapt from the deck cabin, his movement enhanced by his manipulation of the wind. He flew from the door like a bird without wings and then evoked an icy gale-force blast of air. His roc magic knocked the three little thunderbirds around, even freezing their wings so that they crashed onto the deck of the airship, giggling the entire time.

The large thunderbird turned and arched its back.

Then the air tasted of metal. In my bones, I could feel the thunderbird's aura forming all around us. But where was its arcanist? A mystical creature couldn't create the aura without one. If we could find the arcanist, we could stop the thunderclap from shocking any and all metal.

But I saw nothing.

Interrupt it, Luthair advised.

Atty must have had the same idea because she held out her hand and evoked another fountain of flames.

I manipulated the shadows and used the tendrils to cut at the beast like dozens of swords, each shadow-blade piercing deep into its lightning body. The thunderbird wept tainted plague blood across the deck, sparks of electricity hopping from one pool to the next. At first, I thought it would spread to the lower decks, but a wave of frost coated the crimson blood before it traveled too far.

I whipped around. Fain stood near the ladder to the hold. His wendigo magic allowed him to evoke ice, and I was glad he had joined us.

And it wasn't only him.

Zaxis rushed up and immediately evoked fire over the thunderbird—he didn't even stop to ask questions. Either he had made a snap judgment or he was just ready to flame the first thing that looked suspicious. Either way, at least he harmed the monster.

But would this be enough? Technically, it was the arcanist who created the aura. The thunderbird could help, sure, but if we weren't targeting the person, this was all moot.

Captain Devlin used another rush of icy winds to put out all fires from the lightning bursts. It wasn't enough to stop the thunderclap aura, however. As soon as the aura gripped the surrounding area, it seemed as though I were suffocating. The air became too thick and too filled with static to breathe right.

The storm clouds sparked and flashed.

Then an eerie stillness.

I slipped into the shadows, slithering through the darkness until I arrived on the other side of the plague-ridden thunderbird. In that short time, bolts of lightning rained down from the clouds, heading straight for any metal. The nails in the planks, the iron on belts or jackets—even the steel rings around the barrels of rum. The lightning arched from one metallic object to another, flashing so fast and bright that it was nearly impossible to keep up. If I hadn't removed my belt, I would've been struck by at least a dozen surges of lightning.

Captain Devlin hadn't been so fortunate. He was struck and hit the deck writhing.

Zaxis continued applying his flames, even with the rain of destruction. His new scaled armor was not only immune to fire, but devoid of metal.

"*Suffer*," the thunderbird said, its voice still an echo in its throat. "I will consume you... I will become... *complete*..."

"*Never*," Nicholin squeaked in defiance.

Illia appeared next to me in a burst of white sparkles. Her rizzel magic allowed her to teleport, but I hadn't realized she had become so proficient with it.

Nicholin stood on the railing of the airship on the other side of the beast. The lightning from the thunderclap aura continued to rain from the sky at odd intervals, but Nicholin was small and stuck to the wood. Then he opened his ferret-like mouth and breathed a cone of white flame. It wasn't hot—it just teleported flakes of things away a little at a time. Parts of the *Sun Chaser*, and the plague-ridden thunderbird, were scattered around the deck.

From the other side, Illia held up her hand and evoked the same white fire.

She targeted the monster's neck, and her white disintegration flames opened a hole in the thunderbird's throat. That was when I saw hints of a full-grown man deep in the monster's gullet. Was *that* the arcanist? The man squirmed inside the esophagus of the monster.

Had the voice of the beast actually been the arcanist trapped inside?

The thunderclap aura sent flashes of light across the deck. More and more of the airship tore apart as lightning hailed around us. Hexa and Adelgis emerged from below deck, along with Karna, Vethica, and my father, Jozé.

Knowing we hadn't much time before our airship tore apart around us, I hefted my nullstone scabbard—and instead of withdrawing the blade and attracting lightning, I decided to use the scabbard itself. I stepped forward and swung at the beast's neck, striking the half-exposed body in the monster's throat.

The moment I struck the man, the thunderclap aura dissipated.

Arcanists needed to have utter control of their inner being and emotions to maintain an aura—that was damn near impossible if the arcanist were suffering from a concussion.

The thunderbird stabbed at me with the top half of its jagged beak. I shifted through the darkness, avoiding it completely. Blood splattered from the gaping wound of its mouth, its tongue stretched out, attempting to grab me.

On instinct, I ripped Retribution from its scabbard and slashed at the monster, slicing its tongue in half.

To my surprise, Master Zelfree *appeared* in front of the giant thunderbird. Blood from the monster's mouth splashed across his black clothing, but the arcanist star on his forehead had the mark of the wendigo. He was immune to the plague so long as his mimic was copying the powers of Fain's wendigo.

With brutal efficiency, Zelfree reached up and touched the neck of the monster bird. Thanks to his borrowed wendigo magic, Zelfree could manipulate flesh. He twisted the beast's throat and tore it open, further exposing the arcanist inside. The thunderbird exploded lightning from its body, and Zelfree leapt away, unharmed but unable to finish his gory task.

Although the winds from roc magic roared across the deck, fire from multiple phoenixes kept the smaller thunderbirds from attacking the crew, and icy blood sloshed across broken planks of wood from the shattered deck. Even amid the chaos, I never lost focus of what really mattered—killing the thunderbird arcanist.

With Retribution still in hand, I slid through the shadow and emerged practically underneath the beast. I stabbed upward, the black blade piercing deep. My weapon cut the body of the bird as though there were no resistance—it almost felt like I hadn't even connected. But I knew better. My sword was the bane of magic. It wouldn't be stopped by the likes of the plague-ridden thunderbird.

With a powerful slash, I cut outward, catching the arcanist and cleaving a chunk through the monster. The man was practically in two once I had finished my swing. Blood poured from both the arcanist and the monster thunderbird, but my inky armor moved and flowed like water, forcing the tainted crimson to wash off me in a matter of moments.

The thunderbird laughed as it leapt and then slashed at me with its massive talons. Its hooked claws caught my arm, but the shadows across my body instantly gathered around the gauntlets and arm, thickening enough to shield me from the attack.

But my control of the darkness couldn't save me from the lightning.

The thunderbird burst its magic outward, catching me with a powerful blast. The shock of the attack staggered me, and when the airship tilted, I hit the deck, my muscles locked in spasms.

The beating of the monster's heart intensified. Somehow, in my gut, I knew it was desperate and clinging to life, its whole body struggling to maintain itself.

The dead thunderbird arcanist hung from the gaping hole in the monster's throat. Now that the beast wasn't bonded, it would be weaker —but all it would need to do was infect even one person and it would have done its job.

"*Get off my damn ship!*" Captain Devlin shouted.

He stood on the other end of the deck and waved his hand in an arch. Instead of evoking a large gust of icy wind, he created a narrow blast of wind that sliced through the sky—and physical objects. His attack clipped some of the railing, sundering it in half. When his magic hit the thunderbird, it practically burst into two separate pieces. The force of the attack sent it off the ship, tumbling toward the ground, its twisted and nightmarish body thrashing the entire way.

Laughter echoed through the clouds as it went, dying away seconds later.

Fain and Zelfree evoked more ice to prevent the plague blood from going anywhere else, but the airship continued to list sideways.

I stood and took a deep breath. The beating of the monster's heart stopped, but the presence of malice still lingered in the air. When I glanced around, I saw nothing. Still—I knew the taint of corruption wasn't far.

"They're under the airship," I said, my voice a haunting mix of mine and Luthair's.

Atty acknowledged my statement with a curt nod. Then she turned her attention to the sky. "Titania! Chase away the thunderbirds!"

Zaxis snapped his fingers. "Forsythe—help her!"

The two phoenixes swooped around to the underside of the flying vessel, their flame bodies trailing embers and soot as they soared through the storm clouds.

Captain Devlin whistled so loud it impacted my hearing.

"*Mesos*," he yelled. "Clear them!"

A screech answered his command from deep within the clouds.

They can be infected, Luthair spoke telepathically. *We should aid them.*

I swept my cape to the side and rushed to the railing. Without fear or hesitation, I stepped onto the broken railing and then dove off the side of the *Sun Chaser*.

7

THE SURGESTONE MOUNTAINS

My cape ripped in half down the middle as the inky darkness of my armor coalesced to form bone frames for wings. I caught my breath as I fell through the open sky, wind and clouds rushing past faster than I had originally expected.

The cape laced itself into the bone frames, creating bat-like wings that held firm when catching the wind. Although I wasn't accustomed to flight, Luthair's presence in my mind kept me from panicking. With clear focus, I tilted forward and glided—the shadows of my armor shifting to help with flight, acting as a counterweight and helping to catch the wind. I dove and then pulled up, maintaining my speed as I angled back around for the airship.

I couldn't see the ground—the dark storm clouds around the Surgestone Mountains had thickened to the point that they blotted out all visibility. It didn't matter. I could still see the *Sun Chaser*, particularly the monstrous thunderbirds attacking the hull.

They were injured and bleeding, but it didn't stop them from blasting the wood and bone of the airship, destroying the magic that was used to keep the vessel in the air.

Titania and Forsythe erupted fire from their bodies, as though the flames came straight from their core and exploded outward from behind their radiant feathers. Mesos came in from the south, her golden feathers bright and majestic even in the gloom of a storm. When she neared the airship, she breathed icy winds like a dragon breathed fire.

The three smaller thunderbirds laughed as they were singed and frosted. Two of them twirled away, unable to maintain their flight, their tainted blood trailing down with them. The remaining thunderbird shot forward—straight for the phoenixes—but that was the moment I joined the fray.

Once close, I manipulated the shadows on the underside of the airship and lashed out with tendrils. I caught the thunderbird by the neck and wing, trapping it in place and preventing it from attacking.

"*Weaklings*," it said with a giggle. "You'll never... clear away *this* plague..."

I hated the odd way the plague-ridden monsters spoke. Just hearing the grate and laughter of the beasts reminded me of all the horrible things they had done—driving Gregory Ruma mad, twisting Rylion the griffin, and almost corrupting me to the point of no return...

I tightened my grip on Retribution and with unconscious efforts, flapped my bat-like wings to head toward the monster. With less-than-elegant precision, I dove and then slashed with my sword. Fighting in the sky wasn't something I was familiar with, and when I swung, it was wide and reckless.

That was good enough, however.

My shadowy tendrils held the bird in place just long enough for me to catch its chest and rend it in half as I flew by. I swooped up and back around afterward, my heart beating hard in exhilaration. Although moving through the darkness brought with it a sense of freedom, flying was a new form of mobility I had never considered.

The two halves of the creature spun down into the clouds below, lightning crackling off the feathers as it went.

I was thankful I was in a wide-open area. My ability to turn was limited, and due to my inexperience, I suspected that any sort of complicated dodging or maneuvering would be out of the question.

Forsythe and Titania flew in close to me, their scarlet feathers and trailing embers a sight that stole my breath. When I had first seen them on the Isle of Ruma, they were no bigger than peacocks, but now they seemed twice that size. Their wingspans were impressive and their tails gorgeous.

Mesos also flew over, though when she drew near, I was reminded that she was large enough to eat me whole, if she were so inclined. Thankfully, she manipulated the wind around us—creating a gust that elevated us toward the airship without the need for much effort.

As we sailed up and beyond the airship, I realized the extent of the damage wrought by the plague-ridden thunderbird and its throat-lodged arcanist. The main deck had been torn open, the starboard side had a gaping hole, and the magic-infused trinkets that lined the bottom of the hull had been cracked.

The *Sun Chaser* was losing altitude...

I glided to the deck of the ship and landed on a clean and unbroken portion near the quarterdeck. The bones of my improvised wings slid back into my armor and my cape stitched itself back together. The glitter of a starry night sparkled from the inner lining of my cape, reminding me of the pure sensation of magic I had experienced when I had first obtained true form with Luthair. But I shook the thought away. It was a pleasant memory, but now wasn't the time.

"Volke," Illia called out. She jogged over, her wavy, brown hair fluttering behind her. "Captain Devlin says the *Sun Chaser* might not be able to continue."

"We're falling," I said, my double voice smooth and confident.

"Will you help the crew? With your shadows, maybe you can secure everything?"

I replied with a nod.

The deck was under control—Fain and Master Zelfree were handling the containment of the blood while Captain Devlin and Mesos attempted to use their sorcery to keep the airship in the sky. I knew it wouldn't work, however. Luthair had said it best—using magic was like using muscles. Eventually, Devlin and Mesos would grow tired. They couldn't maintain this forever, even if it was working now. We'd eventually crash. Our best bet was to land, even if that was dangerous.

I slipped into the darkness and slithered down the stairs and into the hold. The crew of the *Sun Chaser* had gathered in the galley, the largest single room in the whole airship. I recognized a few of them and even knew their names. Surgeon Tammi was the ship's doctor, and the little girl, Biyu, was the ship's cabin girl. They stood among the others, trying to calm everyone as the airship leaned hard to the right, creating a prominent slant to the floor.

"Brace yourself on the bulkhead," Tammi instructed the others.

She wasn't tall, nor was her voice boisterous, but the crew listened. Tammi wore loose pants with half a dozen pockets on each leg, all stuffed with medical supplies. She reached into a few and passed them to those who had been injured during the splintering of the deck.

"Use this to apply pressure to your injuries," Tammi said. "And focus on maintaining your balance."

Biyu chimed in, "Everything will be okay." She wasn't even ten years old, yet she still tried to help the adults around her, some of whom were gulping down air in their panic. "Captain Devlin and Mesos will protect the ship! You'll see!"

Biyu wore an eyepatch over her left eye, similar to Illia's. Despite that, Biyu held herself with confidence and continued to say words of encouragement as everyone braced themselves.

"Hang on," she said. "I'm sure we'll land soon."

I strode into the galley, and everyone's eyes collectively widened, their attention focusing on me. Of course. They had yet to see Luthair's and my true form. I knew I was imposing—dressed completely in liquid shadow armor, my face covered, and my cape flowing with the mystic presence of the night sky—but I never wanted to frighten innocent people. I lifted a gauntleted hand, taking control of the shadows haunting the corners of the room.

"I'm here to help," I said, though I suspected my odd voice only added to my intimidating aura.

Perhaps the crew *would* have remained fearful, but Biyu's one eye lit up the moment she whirled around to face me.

She practically gasped as she said, "*Volke!* It's you! Thank all the good stars." She reached out a hand. "You should stay here with us."

Biyu's acceptance was all that was needed for everyone to relax. Even when I moved the shadows to hold people in place, they didn't cringe or flinch away. I used the tendrils to secure the crates of food and barrels of rum. Technically, everything had already been tied down with rope, but this was a secondary measure. The last thing we wanted was for our supplies to topple down the mountainside when we landed.

"The shadows are cold," Biyu muttered as she hesitantly touched one of the tendrils.

My shadow had a physical presence thanks to my magic, but I had no control when it came to the temperature. If they were cold, it was only because the void itself was that way.

The *Sun Chaser* tilted further, creating a harsher slant to the floor. The crew—a few dozen individuals—hugged close and braced themselves on the bulkhead, all the while supported by the darkness.

The galley door opened, and a man limped inside.

Jozé—my father.

His left leg didn't move as it ought to have, causing him to put most of his weight on the right. We appeared similar in many regards. Both tall. Both with dark hair and eyes. Both with honeyed skin, though his was paler from a life dwelling in the hold of a ship, rather than in the glorious daylight of the ocean sun.

He rubbed at the rough stubble on his jaw as he attempted to cross the room and join the rest of the crew.

"Father," I said, startling him with my double-voice.

Jozé glanced up and took stock of the situation as the airship tipped another few degrees. It was clear Jozé wouldn't be able to walk in this situation, not with his bum leg.

I stepped close and offered my shoulder. He gave me the once-over, examining Luthair's true form before placing a hesitant hand on the liquid darkness that made up my plate armor. He seemed intrigued by the sensation, even going so far as to take his hand off and examine the palm, as though he'd be marked with ink. But the armor didn't leave marks—it just flowed with magic beyond normal limits.

Then the airship shook, and the wood of the hull creaked in agony.

Jozé tumbled, but I grabbed him with a quick shadow tendril before he hit the floor.

"Thank you, boy," he said as he eyed the darkness. "You're gettin' better with these, I see."

Another tremor. Another painful creak.

"Stay here," I commanded, loud enough for all to hear.

My first thought went to the many holes in the vessel. Would the *Sun Chaser* break in half? It was a possibility. If that happened, I would need to be on deck to help with whatever Master Zelfree and Captain Devlin had planned.

With a swish of my star-marked cape, I left the galley and stepped into the darkness. With all the freedom and maneuverability of a shadow, I darted back up the steps and emerged on deck.

Captain Devlin and Mesos were busy controlling the winds, but the storm had its own priorities. A bluster of currents clashed all around us, and the *Sun Chaser* couldn't seem to withstand the force of it all. Howling winds made it difficult to hear. Every crack and hole created a whistling effect that added to the cacophony.

"You need to land!" Zelfree shouted through the gale-force winds. "There! On the other side of the rocks."

Captain Devlin offered a string of curses that flew off with the storm. Then he whistled, so loud it cut through all other noise. Mesos understood, and with a few flaps of her giant golden wings, the *Sun Chaser* descended closer to the Surgestone Mountains.

I glanced around, looking for something or someone to help while the airship made an impromptu landing.

Zaxis was healing anyone who seemed injured before sending them to Illia so she could carry them below deck. He grabbed crewmates and yanked them across the deck, keeping them close and preventing them from falling overboard, but he did so in such an aggressive manner that it was difficult to tell if he was doing more harm than good.

Illia was teleporting the last of the crew into the galley. One by one, Zaxis shoved them her way, and she used her rizzel magic to send them to safety. Unlike Zaxis, she held each of the deckhands for a moment, as if to reassure them everything would be all right.

Hexa and Adelgis secured the last of the cargo with the excess rigging on deck. Although Adelgis wasn't particularly fast or strong, Hexa put in the extra work to compensate—she seemed determined to lash down the cannons and crates. Even her four-headed hydra helped, each of its mouths holding rope for her.

"Volke!"

I turned around and found Atty. She grabbed on to my arm and then pointed to the bow of the airship. I followed her finger and watched as the *Sun Chaser* just barely made it over a cluster of boulders. Once on the other side, we descended again, blocking out some of the winds by using the mountain as a shield. Sure enough, a flat outcropping of rocks below was just large enough for the airship to touch down.

"We're almost there," Atty said as she tightened her grip on my elbow. "I think it'll be a rough landing."

And it was coming faster than I had expected.

Too fast.

I grabbed Atty and pulled her against my armor-covered chest as the *Sun Chaser* practically dove for the rocks.

"Hang on," I commanded, bracing for the inevitable impact.

8

SUPPLY RUN

The ship shuddered as it scraped against the mountainside. Then it shook. Then quaked. For a brief moment, I thought the whole airship would crumble into a thousand tiny pieces as it collided with the rocks. Atty held tight as I used the darkness to steady us, but I was to slip us into the shadows if things became too rough.

Thankfully, the airship slowed, grinding against the rough terrain until it stopped. Dust and bits of rock surrounded the *Sun Chaser* as everything settled into place. Then the ship—whose hull was curved for sea travel—tilted to the side. The port side of the ship hit the mountain, keeping it upright, but at a slant. The roc magic that kept the vessel in the air had been damaged, yet not completely removed. The airship remained in one piece and mostly upright.

Captain Devlin sighed hard enough for three people. It practically echoed down the mountain, creating a chorus of his frustrations.

At some point during the fall, Devlin had lost his tricorn cap. His curly hair, windswept and everywhere, combined with his ripped trousers and singed shirt, made it look as though he had been through a tornado—a tornado filled with fire and sharks.

And while I wanted to congratulate him on knocking away the thunderbird and guiding the airship down to the ground without losing anyone, my thoughts immediately turned to the arcane plague. The blood could taint others. If it accidently splashed across an injury or entered someone's system, we'd have no way to cure them.

Captain Devlin took a deep breath, straightened his posture, and then motioned to everyone else on the deck. "If you have any injuries, head to the top of the quarterdeck. I'll get Tammi to look ya all over."

The captain—despite having been struck with lightning—didn't seem to be actively bleeding. Then again, the whole fight and crash had been chaotic. I hadn't been watching him the entire time. Perhaps he was.

"Fain, help me with this," Master Zelfree said. He pointed to the remaining frost across the ship, especially the crimson puddles. "We need to keep everyone away from this area and the deck directly below until this is cleaned."

Fain jogged over, his frostbitten hands shaking. Although he had helped the whole crew with his magic, I knew he wasn't entirely confident with it yet. He hadn't been trained as an arcanist when he was younger, and his time as a member of a pirate crew hadn't helped.

When Fain approached Zelfree, his shoulders were bunched at the base of his neck and his gaze was on the deck. His hesitation didn't stop him from following orders, though, and for that I was grateful. He was the only other one on board—beside me and Zelfree when his mimic transformed into a wendigo—who didn't have to fear the plague.

Atty glanced up at me. "We should check on the others."

I released her from my hold and then unmerged with Luthair. The darkness rippled and then fell away from my body, leaving me with a dull sensation of loss. It only lasted a moment, but the decrease in power always left me feeling odd after Luthair and I separated.

Luthair formed again as empty plate armor and stood next to me, his star-marked cape fluttering in the winds of the storm.

When the shadows moved around us, I thought it was Luthair's doing, but a moment later, Evianna emerged from the darkness, stepping out of the void as though it were a tunnel only she could traverse. I knew the power well—I shadow-stepped all the time—but it still fascinated me to see others use it.

"Volke," Evianna said as she hustled over to me.

She carried an ebony heater shield in her arms, one that was small enough to mount on a single arm. I recognized the shield—I had crafted it from a world serpent scale, after all. It felt like an eternity ago when I had fought with the Dread Pirate Calisto and stolen the scale. Turning it into a magical item was the only way I had known to keep it from him.

Evianna stopped next to me and held out my shield, presenting it like a delicate offering. "Here. I'm sorry I didn't get it to you earlier, but Master Zelfree said I couldn't leave the captain's quarters until the airship was settled." She huffed and turned her attention to the stairs below deck. "A certain *phoenix* wouldn't let me sneak out, not even for a moment."

Right as she made her statement, a third phoenix emerged from the bowels of the ship. Unlike Titania and Forsythe, who were both red phoenixes, Tine—my father's eldrin—was a *blue* phoenix. Her sapphire feathers glittered as she flew from the stairs and glided over to our location. When she landed, a small dusting of soot fell to the deck of the *Sun Chaser*.

"Lady Evianna," Tine said, her voice as beautiful and regal as her feathers. "Master Zelfree didn't want you to wander far. We're in dangerous territory. Too dangerous for an apprentice."

"Why weren't you in the galley with the others?" I asked as I took my shield from Evianna. "It'd be safer there. Even now."

I had forgotten how lightweight my shield felt. It could block almost any magical attack, but because I had been an amateur when I crafted it, the magic reflected off of it in a haphazard manner. Still, it was reliable— I had missed having it.

Evianna crossed her arms. "Master Zelfree said I had to watch over your shield, so I kept it in the captain's quarters." She pursed her lips. "I'm starting to think it was a fake errand meant to keep me busy while the fighting happened on deck."

"I don't think you're ready to handle plague-ridden beasts," I said as I slid the shield onto my left forearm. "They're dangerous beyond compare. If you can avoid them, you should."

"*You* don't." Evianna lifted her head high. "And everyone in the Frith Guild said you were fighting plague-ridden creatures even before you were an arcanist. I don't need to be coddled. I can hold my own like everyone else."

Technically, I *had* fought a plague-ridden white hart before I bonded with Luthair, but that was different. And I had come within inches of losing my life.

"Volke," Atty said, drawing my attention away from the conversation. "I'm going to help heal anyone who needs it."

I glanced over to the quarterdeck. Zaxis was already there, using his magic to help anyone and everyone. Atty's assistance could certainly help.

"Okay," I said.

She hurried off and started helping people climb out of the hold. Everyone she offered a hand to gained some of her healing. Although that wasn't her most proficient technique, it was enough to remove minor scrapes and bruises.

"My master doesn't have the ability to heal others," Tine said, her blue phoenix feathers shifting with the winds. "He said he would wait in the galley until the repairs were made or until his imbuing mastery was needed for trinkets."

Blue phoenixes were slightly different than their red counterparts. Their fire burned anything—even creatures supposedly immune to the cruel touch of heat—but in exchange, they couldn't heal others. The powerful flame made my father a talented crafter of items, especially anything to do with metal or bone, but those skills weren't as useful in the current situation. He could repair the ship later, when we had the tools and resources.

"Where is Vethica?" I asked. "She's a khepera arcanist—don't they specialize in renewal magic? Couldn't she help physically repair the ship?"

Although I didn't know much about the mystical scarabs we found under New Norra, I remembered watching the traps laced with khepera sorcery repair themselves once they had been triggered. Surely that could aid us in some way?

Tine nodded, her heron-like face alight with amusement. "Vethica has already begun her work. Look there." She pointed with the tip of her sapphire wing.

I followed her gesture until I spotted a woman with short, reddish-blonde hair. She stood near the stern of the airship, on top of the railing, like heights were the least of her concerns.

Her eldrin, the khepera, Akhet, scuttled across the deck, his scarab exoskeleton bright with an iridescent sheen, much like oil on water. When he touched bits of the wood, they seemingly stitched themselves back together, each splinter shifting back into place until the boards were whole again.

But his magic only worked on things nearby—any wooden boards that were lost in the storm and battle weren't regrown or made anew, they were simply gone.

To my surprise, the last four remaining khepera buzzed around the deck as well, flying and landing on broken bits of railing. They were young—none of them had yet to bond—and their magic worked as well as a child nailing together a piece of furniture. Normally, mystical creatures didn't travel the world on airships. They found homes near their breeding grounds, or perhaps they were born from an event, like knightmares were from the corpses of rulers, which didn't allow for much mobility. The fact that we had four unbonded creatures with us—and not in cages—was a rarity.

But it had to be done. Khepera magic was one of the few ways we could combat the arcane plague. As soon as Vethica became strong enough... or as soon as someone else who had bonded with them had... we could create a cure.

I shook the thoughts away. Now wasn't the time for future hopes. We had an immediate crisis. However, unlike the phoenix arcanists who could offer healing, knightmares were almost entirely combat-oriented. Evoking terrors wouldn't be much help for the ragged crew. I had to do something else.

With only a few options available, I shadow-stepped off the ship, shifted down to the mountains, and looked for bits of the *Sun Chaser* to bring back. The more we had, the more Vethica and Akhet could repair. It wasn't the most pressing of missions, but at least I could do it alone.

Well, I would've done it alone, had Evianna not followed me.

We both stepped out of the shadows, but I had traveled farther. It was hard evidence of my mastery over the magic—she could only go so far before she had to emerge from the shadows, but my travel distance was nearly double hers.

"Volke," she said as she walked the last of the way to my side. "I'll help."

"You should go back to the *Sun Chaser*," I said.

"But I need to learn knightmare magic. Master Zelfree said you would assist in training me."

"Master Zelfree also said you should wait on the ship—yet here you are."

For a moment, Evianna said nothing. Then she motioned to our surroundings. Lightning crackled off the rocks in the distance, and the winds swept over the mountain at a powerful rate, disturbing her white hair.

"There are no monsters," she said. "And Master Zelfree is preoccupied. Let me accompany you."

A part of me feared Evianna would make another declaration of love or put me into another position in which I had to reject her advances. Was that enough to deny her training? We were up against the Second Ascension. We couldn't afford to slack off, not even to avoid awkward encounters.

"We're only going to discuss magic," I said. "And knightmares and how best to utilize powers. Understand? Nothing else."

Evianna swept her white hair over her shoulder. "You have my word."

"I'm being serious."

She narrowed her eyes. "I was raised a princess, thank you very much. My word is my honor. We shall focus purely on magical training and nothing else."

Although I remained skeptical, I wasn't about to put her honor in question. "Very well," I said with a sigh. "Come with me. We'll manipulate the shadows to gather up broken bits of the ship."

Evianna's eyes went wide as she jumped to my side. She clapped her hands once as we made our way up the mountain, toward fragmented bits of wood atop sharp boulders. I had never seen her so genuinely delighted, but the moment she noticed my staring, she hardened her expression into something serious.

"I'm ready," Evianna said with a *hmpf.* "Show me how it's done, Journeyman Volke."

I had never trained someone in knightmare magic before. It was a fulfilling experience as I pointed out how the shadows could be manipulated into fine threads or how larger objects could be dragged and carried back. Somehow, even though I showed Evianna the most basic of techniques, it strengthened my own understanding and proficiency.

The few hours we worked together made me think I should've been training with knightmare arcanists from the beginning. But I knew, deep in my gut, I would never leave the Frith Guild. This was where I belonged—and at least now I would have *one* other knightmare arcanist to help me train.

Evianna manipulated the shadows to drag a chunk of wood lodged between rocks. Lightning flared in the distance, and static rushed through the air. She lost her concentration, and the darkness released its hold on the fragmented hull.

I lifted a hand and willed the shadows back into a solid form, catching the wood before it fell and shattered further.

"You need to pay attention," I said. "It's important you maintain focus, even with distractions nearby. It'll make the difference in a fight— I guarantee."

"Volke is wise to point this out," Layshl said from around Evianna's feet. "A strong will can make the difference in an otherwise unwinnable situation."

I enjoyed the way knightmares spoke from the darkness, their voices majestic and dark in tone. It almost seemed haunting, and when I turned to my own shadow, I had hoped Luthair would say something to me. But he remained silent.

"I'll master this," Evianna stated as she stared at her hand. "Right, Volke?"

I nodded. "Of course."

She smiled, a hint of pride in her expression. "He said, *of course,* Layshl," Evianna whispered to the shadows. "Didn't you hear?"

"Yes, my arcanist," Layshl replied.

I guided the wood down to our pile of pieces. "We should head back to the *Sun Chaser*." Then I gestured to the stack. "Help me carry this. It'll be good practice."

We used our combined efforts to move everything along the speckled surgestones in one trek. When the lightning flashed closer than before, I knew it wouldn't be long until this area was beset with random sparks of electricity.

Hopefully, the repairs to the *Sun Chaser* would be done soon.

It didn't take us long to return. When we did, it seemed as though a good portion of the main deck had been cleaned, and everyone had been healed, but the airship wasn't yet in the sky. Evianna and I dropped the wood off near the quarterdeck and then shadow-stepped to the bow, closer to where most of the arcanists had gathered.

When I emerged from the darkness, Master Zelfree turned to me, as though waiting for my arrival. His mimic, Traces, sat in cat form on his shoulder, her extra-long tail swishing back and forth.

"There you are," he said. "You've returned just in time. We need a team to gather supplies."

All the other arcanists on the ship—Devlin, Vethica, Jozé, Karna, Zaxis, Atty, Hexa, Adelgis, Illia, and Fain—were grouped by the bow, talking amongst themselves in quick and quiet tones.

Mesos, the captain's roc, sat perched on a nearby boulder, her golden feathers puffed out, making her twice as large. The other eldrin—Akhet, Tine, Forsythe, Titantia, Raisen, Felicity, Nicholin, and Wraith—stayed close to their arcanists, each listening intently to the conversation. The only eldrin I didn't see, and who was always hidden, was Karna's doppelgänger, Karr. He hid himself as a member of the airship crew—he was probably nearby, I just didn't know which one.

Master Zelfree pointed down the cliff side. "We need star shards for Jozé and Captain Devlin to repair the last of the hull. Can you and a few others head to the port down at the base of the mountain? We should be close to Port Akro. It's small, but it'll have something."

"You want *me* to go?" I asked.

"I want you to lead a team," Zelfree corrected. "Take at least two of them, probably one of the red phoenix arcanists, or even both. Their healing can be used as payment in some situations. Or, if you're lucky, you'll find a crafter who wants their phoenix magic imbued into an object. Phoenixes are rare and strong enough that it's always in demand."

"You want me to lead it?"

"Must I repeat everything in simpler terms?" Zelfree snapped.

I gritted my teeth. "I'm sorry."

Zelfree exhaled and ran a hand through his short hair. "No. It's me. The storms are moving closer, and I'll need to find a thunderbird in order to mimic its magic. I don't relish the idea of leaving the ship, but it's only with the lightning manipulation that I'll be able to protect the *Sun Chaser*. It's got me on edge."

That was why I had been confused about leading a team—I had just figured that Zelfree would do it himself. But if he was needed to protect the *Sun Chaser*... everything made more sense.

Evianna stepped closer to me, drawing my attention back to the present. "Can I go with Volke?"

Zelfree nodded. "Yes. It would be better, actually. You're the least experienced, and this area is dangerous and tainted with the plague. Volke will watch after you."

She held her head high once again, clearly pleased with this decision —or perhaps with her ability to add herself into the mission.

"I'll go right away," I said. "How long do you think it'll take us to get to the town and back?"

"Two days. Maybe three, if there're problems. And that's assuming you can make the trades quickly." Zelfree turned his dark eyes on me, his expression hard and cold. "Do you think you can do this?"

I nodded. "Of course."

"Good. Then I'll await your return."

9

MOUNTAIN TREK

While most mountains had some form of vegetation—trees, shrubs, weeds—the Surgestone Mountains were entirely rock. Not all of it was the magical lightning-zapping kind, though. The majority of the mountains were comprised of black and reddish stone— some smooth, some jagged. The speckled stones, the ones that appeared to be a mix of the black and red, were the actual surgestones. The lightning that crackled off of them killed all plant life, creating our bleak surroundings as we descended the side of the mountain.

Forsythe and Titania had no problem descending the mountain. They glided down on the winds, making sure to keep our pace so as not to get separated.

"Watch your step," Zaxis said as we leapt from one narrow pathway to the next. "See these little rocks here? Don't step on them. You'll slip." He motioned to pebbles on the edge of a flat boulder.

When had Zaxis ever been so forward-thinking about the needs of others? He jumped ahead of us, checking every crevice and steep incline, as though it were his duty to act as scout. I hadn't asked that of him—he had just done it.

Zaxis landed on a rock that toppled underneath him. He sucked in breath as he fell and hit the rocks, skidding down a portion of the mountainside.

"My arcanist," Forsythe called down from the sky. "Are you injured?"

Zaxis leapt back to his feet and rubbed at his ribs. "I'm fine." Then he pointed to the unstable rocks. "Watch that whole area when you come down."

His phoenix magic allowed him to quickly heal his minor injuries, so I wasn't worried. Actually, I couldn't help but be impressed. I thought Zaxis would've been a pain on the trek—fighting with me the whole way, like when we had been back on the Isle of Ruma—but he hadn't made one snide remark or asked a single sarcastic question yet.

"I can shadow-step," Evianna declared before she slipped into the darkness and the reappeared at Zaxis's side. "Knightmares have the advantage in this situation. Perhaps Volke and I should take everyone down ourselves."

Atty and I made our way down at a slower pace. She slid on an incline to join me on a plateau, but we were still twenty feet above Zaxis and Evianna. Atty was graceful, but not as burly as Zaxis, and she seemed concerned with keeping out of the surgestone areas. It slowed us down.

"Can you take us all in the shadows?" Atty asked me, lifting an eyebrow.

"Well, I know I can take one person," I said. "But more than one caused me pain the last time I tried. It's also a drain—I get tired quickly."

Evianna stared up at me, her white hair fluttering in the storm winds. "But *I'm* here. I will carry some of the burden."

"Have you taken anyone into the shadows before?" I asked.

"Well... no. But that's why you need to teach me."

"When I first learned, it was exhausting. I don't think *now* is the time for that lesson."

"Now is the perfect time," Evianna said, her half-shout bouncing off the rocks and disappearing into the heavy breeze.

"*Enough,*" Zaxis barked. "You want plague-ridden thunderbirds to find us? If Volke said now isn't the time, *then now isn't the time.*"

He had a hard edge to his voice that I recognized. That was the Zaxis I knew—angry and impulsive. But now he was using that to scold people into compliance? How long had I been separated from the group? When had he learned these skills?

"If you can take one person, why don't we go together?" Atty asked as she stepped closer to me. "Then we can keep up with Zaxis and Evianna." She placed a delicate hand on my shoulder and offered a half-smile.

A piece of me wondered if she just wanted to experience shadow-stepping—or perhaps this was an excuse to be close together. Either way, I wasn't about to deny her.

"Sure," I said.

I wrapped an arm around her waist, slow and cautious, waiting for an inevitable flinch or grimace that would signify her disapproval. But it never came. Instead, Atty wrapped her arms around my neck, pulling me closer.

My face heated, and I immediately stepped into the shadows to hide my flustered state. In the darkness, there was nothing to see, and when I emerged, I plunged us back into the shadows as soon as possible.

"V-Volke," Atty gasped when we surfaced a second time.

I stopped my sorcery and glanced over. "Are you okay?"

"I can't breathe in the darkness," she said, gulping down a bit of air. She released her hold on my neck and straightened her golden hair.

I gritted my teeth, feeling foolish. No one could breathe while swimming through the void, but I had gotten so used to the travel that I didn't even notice when I was holding my breath anymore. I should've explained to Atty I was planning on diving through the darkness multiple times so that she'd had a chance to prepare.

"I'm sorry," I said. "I'll stop more frequently."

Luthair sighed, his voice echoing out from between two boulders, even though I couldn't see his shadows. "My arcanist. You should wait for the others."

I turned around, shocked to see Zaxis and Evianna so far behind us. I had only jumped through the shadows twice, yet I was already a good hundred feet below them on the mountainside. When had my shadow-stepping gained such... distance? Was it because Luthair was true form now?

"Volke," Evianna called down from the rocks. "You shouldn't leave without us! You need to wait."

"We will," I replied.

She glared at us from atop her boulder, her bluish-purple eyes distinct and rather unique. Thanks to my ability to see through darkness, even the low light of the storm didn't stop me from admiring them. They were the same as Evianna's sister, Lyvia—and my thoughts immediately went to her and her duel to the death in Thronehold.

I had been so distracted that I didn't comprehend Evianna's next actions. She placed a hand on Zaxis's chest, hooking her fingers into his crimson-scaled armor. Then she dragged him into the shadows, taking Zaxis along for one of her shadow-steps.

"*Evianna*," I said, taken aback.

She appeared ten feet down the mountainside, emerging from the shadows like someone who had just realized they couldn't swim and that they were also in deep waters. She gasped and flailed her arms, confusion written on her face.

I knew the feeling. The first time I had taken someone, it had left me weak and shaken.

Evianna stood straight after a moment of recovery. I had taken considerably longer to regain my bearings, but that had probably been because I was second-bonded to Luthair. My magic was harder to use, whereas Evianna didn't have to contend with that problem.

Zaxis stumbled to the side. He shook his head and then growled something under his breath.

"What's wrong with you?" he snapped. "You just do whatever you want, whenever you want? Huh?"

"I—" Evianna began.

Zaxis snapped his fingers, cutting her off. "When you're part of a guild, you aren't *Princess* Evianna anymore—you're *Apprentice* Evianna. Learn the damn difference and follow the instructions of your superiors. Especially in crucial missions where others are depending on you."

I still couldn't get over how odd it was to hear Zaxis give a decent lecture. Still—the level of his anger was unwarranted.

"Calm down," I said. I knew why this had happened, and I silently scolded myself. This was the first time I was an instructor, and already I could see my mistakes. "It's my fault. Evianna saw me move through the shadows with Atty right after I said she couldn't practice the same technique. I should've known that would have bothered her—and goaded her into imitating me."

"I wasn't *goaded*," Evianna said as she crossed her arms. "I was practicing of my own accord, thank you. Your actions had nothing to do with it."

I almost laughed, but I bit back the urge. Was acting recklessly really better than admitting to imitating me? Or was she upset because I had accurately described the reasoning behind her behavior?

Zaxis huffed and then shook his head. "*Kids.*"

"*Zaxis*," Atty stated. "That isn't helping. Evianna, please—now isn't the time for infighting. We should work as a team to complete this mission as quickly as possible."

Although I thought this would trigger another round of haughty resentment, Evianna inhaled and then exhaled, seemingly clearing her system of the desire. She replied with a soft nod. "You're right. Layshl said the same thing. It won't happen again."

Relief washed through me. At least this wouldn't be a needless argument that stalled our trek to Port Akro.

I gave Atty an appreciative nod. "We should continue," I said. "I don't like the idea of sitting around for too long."

The journey down the Surgsestone Mountains took longer than I had expected, and halfway to the base, I reconsidered using my shadow-stepping abilities to get us there faster. No matter how many times I thought it over, I came to the same conclusion—walking down was fine—but after further consideration, I decided I would use my abilities for the trek back *up* the mountain. I would be able to return with the supplies faster, and Zaxis and Atty weren't weak or apprentice arcanists—they could handle themselves, and Evianna, while I ventured ahead.

The farther down the mountain we got, the more the skies cleared. The clouds never went away, but the storms had thinned, and the gale winds rested. The evening sun shone through in pillars, illuminating part of our path with sunset colors. The black and crimson rocks shone when graced by the rays of the sun, glittering with beauty I hadn't known they'd had. What would the whole mountain look like without the storms? It was a sight for artists and their paints, no doubt.

My legs ached by the time we neared the base. How long had we been walking? Eight hours? Perhaps more. Evianna, the youngest of our group, took in deep breaths, but she never complained. Whenever I glanced over, she lifted her head and walked with a confident gait. I snuck glimpses of her from time to time, and whenever I wasn't paying attention to her, she slouched her shoulders and trudged along, clearly on the edge of exhaustion.

"My arcanist," Luthair said, his voice echoing between nearby stones. "Look there."

I turned my attention to the horizon. Smoke trailed upward in thin lines, and I could detect the faint outline of uneven roofs.

"Is that Port Akro?" I asked.

"I believe it is."

Once we reached the base of the mountain, it would probably be about three or four miles of walking over rocky and desert-like terrain, but at least we were close.

Both Forsythe and Titania swooped down close.

"We found the city, my arcanist," Forsythe said to Zaxis. "Ships are in port."

Zaxis nodded. "Perfect. Fly ahead and inform the locals we're on our way. If you can, find out who has star shards for sale and what they want for them. Our goal is to be in and out of there as fast as possible."

His phoenix replied with a gentle screech and then soared toward the port town.

"Go with him," Atty said to her eldrin.

Titania took off as well, soot trailing behind her.

"We'll need to rest," I said to Zaxis. "It can't be avoided. The moment we get to town, we'll need to find a place."

"I'm not tired. If *you* need to rest, that's fine, but I'll continue with the mission."

Ah. This was the Zaxis I was more familiar with. Then again, perhaps his phoenix magic kept him more active? And if he *could* maintain himself at peak longer than everyone else, perhaps it *would* be better if he continued while the rest of us recuperated.

"It would be better if we stayed together," I said, uncertain if this was the right decision, but confident in my stance to remain a team.

"It's a quaint port town." Zaxis shot me a glare, his green eyes searching mine. "What do you think will happen? I'll become a victim of a pickpocket? I can handle walking around on my own."

Evianna huffed and crossed her arms. "When you're part of a guild, you aren't *Solo Specialist* Zaxis—you're *Journeyman* Zaxis." She said every word in a sarcastic imitation of Zaxis. "Learn the damn difference and follow the instructions of your superiors. *Especially in crucial missions where others are depending on you.*"

I ran a hand over my chin, hiding the smile I couldn't control. Atty looked away—but not before I caught her biting back a laugh.

Zaxis clenched his jaw, his face becoming as red as his hair. He glowered ahead, not bothering to say another word or even meet anyone's gaze.

With a smug little smirk, Evianna tilted her chin up and continued on the downward path.

But then I felt... something.

I stopped dead in my tracks, my pulse quickening.

It wasn't a plague-ridden monster. No. I knew that feeling now—the dreaded heartbeat of a creature filled with malevolence. This was something different. Something... *sneaky.* It crept up my spine and tingled my scalp.

Something...

Was nearby.

I placed my hand on the hilt of Retribution.

"Volke?" Atty asked as she turned to face me.

Before I could respond, the clacking rang from the base of the mountainside. Everyone turned to face the disturbance, and I tightened my grip on my weapon.

A man stepped out from behind a giant boulder of black stone. He wore plain trousers and a thick leather coat. A backpack hung from his shoulder, and he shielded his eyes and hair with a large hat.

"Hello there," he called up to us. "I thought I heard someone talking."

Atty, Zaxis, and Evianna relaxed.

"Greetings," Atty replied. "Are you from Port Akro?"

"Indeed, I am."

"We're travelers from afar looking to trade for supplies. Do you know whom we could speak to?"

Her voice and careful cadence were perfect for a diplomatic mission. Atty had a trustworthy presence I found appealing.

But I couldn't appreciate it long. The feeling of dread didn't leave me. If anything, the shivers down my spine grew worse—like claws running the length of my back, threatening to cut me. It was just a sensation, but it grew worse with each passing second.

"What kind of supplies?" the man asked.

"Star shards," Zaxis called back. "We need several. Do you know of anyone who can help us?"

The man nodded and motioned with a wave of his arm. "There's an artificer who lives just on the outskirts of town." Then the man gestured for us to join him at the base of the hill. "Come. I can take you there."

I can take you there.

Those words rang in my ears like a terrible chime.

Evianna clapped her hands together once. "Perfect. This will make our mission easier."

"Thank you," Zaxis said. He heaved a sigh of relief. "I'm glad they're friendly here."

When everyone started to head toward the man, I held out an arm. They all froze. Then Atty dropped her gaze to the hand on my sword.

"Volke," she whispered. "What's wrong?"

"He's... lying," I muttered under my breath. "He's here... to kill us."

I didn't know how or why, but I could taste it on the air like the bitter fragrance of rotting fruit. This man with the backpack intended to end our lives.

SKULL SCORPIONS

"What?" Zaxis asked. He lowered his voice and stepped closer to me. He wasn't quite as tall as me, but he stood on a rock next to me, gaining some height. "How do you know he's out to get us? Is this guy with the Second Ascension?"

I shook my head, struggling to find the words. It was a *feeling*. A deep, terrible sense. It gripped my thoughts and clawed at my lungs, much like a sickness taking hold.

"I just *know*," I muttered.

"I sense it as well, my arcanist," Luthair said again, his near-invisible presence hard to place.

Atty furrowed her brow. "I sense nothing."

Why did this sensation grip Luthair and me? It reminded me of the plague-ridden thunderbird. I had felt that monster swooping in before I could even see it. Now I could sense this man's intentions before he voiced them. A part of me feared I still had lingering effects of the arcane plague in my system—when I had been plague-ridden, I had sensed others with the disease whenever they had been close—but this was different. More thorough. Like the rattle of a snake's tail in my mind, warning me to *all* dangers, not just those of a magical or plague nature.

I glanced over at Evianna. She stared at me with her distinct eyes, her gaze searching mine. She looked just as confused as the others.

So—this wasn't unique to knightmare arcanists. There had to be another explanation.

"It'll be dark soon," the man in plain clothing called out. "It's not wise to be on these mountains when that happens."

He was urging us to move.

My instincts told me to cut him down, but my heart couldn't stand the thought of killing a man without unequivocal proof of his misdeeds.

"I'm sorry," I said, my firm voice traveling down the mountainside. "It's getting late, and we need to rest. We need to head straight into town."

Zaxis huffed. Still close to me—enough that our shoulders were nearly touching—Zaxis muttered, "There's no way he's thinking of killing us. We're a group of four arcanists. Look at him. He has no arcanist mark on his forehead. What is he going to do? Even if he has something like a rifle, he has no hope of defeating us."

"I just don't trust him, all right? It will be better if we avoid him."

The man grabbed the brim of his large hat and tipped it down in a polite gesture. Even from here, I could tell he forced a smile. "Suit yourself. But I still recommend you move quickly. Nightfall brings with it strange occurrences."

"Thank you for the advice," Atty said with a slight bow of her head. "And safe travels."

Before anyone else could say anything, the man continued on his path, disappearing around a boulder.

"Luthair," I said. "Follow that man and check the surrounding area while you go."

Luthair was basically invisible and could move without being detected. Perhaps he would bring me the proof I needed.

"Yes, my arcanist," he replied, his voice traveling by as he spoke. I saw nothing, not even a flicker in the darkness.

Satisfied with everything we had done, I continued down the mountain. Atty and Zaxis flanked me, neither offering any more commentary on the matter, but Evianna hurried to my side, her long, white hair fluttering with her movement.

"Why did you let him go?" she asked. "If he was going to kill us, we should've used our powers on him—we should've made him regret every decision that brought him to this moment."

"I have no proof," I said.

"But you sensed something, right? With your magic?"

"I don't know if it was my magic." That was the truth—and all I could think about. How had I felt this?

Evianna stepped onto one large stone and then leapt down five feet to another. She had a fair amount of grace, but I still worried she would slip and tumble the last bit of the trek. That was silly, of course— Evianna could dive into the darkness if ever she had a problem. Shadows didn't fall.

"Surely, your true form knightmare magic is the source," Evianna said. She whirled around on her heel and faced me. "It's the only explanation."

I caught my breath.

I hadn't even thought of that.

One of the major changes to a mystical creature when it gained its true form was the addition of a magical power it had never had before. Plain phoenixes couldn't resurrect people, but true form phoenixes *could*. Did true form knightmares have the ability to sense evil and malice? Was this the peak of my eldrin's magic?

"That would make sense," Atty said as she followed Evianna's lead and leapt down. She, too, landed with grace. After straightening her pants, Atty continued, "You didn't have this ability before, right? Perhaps this ability of yours is something fundamentally magical and unique to knightmares."

"If it *is* magic, we should just attack, attack, *attack*," Evianna stated. She grabbed at a dagger hanging on her belt and then thrust it through the air. "We can't let the enemy win. Ever."

I placed a hand on her wrist, stopping her from slashing her nonexistent foes. "*Restraint*," I said. "*Without it, we harm ourselves and our surroundings.*"

Attacking everything I *thought* to be a danger was a poor way to conduct myself. It would lead to trouble—other people wouldn't understand—and I needed to be more than a force that removed evil. I needed to be an example of justice for other arcanists, especially now that I was no longer an apprentice.

Evianna stared up at me, her lips pursing as she mulled over the wisdom. I hoped it would sink in.

"You *still* quote the Pillar?" Zaxis asked with a huff and a stifled laugh. "You'd think you'd start to forget one hundred and twelve random phrases, but I guess once they're ingrained, they might as well be a tattoo on your mind."

Atty lifted both her eyebrows and gave Zaxis a long look. "Don't pretend like *you* don't still have them all memorized."

"I never said I didn't." Zaxis walked by me and then leapt down the remaining stones, using his momentum to carry himself to the bottom of the mountain. He stumbled on the last landing, but he quickly recovered and brushed the dust off his crimson scale armor. "I just don't go around quoting the damn thing anymore. That's for children."

"I think it's great you still voice some of the lessons," Atty said as she touched my shoulder. "Especially now that you're training an apprentice. I find it admirable and quite attractive."

My chest tightened when Atty finished her statement with a smile. The interaction felt more flirtatious than normal, and I couldn't help but dwell on her words.

I wanted to say something clever in return—another quote from the Pillar, maybe about love or how when people admire each other it was a good starting point for a relationship—but I grasped at too many ideas and then vomited them all out at once with, "Pillars are perfect for starting pillars."

I must've sounded as though I were struck in the head and half-conscious. I knew the moment I uttered the statement that it was wrong, and the look Atty gave me confirmed it. A part of me wanted to throw myself down the mountain and end it all—but another part of me said, *I fought and killed members of the Second Ascension; I can handle this.*

"Er, what I meant to say is..." I hastily muttered.

Atty held up a hand and chuckled behind it, adding to my frustrations. Before I could blurt something else out, or exit the conversation, she said, "It's okay. I think I know what you meant. You don't need to be so tense around me." When she lowered her hand, she smiled again, genuine and reassuring. My anxiety melted away a moment later. "It's cute you still get flustered after everything you've been through," Atty added.

"Well, uh, that's not—"

"*Look out!*"

I spun on my heel just in time to catch sight of Zaxis and Evianna. Both were at the base of the mountain, standing in dirt and lightning-struck grass. Evianna had been the one to yell—she pointed at the ground as she leapt away from Zaxis.

Something *giant* shifted the ground, moving as though hidden underneath. I didn't have to wonder long. A second later, a scorpion the size of a small shed burst from the earth, its pinchers open to strike.

It wasn't just any scorpion—its ebony body was covered in skulls of various creatures, including humans—and its pinchers looked more like bone shears, the type of scissors meant for cleaving carcasses in half. It was a *skull scorpion*, a mythical creature that typically lived in the sands of the Amber Dunes. They were aggressive and violent—maneaters that wanted flesh more than anything.

This one was big, which meant it had to have an arcanist.

The beast slashed its bone-shear claws straight at Zaxis. I caught my breath, fearing he'd be sliced in two, but Zaxis stepped back and then tumbled to the ground, narrowly dodging a quick and certain death. When the pincher slammed shut, it screeched with a metallic quality, causing the hairs on my neck to stand on end.

The skull scorpion surveyed the scene with its six eyes—two on top of its body, four underneath—all of which appeared human instead of animal. It wasn't plague-ridden, since being a maneater made it immune, which meant the skull scorpions *normally* had a freakish number of eyes.

Zaxis didn't even give the monster a warning. He held up a hand and blasted the skull scorpion with a wave of fire so bright, it lit up the surrounding area in orange and red.

The scorpion screeched as its exoskeleton baked, but before any *real* damage could be done, the scorpion dove back into the ground, swimming through the dirt like I swam through the shadows.

I withdrew Retribution from its nullstone scabbard and leapt down the side of the mountain.

"Zaxis!" I called out. "Are you okay?"

Zaxis jumped to his feet, his teeth gritted. *"What was that?"*

"A skull scorpion," Evianna replied before I could. "Careful! It'll—"

The monster burst out of the earth a second time, its claws outstretched for Evianna. The beast was large enough that it could easily slice any of us in half, but Evianna was so much smaller—she looked like a doll in comparison.

Evianna stepped into the darkness and managed to escape. The skull scorpion's claw slammed into a boulder, cracking it along the side.

When Evianna emerged on top of another boulder, her knightmare, Layshl, rose up around her, forming a suit of black leather armor. The armor itself wasn't complete—Evianna didn't have a gauntlet on one arm, and her trousers had holes—but Layshl covered the majority of her. It looked dragon-like, with scales and a wing-shaped cape. Once merged, Evianna and her eldrin would live and die as a single being, and their combined strength would improve their magic.

"Luthair!" I shouted, hoping he had heard me from wherever he was.

Fortunately, he made himself known to me as he shifted through the darkness. He slithered over—straight to my feet—so we could merge.

Just as the inky darkness was rising up around me, a *second* skull scorpion lunged out of the dirt. It went straight for me, its six eyes focused sharp.

Even while Luthair's liquid armor formed around my body, I slashed with Retribution. My blade cut through the monster's face and pincher as though they weren't there—no resistance or physical contact. My sword sliced magical creatures the same way a knife cut through water.

The skull scorpion gurgled a blood-filled screech as the main part of its body slammed into mine. His momentum carried us into the side of a large stone, crushing me between the scorpion's massive body and the mountain. I couldn't breathe, and my ribs hurt as I twisted against the beast.

Luthair finished merging a moment later, his cold power seeping into my body. I disappeared into the shadows and reappeared a good twenty feet away, on top of a stone and high enough to survey the battlefield. I took a deep breath as my body slowly healed.

My star-stitched cape fluttered in the evening winds, and my shield hung on my arm.

The plain-looking man who had offered to guide us to a trader was standing behind a boulder, accompanied by two other equally-as-innocuous-looking companions. This was their trap. They lured people away from town and then ordered their skull scorpion eldrin to surprise them from the depths of the earth.

The worst kind of evil—the pathetic and cowardly kind.

"You there," I said, my double-voice a thing of intimidation. "Stand down."

The three men spun around. None of them carried weapons—not that I could see—and they stared up at me on the boulder, their eyes wide. Two of them had arcanists marks on their foreheads, both with skull scorpions wrapped around the star. The third man, the one who had approached us, was the non-arcanist meant to catch people off guard. They all seemed scrawny, or perhaps malnourished, I wasn't sure.

For a fraction of a second, I wanted to tell them to surrender and send them on their way, despite their blatant attempt to kill us.

But one of the skull scorpion arcanists dove into the dirt and the other held out a hand to evoke a splash of scorpion venom. He threw the venom in my direction, and while it wasn't as deadly as *some* venoms I'd had to deal with in the past, it wasn't something I could ignore, either.

I held up my shield and blocked the attack, the venom splattering against the face and spilling onto the ground with little effect.

My arcanist, Luthair said telepathically. *Behind us.*

The other arcanist emerged from the ground and then yanked himself onto my stone with a stealthy guile I hadn't expected. He didn't frighten me, though. Not with how long it took him to get up to my height. He held a dagger with some skill, but not enough to be a threat. This man was a brigand—a pirate of the land—a lowlife who thought he could cut me down and take my possessions.

Too many people were relying on me. I wouldn't fail here.

The skull scorpion arcanist lunged for me, and I nimbly stepped aside, allowing him to stumble. With a wave of my hand, I manipulated the shadows to grab him and hurl him from the rock. He flew down a good five feet before colliding face-first with a pile of shattered stones. Blood exploded from his nose and forehead, coating the area in wet crimson.

A shriek caught my attention. I turned toward the sound and spotted the skull scorpions rushing Zaxis, Atty, and Evianna. Phoenix fire slowed the monsters, but it wasn't enough. Their exoskeletons protected them from the heat.

Even the scorpion I had wounded—the one with the slashed face—was unrelenting in its assault.

Evianna attempted to use her terrors, but faltered at the last moment. Nothing happened—her evocation failed. And when one of the scorpions went for her, my heart stopped in my chest.

Under no circumstance could I let her die.

1 1

PORT AKRO

I gritted my teeth and waved my arm, the icy power of my magic running through my veins with my anger. The darkness in the area rose up like an inky tide, reaching everyone's ankles. Then I manipulated the new water-like shadow right off the ground, the blackness coalescing together to form solid matter. For a split second, the darkness resembled the head of a dragon—or perhaps a sea serpent—rising from the depths and "biting" down on both the skull scorpions.

I had never manifested magic like that before. When I had manipulated the shadows in the past, they had been tendrils or nets or hooks, but never a *creature*. Or perhaps this was better described as a *monster*.

The visual effect of my manipulation left me startled. *I* faltered with my concentration, causing the dragon-esque formation to slam into the ground and break away like a wave on the beach.

It had been enough to knock the skull scorpions onto their sides, but they weren't defeated. Both sunk into the ground, protecting themselves from my sorcery. Evianna, Zaxis, and Atty stared at where the scorpions had disappeared, their confusion apparent in their knitted eyebrows and slightly open mouths.

You must focus, Luthair telepathically spoke, his voice like a growl in my mind. *Battle is never the place to hesitate.*

I shook my head, clearing my thoughts.

A skull scorpion burst from the ground next to the rock I stood on. It swung its tail at me, the needlepoint of its stinger aimed for my neck. With little thought for my actions, I slashed with Retribution, cleaving the tip of the tail clean off. Then I danced back, held up a hand, and evoked my terrors. The nightmare visions I created gripped at the scorpion's mind. It thrashed and hissed and snapped its scissor pinchers in terror.

"Behind you!"

I turned to spot Zaxis lunging for one of the skull scorpion arcanists. Apparently, the brigand was preparing to splash more of his venom, but Zaxis evoked enough flame to catch the man on fire.

Atty—a good ten feet away—also evoked her flames, but hers burned so bright and hot that they quickly overwhelmed the skull scorpion arcanist. He screamed as the combination of two phoenix arcanists charred his flesh.

The non-arcanist turned to run into the rocks, no doubt to hide himself as he fled. Evianna shadow-stepped closer to him and then motioned with her hand. The shadows answered her summons. She manipulated the darkness to grab his ankle. Although it was clear her magic was still new—the tendril she'd created was small and weak—she managed to trip the man, preventing his escape. It was a clever move for someone with limited capabilities, and I took note of it as I used my own manipulation to tether him to the dirt.

The skull scorpions, both injured, dove underground. The last arcanist attempted to do the same, but Zaxis and Atty got him before he could slide into the dirt. When the flames washed over him, he shouted and tried to run. He likely couldn't use his magic to sink into the ground when he was on fire—the shock and pain would've prevented him from focusing.

It wasn't long before he collapsed to the ground, thrashing and screeching. He wore simple clothing—nothing that would protect him from the embers of a talented arcanist. When the man stopped moving, I almost felt pity for him, but then I remembered how Evianna had almost died, and all sympathy disappeared.

I had promised Evianna's sister, Lyvia, that I would watch over Evianna should something terrible happen. Although Lyvia and I hadn't been the closest, I felt a twinge of guilt when I remembered how she'd died in the Thronehold Coliseum. No matter what, I would make sure Evianna was safe—it was the least I could do to honor Lyvia's memory.

After a quick exhale, I glanced around.

The wounded skull scorpions were nowhere to be seen. Both had lost their arcanists, and a part of me suspected they would be enraged—that would be my state of mind—but perhaps they were different. Eldrin typically grew to be more like their arcanists. If the brigands had been cowards who lured people into traps for easy kills, then it was likely their skull scorpions were cowards, too.

I waited, my body tense.

But the beasts never emerged from the ground. They had fled.

Evianna stepped through the shadows, slithering up onto the stone with me before emerging from the darkness. While she was merged with her knightmare, she reminded me of an assassin—her armor was sleek and quiet. The black scales on her armor glistened under the light of the distant moon.

"Are they gone?" she asked, her double voice with Layshl all too familiar.

I nodded.

Atty and Zaxis walked over to the base of the stone. They glanced around, still on high alert, but they quickly came to the same conclusion. The monster scorpions likely wouldn't be a threat.

The non-arcanist I had tethered didn't squirm or plead for his life. He just waited, his head hung.

Evianna's knightmare slid from her body, leaving her in her tailored outfit.

"What're we going to do with *him*?" Evianna asked, glaring at the man.

"We'll take him to Port Akro," I said, still merged with Luthair. "He will face judgment at the hands of the local authority."

Evianna pursed her lips, but she didn't object. Did this displease her? I couldn't tell.

Atty and Zaxis both seemed to approve of my decision. They turned their attention on the town in the distance. Thankfully, it wouldn't take us long to reach it. I imagined the walk—and the fight—had left everyone drained.

"Let's go," I commanded.

As I had assumed, the trek to Port Akro was short, but by the time we entered through the main gate, my feet ached and my back pulsed with a dull pain. Luthair had unmerged with me a long time ago, and I missed the added strength he provided. Still, I soldiered on, refusing to acknowledge my fatigue when the others kept looking to me to be the leader.

I didn't want them to feel like I couldn't handle this.

We left the non-arcanist brigand with the gate guards. I explained his crimes and the incident with the skull scorpions, and they acknowledged that the arcanists had been targeting small groups that were traveling over land. I stood a little taller when the guards thanked us for helping keep their citizens safe. This was the type of situation I had always imagined when I had been younger—I would be an arcanist stopping thieves and cutthroats, saving the innocent from the darkness of the world.

I was a star in the night, providing light to those who needed it. Just like all the old legends of swashbucklers and hero arcanists. Perhaps someday my name would be read beside theirs.

The winds off the Shard Sea swept into town from the port, and I hadn't realized how much I missed the smell of saltwater. It felt like forever since I had been in a proper port, with actual sailing ships. Early morning dockhands unloaded barrels of fish, preparing for market, and I smiled to myself as I remembered my time on the Isle of Ruma. It amused me how smells could trigger such memories.

Atty tucked her blonde hair behind her ear. "Should we find lodging?"

I nodded. "We'll rest for a bit and then gather the star shards we need."

Port Akro wasn't a complicated place. The streets were narrow, but organized into a grid. The buildings were one-story and simple, built mostly from stone, with wooden supports and shutters. A few taverns were positioned near the docks and around the outer wall, which meant the town had a great many travelers passing through.

Zaxis clicked his tongue in disappointment, but instead of voicing his disagreement with my plan a second time, he pointed to a building with a sign. There were no words, just an engraved picture of a bed.

"There," he said. "We found it. Let's do this as fast as possible."

"Rest can't be *powered through*," Atty said, lifting an eyebrow.

"*Anything* can be powered through if you try hard enough."

They gave each other hard glances. Fortunately, they didn't continue their argument.

Forsythe and Titania swooped out of the sky and flew down toward us, the flames of their inner bodies glowing like lanterns concealed by feathers. They landed on the street, their majesty a harsh contrast to our humble surroundings. The few dockhands who were awake and working stopped everything they were doing to point and whisper.

"We've found some people you should speak to, my arcanist," Forsythe said with a slight bow of his heron-shaped head.

Titania nodded along with his words. "Several traders from distant lands are here. Our mission will surely be a success."

"I'm glad to hear it," Atty said, weariness in her voice. "We'll head there as soon as we're ready."

"As you say, my arcanist."

It occurred to me in that moment that I hadn't heard from Evianna in a while. I glanced around and found her standing behind me, her eyes half-lidded and her shoulders drooping. It wouldn't have surprised me if she had fallen asleep while standing.

"Are you okay?" I asked.

Evianna snapped her eyes open and took a deep breath. "What? *Of course*. I'm fine. Everything is fine." She rubbed at her face and then glowered up at me. "I think you should tell me how you manipulated the shadows so well back when we were fighting those blackhearts. I want to do that—to defeat all my enemies in a single stroke."

"It takes time and practice. Perhaps we'll go through some exercises once we wake."

In truth, I didn't know how I had created something so massive, and so quickly, but I suspected there were multiple factors. My powers were always stronger at night, and now that my magic didn't hurt when I used it, I had an easier time using my abilities to their fullest. That, and Luthair was true form.

Atty and Zaxis entered the inn with their phoenix eldrin in tow. The soot that followed created a faint trail, and I wondered if the owners of the establishment would be irritated or honored.

Evianna stayed close to me as we entered, her eyes drooping the moment she thought I wasn't looking.

12

TRADERS FROM DISTANT LANDS

W e slept on simple beds made with cotton-stuffed mattresses. It was infinitely better than a hammock on a sailing ship, and I fell asleep the moment I made contact with the pillow.

But anxiety wouldn't allow me to rest long. Four hours later, I awoke to the sounds of a busy morning market. It seemed as though everyone in town was out and about, gathering food for the day or delivering new supplies. Part of me wanted to rest a little while longer, but Master Zelfree's voice echoed in my thoughts, reminding me of the urgency of our mission.

I was about to sit up when I noticed the shadows in the room shift. Was it Luthair? No. It couldn't be.

With adrenaline in my veins, I leapt out of bed, grabbed my sword, and drew it from its scabbard.

Evianna emerged from the darkness in the far corner. She must have shadow-stepped under the door to enter my room. The moment she appeared, her eyes went straight to the weapon in my hand, and she grimaced as she moved backward a step.

"V-Volke," Evianna said. "What're you doing?"

I exhaled, allowing a bit of my combat readiness to slip out with it. I returned Retribution to its scabbard.

I had long become accustomed to sleeping in my trousers just in case I needed to spring from my bed and act. And while I wasn't indecent, I didn't enjoy the thought of someone walking in and seeing me with Evianna like this. The last thing I wanted was to give the impression of impropriety.

Instead of answering Evianna's question, I asked, "Why did you enter my room without knocking first?"

Evianna straightened her posture and then crossed her arms. "I thought I would feel safer with you around, but instead you had your sword at the ready like I was some common thug you needed to dispatch."

"Feel safer?" I asked. "Are you okay? Is there trouble?" I almost unsheathed Retribution a second time, my heart rate increasing.

"I had unpleasant dreams," she said matter-of-factly. "And while I don't normally require anyone to talk me through them, I just thought *you* might understand." Evianna faced the door, half-turning away from me. In a whisper, she added, "They involved my sister."

The mere mention of Lyvia had me regretting my actions. I placed my sword on the bed, and before I could search for my shirt, the shadows lifted up, holding my clothing like the hook of a hat rack.

"Thank you, Luthair," I muttered as I pulled my shirt on and buttoned it down. "Evianna, if you want to speak to me, you can always send your eldrin to contact mine. There's no need to barge into my room —unless it's an emergency. But that's the only time."

With the darkness acting as his hands, Luthair handed me my belt and pulled my boots over.

Evianna shook her head, swishing her long hair back and forth. She relaxed her tense stance as she turned back to face me. "I didn't realize a visit from me would be this upsetting."

"The last time you appeared in my room, we became *betrothed*," I quipped.

Her expression softened with a smile, and she clapped her hands together once. "Wait, you're acknowledging it? So, you'll accept my betrothal? Oh, Volke, I'm so—"

"That's not what I meant," I interjected. "I was just being sarcastic."

Her jovial demeanor vanished as quickly as it had arrived. Evianna frowned, her expression more genuinely twisted with sadness than I'd thought it would be. "First you hold a weapon on me, and then you make jokes about my romantic intentions?"

I had been prepared for Evianna to be huffy or flounce from the room—or even demand that I act a certain way, because she was a "princess"—but the hurt in her voice caught me off guard. I stepped closer, wondering if Evianna's nightmares had left her emotional, and I was just exacerbating the problem.

"Evianna," I said, gentler in tone. "I'm sorry. I didn't mean to be disrespectful. If you need to talk to someone, I'm always willing."

"No one else here understands," Evianna snapped. She rubbed at her arms, her voice unsteady, her gaze falling to the floor. When she spoke again, it was slower and more purposeful. "For months I've been with the arcanists of the Frith Guild, but none of them knew Lyvia, and they certainly don't know me. I... I just want something familiar. My old room, my clothes, my tutors—*my sister*. But they're gone now."

I ran my hand through my disheveled hair. It had gotten long, and the locks covered most of my ears. I needed to cut it soon, but I only half dwelled on that as I mulled over Evianna's comments. She was alone. And she had been since the incident in Thronehold. I hadn't even thought of that until now, and a part of me understood why she would be so *insistent* on seeing me the moment I had returned.

Evianna walked away from me and placed her hand on the door handle. "The cruelty of dreams is that they twist reality and show you things you can never have." She stared down, allowing her long white hair to cover most of her face, hiding her expression. "You remind me so much of Lyvia sometimes... I just..."

But she never finished her thought.

Instead, Evianna opened the door. "I'll knock the next time I come to speak with you."

"Wait," I said.

Evianna hesitated, stopping halfway through the doorframe.

I continued, "Why don't we wake the others and scour the town together?"

"Zaxis and Atty already left with their eldrin," she stated.

Already? The information didn't sit well with me. Why hadn't they bothered to wake me?

I sat on the bed and yanked on my boots. "We'll go together, then. It'll give us a chance to talk, and I might be able to speak to you more about knightmare magic."

Evianna leapt back into my room, fueled by enthusiasm she had conjured out of thin air. "Yes! This is the perfect plan. Quickly, then—we should start before the others find the star shards we require."

She grabbed my upper arm and pulled on me the moment I was done lacing my boots.

"All right," I said, wiping the tiredness from the corners of my eyes. "Let's go."

The main market of Port Akro was a road that stretched from one end of the city to the other. Port Akro wasn't gigantic, so the market wasn't as impressive as it sounded, but there was plenty of selection. Every merchant ship around the Shard Sea stopped in before heading to New Norra, apparently, and that brought opportunities to trade for exotic goods.

It wasn't difficult to locate Zaxis and Atty among the dockhands, merchants, and denizens of Port Akro. Their phoenixes were large enough, and bright enough, that I could spot them from blocks away, even when they stood on the ground. Not only that, but Zaxis's fiery red hair was unique in these parts. He hadn't been so unique on the Isle of Ruma, where most people had red or blonde hair, but he was one of only two here. Atty's longer hair, and choice of pure white clothes, often made her a standout, and today was no exception.

They stood in front of a stall built into the side of a building. It was an artificer's shop—a place where arcanists would sell magical items. Sure enough, there was a stamp of a guild on the nameplate above the door. It read: *The Tinkerers Guild.*

That was a good place to start if we wanted star shards in a hurry.

Although I wanted to approach Zaxis and Atty and inquire about the deals they were making, Evianna touched my elbow and then pointed to a far stall near the city wall. I glanced over and caught my breath.

The white pelts the merchant had on display glittered with silver stripes, each one no bigger than my forearm. They were rizzel hides, no doubt in my mind.

"Why are they selling those?" Evianna asked, an edge of indignation in her tone. "I mean, I know arcanists use parts of mystical creatures to make trinkets and artifacts, but..."

"The merchant is probably selling those pelts to mystic seekers," I said, turning away from the stall. I didn't enjoy the sight. "Rizzels can be used as lures for other creatures. The pelts help mystic seekers find rarer creatures."

Evianna held up some of her white hair. "Nicholin said I was *part rizzel* because of my hair color. He was joking, of course—I know why my family has this hue—but now I feel somewhat... connected... to the poor creatures who lost their pelts." She stared at the hair in her hand for a long moment. "Can you imagine if someone killed me for my pelt?"

"Humans don't have pelts, my arcanist," Layshl said from the darkness.

Her darker voice startled me for half a second, and I was reminded of how I had first felt when Luthair would speak. *His* voice was a comfort now, but Layshl's I would have to get used to.

"You know what I meant," Evianna said, staring down at the shadows around her feet. "Killing me for my hair."

I glanced around when she said that, surprised to see several people staring in our direction. They all turned away once they noticed my gaze. Most hurried off as if they were late for an important meeting.

It hadn't occurred to me to until then, but perhaps some people here *would* try to kill Evianna. Not because of her hair, but because her brother, Rishan, had ordered her death. The Second Ascension had attempted to carry out his will, and if I hadn't been there, I was certain they would've been successful. I was a fool to think they would stop at one attempt.

The Second Ascension could be anywhere, even in this port town. And Evianna was so distinct.

"Evianna," I muttered under my breath. "Stay close to me at all times. At least until we return to the *Sun Chaser*, all right?"

She stared up at me with a raised eyebrow. "First you seemed awkward about my presence, and now you can't go without it?" She huffed and tossed her hair over her shoulder. "And they say *women* are fickle."

I wanted to offer a retort, but I swallowed the words. Evianna had been so hurt this morning—I couldn't bring myself to do that all over again. She could believe whatever she wanted to believe.

"Oh!" Evianna said with a gasp.

"What is it?"

"Look there! Star shards."

She gestured to another stall. Sure enough, five small crystals sat out for display. The dark velvet they rested on contrasted nicely with their golden coloration. They glittered with a deep inner power, even if they were only thumb-sized.

"Come," Evianna said, tugging at my sleeve. "That's what we're here for, isn't it?"

Although Master Zelfree had said that the phoenix arcanists could potentially trade their healing and imbuing for the star shards, that didn't mean I was to sit out. Evianna was correct—we should attempt to gather as much as possible.

I followed behind Evianna as we made our way through the thin crowds of Port Akro. There weren't many people at our desired stall. There weren't many goods for display, either. Besides the five star shards, there were eight sparkling geodes cracked in half, twelve scales from a sea serpent, and three compasses, each of which looked as though it were made with a creature's claw for the dial.

There was a story behind this collection of items, but I couldn't quite piece it together.

The man behind the table wore a long cloak, his hood back, exposing his sandy hair, sun-darkened skin, and stubbled face. He had bags under his eyes, and he rested his chin in one hand, no doubt fighting the powers of fatigue.

"Greetings," the man said as he placed three fingers over his heart.

Evianna stared at the man's hand for a long moment, her eyebrows knitted.

I recognized the gesture from my time in New Norra. Perhaps that was where the man hailed from originally? I decided to use that information to my advantage.

"Greetings," I replied as I placed three of my fingers over my heart. "It's a peaceful day. I prefer it to the sandstorms."

The man lifted his head off his hand and then offered a genuine smile. "You won't believe this, but when I was last in New Norra, there was a storm so powerful, it crept *over* the city walls. It didn't cause much damage, but the sand and winds were enough that we had to keep indoors."

"I was there for that," I said. "A strange day indeed."

I had also been partially responsible for *starting* the sandstorm, but I wasn't about to mention that to the man.

Evianna tilted her head, but said nothing. She watched with her bluish-purple eyes locked on me, like she was seeing a whole new person.

"What can I do for you, friend?" the man asked, more awake than ever.

I motioned to the star shards. "I was hoping to make a trade."

"Those are ten gold crowns each," he said. "Or eleven gold leafs, if you have that island currency on you."

"I don't have that much coin, unfortunately."

"What *do* you got?"

I opened my mouth, but closed it right after without saying a word. Although I had valuable items—like my shield and Retribution—I wasn't about to trade them away for five star shards. What else could I use? What else was there?

With a sigh, I crossed my arms. At the edge of my peripheral vision, I noticed a man staring. I shot him a glance, and he turned away, his attention suddenly focused on an old oil lamp someone had out for sale.

"Evianna," I whispered. "Perhaps you should wear a hood when we're out."

She frowned. "A hood? What for?"

The man selling the star shards chuckled. Then he knocked his knuckles against the wooden stall table and shook his head. "Don't you worry, friend. No one is staring at your companion."

"Huh?" I asked. "What do you mean?"

"They're not staring at her. They're staring at *you*." The man tapped his forehead, right where an arcanist mark could have been. His head was blank—he was a mortal man without magic—so why did he—

My throat tightened once I realized what he meant. I lifted my hand to my forehead and grazed my glowing mark. No one in this town had a true form eldrin. The phenomenon was so rare that even I hadn't really understood what a glowing mark meant until recently.

"You're a knightmare arcanist?" the man asked. He scratched at the stubble on his chin. "I'm not familiar with knightmares, but I know they're few and far between. Not many born, and a lot of them die early deaths. If you give me a part of your eldrin... I think that's worth the shards."

13

FRITH

"Apart of Luthair?" I whispered.

The merchant's words sank into my gut. I didn't want to *cut up* Luthair just to get resources, but at the same time, we needed them to leave this place. What if these five shards made the difference?

And others in our group had already sacrificed for the benefit of everyone else. Fain's wendigo no longer had his antlers. He had cut them off to make plague-immune trinkets, and even though they had been destroyed by the agents of the Second Ascension, that didn't change the fact that both Fain and Wraith had been willing to go the distance when we had needed them to.

"I need to speak with my eldrin first," I said.

The man nodded and ran a hand over his chin.

Evianna and I stepped away from the stall. She hovered close, her eyebrows knitted in a semi-glower. "You aren't actually going to go through with it, are you?"

"Luthair," I said. "Do knightmares have any part of them that can be easily made into an artifact or a trinket?"

When he spoke, his voice lifted from around my feet. "When a knightmare dies, it typically leaves behind its cape. It contains the purest form of our essence."

"Can it be... cut into pieces?" I felt disgusted even asking the question, but I needed to know.

"If you want to give this man something, I can separate a part of my armor. It won't be as powerful as a shred of knightmare cape, but my new form allows me to compensate for the loss."

The liquid shadows roiled throughout him, shifting and moving themselves as needed. Even if I gave the merchant a gauntlet, I was certain Luthair would "make" a new one, and I would probably never notice.

"Won't you be weaker afterward?" I whispered.

"Yes, my arcanist," Luthair replied. "But the loss will be slight."

Evianna shook her head. "I don't think this is necessary. I wouldn't do it if I were you."

Her shadow shifted beneath her feet. "My arcanist," Layshl said. "Star shards are essential to imbuing and are always useful. In theory, Luthair can regain his lost strength. Knightmares are mystical creatures of pure magic. Our bodies are different—more transmutable than others."

I had been hesitant before, but hearing Layshl's logic helped me understand.

"Luthair, are you okay doing this?" I asked.

"Of course, my arcanist."

Without another word, Luthair rose up from the shadows around us, his imposing plate armor moving with an arcane fluidity. The star-marked cape twinkled like the dead of night as he plunged his gauntlet hand into his chest. It looked like inky clay as he withdrew a hand-sized chunk of black metal from the depths of his void. I had thought he would've removed a piece of his armor, but perhaps that wasn't necessary anymore.

Luthair held out the piece of himself. I held out my hand, and he placed it in my palm. The icy chill of the knightmare metal sent a shiver up my spine.

"This didn't hurt?" I asked.

"No, my arcanist. It was freely given."

"Thank you."

He nodded his helmet head. Before he had been true form, I could see inside his body—into the emptiness of his armor. Now there was no opening. He looked like a man clad in armor from head to toe.

Evianna watched the whole event with wide eyes. Even as I turned to go back to the merchant, she kept her gaze on the chunk of metal.

I placed the fragment of Luthair on the merchant's stall. His eyebrows shot to his hairline as he leaned forward to get a better look at it.

"Now that's something you don't see every day," he muttered. "I'm impressed, friend. Quite impressed." He placed his hand on the metal and then recoiled. After a long second, he chuckled to himself. "It's cold. Didn't expect that." Then he scooped it up and tucked it away into his robes.

I picked up the five star shards.

"They're yours," he said, motioning for me to take them faster. "It's a fair trade."

I nodded as I tucked the shards into my pocket. I had forgotten how powerful they felt in my hand—something about their inner power spoke to me. I kept my hand in my pocket the rest of the walk through Port Akro, both to make sure the shards were still there and to enjoy the tingling sensation of their magic.

Evianna stayed at my side. She said little, but her eyes panned over our surroundings often, and I figured she was intent on finding more star shards.

When it became clear we had searched every random stall, she motioned back toward the Tinkerers Guild.

"We should check on Zaxis and Atty," she said. "I'm sure they've found more shards for us."

With only the five I had in my pocket, I feared we wouldn't be able to find enough. If we had to travel elsewhere to find the shards, would the *Sun Chaser* last?

I shook my head, dispelling the negative thoughts. "All right. Let's head back."

The inside of the Tinkerers Guild reminded me of the Grand Apothecary in Fortuna.

Gillie, the fabled apothecary and a caladrius arcanist, had kept her shop and guild in a constant state of disarray. She had left books and vials everywhere, stacked on bookshelves that lined every wall. Similarly, the Tinkerers Guild felt like a library. Rows and rows of shelves, most of which had no books—just pieces of metal and bits of mystical creatures.

But unlike Gillie, who labeled nothing, the tinkerers kept organized notes and nameplates for every space. The bits of mystical creatures were organized by color, shape, and power of magic. The metals were categorized by their density. Even the vials of assorted liquids were kept together in groupings based on rarity.

I craned my head back, impressed by the vaulted ceilings and shelves that went ten feet high. The tinkerers needed ladders to get anything from the top few, and to my surprise, some of their eldrin made their beds on the very top of the bookshelf.

Over half of the arcanists in the guild were bonded with *bluecaps*. They were a type of fairy, or so I had heard. They appeared humanoid in shape, just a foot tall, with bright blue caps and dragonfly wings. Unlike redcaps, which were violent and sometimes deadly, bluecaps were said to be helpful in crafting and mining. It made sense for the tinkerers to favor them—bluecaps had the magic to strengthen and empower metal.

The guildmaster, Neeson Gray, was bonded to a *miku*—a stout little goblin nearly three feet tall. Miku were quite rare, and from what I could recall from my reading of old legends, they sometimes hid in the nests of bluecaps, as they were attracted to powerful metals and rare gems.

I doubted the creatures here were extremely powerful, but they were all so specialized. I admired the guild for sticking to their strengths, especially since crafting magical items was such a tricky skill.

Evianna and I waited in the main room of the guild. A non-arcanist sat at the front desk and allowed us to mill about, but we were forbidden from touching anything. I walked between the shelves, awestruck by the wondrous materials the guild had gathered.

"This stuff looks valuable," Evianna said. She eyed the resources with a skeptical expression. "Why not keep it all in a chest or box?"

"I read a legend about Gilda the Golden that said her eldrin, a miku, liked to have its horde of valuables on display," I muttered as I continued my trek through the guild. "This is probably the guildmaster's horde. Isn't it impressive?"

"It seems like they want their things stolen. They let us right inside!"

I touched the guild pendant around my neck. "We're members of the Frith Guild, and they know that. We're not complete strangers. Most guilds open their doors to other arcanists registered in guilds."

Evianna pulled on the thin chain holding her bronze pendant. She spun it around in her hand, examining it closely. "I never thought I'd be in a guild. I had always assumed... I'd be..."

Melancholy crept into her tone, and I didn't want a repeat of earlier this morning. "Did I ever tell you how the Frith Guild got its name?" I asked. I didn't wait for her to reply. I took a quick breath and continued with, "The word *frith* means *peace, protection,* and *freedom.* It encompasses all those ideals and was the word spoken by knight arcanists who lived thousands of years ago."

Although I hadn't known if this would interest her, Evianna listened intently.

"You see, there used to be these barbarian pirates," I said, remembering all the wicked tales. "They were arcanists, and they looted and plundered small villages that dotted the coastlines. When they came across wealthy towns, they threatened them instead. The barbarian pirates would make a deal—*give us your gold and we'll leave, but if you don't, we'll burn everything to the ground.*"

"Terrible," Evianna stated. "What brutes."

"Exactly. And for the most part, the people of these towns weren't arcanists, so they had no way of fighting back against the pirates."

Evianna swished her hair back. "And that's when the Frith Guild stepped in to help?"

"Well, the Frith Guild wasn't around yet. It was started when a young man in one of the smaller villages decided to become an arcanist. He rallied others, and they ventured out into the mires around their homeland until they had all bonded. Once familiar with their magic, they fought off the pirates. The first guildmaster said he stood for the *frith of humanity.* So that's how it became known as the *Frith Guild.*"

"I see," Evianna said. She tapped her chin with a single finger. "I didn't realize that word carried such weight. It should be used more often."

"It's very old. Most people don't know its meaning."

"But *you* know it." Evianna glanced away. "And I'm sure Lyvia knew it."

I wanted to respond with something uplifting, but words failed me. Lyvia probably *had* known the meaning behind the word *frith*.

A door opened on the far end of the room, drawing my attention. Zaxis, Atty, and Guildmaster Gray—a stout man with a head of lush, black hair—walked into the room. When the guildmaster chuckled, the slight pooch of his belly jiggled. He wore fine leathers, the type to protect him from heat of a forge, and his arms were muscled, so it amused me that he had any excess fat on him whatsoever.

"That's all I can spare," Guildmaster Gray said, his voice loud and distinct. "I hope that'll be enough to repair the airship."

Atty offered a slight bow of her head. She was a good foot shorter than the man, but she held herself with such a regal presence, it almost didn't matter. "Thank you, Guildmaster. Your assistance has been beyond valuable."

"Yes, thank you," Zaxis added. He also bowed his head, but his speech and mannerisms were curt. Still, I appreciated his show of gratitude. Master Zelfree would be proud.

"No, thank you two," Guildmaster Gray said. "Those healing trinkets will come in handy. And the fire resistance always helps with the forging. This has been a good day. Not many phoenix arcanists make it to Port Akro."

Zaxis grazed a hand over his salamander scale armor. "Trust me. Those fire-proof clothes will last a long time. I've tested the material myself."

The guildmaster chuckled again, and there was another jiggle from his small gut.

Forsythe and Titania hopped into the room, their glowing bodies easy to spot in the dimly lit tinkerer horde. The moment they spotted me, they made their way over like only birds could—a slight waddle, their wings half-opened. They left soot trails, but the arcanists of the guild didn't seem to mind.

"We procured thirty star shards," Forsythe stated. "Are you proud?"

Titania nodded. "So many. It was all the Tinkerers Guild had to offer."

"I hope it's enough," I said. "But we won't know until we get back."

Luthair spoke from the darkness. "We mustn't delay a moment longer, my arcanist. Now is the time for our departure."

I nodded. Zaxis and Atty must have felt the same because they bid the guildmaster a good day and motioned for me to join them. With Evianna in tow, we exited the fascinating guild. Fatigue ate at me, but excitement pushed me forward. My first assignment as a journeyman—the first one with Luthair, a true form knightmare—had taken its toll, but it wouldn't beat me.

14

FORFEND

The trek *up* the Surgestone Mountains was too much. I considered myself physically fit, but the combination of terrible sleep and the steep incline of the rocky terrain, made everything difficult. We made it a fourth of the way up, but my legs and lungs burned, slowing my pace to a crawl.

Zaxis was the only one ahead of me. He climbed the mountain like he was punishing himself for his own weakness—scraping himself on jagged rocks and never resting. After every step, he muttered curses under his breath, and I suspected he would rather walk until collapsing rather than admit he needed to take a break.

Atty and Evianna were behind me, but not by much. Evianna's age was the most apparent when it came to this strenuous task. She was the first to become exhausted, and Atty stayed with her, using her phoenix augmentation of healing to help Evianna through the most difficult portions of the trek.

The phoenixes flew overhead, keeping an eye out for any other brigands in the area. Although I didn't *want* to delay our mission any further, I liked the thought of clearing away blackhearts from the mountainside. Anything would be better than climbing the rocks at this point.

At a small plateau, I stopped to catch my breath.

"Zaxis," I called up to him. "Come back. This isn't going to work."

"I can make it," he snapped, his own breathing heavy.

"I'm not saying you can't. I'm saying we need to do something else."

Zaxis stopped once he hefted himself on top of a reddish boulder. "Such as?"

Although I hadn't wanted to use my shadow-stepping when going down the mountain, this was a different situation. "I'll take us. Luthair and I will use our magic to travel through the darkness."

Zaxis wiped the sweat from his brow before nodding. "Fine."

He leapt off the rock, landed on the ground, and then slipped on a pile of loose pebbles. If it had been anyone else, I was certain they would've tumbled down the side of the mountain, but Zaxis recovered quickly. He managed to stand and grab hold of a lightning-burnt root in order to balance himself.

Then, like a cat pretending they never made a mistake, Zaxis sauntered over to me.

"Well?" he said. "Let's go."

I glanced back to Atty and Evianna. "We're going to shadow-step the rest of the way," I called to them. "Evianna, this is good practice for you. Atty, you and I will go together." I gave Zaxis a sideways glance. "Luthair will carry you."

Technically, I *could* take two other people with me when I dove into the darkness, but the drain it took on me physically was too much, especially with the amount of hiking we had already done. Much like muscles, a person's magic could be overworked, and I still remembered the agony that came from exerting myself too much.

Then again, I hadn't tried that technique since Luthair had achieved his true form...

I shook away the thought. Now wasn't the time to push myself. Now was the time to return to the others.

Evianna entered the shadows, slithered up the mountain at an impressive speed, and then emerged next to me, stepping out of the void as easily as someone stepping off a flight of stairs. "I think I'm rather good at this," she said as she fluffed her ivory hair. "What can I do to get better?"

"Go farther each time." I pointed to the mountain ahead of us. "Even if it's just an inch. Hold your breath longer and longer."

"Really? What if I practiced other magic while I went through the shadows? As in, what if I evoked terrors every time I emerged, or—"

I shook my head. "Don't practice until you get something right—practice until you can't get it wrong."

Master Zelfree had uttered those words to me a while back. They stuck with me, just like the 112 steps of the Pillar. If Evianna wanted to master her magic, she needed to keep doing it until everything became second nature.

"I agree with Volke," Zaxis said as he crossed his arms.

Evianna narrowed her eyes.

"Got something to say, *kid?*" Zaxis taunted.

The last word had Evianna pursing her lips. With red in her cheeks, she placed her hands on her hips. Then she turned to me. "Volke—that was immature behavior, and we both know it. Reprimand him." She motioned to Zaxis with a flick of her wrist. "Go on."

I rubbed at the back of my neck, at a loss for words. On the one hand, it *had* been immature. On the other, I couldn't let Evianna *command me* like one of her castle servants.

Zaxis snorted and huffed out a laugh. "You are way too easy to rile." Then he smirked. "As an arcanist of the Frith Guild, you need to be able to keep a calm focus. If you let your enemies taunt you—or get angry at just a few words—you're giving *them* control of the situation." He tapped at his temple. "Think about it. You act reckless when you're upset."

I wanted to dive head-first into a tirade about how Zaxis *always* allowed his opponents to rile him, but I held back the urge. He had gotten better, and I didn't want to chide him for past mistakes. Besides, if he was voicing this wisdom now, perhaps he had learned something valuable while I had been out searching for a cure to the arcane plague.

Atty climbed up a collection of rocks and made it close. "I'm ready, Volke."

"So am I," Zaxis said.

Without me needing to voice a command, Luthair stood from the shadows as a massive suit of plate armor. He was taller than Zaxis, and when he placed a gauntleted hand on Zaxis's shoulder, he almost looked like a vengeful ghost coming to claim the ultimate toll. Zaxis didn't react with any sort of fright, however.

"Hold your breath," I told him.

"I will."

Zaxis allowed himself to be dragged into the darkness and whisked away up the mountain. I watched as they went, their movements nothing more than shifting shadows.

When Atty stepped close, I glanced over and held out my arm. She placed her hands on my chest and leaned against me, a slight smile on her face. I pulled her into an embrace.

"*Excuse me*," Evianna said, mere feet away. She raised an eyebrow. "Is that really an appropriate way to transport someone through the darkness?"

Atty's face brightened. She took a step back, distancing herself enough that she had to hold my hand. "I suppose it's more proper to travel like this."

A harsh wind rushed down the side of the mountain. I shivered, both from irritation and the chill. A part of me wanted to tell Atty about my "betrothal," but another part of me never wanted to mention it to anyone. I feared everyone who heard the story would think I had somehow instigated the situation.

Evianna moved closer to Atty, her arms still crossed. "Volke, you should be setting a good example for a young apprentice like me. Holding someone in such an intimate manner might give me the wrong idea." She spoke every word with a sardonic glare. She wasn't confused —she was just saying all this to make it uncomfortable for everyone. Was she jealous? Was she just trying to upset Atty? Again, if I said anything, I'd have to explain the whole story to Atty, so I held back the commentary. I really didn't want to deal with the situation at the moment.

Unaware of Evianna's true motive, Atty nodded along with her words. "I suppose it was a bit inappropriate. I apologize, Volke." She rubbed at her face. "I can already hear my mother's chiding. She would never let me live something like that down."

"It wasn't egregious," I said. "Let's just... put this behind us and get up the mountain."

Satisfied with her victory, Evianna slid into the darkness with a smug smile and left us.

I turned my attention to the long trek up the mountain. I spotted Zaxis and Luthair quite a distance ahead of us. Luthair wasn't one to wait, and I was certain that Zaxis was urging him to move quicker.

I dove into the darkness, taking Atty with me. The cold power of the void was pleasant. It soothed my sore legs, and I enjoyed the powerful sensation of gliding through the inky shadows. Unaffected by gravity, I made my way up the mountain, snaking between rocks and traveling at lightning speed.

When I emerged to take a breath, it was at a small outcropping of rocks. I had to take a second to regain my balance.

Atty gasped for air when she emerged. After a moment of steady breathing, she glanced around. No one else was nearby. A quiet howl of wind was our only company.

With a sheepish smile, Atty leaned against me again, this time wrapping her arms around my neck. My face heated, but at the same time, the excitement of the action had me smiling.

"Atty?" I asked.

"My mother would be so furious," she muttered. "She disliked the thought of me being with anyone. But let's keep it quiet, okay?" Atty rested her forehead on my collarbone. "If no apprentices are watching, is it really harming anyone?"

I wrapped an arm around her waist, holding her close. "I suppose not."

"Then... let's just spend a moment together. Okay?"

It almost felt irresponsible to sit on the rocks for a few seconds, but I couldn't deny Atty's request. She felt warm. And I enjoyed the way she relaxed against me. For most of my life, I'd had *awkward* relationships with women, to put it mildly, but this didn't feel like that. This felt more natural. More genuine.

Once enough time had passed, I dove back into the darkness, my insides twisting and my heart beating harder. Although I knew it was an illusion brought on by excitement, my fatigue had vanished, and in an attempt to impress Atty, I pushed myself harder than I had before, determined to get to the top of the mountain as quickly as possible.

We made it back to the *Sun Chaser* much faster than I had anticipated. The sun had yet to set, and the storm clouds were still in the distance. Vethica and the khepera had done wonders at restoring the airship. Their magic of renewal truly was amazing, and I suspected the ship wouldn't have been repaired as quickly without them.

Zaxis and Luthair had made it to the ship first. Atty and I would've been close on their heels, but Evianna couldn't travel as far in the shadows, and I had slowed my pace to keep a close eye on her. At some level, Evianna must've known that because as we reached the summit, she murmured a quiet apology before disappearing into the darkness and making her way into the hull of the airship.

Once on the summit, Atty took the star shards and headed for the *Sun Chaser*. I would've gone with her, but Zaxis jogged over to me and held a hand up as though to stop me. I hung back, ready to hear his questions, but instead, he approached with a playful grin.

"Do you realize how useful traveling through the shadows is?" Zaxis asked as he neared me.

I lifted an eyebrow. "Yes?"

"I wouldn't trade bonding with Forsythe for anything, but I must admit... that was amazing. I wish I could do that all the time."

"Maybe I can make you a trinket," I replied as I rotated my shoulders, stiff from our travels.

"Oh, yeah? Something that'll let me do this? All the time?"

"Yeah. I made one already. It worked like a charm."

"For whom?"

I caught my breath. I had made the shadow-stepping boots for the Dread Pirate Calisto—but I couldn't bring myself to say that. I hadn't done it knowingly. Karna and my father had had me create the trinket as payment for a ship ride without my permission.

"Never mind," I said. "It's not important. I'm just saying that I can help you."

Zaxis nodded. "Well, I've gotten better at my imbuing as well. My armor is immune to flames—I could make something like that for you.

Or better yet, I could give you something to improve your healing. It'll make you sturdier."

"Really?" I asked.

He shrugged. "Of course."

I offered him a weak smile. "Thank you."

"Don't get weird." Zaxis smacked my shoulder. "We have to help each other. If something happened to you, Illia would never be the same. I can't let that happen. Plus, we need to make sure we're ready for those goons from the Second Ascension."

"I suppose."

Zaxis replied with a click of his tongue. "Tsk. *You suppose.* Don't get like that. You know I'm right."

"Okay. You're right." I half-smiled. "Happy? We'll craft each other trinkets once we're back at a major port and we can get more star shards."

Thinking about the shards brought me back to the biggest problem at hand. I turned my gaze to the airship.

Now with star shards, my father and Captain Devlin had started working on the ship. They only had the thirty shards that Atty and Zaxis had worked for, since I had yet to add my five to the mix.

To my surprise and fascination, Karna leapt down from the rope ladder hanging on the side of the airship. She headed right for me, her grace evident, even in her gait.

As a doppelgänger arcanist, Karna had the ability to change her appearance—almost at will. Despite that, she had a standard look that I had become familiar with. She almost always gave herself long, golden blonde hair, the lithe body of a dancer, and sun-kissed skin that glowed with healthy radiance. Today was no different. She wore puffy pants and a shirt that was twisted close to her body, but otherwise it was the "normal" Karna.

Zaxis kept at my side, one of his eyebrows raised. "She looks like she wants something," he whispered. "Watch yourself. I don't trust her."

I wanted to give Zaxis a questioning look—why wouldn't he trust her?—but Karna reached me before I could voice my concerns. I was prepared to greet her with a standard bow of my head, but she didn't give me an opportunity. Instead, Karna threw both of her arms around my neck and pulled me into a tight embrace. She smelled of flowers and honey, and my face heated from the sudden and unexpected contact.

"Volke," Karna said into my neck, her voice practically a purr. "I wish I had gone with you, but I'm glad you're back now. I feel like you've been avoiding me."

"Uh, Karna," I muttered as I softly patted her back. "I've just needed to rest. I haven't—"

"*Someone* from the *Sun Chaser* should've gone with you. It's our airship, after all. We've never needed the help of the guilds to solve our own problems."

When I tried to separate us, Karna held tighter. Not wanting to struggle against her, I opted to pat her back a second time. "You're helping the Frith Guild. Of course we would help you in return. That's how we operate."

Finally, Karna released me and took a step back. She flashed me a smile, but when her gaze shifted to Zaxis, it turned into something cold —a fake smile, maintained through willpower.

"Don't you have somewhere to be?" Karna asked. "A big, important arcanist like yourself should probably help the crew. Am I right?"

Zaxis tensed as he stared down at her. With a sneer, he said, "As journeymen arcanists, *Volke and I* have many places we need to be." He grabbed me by the upper arm and yanked hard. I half-stumbled, shocked by the brashness, though I probably shouldn't have been. This was Zaxis—some things never changed.

I allowed Zaxis to lead me toward the airship, still bemused by the whole situation. "I can speak with you once we're back in the air," I said over my shoulder to Karna.

She didn't reply. She just stared at me and Zaxis, her expression neutral. Despite her ability to maintain an unreadable exterior, I knew how she felt. Karna had certain tells that I had come to learn while traveling with her—and she was angry.

I wasn't sure why, but I could see it in her blue eyes.

Zaxis motioned to the deck of the *Sun Chaser*. I nodded and slipped us both into the shadows. A moment later, we were on the deck. My father and Master Zelfree stood near the railing while Captain Devlin and his giant roc eldrin were down on the ground.

While my father was a talented artificer who could craft metal and bone, it was Captain Devlin's roc magic that would allow the airship to fly once again.

As such, Jozé used his flames—and his skilled hands—to mold metal around the shattered bones used to keep the ship afloat. The white-hot steel was like clay in my father's hands, and he used his magic to coat the broken bits of airship in a careful casing. When he was done with a piece, he handed it over to Master Zelfree.

I thought the white-hot metal would burn him, but Zelfree's arcanist mark had a phoenix interwoven in the star, which meant he had copied Jozé's blue phoenix and was now capable of handling fire without risk of harm.

Master Zelfree took the reinforced bone and slid down the half-busted gangplank. Then he used his borrowed magic to rapidly cool the metal and attach it to the underside of the airship. Captain Devlin placed the star shards against the mended bones and imbued them with his roc magic, creating a constant wind that would uplift anything.

"You should stay away from the doppelgänger woman," Zaxis muttered as we watched the three of them work.

"Why?" I asked.

"Ever since you met her in Thronehold, you haven't been the same. Even Illia thinks so. And if it hadn't been for Karna, I doubt you would've taken off the moment you were infected." Zaxis tilted his head to the side and shot me a glower. "She's the type of person who will try to manipulate you."

"You don't know her like I do." But Zaxis wasn't wrong. Karna *was* the type to try manipulation, but that didn't mean she couldn't be trusted. "Karna isn't someone you need to worry about."

"Heh. We'll see about that."

The moment Zelfree climbed back up the gangplank and onto the deck, his attention snapped to me.

"Volke. There you are."

"Yes?" I asked.

"You did good," he said as he walked over, his expression softening. "You gathered more star shards than we needed. It won't be long now until we're ready."

"How many did we end up requiring?" I asked as harsh winds blasted down the nearby rocks.

Zelfree held up an arm to shield his eyes. "We only needed twenty-two."

I reached into my pocket and withdrew the extra five. "I gathered a few on my own."

"Oh? How's that?"

"I gave up a piece of Luthair to purchase them. Perhaps we should give these to the crew of the *Sun Chaser*?"

Zelfree's brow furrowed as he stared at the star shards in my hand. "You gave up a piece of Luthair for these?" Then he shook his head. "By the abyssal hells—even you need a keeper sometimes."

"I didn't want us to return without having enough," I said.

"Enough? Clearly, I've neglected my responsibilities as a master arcanist because you should've known that *thirty* would've been plenty. Thirty-five is overkill, and I definitely didn't want you to weaken your eldrin for this task."

"Luthair said he could handle it."

Zelfree ran a hand down his face, his gaze on the dreary skies above. It took him a full five seconds before he exhaled and brought his attention back down to me. "Keep those. They're yours. Use them to make a trinket or something useful."

"No," someone said.

Jozé walked over to us, his gait off from his bum leg. It took him longer than most to cross the deck, but I didn't mind. He had an expression that said he had a clever idea.

When he neared, Jozé said, "You should use them to repair your shield."

I caught my breath. I hadn't even considered that. It had been nearly a year since I had failed to create my shield properly, and since then, I had never had the time or the resources to fix it. Well, I also hadn't had the expertise.

"Can I do that?" I asked. "I mean, I'm not entirely sure how."

My father smirked as he stepped close. He held up his hand and gestured for me to bring out my shield. I did as he wanted and reached toward the shadows. Luthair's gauntlet hand rose up, the magical item held tight in his grasp. I scooped it up as Luthair sank back into the darkness.

The heater shield seemed cracked when I examined it in the low light of sunset. Then I handed it over. Jozé turned it around in his hands, his eyes focusing in on certain aspects. Did he know it had been crafted with a scale of the world serpent? I doubted it, and since my knightmare magic coated the base material and made the whole shield black, it would be difficult to deduce.

"Let me help you," Jozé said as heat flared from his palms.

The shield didn't have any metal, but his blue phoenix magic seemed capable of bending anything with its heat. Despite that, the shield didn't budge. My father had to focus—practically strain himself—to heat any portion of the shield. As he did so, crackles of magic shot up from the surface of the face. The shield could reflect magic, after all. Would the heat turn back on him?

But that wasn't the case. My father instead used his powers to mend the small cracks. The bright white-hot edges melted together, and Jozé took the time to smooth everything afterward, using his fingers to shape the surface of the shield like a sculptor did clay.

"There," he said, his voice strained. "Now... use your shards."

I waited until Jozé cooled the shield before reaching out for it. The whole thing was still warm, but I could handle it.

Zelfree and Zaxis watched the whole event a few feet away, both of them with their arms crossed as their attention locked on the heater shield. Having an audience didn't bother me, but I did fear Zelfree's judgment. What if I failed this a second time, and he thought I wasn't worthy of the *journeyman* title? I hated that thought, and it took some of my willpower to push it aside.

Luthair rose out of the shadows and instead of taking his place by my side, he merged with me, his liquid armor coating my entire body and forming into a solid metal-like suit of armor that both filled me with power and sent a shiver down my spine. With his power and his guidance at the edge of my thoughts, I placed the five star shards on the face of the shield.

Imbuing an item with magic was like pouring water from a jug. My soul was the container, and I needed to allow the star shards to absorb my essence. The shards acted as a type of adhesive that kept the magic inside the item, even after I was done offering it.

The draining sensation hit me hard. I needed sleep, and every drop of power that the shield took was like another hour of hard labor added to my fatigued body. Still, I gritted my teeth and held firm. This was to repair the shield, not make it from scratch.

Fortunately, the process didn't last long. My shield glowed, and as soon as I felt the last of the star shards dissolve fully into it, I stopped my magic.

The whole piece of armor practically sparkled afterward.

Zelfree and Zaxis both raised their eyebrows, and although I had to take ragged breaths, it still made me smile.

"You've done it," Jozé said. "Now it's perfect."

I lifted the heater shield and slid my arm through the straps on the back, attaching it in place. It felt... lighter. Easier to move. I was half-tempted to swing it around—really test out the weight—but soreness prevented me from acting out my inner excitement.

"What's its name?" Jozé asked.

I turned to him. My head was completely encased in a helmet, but still I was able to see everything.

"I hadn't thought about it," I said, my double voice echoing slightly.

Jozé motioned to the shield. "It's an artifact, boy. It needs a name, just like your sword."

While the name of my sword had come quickly, I didn't know what I would do for the shield. Something to do with defense. Something with protection. Something striking and powerful—a single word that embodied all those qualities.

Luthair's presence in my mind helped to guide me to the word I was looking for.

"Forfend," I said. "I'll name the shield *Forfend*."

The word *forfend* meant to protect things from evil—the perfect name for a knightmare arcanist's shield.

A NIGHT TOGETHER

The *Sun Chaser* was repaired in less than two hours once we had the necessary star shards. My father, Master Zelfree, and Captain Devlin worked tirelessly until it was capable of flight, and only afterward did they rest.

When the airship took to the sky, I breathed a sigh of relief. Finally, we could leave the storm-ridden mountains behind. Now we needed to focus on reuniting with Guildmaster Eventide and helping her protect whomever she deemed worthy to bond with the world serpent. As long as the Second Ascension couldn't get their hands on the legendary god-creature, we still had a chance of thwarting their schemes.

I paid careful attention as we rose into the air. Night descended, and I worried about running afoul of a second plagued thunderbird. Although fatigue ate at me, I just leaned against the ship's railing and kept my watch over the passing clouds.

"I found the last person!"

I turned toward the high-pitched voice of a child.

Biyu stood a few feet away from me, a heavy book in one arm while she wrote something with her free hand. I knew the *Sun Chaser's* cabin girl well, and seeing her again had me smiling. Biyu returned the smile when she glanced up, her one eye bright with tireless optimism.

"Everyone is accounted for," Biyu said as she tucked her quill away.

She wore rough trousers and a coat with several large pockets. Her eye patch was the most striking part of her outfit, however. Not because it was brightly colored or gaudy, but because it didn't quite cover the gnarled scars that ran from her hairline to her jaw. The Dread Pirate Redbeard had cut out her left eye, leaving Biyu with the "souvenir" of their encounter.

Her missing eye reminded me of Illia, and for that reason, I had always felt more protective of Biyu than I probably should have. She was only ten or eleven, and she hadn't deserved the pain of a pirate's knife—and neither had Illia.

Biyu's shoulder-length brown hair, silky and straight, fluttered in the evening wind, but it didn't seem to bother her. She was too focused on her book. It had a leather strap attached to the spine that allowed her to carry it like a satchel, and Biyu carefully closed the tome in order to heft it onto one shoulder. The book itself was as thick as her arm, and I suspected it weighed more than five pounds.

Biyu furrowed her brow. "Volke, why are you up on deck?"

"I'm just keeping watch." I gestured to the landscape of sky all around us. "I can see in the dark, and—"

"But *Mesos* is keeping watch," Biyu interjected.

She pointed in the opposite direction, off the starboard railing. There, among the swirling nimbus, was Captain Devlin's roc. Mesos soared at the same speed as the *Sun Chaser*, just a few hundred feet in the distance.

I would've been content to watch the majestic roc fly for hours, but the sounds of heavy bootsteps drew my attention. Each stomp on the deck betrayed the anger behind the movement.

Vethica approached me with her scarab eldrin, Akhet, perched on her shoulder. Akhet's shiny exoskeleton contrasted nicely with Vethica's pixie-short, reddish-blonde hair, but I couldn't enjoy the range of color —not when Vethica scowled at me like she had caught a thief in the act.

"Here you are," she said with a single snap of her fingers. "I should've known. C'mon. Food is ready."

Her khepera eldrin buzzed his scarab wings. "Everyone is worried."

"Worried?" I asked. "About what? I've been here the whole time."

Vethica smacked my shoulder with the back of her hand. It wasn't painful, but there had been force behind the strike.

"What's wrong with you?" she asked. "You disappeared on your guild in the blink of an eye and now you're wondering why they'd be worried if you vanished for a couple of hours?"

Biyu nodded along with Vethica's words. "That's right! They told us the whole story about how you disappeared after you got the plague." Biyu stood as tall as a ten-year-old could. "You shouldn't leave them. Crews don't leave their ships, and guild arcanists don't leave their guilds. Everyone knows that."

With a playful bounce to her step, Biyu bounded to my side and took hold of my hand. "We can go together." She smiled again, bright enough to chase away the evening gloom.

Vethica forced a quick exhale, her breath coming out as a visible fog. "You heard the cabin girl."

The two of them escorted me to the stairs and then below deck. Neither was part of the Frith Guild, so why did it matter what the guild was doing without me? Then again, the *Sun Chaser* had become like a second home—with the crew, the officers, the eldrin—my short time with them had had an impact. Perhaps Biyu and Vethica were just looking out for me.

We entered the galley to find everyone from the Frith Guild already gathered and eating their meal: bowls of goat soup. I could smell it from the corridors. The pungent odor would linger for hours afterward, and I swear it also sank into the wood itself, sometimes lasting days.

When I approached, the group of arcanists glanced up from their bowls. Atty, Adelgis, Fain, and Hexa sat on one side of the table while Illia, Zaxis, and Evianna sat opposite. Technically, Master Zelfree was at the head of the table, but he wasn't engaging with the others. He ate his food while he read over a piece of parchment, his focus away from the idle conversations of the journeymen around him.

Their eldrin crowned the benches, or the space near their feet, or their shoulders, if small enough. It was packed, even though there weren't many people. I almost didn't think I'd be able to fit amongst them.

To my surprise, Karna circled the table, as though playing the role of serving girl. It was odd to see the members of the *Sun Chaser* mixing with arcanists in the Frith Guild. I wasn't accustomed to interacting with them all in the same place.

Karna stopped her work and gave me a coy smile the instant she noticed my presence. I gritted my teeth, already on edge. That look she gave me always preceded some sort of mischief.

"Oh, Volke," Karna said. "And here I was about to come get you."

I motioned to Vethica and Biyu. "It's fine. Other officers of the *Sun Chaser* came to inform me dinner was ready."

Biyu puffed out her chest and smiled, unable to contain her pride. Being called *an officer* probably didn't happen often.

Karna swished back her lovely hair and sauntered straight to me. "I wasn't going to come get you for dinner. I wanted to see if you were ready for bed."

"Why would you care?" Hexa piped up with a snort and a laugh. She leaned on the wooden table, her eyes narrowed.

Raisen stuck one of his hydra heads up from under the table, its snake-like neck making the movement easy. "Yeah, why would you bother?"

"Volke and I are close," Karna said as she gently placed a hand on my shoulder. "I wanted to ask him if he wouldn't mind sharing my bed again —he's so warm, and it can get chilly on this airship at night." She flashed me a subtle smile. "As long as you don't steal the blankets this time."

"*Karna*," I snapped, practically choking on all the words I wanted to say but couldn't seem to voice.

The expressions of every person at the table shifted all at once, their eyes locked on me and Karna, their own conversations dead in their tracks. I had never felt my body heat with unbridled embarrassment quite so quickly.

Without allowing a second to go by, Master Zelfree hastily stood, his parchment in one hand and his soup bowl in the other. "Whelp—this isn't where I left my work materials..."

Traces leapt from the table and onto Zelfree's shoulder as he strode away. He didn't even give me a second glance as he retreated from the situation. Was that really what a master arcanist should've done? I needed his help and he just *left*?

"I can explain," I said, my attention on Atty.

She stared at me with knitted eyebrows, her posture stiff.

"What's to explain?" Vethica asked. "It's pretty straightforward."

She and Biyu were the only ones in the group not stunned into silence. Vethica glanced between Karna and me, and then to the members of the Frith Guild. Her khepera eldrin did the same with his beetle-like eyes.

"It's not a complicated story," Karna said as she walked around behind me and took a position on the other side. "And our time together was rather chaste, just in case any of you were getting the wrong idea. You see, during our travels, I asked Volke to stay in my quarters for a few evenings, and with all the respect and grace of a gentleman, he obliged. It lasted longer than expected, but I wasn't complaining. Volke's a compassionate companion. He made the cold nights bearable."

When Karna placed her hand on my arm, I jerked away, on the edge of fury. Why did she have to make the story sound so intimate? Even if she said it had all been chaste, that wasn't how the others would take it. Especially Atty.

But I could see the hurt in Karna's expression—like my reaction to her touch had been a slap to the face.

"You slept with a harlot?" Evianna asked, more incredulous than shocked.

"Volke said she *wasn't* a harlot," Illia interjected before I could get a word in. "He told us in Thronehold that Karna is a songstress."

"*Yeah*," Nicholin chimed in, his fur puffed up to make himself look bigger. "What my arcanist said!"

"But she has a harlot's mark." Evianna pointed to the side of Karna's neck. "That crescent moon is for the women of the Moonlight District. Everyone knows of them—Thronehold is a haven for their kind."

The tattoo on Karna's neck was coin-sized and easy to miss, due to her long hair. I often forgot it existed, but Evianna was correct. The crescent moon shape marked her as a woman from the infamous Moonlight District.

"And you have a problem with that?" Vethica barked. She withdrew a zigzag dagger from a sheath on her belt. The blade sparkled with inner thunderbird magic. "Don't guild arcanists claim to be *saviors and knights*? Yet you'd sneer at the first *undesirable* you run across, wouldn't you?"

Atty stood from the table. "Wait, please. I apologize if our reactions were offensive. That's not our intention. We just... were unaware Volke had such a relationship." She gave me a weak smile. "That's fine. I just wish I had known ahead of time."

"I can explain," I said. "I—"

"It's okay." Atty shook her head. "You're obviously important to Karna. Perhaps you should discuss this with her first before explaining anything further."

Sure enough, when I faced Karna completely, I could see the distress in her demeanor. She hid everything so well—I hadn't noticed it previously. Her shoulders were tense and her face was set in a forced neutral. Had Atty sensed Karna's displeasure? Was she trying to give me a chance to make things right before I could shove my foot deep into my gullet?

Hexa clicked her tongue in semi-disapproval. "Well, uh, I think it's time to retire. Raisen, come along." Hexa stood, stretched her scarred arms, and then headed out of the galley.

Her hydra lumbered out from under the table, crashing into and dragging some of the benches along the way. The sound of wood scraping against wood echoed throughout the room until Raisen was most of the way to the door.

Fain and Adelgis stood from their bench a moment later.

"Moonbeam," Fain whispered as they went. "You can read minds—you have to tell me the interesting bits."

"That's really inappropriate," Adelgis murmured afterward. "And some of it is too scandalous to repeat, to be honest."

"Seriously? Those are the best damn parts."

But as soon as they got a few feet away, I couldn't hear their murmurings.

Illia and Zaxis got up from the table next. They had a silent conversation between them, conducted in glances alone. When they had finished, they turned to me. Zaxis smirked. *I told you the doppelgänger arcanist was trouble,* he mouthed, though he didn't voice anything.

Illia shook her head. "Volke, I'll be in the storage room with the hammocks. If you need me."

I nodded.

The two of them left, much quieter than the rest. Even Forsythe and Nicholin remained silent, which surprised me more than anything else.

Vethica sheathed her zigzag dagger and then motioned to Biyu with a jerk of her head. Biyu saluted and held her book tight as the two of them departed.

While there were still cooks and deckhands in the galley, they kept to themselves, either cleaning, cooking, or eating. None of them seemed concerned about the minor drama of arcanists bickering, and some of them even seemed to avoid glancing in our direction.

Which basically left me with Karna, Atty, and Evianna at the table.

"Perhaps once you have this settled, we can talk in the morning?" Atty asked. "I know I don't quite have the full story, but I'd love to hear it from you, Volke."

Evianna quickly stood from the table. "If you have time, you should also speak to me in the morning. I... would like to know what kind of relationships you have."

Without another word, Evianna glared at Karna and then swished back her white hair with a mild amount of flair. A moment after, Evianna fell into the darkness, disappearing from the table in one movement.

Atty didn't have the same style of exit. Instead, she offered me a smile before motioning to her phoenix to depart. They left as a pair, and I wished I had the social graces necessary to prevent her from leaving, but I couldn't think of a way. Atty had been correct—I probably needed to speak with Karna. I hadn't since I had returned to the *Sun Chaser*, and while I hadn't been avoiding her, I was starting to suspect that *Karna* thought I had.

Finally alone with Karna, I rubbed at the back of my neck.

"Listen," I said.

I stared down at her and caught my breath.

Out of all the things I had expected, Karna crying hadn't been one of them.

ARRIVAL AT FORTUNA

"Karna." I gently placed a hand on her shoulder, uncertain of how to conduct myself.

Her tears weren't accompanied by hysterical sobs—they ran cold and silent. When Karna finally registered my touch, she glanced up at me, the last of her misery slipping out of the corner of her eyes. After she wiped her face dry, there were no lingering hints of her sadness.

Karna didn't pull away from my touch. If anything, she moved close enough for me to smell the lilac fragrance woven into her hair.

"It's been a decade since I've cried over a man, I'll have you know," Karna whispered. "I never expected that you, of all people, would be the one to remind me how callous men can be."

"Karna, I didn't mean to—"

"You didn't mean to recoil away from me?" she asked. Karna pulled away from my touch, almost in the exact same manner I had done with her. "You didn't mean to look disgusted? To act like I was a diseased whore reaching for your coin purse? You didn't mean for all that?"

"*Of course not.* I just—"

"You just did it anyway," Karna interjected. With a hard-edged look, she continued, "You were the man who took me to the Queen's Gala. The one who said he didn't care where I had come from or what my past had been. But the moment you could get away from me, you did. And the moment it might have appeared as though we were close, you had to clarify to everyone that *of course you'd never be with the likes of me.*"

Her words left an odd buzz and sting in my thoughts. It reminded me of the skull scorpion arcanists we met on the road. An unusual feeling...

"Listen," I said. "I've never conducted myself in a manner that's implied we're more than just friends."

Karna kept her narrowed eyes on mine. "We're closer than that. We shared the same bed and kissed on more than one occasion. Why would I hide that? Are you disgusted by my feelings for you? You can admit it."

Her words continued to sting my mind and leave a bitter taste in my mouth. Something about this was wrong. My reactions didn't feel natural.

Was it my magic? Was it telling me when someone was lying or concealing the truth? I had to take a moment to mull over the situation, and thankfully, Karna didn't say anything as I stared into her ocean-blue eyes.

"You know none of that is true," I whispered, keeping this part of the conversation between us.

Karna opened her mouth to speak, but I cut her off with a single word.

"*Don't*," I growled.

She fell silent, her eyebrows knitted, her eyes searching mine, like she couldn't believe I'd act in such a manner.

"Don't play this game," I finally said, my voice low. "I never want to hurt you, Karna. Ever. But you know why I reacted the way I did—and you were hoping for that reaction, weren't you? You wanted my attention, and you wanted the drama between me and the others. Maybe you even wanted me to apologize. That's the sense I'm getting."

And not just an intuitive sense, but something deeper. When the skull scorpions attacked, I understood that they wanted our deaths. But now, with Karna, I had a feeling of manipulation. This was a ploy to get me to act a certain way—and to consume my time. Perhaps it would've worked on me months ago, when I had been more naïve and without my knightmare magic to detect these lies and falsehoods, but it wouldn't work on me now.

Or ever again.

Karna went to speak again, but I held up a hand, cutting her off.

"Please, think about this," I said, my anger fading the longer I stared at her. "I told you—be honest with me. If you want my time, just... ask. There's no need for *this*. It's only going to push us apart."

I lowered my hand, and Karna exhaled.

"You want me to be honest?" she asked. "It *did* hurt when you pulled away from me."

When she had mentioned that earlier, I'd had no sense of deception. Even now, her voice carried a genuine tone.

I gritted my teeth and replied with a curt nod. "I'm sorry. I was just caught off guard by your statements. You were implying so much more had happened between us, and you know that."

Karna stepped closer and placed her hands on my chest. I didn't move away, even if this was more intimate than I'd like. Karna was a more physically affectionate person. It was just... who she was.

"I apologize," she said, staring up at me through her lashes. "To be honest, I had no *plans* for drama, but the moment you hurt me, all I wanted was... to make you feel the same way."

Again, my new sense for deception didn't register with her words. Thankfully, she was being honest, and we were having a real conversation, not something manipulated or crafted. In that moment, I finally saw her again—beautiful, striking, compassionate. It was difficult to remember all that whenever she was acting out her usual ploys.

"Have you spoken to the others much?" I asked. "In the Frith Guild, I mean."

Karna lifted an eyebrow. "They're utterly convinced it's my fault you disappeared from the guild. Their odd glances give away their true feelings, even if they're cordial when I walk by."

"It was my choice to go with you after I was infected with the plague."

"They don't know that. And I doubt they'd believe me if I told them."

"I'll make sure they know," I said, determined to make good on that promise.

Karna shook her head. "It's not important. Let them think what they will."

"It *is* important."

She narrowed her eyes, but didn't comment.

"We'll need your help," I continued. "And Vethica's, and Captain Devlin's—and my father's. You saw what the Second Ascension was doing with your own two eyes. Now isn't the time for pointless bickering."

Or needless drama—but I didn't mention that part. Thankfully, Karna didn't have the extraordinary mind reading skill that Adelgis did.

Karna brushed her blonde hair over her shoulder. With the grace of an expert dancer, she turned on her heel, her movement fluid. Then she took a seat on the edge of the table, half-jumping up and landing without much noise.

"Very well," she said, her head high. "I'll attempt to bridge the gap between your guildmates and the crew."

"R-really? The whole crew?"

She smiled. "I'm not fond of the guilds, but I am fond of *you*. If you think this is important, I'll ignore my gut feeling and put my faith in your plans."

I rubbed at the back of my neck, uncertain of what to say. Was she doing this as an apology? Or did she really trust me? My newfound ability to detect falsehoods wasn't alerting me to anything, but then again, I wasn't sure if it would detect white lies and general politeness. I hadn't felt the magic until there had been genuine instances of people trying to manipulate or trick me...

"Thank you," I muttered. "That means a lot."

Maintaining her smile, Karna replied, "Well, now I'll have more chances to ask for your time, so it works out for everyone, doesn't it?"

Knowing that was a reason eased my doubt. "Yes, I suppose we'll have more opportunities to spend time together."

It would only take us a week to reach Fortuna, the capital of the Isle Nation Perphestoni. Although I had grown up on the Isle of Ruma, I knew Fortuna well, and I couldn't wait to return. It had been *the city* when I had been younger—the place everyone had wanted to move to and make a name for themselves. Fortuna also had a collection of guild headquarters, and I had wished with all my heart to visit them all.

Thinking back on those memories made me smile.

The evening winds rushing over the *Sun Chaser* picked up in intensity. The chill brought me out of my musings, and when I turned my attention to the horizon, I took a moment to admire the Shard Sea stretched out below us. The moon transformed the surface of the water into a glittering landscape. Few things were as breathtaking as water.

I exhaled.

Fortuna was far to the north, past the Argo Empire. We were a single airship, and I doubted our enemies would find us, but I worried. Prince Rishan—or perhaps now *King* Rishan—would kill us all if he knew I had taken Evianna from the Thronehold castle.

"You're distracted, my arcanist," Luthair said from the darkness. "You came to the deck to practice your magic."

"I'm sorry, Luthair. I can't help but dwell on the timing. I wish we were already in Fortuna."

"Patience isn't about waiting. Patience is about understanding that you can't force events, so you must use your time between each wisely."

"I'll try to keep it in mind, Luthair."

I turned around, attempting to focus, but that came to an abrupt halt the moment I spotted Hexa striding over to me. Her hydra lumbered up the stairs and crawled onto the deck, his four heads glancing around in all directions. Hexa had already reached me by the time Raisen managed to locate us.

"Volke," she said as she approached.

The chilly winds whipped across her skin, creating goosebumps in their wake. She rubbed her shoulders down to her elbows and then shrugged off the chill.

"Are you okay?" I asked.

Hexa replied with a sardonic frown, as though she had heard the most ludicrous statement. "Are you serious? The last I saw, you were being scolded by a harlot, and everyone got upset." She smacked my shoulder. "What's going on with *you*?"

I furrowed my brow. "Don't worry. I've already handled it."

"You spoke to Atty? Because she was upset. I mean, she didn't say anything, but I could tell."

"You could? How?"

"It's a special power women share," Hexa said with a snort and a laugh.

"Well, I spoke to Atty a few moments ago. Briefly. Even so, she didn't seem upset."

She had been in her room, and when I had told her that Karna had just been acting out to get attention, Atty had nodded and said we could talk more in the morning. That had been it. No anger.

And when I had told Evianna, she hadn't reacted much, either. She had simply acknowledged my statements and smirked, like Karna's actions and apology had been the desired outcome.

Hexa pressed her lips into a fine line. "Ya know, this is why we've never spent much time together."

A prolonged moment of silence passed between us.

"What?" I said, unable to string together her logic. "We haven't spent time together because... I speak to women?"

With another sarcastic frown, Hexa struck my shoulder a second time, harder than the last. "What's wrong with you, fool? That's not what I'm talking about. I'm saying you're... how best to put this... You're sometimes naïve. And way too trusting."

"*That's* why we've never spent time together?"

She nodded, her eyebrows lifted as though she were mock-surprised it had taken me so long to get the clue. Then she grazed her fingers along the scars on her arms. "See these? In my hometown, we had a saying. *You can tell how old someone is, not by their age, but by their scars.* My grandpap said people without scars can't be trusted because they don't yet understand how painful life can be."

"Okay?" I said.

"He was sayin' that people who are naïve shouldn't be relied on," Hexa said. "But that's not really you anymore. Even if you don't have scars like mine, you still have them on the inside. You're not the same person. You're more confident. You have a true form eldrin. Don't go making yourself looking naïve. Be proud of your scars—show them off so everyone knows you've grown."

I didn't understand how our conversation had gradually become a motivational speech, but I enjoyed it more than being berated for associating with the wrong people.

Before I could acknowledge Hexa's statement, she laughed.

"Okay, now that we're closer, it's time to train."

"Wait, what?" I said.

"You heard me. I have new techniques I need to try, and you're the only one awake."

"Why aren't *you* sleeping?"

"Hydra arcanists don't have to sleep as much as everyone else," Hexa said with another shrug. "Hydras barely sleep. Didn't you know that? Well, only the ones with multiple heads. They keep each other up. So, hydra arcanists don't sleep that much, either."

"All right. I suppose I could use a training partner."

For a third time, Hexa smacked my shoulder. "That's the spirit. And while we're at it, I might teach you some *woman magic*, okay? It'll help you with Atty."

I held back a roll of my eyes. "Very well," I said with a groan.

The next week took its toll.

I didn't see much of Atty or Karna. At meals, they insisted they were busy with their own magical training. Master Zelfree confirmed this, but it wasn't a gigantic airship. Were they training in their rooms? I spent most of my time with Hexa on the deck, yet I never saw them. I had to admit to myself there were logical explanations. Not all forms of magic were combat oriented. Perhaps they were meditating, to create their auras, or perhaps Atty was practicing her healing abilities since she had struggled so much with those in the past.

But I dwelled on their whereabouts more than I should have, which made training with Hexa especially painful.

Somehow, over the past few months, she had drastically improved with her throwing knives. She would coat them in hydra venom. In large enough doses, it was deadly, but with minor cuts, it just sent pure agony throughout the victim's body. And it acted quickly. In a matter of moments, the venom could incapacitate an adult man.

I knew that for a fact—Hexa struck me twice during our training. Both times it was because I had been distracted. There was just too much to think about.

Fortunately, each time I got struck, Adelgis came running from below deck. Apparently, my thoughts had turned rather desperate, and he had heard them, even from the other side of the *Sun Chaser*. He had rushed to my side to make sure I was all right. The second time he brought Zaxis along to help me recover, though that wasn't much help. Phoenix healing didn't do much for venoms and poisons.

The last day of our training, I walked onto the deck with a resigned sigh. I had to keep my thoughts in order—Hexa wouldn't catch me with her blades then.

"Volke," Hexa shouted from across the deck. "Come look!"

I ambled over, still groggy from a night of poor sleep. Hexa didn't share in my fatigue, though. She had enough energy for five men, and when I drew close, she clasped my shoulder and then pointed to the horizon.

"See? It's Fortuna."

Sure enough, there it was.

Fortuna had been built upon a massive hill. Buildings lined the flatlands around the base, and roads led up to the step-like terraces, but all of that was difficult to see from this far away. I pictured it in my mind's eye, anxious to walk those roads again. At the top of the city stood a massive clock tower, complete with bells and a representation of the stars in the night sky etched on a steel dais—a gigantic machine to keep track of the celestial changes throughout the year. It glinted in the sunlight, almost like a lighthouse, and even from this distance, I knew exactly where it was.

"And look there," Hexa added.

I followed the direction of her finger.

Floating out in the bay, near the many ports, was a massive island-sized turtle. It was Guildmaster Eventide's eldrin—the mighty atlas turtle, Gentel.

If she was in Fortuna, it meant only one thing...

Eventide had found the person to bond with the world serpent, and we could finally head straight for it.

A MAN NAMED RYKER

The *Sun Chaser* descended into Fortuna at a steady pace. Mesos landed on the city wall, her giant roc feathers shining in the seaside sunshine. The nearby dockhands stopped their work to watch the airship approach one of the piers. Although Fortuna was a capital city with an impressive population, airships weren't so commonplace here as to warrant a sky dock.

I stayed on the deck the entire approach. Hexa stood next to me, smiling. Even her hydra observed the descent with all four heads. He stretched his long necks out so that he could get a better look over the railing.

Atty, Illia, Zaxis, Adelgis, Fain, Evianna, and Master Zelfree joined us on the deck a few moments before the ship's crew secured us to the pier. The *Sun Chaser* never entered the water—it floated in the air a few feet above, gusts of wind whipping around so fiercely that they disturbed the calm tide enough to rock nearby dinghies.

Illia approached me with Nicholin on her shoulder. The winds played with her wavy brown hair, and for a moment, she looked like how I imagined swashbucklers might look from the old tales. Determined. Adventurous.

"Master Zelfree believes we'll be stopping at the Isle of Ruma after this," Illia said.

Nicholin nodded. "Maybe we'll get to see Gravekeeper William before we save the world serpent."

"I'd like that," I said. "But I hope we don't stay there too long."

In my core, I hoped we'd just meet Guildmaster Eventide and leave immediately. We couldn't afford to delay any longer than necessary.

As if he had the exact same opinion, Master Zelfree snapped his fingers to get the group's attention. He swept back his short, black hair with his other hand as he said, "Listen up. We're heading straight for the guild manor house on Gentel. No stops. Understand? Everything we need, we already have."

I nodded. In my shadow, I had Forfend, my shield crafted from a world serpent scale. In Illia's pocket sat the Occult Compass, the trinket that would point us in the direction of the world serpent's lair. And in Eventide's possession was the world serpent runestone—the object required to enter the birthplace of the serpent.

We had everything.

Once the *Sun Chaser* was secured, and the gangplank was lowered, Zaxis and Illia disembarked first. Adelgis, Fain, and Hexa followed afterward, each with their attention on the far-off atlas turtle. Atty and Evianna waited for me, and I appreciated the gesture, but I noticed Master Zelfree heading to the quarterdeck. Curious, I kept my gaze on him, wondering why he didn't disembark with the rest of us.

Zelfree approached Captain Devlin with a stiff stride. Although I was on the main deck, a good forty feet away, the winds carried their voices.

"Come with us," Zelfree stated.

The captain scratched at his chinstrap beard. "You know how I feel about the guilds."

"We need your skill. Any arcanist in your crew could be the one to change the tide of this war."

I had never heard Zelfree so insistent. Normally, he had a gruff, almost jaded tone to his commands and comments, but this sounded more desperate.

"The Frith Guild needs as many good arcanists as it can find," Zelfree continued. "I swear to you that our association can end once this task is completed."

When would that be? I had no idea, and I suspected neither did Devlin nor Zelfree. It was a lot to ask someone to sign up for an indefinite amount of time. I held my breath, hoping the captain and his crew would join us, even if that were unlikely.

Captain Devlin mulled over the request, his hard gaze set on the atlas turtle in the distance. With a powerful exhale, he finally stated, "We'll go with you to meet your damn guildmaster."

"Thank you," Zelfree immediately said, a sigh of relief on his breath.

"But if we rub each other wrong—or if we're as compatible as jellyfish and land—I'm taking my crew and we're leaving. Got me?"

Zelfree replied with a curt nod. "Again, thank you."

"Don't thank me," Devlin growled. "You wore me down, that's all that happened here. Can't take a damn *no* to save your life." He threw up his hands and turned away. "Throw me into the abyss—this isn't how I saw my life turning out."

"Let me help you transport the unbonded khepera," Zelfree said, completely ignoring Devlin's cursing. "I'm sure the Frith Guild can find suitable individuals to bond with them."

"Fine. You handle it."

Thankful that Vethica, my father, Karna, and Devlin would be joining us, I turned for the gangplank. Atty smiled as I approached, and relief mixed into my state of being.

"It's felt like forever since we've been in Fortuna," I said as we walked onto the pier. "I can still remember our first time here."

Atty's phoenix soared off the railing of the airship and headed straight for our destination, soot trailing down to the ground behind her.

"My first time here, I found it difficult to concentrate," Atty said, lacing her fingers together. "All I could think about was the guilds and how we'd have a dozen adventures on the high seas."

"I felt the same way."

We shared a smile, dispelling the last of my doubt. Atty wasn't upset. She *had* been busy with Zelfree during the trek. We were still as close as we had been before Karna had complicated matters.

Fortuna's city wall stood tall and impressive. I barely glanced at it, however. I had eyes for Atty, and her blonde hair waving in the ocean winds. She said a few things, and I answered them, but I honestly couldn't remember what we said. I was too distracted.

The cobblestone streets were crowded with people and horses. Some of the town bulletin boards had news posted about the change in rulership of the Argo Empire, but we didn't linger long enough for me to see the details. We wove through the throngs of Fortuna citizens as quickly as we could, making our way to the northern piers, closer to the atlas turtle.

"Volke," Atty whispered as she glanced over her shoulder.

I followed her gaze and spotted Evianna trailing behind us. She had her arms crossed, and her attention was on the ground in front of her. Her shadow shifted with the presence of her knightmare—a sight familiar to me—but I didn't stare at it long. I was more concerned with Evianna's melancholy expression.

"She's really young," Atty muttered under her breath. "She tries to act as though she can handle adulthood, but Master Zelfree noticed she was having terrible dreams and sleeping poorly."

"Adelgis should help her," I whispered. "His dream manipulation is beyond compare. I've seen it in action many times."

"He's helping her now, but... that won't solve the problem. I was hoping that maybe *you* could be kind to her—help her out. She admires you, and you're a fellow knightmare arcanist."

"Evianna asked that I marry her," I stated.

It wasn't the most eloquent way to impart the information, but I didn't care. My hopes were that Atty would have a solution.

"Oh," she said, both her eyebrows heading for her hairline. "How... interesting."

"Don't you mean *unexpected*?"

"No." Atty tilted her head and combed her blonde hair with her fingers. "Evianna's audacious in a good way. But I think that's just another piece of evidence that she needs someone. You don't have to marry her to help her, Volke. Just be there for her. And be understanding —she's still a child, even if just for a few more months."

I couldn't deny any of Atty's observations. Even when I glanced over my shoulder to watch Evianna, I knew Atty was correct. Evianna had lost so much.

"I'll try," I said.

Atty smiled—reward enough for the task.

When we arrived at the northern dock, my chest tightened, and my pace quickened. The atlas turtle was too large to be in the port itself. Everyone had to take dinghies to Gentel's shell, and the anticipation ate at my patience.

"Evianna," I called back. "Let's use the shadows."

She perked up when I called her name, her bluish-purple eyes alight with excitement.

"Understood," Evianna replied.

I held out a hand for Atty. She took it, and I fell into the shadows in dramatic fashion, taking her with me to travel through the void of darkness. We snaked our way down the main street, past the city wall, and onto the pier. In a matter of moments, we were at the tiny vessels that would take us the last leg of the trip.

If I could slip through the water using my shadows, I would've, but liquid wasn't a suitable surface for my magic.

Evianna appeared next to us a moment later, her white hair caught by the breeze and fluttering behind her like a war banner. For a brief second, she reminded me of her sister, Lyvia. I stared, and she held her head high.

"I'm getting better," Evianna said. "Don't practice until you get it right —practice until you can't get it wrong. Right, Volke?"

I nodded. "That's right."

The three of us boarded a dinghy and rowed the short way to the atlas turtle. The waves and smell of saltwater did my soul good. I had missed the ocean.

Evianna leaned over the edge and stared at the water as we went. She had grown up in the Argo Empire—specifically in the capital, where the docks were connected to a river—so I suspected she hadn't traveled much on the ocean. It would be a new experience for her.

When we arrived at the floating dock on Gentel, we quickly leapt out of the dinghy and headed up the path on the shell of the massive turtle. Grass grew lush and emerald green. A tree and a pond sat near Gentel's head, reflecting the sun. And at the back of the shell, standing three stories tall, was the Frith Guild manor house.

The building had been constructed with red bricks, dark wood frames, and pale white ivory. It all contrasted perfectly with the ivy growing up the lattice fencing, and I slowed my pace just to admire the manor house a little longer. All three stories had pristine windows and decorative clay designs interlaid with bricks. Etchings of mystical creatures—from the phoenix to the sphinx—were hidden in every detail. The shrubs in the garden were cut to appear like unicorns, harpies, and bugbears. One shrub, which I hadn't noticed before, had been shaped like a suit of armor. A knightmare? Was that for me?

Positioned right before the front door, prominent and beautiful, was a birdbath with a statue of an atlas turtle holding up the dish, larger than three full-grown men.

Guildmaster Eventide stood in front of the birdbath. She had all the presence of a buccaneer, from her long coat to her tricorn hat. Her arcanist mark, the star and atlas turtle, glowed with an inner power, just like mine. Gentel was true form, which was why she had become large enough for a manor house to be built on top of her to begin with.

Eventide also had long, graying hair, which was braided neatly to keep it from flying about. Just seeing her again put me at ease.

Then I noticed someone standing next to her. It was a young man, perhaps my age, maybe a year younger. He had black hair, windswept and wild, with honeyed skin and dark eyes. He stood taller than most— almost my height, which was rare—and I wondered who he could be. The man had no arcanist mark.

Guildmaster Eventide turned her keen gaze to Atty, Evianna, and me as we approached.

"Ah, here are some of our arcanists now," she said. Then she patted the strange man on the shoulder. "Ryker, I'd like you to meet Journeyman Knightmare Arcanist Volke Savan, Journeyman Phoenix Arcanist Atty Trixibelle, and Apprentice Knightmare Arcanist Evianna Velleta. They'll protect you on our journey."

Ryker what? Eventide hadn't mentioned a last name.

The man offered a reserved smile and a slight bow of his head. "It's a pleasure to meet you," he said, his words precise, like they were practiced.

Ryker wore a swashbuckler coat—long enough to reach his knees—but he also wore a vest and fine shirt underneath. His trousers were sturdy and had several pockets, though none of them appeared used. His boots shone with a brand-new luster, and the gloves he wore had yet to be broken in.

"The pleasure is ours," Atty replied. "Ryker, you said? An unusual name."

"Forgive me," Ryker said with a smile. "My mother was a traveler. She said she had met a man on a tiny island with the name and was so smitten with it, she swore to herself a child she bore would also carry the name."

"No need to apologize." Atty stepped forward and also bowed her head. "It was rude of me to comment."

Guildmaster Eventide placed a hand on her hip. "Ryker's safety will be our primary concern until we reach the lair of the world serpent."

"Why?" Evianna blurted out, her eyes narrowed.

I already knew, and the words caught in my throat, almost in disbelief.

"I spoke with the future-vision sibyl arcanists of Fini Isle," Eventide replied. "They informed me that Ryker is the rightful world serpent arcanist."

18

THE RIGHTFUL WORLD SERPENT ARCANIST

I stared at Ryker as if seeing him for the first time all over again. Yes, his clothes were new, but now all I could focus on was his facial expressions and mannerisms. Ryker noticed my staring and then met my gaze with an inquisitive eyebrow lifted in a silent question. I was certain he wanted to know what I found so fascinating, but I couldn't bring myself to voice my thoughts.

Ryker had an expressive face with a clear and focused gaze. He didn't appear nervous, not even when he stepped forward to offer a small bow of his head to me, Atty, and Evianna. And it was more than that. He displayed a bit of confidence when he met my eyes and smiled. That one fact eased my anxiety. Confidence in the wrong hands could lead to disaster, but if it were wielded by someone talented, it could be a fuel that propelled them to greatness.

I hoped Ryker was talented enough to bond with the world serpent and help us defeat the Second Ascension. He had to be.

"It's a pleasure to meet so many arcanists from the legendary Frith Guild," Ryker said.

"The pleasure is ours," Atty replied with a smile. "It's not every day you meet a god-arcanist." She said the words with a hint of awe, and it was one of the few times I felt a twinge of jealousy burning through my chest, threatening to escape through my throat as a derisive comment.

Obviously, that was childish, and I held my tongue.

The corner of Ryker's lip twitched into a nervous smile. "Well, I'm not yet anyone so important. Until then, I'm just a young man who's been thrust into an interesting situation. There's no need to treat me with any sort of reverence."

"As a god-arcanist, you *should* be treated with reverence," Evianna chimed in. She fluffed her white hair. "You're even more important than kings, queens, and princesses—you're here to restructure the world. That's a station that should be respected."

"Perhaps, when I actually take on the responsibility, I'll change my mind... but until then, there's no need to go out of your way. Please. I'd prefer it that way."

Guildmaster Eventide patted Ryker's shoulder. "You'll be given your own quarters. If you'd like, you can rest there most of the trek. No one will bother you then."

He nodded once. "Thank you, Guildmaster. It sounds pleasant."

"Fantastic." Eventide glanced in my direction and then motioned to the guild manor home with a jut of her chin. "The rest of you should get settled. But don't sleep just yet. Once we've gathered everyone, we'll be meeting in the map room."

Atty and I replied in unison with, "Yes, Guildmaster."

It took Evianna a second to mutter the same acknowledgement, no doubt because she wasn't accustomed to interacting with Eventide. She had trained at Zelfree's side for the last few months, after all—far from the Frith Guild.

Had Evianna ever seen the atlas turtle up close? I suspected she hadn't. Eventide had been in Thronehold, but her eldrin couldn't leave the ocean. As far as I knew, Evianna had never returned to the Frith Guild headquarters, even though she had been a member for several months.

I walked past Ryker, still fascinated he had my height. Atty and Evianna flanked me on either side as we traveled around the birdbath and into the manor house.

The vast entrance room greeted us with a rush of warm air. The pleasant temperature contrasted nicely with the ocean misting outside. Instead of basking in the new temperature, I headed straight for the main stairs. Everyone except the master arcanists lived on the third floor, and although I wasn't an apprentice anymore, I knew where all the personal quarters were.

Atty, also familiar with our surroundings, kept my pace. Evianna, on the other hand, craned her head back to get a better look at the manor house. Her mouth hung slightly agape as she admired the etchings of mystical creatures in the stair railings, and in some of the walls. The lengthy staircase wasn't as imposing as the one in the castle in Thronehold, but it was still gigantic. Evianna had to slow her walk to take in all the details.

"I can't believe this all fits on the back of a single eldrin," Evianna muttered as she started up the stairs.

Smiling to myself since I had guessed correctly, I glanced back from at least twelve steps ahead of her. "Guildmaster Eventide's atlas turtle has achieved its true form. That's why Gentel is so large."

"The size is just... so impressive."

We continued up the steps until we reached our desired floor. Then I pointed to the left. "That side of the manor is designated for women," I said. "And this side over here is for men."

Atty waited at the top of the stairs for Evianna. Once together, Atty smiled and tilted her head. "Evianna, why don't I help you locate a room? It can be close to mine so that you can find me easily if you have any questions."

After a quick moment of contemplation, Evianna replied with a curt nod. "I find this acceptable."

The two of them headed off toward the main hallway of bedrooms, but before they rounded a corner and went out of my sight, Atty glanced back and gave me a small smile.

I couldn't help but return the gesture.

Once they were no longer in my line of sight, I exhaled and paused at the top of the staircase.

"Luthair," I muttered, "are you happy to be back in the Frith Guild?"

"Of course, my arcanist," he replied, seemingly from nowhere. "Are you?"

"It's like stepping into the past. Or maybe like... a pleasant dream. It feels like forever since I was here."

"Indeed."

As I recalled happy memories, my thoughts took an odd turn. I dwelled on the worst hypothetical scenarios. What if we couldn't stop the Second Ascension? What if the manor was destroyed? What if everyone here were killed? I had to have been standing at the top of the stairs for five whole minutes before reality came back to me.

"Luthair..." I hung on the word, hesitant to voice my desire. But I couldn't help it. "Can you... keep an eye on Ryker? Even while he's in his room? Without being noticed, I mean."

"With ease, my arcanist."

"You should do that."

The shadows in the corners fluttered with a bat-like quality.

"You're not asking me to protect him," Luthair said—no question in his voice, just a statement.

I rubbed at the back of my neck. "I'm worried," I said under my breath. "What if he's not the right man to bond with the world serpent?"

"You doubt the guildmaster?"

"Of course not." I crossed my arms and headed for the men's portion of the house. "That's not what I'm saying. It's just... maybe I don't trust the sybil arcanists. How can they possibly know who should bond with the world serpent? What if they're wrong? What if Ryker is actually a terrible person who... who..." I grasped at examples and finally blurted out, "Who tortures puppies in his free time?"

"Ah, yes. The Dread Pirate Ryker—torturer of canines. He once collected dozens of pooches to fashion a buccaneer's coat."

"You know what I meant," I said as I reached the door to my old room.

"Indeed. But it was still amusing."

I half-smiled and held back a laugh. I supposed it was *somewhat* funny.

Then I stared at the door in front of me. Was this room still mine? I had been away for so long, I wasn't sure.

I cautiously opened the door and peered inside. To my relief, everything was exactly the same—my bed, my dresser, my small desk, and even my bookshelf stuffed with magical information and tomes about historical arcanists. It was a shame I no longer had Theasin's book detailing mystical creatures. Although Theasin was a member of the Second Ascension, I had found his guide useful while I had been in Thronehold.

Perhaps I could find another copy at some point?

Afternoon sunlight streamed in through the window, shining down on the oak wood that made up the furniture. The white linens practically shimmered. The room had been cleaned, but not bothered. At some level, they had always expected I would return.

"Shall I spy on Ryker now, my arcanist?" Luthair asked.

I grimaced at the word *spy*—not because it was inaccurate, but because it felt deceptive and disgraceful. At the same time, Master Zelfree had been a master spy who had infiltrated the ships of dread pirates. And wasn't my reasoning noble? Shouldn't I make sure Ryker was the right man?

"Keep an eye on him after we meet in the map room," I said, still reluctant, though not enough to abandon my plan. "Just in case."

The Frith Guild needed a bigger map room.

Even with two of the Frith Guild's master arcanists away from the manor—Gallus the Gray and Master Yesna—we were still packed to the gills from one wall to the next. The officers of the *Sun Chaser*, along with several journeymen, new apprentices, Master Zelfree, and the arcanists of our group, had to stand shoulder-to-shoulder. In total, at least twenty-two arcanists and their eldrin were gathered. Fortunately, Captain Devlin's roc remained outside. Last I had seen, she had curled up near the giant birdbath and was using it as her own personal drinking dish.

A giant map table was in the center of the room, taking its fair share of space. It was an artifact or trinket of some sort—a magical piece of furniture that the guildmaster used to instruct Gentel on where to head next.

Somehow, while everyone had been packing themselves into the room, Zaxis had managed to position himself right next to me. I had hoped for Atty, but at this point, I knew that fate just wanted to make everything difficult. If I wanted to see her, I would have to *make* time to see her, and I intended to do that at the earliest opportunity.

Zaxis stood so close, I could smell charcoal and ash. His flames had become intense lately, and he burned up wood, grass, and moldy food within seconds if he managed to get his hands on them. In the future, I would recommend he burn a few flowers, or perhaps some incense, so that the odor he carried wasn't so irritating to the nose.

The whispered conversations of everyone in the room mingled together into a constant noise that hummed in the background. I couldn't distinguish one conversation from the next, not with all the people present, but I attempted regardless. It was just a jumble of words.

After jabbing me in the ribs with a sharp elbow, Zaxis asked, "Where is Guildmaster Eventide and our world serpent arcanist?"

I sarcastically glanced around the room and then returned my attention to Zaxis. "Using my *eyeball powers*, I've determined they're not here yet."

"I thought the guildmaster summoned us? She has to be nearby."

"And?" I asked.

"And use your *shadow powers* to locate her or something," Zaxis quipped. "I want to get back to practicing."

I sighed as I stepped backward, slipping into the darkness as though falling into a hole that had been placed into the room. Once wrapped in the cold power of the shadows, I slithered out of the map room and into the entrance hall, just in front of the staircase. When I emerged, I took a breath, allowing the warmth of the manor to soak into me once again.

"—and you're certain everything was to your liking?" I heard the guildmaster ask.

"Yes, thank you," someone replied.

It was Ryker. I hadn't known him long, but his voice was distinct.

Where were they? I glanced around, curious but quiet. Then I stopped once I realized they were standing on the opposite side of the staircase, just out of sight. I held my breath and waited near the first step.

"Well, as long as everything is settled, I think it's time for you to meet everyone," Eventide said. "I'll formally introduce you, so don't worry about that. The fewer questions about your birthplace the better. Then I'll demonstrate how we're going to find the world serpent."

"What if you can't locate the creature?" Ryker asked.

"There's no need for you to concern yourself with that. The Frith Guild will handle all the details. I just want to make sure you're safe and protected until the time comes to bond."

Ryker let out a short exhale. "You're much too kind, Guildmaster."

"Nonsense. You'll find that everyone here will be equally accommodating. Now come along. The map room is this way."

My heart leapt into my throat the moment I heard Eventide's first bootstep. On instinct, I dropped back into the darkness and shifted up the steps until I was at the top. I emerged just as Eventide finished walking past the bottom step of the staircase.

But Ryker wasn't with her...

Although I didn't think eavesdropping on someone's conversation was a knightly thing to do, I was still uncertain about Ryker. Too much depended on him being the appropriate man for the task, and I *needed* to know for certain his intentions were pure.

I shadow-stepped back downstairs, then around to where the two had been speaking, and rose out of the darkness near the corner of the room. To my surprise, I had exited just behind Ryker. He stood—not moving, his gaze on the floor in front of him.

My ability to shift through the shadows was damn near silent, and I suspected he didn't realize I was behind him. With my breath held, I did nothing. I wasn't certain what I should do, as I was still taken aback by his presence.

Ryker's hands shook as he brought both of them to his hair. He swept back his black locks, his breathing shallow. He seemed paler than before.

"Ryker?" the guildmaster called from the other side of the room, beyond the staircase and just out of sight. "Are you coming?"

After two deep inhales, Ryker whispered to himself, "You can do this." He steadied his shaky hands, straightened his posture, and then strode out to meet the guildmaster. "I apologize. I was just admiring the lovely architecture."

In that moment, I learned more about Ryker than I had in all our other interactions combined. He was nervous. Genuine. Someone who, a few weeks prior, probably had had no plans to become a god-arcanist. And now he had the weight of the world on his shoulders. It was almost unfair.

My fears felt foolish now.

"Luthair," I whispered. "Never mind about watching Ryker. We don't need to violate his privacy."

"As you wish."

"Thank you."

The darkness fluttered as Luthair asked, "My arcanist?"

"Yes?"

"The guildmaster is starting the meeting."

"R-right."

I shook my head and traveled through the shadows, returning to the map room in a matter of seconds.

19

FORFEND AND THE OCCULT COMPASS

I almost couldn't squeeze myself back into the map room. I hadn't realized it until then, but there were two griffins awkwardly jammed into the crowd. When had griffin arcanists joined the Frith Guild? I made a mental note to myself to meet them. Griffins had always fascinated me, and I was certain their arcanists would be a noble breed.

Guildmaster Eventide stood at the head of the map table. She brushed her gray braid over her shoulder and cleared her throat. The murmured conversations came to a sudden halt. Eventide stood a little straighter, her expression stern. Her long coat, sewn with various parts of mystical creatures—including phoenix feathers and unicorn hairs—gave her an eldritch, almost arcane, appearance.

"Now that we're all gathered, it's time to leave Fortuna," the guildmaster stated. "From here, we're traveling straight to the lair of the world serpent. I can promise you that this is one of the most important tasks that will happen in our lifetimes, and one I'm proud to participate in."

Eventide took a deep breath and exhaled. "But I can't promise it'll be a short journey, nor can I promise it'll be an easy one. It's more than likely that we'll encounter plague-ridden arcanists and their twisted eldrin."

The mere mention of the plague sent shivers throughout the room. I held my position, unafraid. This was how I would help the Frith Guild— I would have to be a shield for the others. If a plagued creature attacked, I had to be among the first to deal with it.

"It's also likely that we'll run afoul of the Second Ascension," Eventide said. "The king basilisk arcanist who assassinated Queen Velleta has been tasked with my assassination, which means there's a chance he could turn his poison on the rest of you. One mistake and your death will be a swift one."

Her grim tone didn't sit well with me. Guildmaster Eventide had always been cheerful and bursting with charisma. Why the doom and gloom now?

She continued, her tone solemn, "The leader of the Second Ascension, a man they call the *Autarch*, will have more than one eldrin, and his golden kirin will empower whatever he bonds with. He is a man shrouded in mystery and one who may be too powerful for a single individual to handle—one who may be able to kill master arcanists by the dozens."

I clenched my jaw as the reality of the situation was laid bare.

Guildmaster Eventide removed her tricorn cap and placed it on the map table. Then she glanced around the room, taking a moment to meet the gaze of the arcanists around her. "If any of this is too frightening—or if what I said took you by surprise—now is your chance to leave. We're still in Fortuna. You can take a dinghy back to port. I'll give you two gold leafs to help you on your way."

The guildmaster paused after that statement, her breath held.

No one spoke. It was as if the very walls were also holding their breath in anticipation.

"If you stay," Eventide said, her voice strained, "then I expect nothing but the best. We'll be in this together, to the bitter end—a type of adventure where we either succeed and come home as heroes or we fail together, our bodies dragged down to the lowest level of the Abyssal Hells. It's all or nothing."

The greatest adventurers, and the great arcanists, were men and women who gambled against death and won. Even though my guts and chest twisted into tight knots, I knew what I had to do.

Eventide ran a hand over her mouth. Then she glanced at Captain Devlin. "This goes for the crew of the *Sun Chaser* as well. I can't bring you along unless I know I can depend on you."

For an anxious moment, I feared they'd leave.

Captain Devlin scoffed. "I'm not afraid of pirates, I'm not afraid of the plague, and I'm *definitely* not afraid of those snakes-wearing-human-skin that make up the Second Ascension. The crew of the *Sun Chaser* is with you until the end."

His confidence—arrogance, really—brought a smile to my face. The other arcanists in the room murmured quick conversations, some impressed, some irritated by his flippant response.

"Thank you," Eventide replied. She glanced back to the rest of the room. "But there's still a chance for the rest of you. If you want to leave— please, do it now."

I looked around, half-expecting *someone* to head for the door. When no one moved, I stood a little taller. In all the stories I had read about the Frith Guild, none of the arcanists would turn away from destiny because it was too *frightening.* And it seemed nothing had changed. We would all be in this together.

"Volke," the guildmaster said. "Please join me here at the map table."

Her summons caught me off guard.

Everyone in the room glanced around until they noticed my position by the door. With intense stares, they watched as I maneuvered my way through the crowd. Gillie, the Grand Apothecary, stood near the table, and she lit up with a bright smile as I walked past. Her short, golden hair had been pulled back into a tight ponytail, showcasing her expressive face. I would recognize it anywhere—she had enough cheer to liven the dead.

When I drew near Guildmaster Eventide, she placed a hand on my shoulder.

Although I hadn't noticed him before, I spotted Ryker a few feet behind her, half-hiding in the natural shadows of the room, as though trying to take up as little space as possible.

"We need the world serpent scale," Eventide said to me, her voice low enough that only I could hear.

I replied with a curt nod and then reached down to the shadows.

Luthair handed me Forfend from the darkness, like a hand lifting out of an oil lake. Once I had my shield, I hesitantly placed it on the map table, careful not to disturb the topography. The many mountains and little figurines of ships always impressed me, and I'd hate to damage them in any way.

To my surprise—and slight embarrassment—everyone was staring. Not at my shield, but at the arcanist mark on my forehead. I almost wanted to hide it, to avoid the many gazes. I couldn't do that, though. Besides, most of them hadn't yet seen my new glowing mark, and I knew they were just curious. Soon this attention would go away.

I hoped.

The guildmaster glanced around. "Illia? Will you also join us?"

Nicholin answered long before Illia. "Aye, aye, Guildmaster!" he said with a squeak. "You can count on us. We're ready for anything. We're even ready to give the Second Ascension a swift kick to the sensitive bits. They're so ugly, they couldn't even arouse suspicion. We'll deal with them like we would deal with—"

Illia placed a hand on her rizzel eldrin's face as she made her way to the map table, her face slightly pink, even if it was half-covered by her eye patch.

She stood by my side and gave me a quick smile. It felt right having her here with me.

Without prompting, Illia withdrew the Occult Compass from her coat pocket. The compass had been made with the eye of an all-seeing sphinx, a mystical creature now extinct. The needle of the trinket was stuck in the iris and didn't move, no matter which direction Illia pointed the object.

Illia placed the Occult Compass on top of Forfend. Nicholin moved from Illia's shoulder, down her arm, and closer to her elbow. His little ears remained perked as he watched the needle twitch and then rapidly spin.

My breath caught in my throat.

In theory, the Occult Compass could find any mystical creature. Even the gods. That was why the Dread Pirate Calisto had wanted it in the first place.

And while I knew all of this was true, the moment still made me nervous. What if something went wrong? What if it didn't work? What would we do then?

The needle stopped hard and fast. It pointed to the east, in a direction beyond the Isle Nation Perphestoni and beyond Port Crown. There wasn't much else in that direction except vast amounts of ocean. In theory, there were more lands beyond those waters, but that journey was so long and harsh that few ever made it and returned to tell the tale. Was the world serpent there? Or was it hidden below the sapphire waves?

Guildmaster Eventide placed a little flag on the map table—the point farthest east. I suspected that her atlas turtle now knew which direction to head.

"Using the Occult Compass, we'll make our way to the world serpent's lair," Eventide stated. She took a moment once again to glance around the room, meeting people's eyes. This time, however, she was smiling—the kind of expression that betrayed her excitement. "Who's with me?"

Everyone in the room responded at the same time, half a cheer, half an actual response. It fueled my appreciation of the guild and chased away any doubt that I had made the wrong decision in joining. This was where I was meant to be.

I took stock of our arcanists. The guildmaster was considered a *grandmaster* atlas turtle arcanist. It was the highest title a guild arcanist could achieve and was granted to those who had supposedly mastered every aspect of their magic and who had an adult, or true form, version of their eldrin.

Zelfree, Devlin, Gillie, and my father, Jozé, were all considered *master arcanists*. They were among the most powerful and had been bonded with their eldrin long enough to have access to the strongest aspects of their magic.

In theory, Yesna and Gallus the Gray would also join us, bringing our number of master arcanists up to six.

The majority of the arcanists in the guild, however, were journeymen, like me. Those were arcanists who had mastered the basics, but were still young—both themselves and their eldrin—and still needed to learn the more advanced techniques of their magic.

Fortunately, we only had a handful of apprentices. I wasn't sure if bringing them on this journey was a good idea, but I knew we couldn't leave Evianna behind and on her own, so it couldn't be helped. Besides, everyone had to have known what the Frith Guild was before joining.

This was a guild of action, and perhaps now was the best time to learn that.

20

ARRIVAL AT THE ISLE OF RUMA

M otivated by everyone's dedication to the guild, I spent my time training. I wanted to feel the burn in my muscles just as much as I felt the burn in my soul. If I had done fifty swings of my sword before, today I did seventy. Each time I shadow-stepped, I tried to go ten feet farther. When the sun set on the horizon, my abilities strengthened, and I used that as further motivation to stay outside and press on.

To my surprise, Evianna trained with me. She didn't give up at the two-hour mark, or the four-hour mark, or even after the stars appeared over the atlas turtle and ocean. Sweat stained her clothing, and she took in ragged breaths, but she never quit.

Her mastery of magic was gradually improving. She stepped through the shadows, she evoked terrors—she even created tendrils from the darkness. It felt as though she were improving faster than I ever had.

It made sense, I supposed. She wasn't second-bonded, and she had me as an example. Why wouldn't Evianna improve by leaps and bounds?

Sometimes she attempted to do multiple magics at once, and I had to stop my own training to remind her to focus. Her ambition was as great as her dedication, which only added fuel to *my* fire. Determination like hers was contagious.

Mist from the waves breaking against Gentel's shell wafted over us.

We were alone on the grassy field outside of the manor house. A few windows shone with lantern light from within, but otherwise, the Frith Guild was quiet.

In the sky, the *Sun Chaser* flew alongside the guild. I suspected the officers of the ship were aboard for the evening, sleeping soundly.

I finished manipulating the shadows, satisfied with my progress. Then I took a deep breath and turned to Evianna. "It's getting late. I think it'd be better if you got some rest."

Evianna lifted her arm and created an arm-length tendril from the darkness—impressive for an apprentice, but nowhere near my level. "No," she said after a long exhale. "I need to do more. I need you to train me with a sword, and I need you to train me to use an eclipse aura, and—"

"Whoa, whoa," I interjected. "You need to slow down."

With a swish of her hair, Evianna stopped her magic and turned on her heel to face me. "*Slow down?*"

"Learning to fight with a sword is a completely different skillset. And I didn't even learn how to make an eclipse aura until recently—years after becoming an arcanist. And even now, I don't think I'm doing it correctly. I've only made a perfect eclipse aura once. It's difficult, and you need to master all the basics first."

"But if you can do it, then *I* can do it."

"I'm older," I said. "I've had more time. You need to remember that."

"If I train, I can catch up," Evianna retorted. She stepped closer to me, fatigue plain on her wan face, her hair soaked with sweat. "I can do this. I *have* to do this."

She spoke in a half-shout, and her words carried over the grassy field.

"The others are sleeping," I said. "And you should be, too. Rest is just as important as training. Trust me. Your muscles need time to recover."

Evianna shook her head. "Then why aren't *you* resting?"

"I... Well... I'm older," I said again, though I knew it was a pathetic response.

With her teeth gritted, Evianna straightened her posture, her whole body tense. "*No.* No. I can't. I have to be better. I can't waste my time. I need to be just as good as you—or better."

Her shadow swirled around her feet, and then Layshl, her

knightmare, spoke from the darkness. "My arcanist, Volke is correct. You've been pushing yourself too hard."

"I haven't been pushing myself *hard enough*."

Evianna's desperation hit a level I had never heard from her before. I placed a hand on her shoulder, and she snapped her gaze to mine, her eyebrows knitted, her eyes glassy.

"Why are you so insistent?" I asked, my voice low. "Is something wrong?"

"Is something *wrong*?" Evianna repeated, as though it were an absurd question. "*Everything* is wrong. I have to make it right. Don't you understand?"

Sometimes I felt like Evianna and I were having different conversations. Or perhaps we lived in worlds with different expectations. Her betrothal proposal, and now this outrage—where had they come from? Was she so lost in her own thoughts that she couldn't see my utter confusion?

Evianna's eyes grew wetter, and she jerked her head to the side, forcing her gaze to the manor house in the distance.

"Everything was taken from me," she said, anger lacing her words, defiance in her tone. "My sister, my family, *my home*—I don't want to lose anything else. I *can't* let that happen. Lyvia trained four hours a day before she was killed in the coliseum. I have to train *eight hours* a day, or else that's just going to happen to me."

Evianna ran a shaky hand up into her hairline as she closed her eyes. Her lip quivered, but she never cried.

Atty had warned me about this. She had said that Evianna was alone and frightened. All of this *acting out* she was doing was just a symptom of the larger problem beneath the surface, and now it fell to me to help her.

With a gentle touch on her shoulder, I carefully pulled Evianna into an embrace. She snapped her eyes open and glanced up at me—so quick and so filled with shock I almost let her go immediately.

"I'm sorry," I said as I removed my hand.

Evianna grabbed it and returned it to her shoulder. Then she rested her head on my chest, and I held back a curse because I hadn't intended for her to take it as something *romantic*.

"Evianna," I said. "I don't feel that way about—"

"I know you have feelings for Atty," Evianna interjected, her voice strained and raw, as though on the verge of tears, but never reaching that level. "I've just lost everything else... and I don't want to lose you, too. You remind me so much of Lyvia, and I feel safe in your presence... I don't want that taken from me."

She wrapped her arms around my torso, and I silently thanked the stars that we were alone and the others weren't watching this. I already had enough troubles interacting with women, and I didn't need to make things *more* complicated.

"Atty won't take me away," I whispered. "I'll still be here to train you in magic. And to help you with—"

"*I know,*" Evianna snapped. She shook her head, half-hiding her face in my shirt. "I'm sorry. I wanted you for myself. As *my* knight, not hers."

"I..."

I didn't know what to follow that up with.

Without any warning, Evianna released me and then shoved me away. I took a step backward, bemused and uncertain of what she was doing.

"I spoke with Layshl," she said, curt. "I know... I'm being immature. And I'm sorry for that. We're not betrothed, and I'm never going to bring it up ever again." The last of her words came out as a shout, almost as if the more her emotions spilled out, the more she lost control of her volume.

"My arcanist," Layshl said from the darkness. "I didn't—"

Before any more comments could be made, Evianna shadow-stepped away, fleeing the conversation. Layshl slithered as a shadow after her. I could've caught up with the both of them, but after a moment's reflection, I opted against it. When I had been her age, I had struggled with the correct course of action as well. I wasn't *much* older, but I felt those few years were crucial to my decision-making process.

"How do you manage to find yourself in these situations, my arcanist?" Luthair asked, his disembodied voice both gruff and amused.

"I don't know," I said with a sigh. "I feel like I'm not handling this well somehow... Do you have any advice?"

"I do not."

I ran a hand down my face. "I should've known."

I'd have to find someone else to discuss this with.

I couldn't sleep.

All the master arcanists in the old stories never had problems of this nature. They instantly fell in love or found themselves married to adventure. I couldn't use their examples as a shortcut to my own problems.

Apparently, Karna and Evianna wanted more from me than I was willing to give. They hadn't hidden it, but in both cases, I thought I had made my stance clear. Not clear enough—I could see that now—and that mistake had caused them distress.

Similar to what had happened between Illia and me.

How did I keep finding myself in this situation?

I paced around the guild manor, my hands on top of my head, my fingers laced together through my hair. Who could help me make things right? Who could offer advice?

Dawn broke, and my heart picked up its pace. Finally—the others would be waking.

I slid into the darkness and traveled to the part of the manor house where the master arcanists slept. I knew the area only because I had snuck around at one point and broken into several rooms. Looking back, it probably hadn't been the best course of action, but at least it made me familiar with the area.

I shifted through the shrubs and then close to the building, making my way to Master Zelfree's room as silent as a corpse in a casket. To my relief, his window was cracked open—only a hair—but that was enough for a shadow to slip in.

With my knightmare magic, I traveled up the wall and into his bedroom, all within a matter of moments. When I emerged, I silently cursed myself for not checking first. Master Zelfree had his trousers on, but he was in the process of pulling down his shirt, and he still didn't have on any boots, nor had he taken the time to shave his face.

He had so many scars—small knife wounds, a place over his

shoulder where skin had been flayed—and the sight startled me, even though I had known they were there.

Zelfree shoved the shirt down and whipped around, all grogginess gone. It took a moment before his dark eyes shifted from anger to recognition. He exhaled and relaxed in one short movement.

"What're you doing in my room?" he asked, equal parts sardonic and annoyed.

"I apologize," I said, rubbing at the back of my neck. "I really wanted to speak with you, and I figured you'd be up already."

"Ugh," Zelfree growled.

Grogginess crept back into his expression as he took a seat on the side of his bed and grabbed for his boots.

His room was simple—a bed, a dresser, a table, and two chairs—but spacious enough that three of my rooms could easily fit within. There were stairs leading down to the first story, where master arcanists shared a sitting lounge, but this was Zelfree's personal domain. It amused me that he didn't decorate with anything personal.

Traces slept in a tightly curled position, like only a cat could. When she exhaled, she purred.

"Go on," Zelfree said, taking me out of my musings. "Is this about Ryker? You don't have to worry. We have several people watching him at any given moment."

"Oh, uh, no. It's not about him. It's more personal than that."

Zelfree narrowed his eyes and shot me a sideways glance. The stubble on his face reminded me of when we had first met—he had been a wreck. Did he always look like this in the morning?

"It's about... interacting with women," I said, ending the sentence with an upward inflection, like it was half a statement and half a question. Zelfree enjoyed the company of other men, but I figured he would have some insight to help me. He had *always* had advice in the past.

Zelfree shoved on his boots and then stood. "Uh-huh," he muttered as he walked over to the window and opened the glass panel wide.

"Recently, I've run into more complications than I ever have before," I said, my face burning just thinking about describing everything. "I don't want to hurt anybody, but things are awkward. I'm not sure what to do."

Without replying, Zelfree leaned over the sill and glanced around the garden down below.

"Are you okay?" I asked.

"Yeah," he murmured. "I'm wondering whether I can leap from this height and avoid hurting my knees."

I clenched my jaw and said in a heated tone, "Are you serious? The conversation isn't *that* bad."

Zelfree turned around, his arms crossed. "Let me save you the trouble—I'm the wrong person to talk to about this. I've *literally* ruined every relationship I've ever attempted. And the one time I didn't ruin it, I failed to protect him from a plague-ridden lunatic. What do you want from me? Advice? *Don't do the things I do.*"

"Er..." I couldn't think of anything to say.

Zelfree lifted an eyebrow. "That's all I've got for you." He motioned to the door. "Now get out of my bedroom and find someone else to discuss this with."

I shuffled over to the window. "Can you recommend someone?"

"*Anyone* else," he quipped. "An upturned broom with a bucket for a head might be better than me at this point." Zelfree patted me on the shoulder with a look of *finality* on his face. "You'll do great. I believe in you. Don't give up. Pick whatever phrase motivates you the best, kid."

His unmitigated sarcasm pulled a single chuckle out of me. "Thank you, I guess," I said right before diving into the shadows.

I traveled as far as I could, returning to the grassy field across the top of the atlas turtle's shell. Perhaps ignoring the problem was another type of solution. When I emerged, I inhaled and huffed, knowing that was a craven tactic. Evianna had been so distraught, and I'd had nothing to say —I didn't want to be in that situation ever again.

"My arcanist," Luthair said. "Look at the horizon."

My body felt lighter the moment I caught sight of the tiny island in the distance.

The Isle of Ruma.

This might be the last time I saw it. And perhaps this was the only opportunity I'd have to say goodbye to my adopted father, Gravekeeper William. Perhaps he could also help me with my dilemma?

"We should go get Atty, Illia, and Zaxis," I said.

They had grown up there with me—they would be just as excited, I knew.

"As you wish," Luthair replied.

21

THE TRIXIBELLE FAMILY

W hen I had been young, the Isle of Ruma had seemed so massive and wondrous. We had a city, a gigantic stone pillar with 112 steps, and a charberry tree to attract phoenixes. Just beyond our civilization lay the Endless Mire—a place I had once truly thought endless.

But each time I had returned, I had seen the isle for what it was. Small. Quaint. Lost in time.

The Isle of Ruma hadn't yet felt the terrible touch of the arcane plague, and there wasn't much here that dread pirates would covet except the phoenixes. What problems did the island dwellers face? The occasional teenager who vandalized the wrought-iron fences by skewering fish on the arrow-like points? That had been a big deal that had rocked the community. Schoolmaster Tyms had called for an investigation.

Once upon a time, it would've been a big deal to me as well. But not anymore.

The guildmaster's atlas turtle couldn't pull up to the tiny docks of Ruma. Gentel waited half a mile away while members of the Frith Guild boarded dinghies. Most people appeared anxious to get to land, fidgeting with their shirts and coats. I suspected they either wanted to grab a few last supplies or to visit with individuals before we made a long trek across the ocean.

I stood on the grassy field of the atlas turtle, on the peak of the shell, overlooking the small dock built onto Gentel's side. I didn't want to board a dinghy until I could go with Atty.

Zaxis and Forsythe exited the manor house and headed straight for me. In the early afternoon light, Zaxis's armor shone with the brilliance of a bonfire, the salamander scales glittering like smoldering embers. Forsythe hopped along, the soot from his body dusting the ground as he went, his peacock tail and radiant feathers another sight to behold.

"My arcanist," Forsythe said, his gold eyes staring up at Zaxis. "May we get a few charberries for the travel? They should be ripe this time of year, and it's been so long since I've tasted one."

Zaxis shrugged. "I don't see why not."

"Thank you! I can already taste them." Forsythe puffed out the feathers around his neck, his body practically doubling in size.

When Zaxis drew close, however, his casual expression and tone shifted. "Volke," he said with an edge of icy seriousness. "Where's your father?"

"Jozé?" I asked.

"Yeah." Zaxis glanced around, his eyes narrowed and his muscles tense. "The blacksmith for the *Sun Chaser*. Have you seen him?"

"Not yet."

I hadn't thought about my father—my mind had been too focused on Atty. Would he be excited to revisit the Isle of Ruma? He had lived here for several years, after all.

Zaxis huffed and crossed his arms. I hadn't realized until then that his biceps were almost twice the size of mine. How had he done that so fast? I would've been jealous, but I knew from watching his training, that the bulk slowed him a bit, even if he had more power. I liked having the speed advantage in a fight, so I never attempted to imitate his muscle training.

"Jozé shouldn't go to the island," Zaxis stated. "He's still a wanted criminal."

I lifted an eyebrow as I mulled over the comment. I had almost forgotten—my father had killed Zaxis's uncle, Hevil Ren. That had been just before Jozé had bonded with his blue phoenix, Tine. Jozé had been rescuing her from people trying to sell her away.

"I'm sure my father remembers," I said. Perhaps that was why I hadn't seen him all day.

Zaxis rolled his eyes. "Yeah, well, knowing you, I figured you were going to try to take him around town and show him the sights. I just wanted to remind you that's a terrible idea."

He said every word as though they were venom.

I stared at Zaxis for a prolonged moment. "My father said it was an accident. He didn't mean to—"

"I remember his trial," Zaxis growled. "I don't need to hear his excuses again." Then Zaxis waved his hand in a dismissive fashion. "Look, I just didn't want *you* to get into trouble, okay? If you bring your father into town, they'll try to apprehend him, and then you'll defend him because *of course you will*." Zaxis scoffed and headed for the dinghies, the rest of his speech more a muttering of annoyances as he said, "You're as predictable as the sun traveling across the sky, Volke, and the *last* thing I want to do is free you from the stockade."

I chuckled to myself. Zaxis would help free me from the stocks if I were being held for a trial of my own? That was... unexpected.

He and Forsythe went straight for the nearest vessel and boarded it.

Once they started their short journey to land, I took another moment to glance around. Jozé was nowhere to be seen. He wasn't even with Captain Devlin, who stood near the manor house, petting his giant roc. Was my father on the *Sun Chaser*? It remained in the sky, like a kite trailing behind the atlas turtle.

Perhaps the Isle of Ruma was nothing more than painful memories for Jozé. Although he had met his eldrin here, he had also been convicted of murder. And while he had technically met my mother here, she had left him a few months after my birth. All the good memories he had of the place were punctuated by terrible events.

My mother...

I didn't know why, but for a brief moment, my mind dwelled on her. My father had said her name was *Aarona*. I'd never had the chance to know her.

"I haven't seen Ryker since early this morning, my arcanist," Luthair said, his gruff and disembodied voice startling me from my thoughts.

"Oh?" I asked. I hadn't seen him, either. "Do you think something's wrong?"

The darkness among the blades of grass shifted slightly. "It's probably nothing. Forget I mentioned it."

A part of me wanted to explore the subject further, but my attention was stolen the moment Atty exited the guild manor house. She wore fine robes of white so brilliant I swear she had stolen the color from the purest of snow. The fabric glowed in the sunlight, practically a beacon. Her phoenix also hopped at her side, but no amount of scarlet glitter from the bird's feathers could eclipse Atty.

I stood a little straighter and smoothed my coat. I tried to hold back a smile, though it probably resulted in a twitchy half-grin that made me look like a fool. I couldn't stop myself. When Atty headed right for me, it made my insides feel light, and I found it hard to breathe.

"Volke," she said as she neared. "Are you heading to the island?"

"I am." I offered my arm. "Would you like to join me?"

For half a second, her cheerful expression cracked, revealing something more akin to disappointment. It was fleeting, and I had almost missed it, but Atty had her same smile back in place the moment I blinked.

"Well, you don't need to accompany me, if you'd rather see your adoptive father," she said.

I lowered my voice and asked, "Is something wrong?"

"Wrong? No. Of course not." Atty took my arm and held the elbow a bit tighter than I had expected. Her last words made it sound as though she would continue her sentence, but she never did.

Instead of pushing the issue, I remained silent. We walked down the grassy hill, her phoenix hopping along behind us. When we reached one of the last dinghies, I helped her in and then grabbed the oars so I could row us to the island.

We had only gotten a few feet from the atlas turtle when Atty said, "I'm worried what will happen if you meet my family."

I lifted an eyebrow. "Because I used to be a gravedigger when I lived here?"

Atty shook her head. "My mother won't care now that..."

"Now that I'm an arcanist?"

"Now that your eldrin is true form."

I caught my breath and held back any commentary. I continued rowing—the ocean was calm, and the trip could be short, but I took my time. The smell of saltwater rushed over us, reminding me of my childhood.

"My mother wants me to have a true form phoenix," Atty said as she patted Titania's head.

"I remember," I said. "You said she insisted you have a *pure heart—* that it was the key to a phoenix's true form."

"That's right. Which means... she'll be delighted that I'm associating with someone who has achieved that. But..."

"But she'll be angry *you* haven't achieved it yet?" I asked.

Atty simply replied with a single nod.

The water lapped against our tiny vessel. I hadn't thought of this situation. Again, I wished Master Zelfree had spoken with me, even just for a moment. As a friend, I could simply avoid Atty's family so they wouldn't know about my accomplishments. But if I wanted to be something more than a friend, I couldn't ignore Atty's family forever. And it was a coward's move to simply avoid the problem.

"Do you think she'll chide you in front of me?" I asked. "Or would she maintain an air of politeness?"

"My mother is a *woman of fine breeding with a noble upbringing*," Atty said, mimicking someone's style of speech, though I didn't recognize it. She continued in her normal voice, "My mother would think it low class to scold me in front of guests."

"Then I'll accompany you. If we stay together, there should be no opportunity for your family to comment."

Atty's smile returned in full force. "I would love that, Volke."

I replied with a nervous laugh as I rowed the dinghy the last bit to the Isle of Ruma. Once we neared the dock, I leapt out, tied our vessel to a post, and then offered my hand to Atty. She placed her palm on mine, and I pulled her up and out of the dinghy, careful to keep her from getting any water on her fine robes.

Titania took to the sky.

Gasps erupted from behind me. I turned on my heel to see the denizens of Ruma staring upward. They pointed at Titania and whispered among themselves. The dockhands even set down their crates and laughed together.

"Phoenix arcanists have returned," someone said.

Another replied, "I saw one earlier! His phoenix was walking next to him."

"We should ring the bells."

The bells on the island signified any sort of great event. Years ago, when Zaxis and Atty had gone through the bonding ceremony, the bells had chimed across the island for the whole morning.

Atty and I walked past the dockhands. I recognized some of them. They were my age—seventeen, perhaps a bit older—and when they got a good look at the glowing mark on my forehead, their eyes went wide.

"Is he that...?" one of them whispered.

"It couldn't be," a fellow dockhand muttered.

I rubbed at the back of my neck as heat flooded my face. A part of me enjoyed their attention. When I had been a gravedigger, they had all ignored me. But another part of me wished they *didn't* know who I was. It felt strange to have so many people's awe and admiration.

When Atty and I stepped onto the main street of Ruma, I took a deep breath and pressed forward.

The two-story houses were built right next to one another, most with stores downstairs and homes above. I had always considered it congested —even now, as I stared at the wrought-iron fences in the shape of fish for the balconies, the potted flowers, and the murals of whales on the sides of some homes. The people of this island imbued life and color into everything. Even mundane cobblestone walkways had jellyfish designs near the main street.

The deeper we went into town, the more people pointed and whispered. Were they just that excited to see me? But no one ever approached...

"Volke," someone called out.

I turned to find Adelgis and Fain standing near a fountain shaped like a sea serpent. It was easy to spot them—most people on the Isle of

Ruma had red, blond, or strawberry hair—and Adelgis's inky waterfall of long locks was distinct.

Plus, Fain's frostbitten fingers and ears made him recognizable no matter what city we were in.

"This place is warm," Fain muttered. Sweat soaked his shirt, and he tugged at it while evoking some ice to help keep him cool. "You islanders deal with this all year around?"

I nodded. "I think it's pleasant."

"I miss the snow."

Adelgis's eyes knitted together, his attention fixed on the stones beneath our feet.

"Are you okay?" Atty asked him.

He looked up and forced a smile. "Hm? Oh. Yes. Quite all right. Thank you."

But he wasn't telling the whole truth. I knew that look—Adelgis had heard someone's unpleasant thoughts. It was an expression he wore often whenever we were near crowds. It was a shame he couldn't seem to control his mind reading.

Adelgis shot me a look, and I was painfully reminded that he was listening *right now*, even when I was lamenting his uncontrolled powers.

"*I'll be okay,*" Adelgis said telepathically, his voice echoing in my thoughts. "*I'm more concerned about you. People keep thinking of you as a son of criminals—as a bad omen—and as someone who had been exiled. No one wants to confront you openly, though. They seem to think you'll turn violent.*"

It had been a long time since anyone had called me *the son of criminals.*

I pushed that from my thoughts. Dwelling on the matter would only get me angry, and I doubted anyone would attempt to enforce my exile. If they did, I'd just return to the atlas turtle and spend time with my father. He would understand the predicament I found myself in.

When I glanced around now, however, I couldn't help but notice that some people avoided eye contact or hurried away the moment my gaze went in their general direction.

Their attention wasn't awe and admiration.

The citizens of Ruma were afraid.

I didn't know why, but their reaction killed my anger. I never wanted to frighten them, no matter how many wrongs they might've done to me.

"This is… a nice town," Fain muttered as his gaze panned over the homes and ocean-themed decorations. "But do they have any *entertainment*?" He said the last word with odd emphasis.

I stared at him for a moment. "Do you mean a tavern?"

"Something like that."

"Uh, there's just the one. It's small. And it mostly sells fish soup."

"There are no women," Adelgis chimed in, matter-of-factly. "This isn't the type of isle known for singers or dancers or anything similar."

Fain turned away and crossed his arms. "I wasn't just asking about that. I meant anything entertaining. Most islands we stopped at always had something unique. Hot springs. Waterfalls. Bizarre fruit. I figured this one had it, too."

"We don't have much here," I said. Then I pointed to the Pillar. "There's a charberry tree at the top, though most people on Ruma don't approve of outsiders ascending the staircase. And you're definitely not supposed to eat the fruit unless you're a phoenix."

Fain scoffed. "No. That's not entertaining."

"We can wander through town," Adelgis said.

"Wandering isn't that amusing, either."

Although I would've loved to show the two of them around, especially to the Endless Mire, which was the Isle of Ruma's unique feature, Atty squeezed my elbow. I gave her a nod, waved goodbye to Fain and Adelgis, and continued with her into the city. We didn't have much time here—less than a day, I suspected. We probably shouldn't dither.

Ruma was a small city—if *city* was even the right word—and the main street would take us to any important destination, including Atty's family home.

In the center of the city was the Pillar, a straight tower of stone that jutted out of the ground like a gargantuan stone golem finger. It cast a long shadow over some of the houses, moving throughout the day like a massive sun dial. I glanced up at the 112 steps, daydreaming about my time spent memorizing the wisdom on each one.

"There he is," someone said as we entered the main square.

I had to drag my attention away from the Pillar to figure out who was talking.

Everyone on the Isle of Ruma knew everyone else, and I recognized the messenger man, Crant. He pointed to me, his wide-brimmed hat shading most of his face from the island sun, but I could still detect the disgusted frown.

"It's the gravedigger boy," Crant said.

Behind him stood one of my least favorite people in the whole world: Schoolmaster Tyms. When I had been a child, he had made it his mission in life to remind me I was scum. Seeing him now almost made me laugh. He seemed so... unimportant to what was going on in the world, yet he strode over to me with a powerful gait and stern, authoritative expression. A sneer. Narrowed eyes. His head high.

Tyms had the face of a man who didn't like to smile, and he was old enough that the wrinkles of his skin had settled into their favorite position—a glower.

"The audacity," Tyms said once he was close.

His voice was naturally loud. I could've heard him from halfway across the island.

"Good afternoon, Schoolmaster," Atty said, her voice cheery. "It's been forever." She let go of my arm and approached Tyms in order to offer a bow of her head.

As though hit in the face with a cold fish, Tyms grimaced and then glanced at Atty. "Oh, my dear. I... didn't see you there. Yes, it has been quite some time." He returned the bow, his half-silver, half-blond hair an odd combination. "I'm pleased to see you're with a guild. I would love to hear the story of your adventures."

"I apologize, Schoolmaster, but Volke and I are here to see my mother."

Tyms's sour demeanor returned as he shot me a glare. "You. This is unacceptable. You are not allowed to return to the island. Not after the stunt you pulled. Not after you defied our traditions."

The messenger man, along with a couple dozen other citizens of the island, lingered on the sides of the street, watching our interactions with rapt attention. Adelgis had told me what they really thought. It both angered and saddened me—I wasn't here to cause trouble.

But I didn't know what to say. I just... stood there. Even if I explained, Tyms would never believe me.

"Volke is an important journeyman in the Frith Guild," Atty quickly said. She took hold of my arm again. "He's my bodyguard for this trip, you see. We're being chased by a villainous organization far worse than any dread pirate."

"*Him?*" Tyms balked. He shook his head. "Surely someone *else* would be willing to escort a beautiful phoenix arcanist through town. Someone trustworthy and reliable." He stepped closer to Atty and offered his arm. "You shouldn't be alone with a man of his reputation. Self-control isn't his strong suit."

The shadows in the nearby area shifted as anger roiled through my system. I gritted my teeth and then resumed my walking. Atty kept my pace.

I couldn't lash out at Tyms or else it'd just prove his point—that I couldn't control myself. But at the same time, I didn't have to listen to his blabbering. I wasn't the criminal he wanted me to be.

Atty glanced back. "Everything will be fine, Schoolmaster. Thank you for your concern."

"He's been exiled," Tyms shouted. He even pointed, his face growing a bright red. "He'll be apprehended!"

Atty held my elbow a little tighter and said nothing in return.

The stares of the nearby denizens became accusatory. It felt like they were talking themselves into grabbing me and dragging me to the stocks, but the moment I glanced in their directions, they went silent and shuffled away, their anger snuffed out by my own.

Perhaps I shouldn't have returned so openly. Last time I had been here, I had just snuck into the graveyard to speak with Gravekeeper William.

"We're almost there," Atty whispered. "We can leave the island afterward, if you want. I didn't realize everyone would be so unpleasant. I'm sure they mean well, though. They just don't know you like I do."

I didn't reply.

She pointed to a large home near the center of town. "There it is."

I knew it well. The Trixibelle House was one of the largest houses on the Isle of Ruma. The Trixibelles' owned most of the buildings, and when I had been younger, I had always wondered what the inside of their home looked like.

With Atty still clinging to me, we walked straight to the gate that led to her family abode. The fence around the property was twice my height —at least twelve feet—and I marveled at the stone and iron used to construct something so impressive for this tiny isle.

But despite having a fence, there was no gate guard. The gate stood ajar, allowing for anyone to enter. The Isle of Ruma didn't have many soldiers or city guards since crime was nearly nonexistent, and while the Trixibelle family was wealthy, even they didn't want to pay a single person to stand out by the gate all day.

"Let me be the one to speak with my mother," Atty said. "She gets irritated with people who don't speak with a certain level of refinement."

I could tell she had searched for just the right words to mean *uncouth* without actually calling me an uncivilized barbarian.

"I'll try to limit how much I speak," I said.

Atty tugged on my arm and forced me to stop right before we reached the front door. Then she gave me the once-over, her blue eyes examining every inch of me.

"Can you comb your hair?" she asked. "And dust off your coat a bit?"

I ran a hand through my black hair, well aware of how shaggy and unkempt it was. But that wasn't entirely my fault. I had been traveling for months, and my hair never wanted to cooperate.

"I don't have a comb," I muttered.

Atty frowned, and my chest hurt just seeing her disappointment.

In an attempt to comply with her demands, I brushed off my coat and then used my hand to comb back whatever hair I could. Without water or pomade—beeswax that mainland aristocrats used to keep their hair in place—I wasn't going to achieve what Atty wanted.

My disobedient hair flopped back into its disheveled state.

"I'm sorry," I said.

Atty sighed. "No need to apologize. As long as your arcanist mark is visible, my mother will likely be distracted."

"Does she know that the glowing mark means my eldrin is true form?"

"I doubt it. But once I tell her, everything will be okay. Until then..."

Atty said the words, but there was no emotion or warmth behind them. Dread crept into my thoughts, and I questioned my decision to accompany her to the Trixibelle family home.

Before I could change my mind, the front door opened.

An old woman with a stained apron stood before us. She had a prominent hunch that reduced her height, but her wispy white hair was pulled up into a bun, adding a little back. With a smile that had left permanent lines in her face, the woman said, "Is that you, Atty? What a pleasant surprise."

"Hello, Ogma," Atty replied with a smile

The woman turned to me, her bluish-gray eyes half-hidden under heavy eyelids. They went wide once she examined my face.

"Aren't you...?" Ogma began, her voice breathless.

"We're here to see my mother," Atty interjected. "I assume she's in?"

"Y-yes. Of course." The woman bowed her head and then shuffled into the house, her steps quiet and tiny. "Right this way."

Titania swooped around the roof of the large abode and then landed on a peak near the front door. She stared down at us, but made no indication she would enter.

Atty motioned for me to go inside. I did as she wanted and entered the Trixibelle residence. The gloomy halls and dark rooms took me by surprise. Odd—it was the middle of the day—yet they had heavy curtains drawn over every window and barely any lit lanterns. It didn't matter much to me since I could see through any darkness, but it made me wonder.

"This is a waiting room," Ogma said, gesturing to an empty room with a small table and plenty of seating. She gave me an odd look. "You can stay here."

Atty shook her head. "Volke will stay with me."

"But... your mother is in the great hall."

Ogma spoke slow and deliberate, almost quiet. Again, the situation felt off. Atty and Ogma stared at each other for a prolonged moment, having a silent conversation. The creaks of the grand house got me on edge. I caught myself glancing over my shoulder and checking the hilt of my blade.

"Volke," Atty said. "This way."

She took hold of my elbow again and guided me through the house, leaving Ogma behind. Atty couldn't see in the dark, but she didn't need to. With the grace of a dancer, and the familiarity of family, she guided me down one corridor and to the next. There were others inside the massive house—I could hear them in nearby rooms, their movements echoing throughout the spacious areas—but I never *saw* anyone else.

When we arrived at the great hall, Atty stopped in front of the tall oak door. When she faced me, it was with a controlled expression —neutral.

"Volke," she said. "My mother is a bit... reserved."

I nodded once. "Okay."

"She rarely leaves the house."

Once Atty had mentioned that fact, I realized she was right. I couldn't remember seeing Atty's mother. Ever.

"I'll be polite," I said.

"Well, that's not what I'm worried about." Atty fidgeted with the hems of her sleeves, her expression shifting into something anxious. "My mother is eccentric. And some people don't understand. I'm hoping you won't judge her too harshly."

I didn't like where the conversation was headed. "I'll try to keep an open mind," I said.

"Thank you."

After a deep exhale, Atty pushed open the door to the great hall—it creaked as it went, heralding our arrival with a soft, metal screech.

For something considered a *great hall*, it felt small. There were two tables, several bookshelves, and walls covered in paintings, but I had seen larger rooms in the past. The vaulted ceiling created a sense of false space, and I craned my head back to get a better look at everything.

All the paintings were portraits. So many blond individuals.

"Mother?" Atty called out.

No answer.

"Mother? Are you here?"

Atty's voice traveled up to the tall ceilings. But still—no answer.

I glanced around, peering into the darkest corners of the room, but I saw no one. Before I could voice my observation, I caught sight of something interesting.

Two coffins.

And not just any coffins—they were specially made from the red wood of the mangrove trees that grew in the Endless Mire. I knew them well because I had helped Gravekeeper William construct both.

They were resting on tables at the far end of the room, elevated high and partially lit with a handful of candles. Cloth had been draped over them, half covering the wood and hiding the hinges of the lids, but I still recognized them. The six-sided design of coffins would forever be burned into my mind after my apprenticeship at the graveyard.

"What are those doing here?" I asked, my eyebrows knitted.

Atty pursed her lips and remained quiet.

"They're... coffins." I walked over to one, just to make sure. "Shouldn't they be—"

"You said you would keep an open mind," Atty muttered.

I stopped a foot away from the coffins and held my breath. I focused my attention on the wooden containers, almost unable to process their existence inside the house. If there were bodies inside, they would be decomposing, and the gases released from a dead body could get trapped in the coffin or leak out and cause a terrible stench. I didn't smell anything, and both coffins were sealed tight—a difficult process some used to preserve bodies far longer than normal. It delayed the terrible process of decay.

Why would anyone keep dead bodies in the middle of their home?

"Who are they?" I finally asked.

Although Atty had never walked over—and even though she kept her voice to whisper levels—I heard her say, "The one on the left is my uncle."

"And the right?"

"That's... my younger sister."

22

RESURRECTING THE DEAD

I wanted to ask a million questions, but they clogged my throat, preventing me from speaking. I didn't need to ask anything. Deep down, I knew what this was. Why they were here.

Since the first day Atty had bonded with her phoenix, she had spoken about obtaining the true form of her eldrin. Why? I had never known—and I had never asked—but now I knew.

Because according to legend, true form phoenixes could resurrect the dead.

After a long exhale, I faced Atty. She stared up at me through her lashes, a slight frown at the corner of her lips.

"They're here to be honored," she said before I could speak. "It's no different than a crypt."

I shook my head. "Don't you remember Gregory Ruma? How his wife, Acantha, was... was dead. And how he tried to force her eldrin to resurrect her?"

The memories still haunted my nightmares. Acantha had been a shambling corpse, and Ruma, driven mad by the plague, had gone to great lengths to revive her. Despicable lengths.

"Acantha's phoenix was also affected by the plague," Atty said. She laced her fingers together, her frown deepening. "Ruma was feeding other arcanists and mystical creatures to the plague-ridden phoenix—to make it stronger. That was an abomination. If my phoenix achieves her true form correctly... Maybe it'll be different."

I opened my mouth to speak, but then caught my breath as I remembered something.

The plague-ridden creatures sought out magic to consume, and once they had enough, they became something different. Something strong. Something twisted. The *true form* of a mystical creature represented them at their best. But the *dread form*—as Adelgis's father called them—were mystical creatures at their worst and most disgusting.

Atty was right. Ruma's wife had had a plague-ridden phoenix. Had Ruma been trying to empower the phoenix until it reached its dread form in the hopes it could *also* resurrect the dead?

"Is this what *you* want?" I asked, keeping my voice low to avoid the echoes from the vaulted ceilings. "Or is this what your mother wants?"

Silence settled between us.

I tensed at the sound of the door groaning open, and snapped my attention to the woman entering the great hall. There was no need for introductions; I knew it was Atty's mother. She had the same elegant face and noble poise. Her eyes were marked at the edges with hard lines, and her blonde hair bore the silver strands of age, but the other similarities were too numerous.

Her forehead was bare. She wasn't an arcanist.

"Mother," Atty said as she straightened her posture just a little more. "Ogma said you'd be here. I apologize for—"

"You brought someone?" her mother asked, harsh and curt.

Then the woman strode into the room, her long legs taking her far with each step. Like Atty, she wore long robes, but unlike Atty, hers were red and gold instead of white. The folds of clothing accented her beauty. I couldn't guess her exact age—she had an unusual mix of *youthful* and *tired* about her appearance.

"Mother," Atty muttered with a slight bow of her head. "This is Volke Savan. Volke—this is my mother, Bayva Trixibelle."

"It's a pleasure to meet you," I said, also offering a slight bow.

Bayva went straight to her daughter, barely giving me a second glance. She grabbed Atty by the shoulder, her spindly fingers hooking into Atty's robes.

"What have I said about this place?" Bayva asked. Her tone reminded me of a parent speaking to a small child.

Atty took in a sharp breath. "I—"

"And you had the audacity to bring the troublemaking *gravedigger*? The one who ruined your bonding ceremony by storming into the phoenix's trial of worth?" Bayva shook her head and then offered me a narrowed glower. Her blue eyes reminded me of Atty—they were almost identical, down to the striation from the pupil. "I can't believe you had the gall to introduce him as though I had no idea as to his identity."

"Mother," Atty said. "Look at his mark." She pointed, her speech much faster than normal. "Volke managed to help his eldrin achieve true form. That's what the glow represents."

Their elevated voices bounced around the ceiling, creating a ghostly effect to their conversation.

Bayva stared at me again, this time her gaze fixed on my forehead. Her expression shifted from cold anger to confusion, her eyebrows lifting at a slow, but steady pace.

"That can't be true," she muttered. "He's... he's not the type."

"But it *is* true." Atty slipped out of her mother's claw-like grasp and moved closer to me. "Volke's knightmare is stronger than ever. And it happened not too long ago. Isn't that right, Volke?"

I nodded, though I didn't speak.

Her mother's condescension reminded me of Schoolmaster Tyms and wore at my patience, but I withheld my commentary. What was the point of starting a fight? And I didn't want to disappoint Atty. She had asked me to keep an open mind, after all.

Bayva's stillness bothered me. I kept expecting her to say something, but she just stared, her face stuck in rigid bemusement.

"Volke is going to help me," Atty said, ending the quiet. She placed a hand on my upper arm. "He's grown since he left the isle, Mother. Master Zelfree even trusts him with an apprentice of his own. This is a fantastic opportunity for me."

Atty didn't hold or touch me like she had before. She remained a respectable distance and never stared at me for too long.

When her mother said nothing, Atty continued, "Volke has even introduced me to a few tomes on the subject of true form eldrin. I've learned so much since joining the Frith Guild, and my magic has improved by leaps and bounds. I was hoping you might speak with the guildmaster before we left. She, too, has a glowing mark to symbolize that her eldrin has—"

"Atty," her mother said, cutting her off. "We should retire to the sitting room if we're going to have a discussion."

"O-oh. Of course."

With a swish of her robes, Bayva motioned to the door of the great hall.

A part of me wanted to glance back at the coffins, but I reined in the urge. I still didn't know how I felt about them—about Atty's goal—and instead of grappling with that issue in this moment, I decided to focus on the immediate.

I opened the tall wooden door, suffered through a third round of metal groaning from the hinges, and then held it open for Atty and her mother. When they stepped into the corridor, I noticed they were both roughly the same height. The similarities never ceased to strike me as interesting.

Bayva motioned with a flick of her wrist. "Atty. Go have Ogma prepare us some tea."

The command left me uncertain. Atty had said she didn't want to be alone with her mother, but now that I had met the woman, I didn't want to be left alone with her, either.

"I'll return momentarily," Atty said, offering a bow as she left us.

I should've insisted on going with her.

Bayva pointed in the opposite direction. With a resigned sigh, I turned to walk down the hall. Bayva didn't move. She just gestured, as though I should go first. When I attempted to step past her, however, Bayva grimaced away with a sneer.

"Don't even think of touching me," she said in a low growl.

Unable to hide my anger, I replied with a glare and then continued down the corridor, making sure to give the woman a wide berth. Clearly, Atty had been mistaken. Her mother didn't care that my eldrin was true form. Bayva hated my mere existence, and she wasn't afraid to share that information.

The sitting room wasn't far—thankfully—and once we entered, all I could think about were the drawn curtains and the window. Was it open a crack? If it was, I could shadow-step out of this room in a matter of seconds. Nothing would've made me happier.

The two maroon couches and the dusty tea table had probably been around longer than I had been alive. Their worn edges and faded coloring gave the room a sad feel—and barren walls didn't help matters.

Bayva and I stepped in, and the door shut with a creaky snap. The air smelled of dust. I almost sneezed.

Stillness filled the dour room. I shoved my hands into my pockets. Part of me thought I should start conversation, but another part knew that would be a mistake.

Bayva decided for me.

"Only arcanists of true integrity can achieve the true form of their eldrin," she said.

I faced her. "Well, I don't think it's the same for every mystical creature. From what I've read—"

"*No,*" Bayva hissed. "I've read the ancient legends. I know what it takes." Her hands curled into fists. "I've spoken with dozens of master arcanists. They all say the same thing."

What was the point of arguing? Technically, I didn't know what *exactly* had triggered Luthair's transformation. Perhaps it had been integrity, like she said. But perhaps it had been something more...

"Okay," I said. "I'll try to help Atty understand the path of *true integrity.*" I couldn't hold back the entirety of my sarcasm, and the last two words came out with the levity of a joke.

Bayva glowered, her lips so tightly pressed together, they had become a white line. "Are you *mocking* Atty's life goal? She has great work to do. Don't you understand? A true form phoenix can change fate—it can change the world. Atty's fame and glory will be never-ending. She'll never have to experience loss. And you would *deride* that?"

I wanted to reply, but the door to the sitting room swung open. Atty and Ogma stepped in, both holding trays. Atty carried small biscuits, and Ogma carried the cups and kettle. They set them on the circular tea table. No one spoke while the dishes were laid out and the spread prepared.

The clinking of the plates was our only entertainment.

"Here we are," Atty said once finished.

She smiled and gestured to the small assortment of food. Some biscuits were yellow, some were small, some had herbs—they all seemed delectable.

"Thank you," Bayva said with a forced smile. "Volke, why don't we sit and enjoy each other's company?"

I hated the way she spoke. It reminded me of someone reading from a piece of parchment. Fake.

Atty motioned me over to the worn couch. I sat next to her out of a sense of obligation, and she poured us tea and served biscuits without saying a thing. Her mother sat opposite us, and from the neutral expression on her face, I knew we weren't going to discuss my true form any longer.

"Why don't you tell me about your time in the Frith Guild?" Bayva asked her daughter. "Tell me about how they're helping you master your phoenix magic. And how they'll help Titania achieve her true form."

It was dark by the time we left House Trixibelle.

Every second there had been torture. Bayva's frigid demeanor and the gloomy atmosphere of the house had seeped into my system like poison and chilled me to the bones. I had walked out with my jaw clenched and my gait stiff. I never wanted to return. Ever. Not when Bayva clearly felt disgusted with my presence.

She had made it clear, in not-so-subtle ways, that she didn't want to hear from me. Whenever I had tried to add to the conversation, she had cut me off to speak to Atty. Whenever I had attempted to correct facts I had thought clearly wrong, she had taken it as an insult to her intelligence.

I had been trapped with no escape. Fighting a plague-ridden monster wouldn't have been as terrible.

Atty and I walked down the main street of Ruma. Most windows stood dark and quiet. The denizens of the isle had long gone to sleep, and I was thankful. I didn't want another run-in with Schoolmaster Tyms.

With a playful amount of energy in her movements, Atty grabbed my elbow and pulled herself close to my arm. "That wasn't nearly as bad as I thought it was going to be."

"We were there for more than five hours," I muttered.

"I know. My mother is never that talkative. I think you brought out her good side, Volke."

I gave Atty an odd glance, confused by her reaction. Did she think I'd had a fun time? Or perhaps she was blind to her mother's antics? Bayva clearly wanted me to crawl into a ditch and die.

"She had always pushed me so hard as a child," Atty said. "And I owe most of my success to her. Now... I want to live my own life, but I do feel an obligation to the family." She smiled wide and exhaled as though content. "And seeing your true form eldrin made me realize something. Maybe this goal won't take me forever. Maybe I can achieve it and finally move on from my family, travel the world without feeling guilty."

I rubbed at the back of my neck, uncertainty twisting my insides. "But most arcanists never—"

"If you can do it, I can do it," Atty interjected. "Right?"

"Well, yes, but—"

"And you'll help me every step of the way, right?"

I slowly nodded.

"Then it'll happen sooner or later," Atty said, a laugh at the edge of her words.

Titania swooped in close as we neared the docks. Her bright glowing body was like a giant firefly in the sky. Whenever she drew close, the shadows shifted all around, fluttering like black moths.

I couldn't help but think of the dead bodies inside Atty's house. Corpses never bothered me much—not after working as a gravedigger—but keeping them around in the hopes someone could resurrect them felt... disturbing. Why not keep them in a crypt? Or underground? Or anywhere but the great hall of their home?

"Are you okay, Volke?" Atty asked as she slowed her steps.

I responded with a weak smile. "I'm tired, that's all."

"Oh. Well, we should return to the manor house."

I nodded.

But Atty stopped and kept me from going any farther. I glanced back at her, one eyebrow raised.

"I really appreciate you taking the time to meet with my mother," Atty said. She met my gaze, her expression set between neutral and serious. "It means a lot. She doesn't leave the house much, and I think you're a positive influence on everyone you meet. I hope my mother will think about you afterward—maybe even think gravediggers aren't what she thought they were."

I almost blurted out my experiences with her mother in private, but I bit my tongue and just nodded along with Atty's words. Did I really want to shatter Atty's illusion? No. If she wanted to think I had helped her mother, then I would allow that.

Even if I knew it was the farthest thing from the truth.

2 3

ATTACK ON THE ISLE OF RUMA

I wanted to visit Gravekeeper William, but the night had already settled. I had so many questions for him—especially about relationships and responsibility. Did I want to disturb him, though? He would be here when I returned. In theory. So long as I *did* return.

Atty and I headed to the atlas turtle in relative silence. It wasn't uncomfortable, just quiet. As I rowed the dinghy, she sat close and kept a hand on my knee. I focused on her touch more than I should've, but I enjoyed the show of affection. Being distracted made it difficult to steer, and I half-crashed our vessel onto the tiny dock attached to the atlas turtle.

"Are you okay?" Atty asked, her eyes wide.

She withdrew her hand from my knee, and I regretted my incompetence.

"I'm okay," I said as I tied down the dinghy. "It's just late." I ended the statement with a nervous laugh.

"Are you *very* tired?" Atty asked, but her voice made me think she was... disappointed.

I shook my head. "Uh, well, I could stay up."

"I was wondering if you wanted to spend more time together? We could walk around the pond."

"On Gentel's shell?"

Atty smiled and nodded. "It's beautiful under the moonlight."

"Sure. That sounds wonderful."

Titania flew to the manor house, her brilliant phoenix body a delight to see soaring in the sky. As Atty and I walked up toward the top of the shell, Titania flew to the roof and landed. Forsythe was likely sleeping somewhere up there, too. They were so large now. Perhaps they didn't want to stay cooped up in a small personal room anymore.

Halfway to the pond, Atty smiled. "I've been practicing my magic." She followed the statement with a soft laugh. "I know, I know. We *all* have. But I've been wanting to speak to you for a while." She glanced up at me. "What do you think about using multiple types of magic at once?"

"What do you mean?" I asked.

"As a phoenix arcanist, I can evoke fire. But I can also augment the body to heal individuals. What if both were used at the same time?"

"Uh, well, I still don't know what you mean. As in, you would burn someone while healing them?"

Atty shook her head. She withdrew into her own thoughts as we reached the edge of the clear pool of water on the back of the atlas turtle. It was a circular pond with a single oak tree on the opposite side, and Atty was correct—the moonlight glittered across the surface, sparkling with an evening luster.

"Do you remember that I had problems learning my augmentation?" Atty asked with a tilt of her head.

Her blonde hair also shone in the moonlight.

"Yeah, I remember," I said. "You mastered your evocation quickly, but you struggled with healing."

"That's right. I spent a lot of time by myself, trying to master my augmentation. I didn't want anyone to know I was struggling, and... Well, that doesn't matter. The important part is what happened. I think... I used both my evocation and my augmentation at the same time."

"What happened?" I asked.

We both stood at the water's edge, mere inches away from the mirror-like surface.

Atty held my arm tight. "I think I created fire that healed flesh."

"Really?" I asked, shock in my tone. "I've never heard of that."

"Neither has Master Zelfree. He asked me to show him, but whenever I tried to replicate the power, I faltered."

Master Zelfree hadn't heard of it? That surprised me more than anything else. Zelfree had traveled the world and seen thousands of arcanists of all types. *He* hadn't heard of someone combining types of sorcery? Perhaps Atty was mistaken—she only *thought* she had created a healing flame.

"I was hoping you would help me," Atty said, breaking me out of my thoughts. "You see... After reading Theasin's tome on mystical creatures, I realized that each one has a different requirement for achieving its true form. As the arcanist, it's my job to exemplify the virtues of a phoenix, and I thought that, perhaps..."

"If you created some new form of healing, it would help Titania transform?" I asked.

Atty nodded.

"Shouldn't you speak to Gillie about this? She's the Grand Apothecary—a master healer beyond compare."

"I want to develop it on my own," Atty said. "I don't want to copy her techniques. I want to make something new. *Discover* something, you know? I know knightmares can't heal others, and you and Luthair are so confident now... I thought you could assist me in getting into the proper mindset to create these healing flames."

"I thought you said you already did it once before?" I asked. "What mindset were you in then?"

Atty's face grew pink, and she glanced away.

The reaction got me curious. I tilted my head and tried to get a good look at her face, but Atty turned more, practically showing me her back.

"It's silly," she said, her voice laced with a nervous laugh and an anxious strain. "But... I created the flame because... Well, because *you* were trying so hard to master your knightmare magic, even though you were second-bonded and your training hurt. I wanted to be more like you—confident and determined. That was the mindset I was in."

My face heated in an instant, and for a long moment, I didn't know what to say. Atty had been thinking about *me* while locked away in her room and practicing magic? *I* had been the one to inspire her?

"I'm, uh, flattered," I said, though I knew that sounded stilted. I wished I had a similar story—about how I had done something because of her. I floundered for a moment before adding, "I always thought *you* were the dedicated one of the group. You always had your magics mastered, and you never hesitated to use them."

Atty turned back around to face me. Her cheeks remained rosy, and she kept her gaze low. "So you'll help me?"

"Yes," I said, probably too quick and eager, but I didn't care. "I think it's a great idea."

She smiled and stepped close. Much closer than before. She placed both her hands on my chest, and I held my breath. When she met my gaze, my throat tightened.

I had never been the one to initiate a kiss before. Every other time, the woman had taken the lead, but this was different. I brought my hand to the side of Atty's neck, brushed my fingers up to her jaw, and then leaned down, bringing my mouth to hers.

My heart hammered like it wanted to escape my chest—the thumping echoed in my ears, even as Atty's soft lips touched mine. She didn't pull away or even hesitate. A part of me relaxed, comforted by relief. Another part of me couldn't settle down. I never would've imagined this happening even a few months prior.

I wasn't sure what else to do. Atty was the one to end the moment. All in all, it was rather chaste, but I couldn't help feeling like it was something intimate. That was foolish, but still. I swear I saw Atty in a different light from that moment on.

She looked away, her cheeks a hot red. She seemed to glance everywhere, so long as it wasn't meeting my gaze straight on.

"How about we sit for a while?" she asked, her tone giddy. "I don't feel like going inside yet."

"Sure."

I sat on the grass, a foot away from the pond, and Atty smoothed her robes as she took a seat next to me. Then she leaned over and rested her head on my shoulder.

"I really appreciate you accompanying me to my family home," she said.

I nodded, still unwilling to comment.

Atty continued, "This whole day has been much better than I ever could've imagined."

I had to agree.

The sun rose on the distant horizon.

Atty had fallen asleep several hours ago. She used my upper leg as a pillow, one of her hands on my knee. I didn't want to move, for fear I would disturb her, and I couldn't manage to fall asleep, not with excitement coursing through my veins. So I just sat there. Staring at the water. Contemplating the future.

"You should rest, my arcanist," Luthair whispered.

I couldn't see his location, but his dark and gruff voice seemed to emanate from the grass slightly behind me.

"She'll wake up if I move," I muttered under my breath. "I'll rest while we travel."

"We have a fight ahead of us. Is it wise to use your time in this way?"

"Uh, well—you see..."

I sighed. He was right. We needed to focus on the world serpent.

"We might not come back from this," I whispered. "What if I never have another chance like this? A chance to just be happy?"

"The essence of sacrifice—of giving up things for the greater good— is about moments like this."

"Are you saying that I need to give up all opportunities for personal happiness?"

"No. I'm not saying you have to do anything, my arcanist. I'm just speaking aloud."

The eighty-third step on the Pillar read: *Sacrifice. Without it, we cannot achieve the greatest of accomplishments.* Deep down, I knew what Luthair meant. I had to protect the world serpent arcanist. I had to train Evianna. I had to hone my own skills and prepare for the inevitable fight with the Second Ascension.

"Just a little longer," I muttered. "After this, I'll remain focused."

"As you wish, my arcanist."

I would've taken a few more moments of contented bliss if I hadn't felt a terrible creeping feeling slithering up my spine. Tense and confused, I glanced around. The morning light cast harsh shadows, and while some would consider that ominous, I thanked the stars I had darkness to manipulate should anything happen.

I recognized this feeling. It was the same I'd had when the plague-ridden thunderbird had descended onto the *Sun Chaser*. It was a heartbeat like a war drum, growing faster in tempo with each destructive thought. The closer it became, the louder the thumping sound grew in my head.

"Do you feel that, Luthair?" I asked, no longer bothering to whisper.

"Feel what, my arcanist?"

Atty shook her head and then rubbed at her eyes. "Volke?"

"I'm so sorry," I said. "But we need to go."

She sat up, her brow furrowed. "Is everything okay?"

"No," I said as I leapt to my feet. "Something is nearby. Maybe plague-ridden creatures... Maybe something else."

The heartbeat—there was more than one.

"Maybe the Second Ascension," I whispered.

24

AKIVA THE ASSASSIN

As if the world wanted to answer my unspoken question, an explosion of fire and smoke erupted from the Isle of Ruma. The atlas turtle was at least half a mile from shore, but the blast of light and flame was clearly visible. A rumble ran through the island city, shaking the buildings and causing a wake of water to rush from the beach and out to the ocean.

"*Luthair*," I shouted, my attention locked on the fire.

He rose from the shadows in an instant, his inky armor flowing like a swift river, his tall and imposing frame an impressive sight. His cape, fluttering in the morning wind, glittered with stars embedded in the inner fabric. Although Luthair had no face—just a helmet with no open visor—his stance told me everything I needed to know. He was ready for combat, Forfend on his arm, his stance wide.

Atty leapt to her feet. "Volke—what're you going to do?"

"I'm going to help fight," I said. Then I motioned to Luthair. "Come. There are plague-ridden mystical creatures nearby. The denizens of Ruma need us."

Luthair's shadow-water body melted in an instant and then reformed up and around me. The cold strength of his power washed away the fatigue of a long, sleepless night. My heart raced, my muscles tensed and coiled, and I whipped my attention back to the havoc. It would take an unreasonable amount of time to row a dinghy to the port.

"I'll fight, too," Atty said.

She placed her hands on the shoulder of my void-like armor. I could feel her touch, as though the shadows themselves were one with my flesh.

"Very well," I said, my voice a mix of mine and Luthair's, but it came out so intertwined that it was difficult to distinguish between us. It was like we were a new person—a new voice, a new strength, a new purpose.

I couldn't shadow-step across water, but that didn't matter. My cape ripped down the middle, and bone-like appendages burst from the armor, crafted from the inky metal that made up Luthair. The cape wove itself between the bones, once again creating wings. Although I hadn't practiced flight, I only needed it for the short distance to land.

With an effortless motion, I scooped up Atty and then spread my new wings wide. She softly gasped as I flapped once, launching us into the air. The power behind my flight was enough to disturb the pond water and tree, and once I had gotten high enough, I glided toward the Isle of Ruma. The morning sun scorched the sky, stinging my back and wings. It reminded me that my magic would only grow weaker from this point forward. The daylight killed the darkness.

Atty tightened her hold around my neck as I soared toward the docks. It was cumbersome to carry someone. The drag of the air, the awkward weight distribution—they made everything difficult. Despite that, I persisted. I gritted my teeth and focused on the task at hand.

The two phoenixes, Forsythe and Titania, flanked me in the sky, reminding me of a flock of gulls. They matched my speed and angle and descended at the same time I did.

Landing worried me, but when I drew close, shadowy claws formed from my greaves, giving me hooks and some ability to latch on to the ground.

I hit the end of the pier hard, but my claws dug into the wood, keeping me from stumbling off and into the ocean. With as much grace as I could muster, I placed Atty on her feet. She stepped away from me, her focus on the city ahead of us.

Forsythe and Titania sailed to the city gates.

Crowds of people rushed around in panic as another explosion of fire rocked the nearby street. Smoke billowed into the sky, creating a black pillar that matched the stone one in the center of the city. Debris swept down the main street. Screams filled the air.

I glanced toward the graveyard in the distance. It was far removed from the devastation—isolated and alone. Gravekeeper William was likely safe, which meant I could freely focus on the threat at hand.

My arcanist, Luthair spoke telepathically. *Wanton destruction of this nature must be ended quickly, lest innocent lives are lost by the hundreds.*

"You should heal anyone who's injured," I said to Atty, my guts twisted in uncertain anxiety.

"The fire won't harm me," she replied. "We can help with the injured after the threat is dealt with."

We didn't have time to argue. I wrapped one arm around her and dove into the shadows. I had forgotten to remind her to hold her breath, and when we finally emerged inside the city, Atty gasped for air.

I released her, and she quickly recovered.

My wings of darkness melted back into my armor. I didn't need flight, and they would only hinder my movement through the narrow streets and alleys.

"Let's go," I said in my double-voice.

Hundreds of people rushed down the road, some carrying personal belongings such as blankets and flintlock pistols. They hurried away from the destruction, their eyes wide. I thought they would run into me, or push me aside, but the exact opposite happened. They parted to either side, avoiding me as though I were the cause of the mayhem. Some even shrieked when they got a good look at me.

Luthair's helmet covered my face completely, including my arcanist mark, so I didn't blame them for being frightened. I just wished that weren't the case.

"There!" Atty shouted and pointed.

I followed her finger until I spotted a magma salamander far up the street. They were typically creatures of extraordinary ability. They nested in island volcanos, and their scarlet scales were said to be impervious to heat and arrows. From the old tales I had read, magma salamanders only bonded with great warriors or daring adventurers brave enough to risk the heat of lava.

But this...

This wasn't the majestic magma salamander of legend.

It was a monster that appeared to be more skeleton than creature. Its scales, muscle, and organs appeared melted and twisted together to form a solid ooze of fleshy tissue that pooled in the monster's stomach, leaving the bones to shamble about, clearly powered solely by magic. The bones of the salamander trembled and shook as it scuttled forward, its gut distended from the mass of flesh it was carrying around like a sac-of-blood pregnancy.

The beast was larger than most horses, and it dragged its fleshy gut out onto the main road. Most everyone in the nearby area had already fled, but screams and frantic panic still filled the atmosphere.

The monster had no eyes in its sockets, but somehow it glanced around—and although it had no throat, it let out a laugh.

"Fools," it hissed. "Everyone here is such... *a fool.*"

Standing on its spine, and gripping the back of its skull, was an arcanist with a magma salamander mark on his forehead. The man wore no shirt, just a pair of trousers, boots, and a belt bandolier over one shoulder. The bandolier carried his pistol, gunpowder, and bullets, all strapped close and ready to go.

To my horror, the magma salamander arcanist hefted the gun and then slit his wrist with a blade to coat the bullets in his tainted blood.

"Get as many as you can, Vetter," the arcanist shouted, a jovial tone to his words. "Make them scream."

Vetter, the magma salamander, dragged his plague-ridden body to the next building over. His jaw opened wide, displaying shark-like teeth on top and bottom. Flames bubbled up from its fleshy sac, glowing bright with unrivaled heat.

Before it could vomit its destruction all over my hometown, I waved my hand and manipulated the darkness. Fueled by rage, the shadows lashed out—not as tentacles, but as barbs, knives, and spears. I punctured the deranged salamander, piercing his half-melted flesh and chipping his bones. The arcanist leapt away before my attack could skewer him as well. He hefted himself onto one of the second-story balconies and then turned to face me, his pistol at the ready.

The man fired, but I already had my shield up. The metal ball slammed against Forfend with a harsh *clank*.

Atty held up her hand.

"They're immune to flames," I said.

She clenched her jaw and instead manipulated the fire that was consuming the nearby building. She snuffed out the embers and pulled the flames away from flammable material, like the bales of hay for the horses and the wooden walls of buildings.

The psychotic arcanist reloaded his flintlock pistol by shoving powder and bullets down the barrel. His magma salamander struggled for a moment, clearly trying to escape my shadow weapons. I waved my hand and evoked terrors, filling the area with nightmarish visions. The salamander laughed harder than I had ever heard a creature laugh, but the arcanist dropped to his knees and dropped his pistol. He clutched both sides of his head, his fingernails digging into his own temple.

"No," the arcanist said, his voice strained. "*No*. I need to... keep going. I have to... kill as many as I can..."

I withdrew Retribution and lunged for the plague-ridden salamander.

Once I had finished with the man's eldrin, I could question him afterward. Perhaps he hadn't been permanently affected by the plague just yet.

The bloated gut of flesh and organs hindered Vetter's ability to dodge, not to mention the several shadow spears keeping it pinned in place. I slashed at his body and cleaved clean through his ribs and forearm, my blade never catching on anything. It was like there was nothing there at all, that was how clean my strike had been.

The magma salamander whipped his head around and snapped at me. I lifted my gauntleted arm, and the liquid shadows rushed to my limb in order to harden and thicken the armor. When the teeth clamped down, I felt no pain—the shadows had protected me, even without a conscious thought to do so.

The monster hissed and released me. "You and your guildmaster," it said with a giddy giggle. *"You're already corpses!* Dead by the venom—we're all dead! I'm... I'm also... dead..."

I lifted my sword to end this beast, but something happened.

My heart fluttered and beat at an irregular interval.

It felt as though I had run 50 miles uphill, and that my body hadn't yet recovered. Every fiber of my being became soaked in dread as my heart continued to beat at an odd rhythm.

I recognized this odd sensation, the bizarre heartbeat in my chest.

This was a side effect of a *requiem aura*—a terrible magical power that only king basilisk arcanists could produce. The aura had a sinister purpose. Each person who died within the aura's range empowered the arcanist. The deaths strengthened them. Made them faster. Deadlier.

Akiva.

These attacks *were* the Second Ascension. King Basilisk Arcanist Akiva had come to assassinate Guildmaster Eventide.

My arcanist, focus! Luthair said, drawing me back to the immediate, but it was too late.

The salamander vomited flames across me. The heat and light from the fire burned at my shadow armor, destroying it faster than almost any other type of attack. For a moment, I couldn't see anything, all I could sense was the searing of my skin. I fell back into the darkness and slithered away, the burning sensation still lingering. When I emerged, I fell to my knees, the liquid shadows thinner and weaker than before.

Another eruption of flames rocked the city—this one on the other side of town. Which meant there were more of them.

I already knew their plan. They were killing innocent civilians so that their deaths would empower Akiva through his requiem aura. He was strengthening himself before confronting Guildmaster Eventide.

Did she even know Akiva was here? Someone had to warn her.

We can't allow this arcanist and his eldrin to continue their dastardly tactics, Luthair said. *We must finish this first.*

My thoughts dwelled on the guildmaster. If she died... would we be able to reach the world serpent?

Now isn't the time for indecision! My arcanist, you must act!

With Luthair's words ringing in my mind, I forced myself to stand. I would kill the magma salamander and his arcanist. I just hoped I finished in time to rush to Eventide's side before it was too late.

25

INFECTED

Determined to finish this fight quickly, I stepped into the darkness and then emerged on the balcony with the magma salamander arcanist. He stood and readied his pistol, but it was too late. He didn't have the wits to whirl around and defend against me—I stabbed him through the chest, the black blade of Retribution shiny with his tainted blood as I withdrew it from his body.

My time was limited. I leapt off the balcony and dove into the shadows instead of hitting the ground. Then I stepped out near the salamander and slashed hard for its boney neck. The beast laughed, even as its head was separated from its body. Thankfully, the monster didn't have much blood. Most of it had congealed in the gross gut that hung from its midsection, like lumpy porridge that had gone rotten.

"Everything is ash," the skull said as it clattered to the cobblestone road. "No one can... see it... *yet.*"

Atty snuffed out the largest of the fires, saving a good portion of the cobbler's home. Her phoenix swooped in from the sky and landed on the street next to us.

"My arcanist," Titania said. "I've located the other blackhearts attacking the city! They're killing everyone, including the children."

"Did you engage them?" Atty asked.

"No. They're splattering their plague-tainted blood across any mystical creature or arcanist who dares to stand in their path."

"I'll handle the villains," I stated, no hesitation. "Titania, lead the way."

I knew Atty had insisted on fighting, but there was no time to argue, and I truly didn't want to see her infected. When Titania took to the sky, I moved through the darkness until I arrived on top of a nearby roof without discussing the plan further.

The sun had fully lifted above the horizon, and the fire from the salamander still affected me. With sluggish movements, I pressed forward. Luthair's armor prevented me from really seeing the extent of the damage across my body, but I knew I would need to take time to recover after this.

When I came to gaps between buildings too large to jump, I slipped into the shadows once again. Having the liberty to use my powers without pain was a blessing. Although magic tasked my strength, I felt twice as strong as I ever had before.

But my heart continued to beat out of rhythm. My chest hurt, and taking in a deep breath resulted in a sharp spike of agony. The requiem aura would affect everyone like this, and I wondered if it would hinder my ability to concentrate.

The citizens of Ruma who ran through the streets were all people I knew. I spotted the messenger man, Crant, holding his seven-year-old daughter close as he hurried to the docks. There weren't many ships in port—not enough to carry everyone—which meant this threat *had* to be dealt with, no matter what.

When fire burst up over the roofs of nearby buildings, I dove into the shadows and emerged on the scene of the action.

Fire whooshed by me, the heat destroying some of my water-like darkness. There was another magma salamander, but this one wasn't as twisted as the last. It looked like a normal salamander should—a wingless dragon with the head of an iguana—and its scarlet scales glittered with the reflection of uncontrolled fire.

The only indication that it was plague-ridden was its manic laugh and disturbing eyes. They bulged out of the sockets and jiggled whenever the creature moved.

The salamander vomited fire and a lava-like substance onto the schoolhouse. The wooden walls burned, and it was only then that I caught sight of the salamander arcanist. He wore a long coat—the type for gentlemen, not sailors—and wielded a rapier. With his slicked-back hair and clean-shaven face, he seemed out of place in the chaos, but the mark on his forehead tied him to his eldrin.

He had to be a member of the Second Ascension. And he was engaged in slaughter on the street while his salamander tore into the schoolhouse.

I rushed toward the arcanist, ready to end the man's life.

To my shock and disgust, the salamander arcanist lunged for a child no older than eight. I almost leapt into the shadows in a desperate attempt to interject myself between them, but it wasn't necessary.

Zaxis appeared from a pillar of flame, like a fire elemental straight from a pyre. With white-hot knuckles, Zaxis punched the salamander arcanist square across the jaw, shattering teeth and sending the dastard to the ground in one powerful strike.

The fire didn't harm Zaxis. His salamander scale armor—the same shade of red as the plague-ridden salamander—remained secure in place, also unaffected by the heat.

I glanced around and spotted Schoolmaster Tyms and a small group of children caught in a narrow alleyway. Flames and broken houses blocked their path of escape. If I killed the salamander, they could flee, but until then, Tyms stood in front of the kids, shielding them, his eyes so wide I feared he had lost his eyelids.

The gentleman salamander arcanist managed to pick himself up.

That was when I held up a hand and evoked more terrors. Both the salamander and his arcanist screamed and fell to the ground. Instead of punching the arcanist a second time, Zaxis used his magic much like Atty had. He manipulated the fire and created an opening on the street —one large enough for several people to get through.

"*Run*," Zaxis shouted. "And keep your heads low!"

The little eight-year-old rushed to join Tyms and the others.

Perhaps they all would've escaped, had it not been for the harpy that appeared seemingly from nowhere.

Harpies were tricky creatures. They were birds—complete with black-feathered wings and sharp talons on the ends of their feet—but their torsos and heads were the visages of women, naked and young. They used the voices of delicate girls to lure men into a trap, often by hiding their feathers and bird-like legs with long cloaks. Their invisibility and ability to create confusion, were well known to travelers. Harpies hunted in packs, consuming human flesh whenever they could get it. Man-eaters, the lot of them, and immune to the arcane plague.

The harpy dove at Tyms. He held up an arm to defend his face, and the harpy clawed through his forearm, resulting in a terrible gash. The children screamed, and several fell to the ground as they attempted to scramble away from the fighting and flames.

I slid through the shadows and appeared at Tyms's side a second later. When the harpy attempted to attack again, I pushed Tyms aside and slashed with Retribution, slicing clean through the harpy's toes and cutting her foot in half.

The harpy hissed, flashing vampire-sharp canines. She flapped her wings, putting a dozen feet between us. Then she smiled, despite her bleeding foot.

"Do you want to play?" the harpy asked in a sweet voice.

Normally, I'd have been unsettled by a naked half-woman attempting to make advances at me, but only anger coursed through my veins. The Second Ascension thought they could harm *my* hometown? They thought they could kill everyone I had ever known?

My hatred for them ran deep.

I waved my gauntleted hand through the air, and although the area was flooded with fire, I managed to manipulate the nearby shadows. They gathered together across the cobblestone road, and when the harpy dove for me with her one good foot, the darkness shot upward like spikes. The sharp tips pierced the harpy through the leg, gut, and wing, but any shadows that touched the flames were burned away, melting like a candle.

The harpy screeched and struggled, her claw and wings thrashing wildly.

With the harpy held, I slashed with Retribution, cutting her in half from the left to the right. She groaned and cried out as her upper torso hit the road. Intestines splattered across the cobblestones. Thankfully, she wasn't a carrier of the plague.

Tyms grabbed at my star-woven cape. "Help us! P-please. You must! Take us to the docks!"

"Titania!" I shouted.

The phoenix emerged from around a burning building. Like Atty, she had been attempting to quell the flames, but she came to my summons without hesitation.

"Guide them far from here," I commanded Titania. Then I pulled my cape from Tyms's grasp. "I'm needed here. Follow the phoenix. She'll lead you to safety."

I didn't stay to hear Tyms respond. Instead, I stepped into the shadows and snaked my way to the salamander and his arcanist. When I emerged, I had to catch my breath.

Zaxis had already killed the gentleman-looking arcanist.

The bruised and bloodied body of the arcanist lay motionless on the ground, face down in a pool of his own blood. But Zaxis hadn't yet handled the salamander. The monster was latched onto his forearm, its razor-fangs buried deep in the flesh of Zaxis's forearm.

My arcanist, Luthair spoke telepathically. *The blood!*

The salamander bled at the gums, its corruption running the length of its teeth.

Zaxis punched the monster salamander straight in the face, his white-hot knuckles unable to burn the creature, but he was strong enough to crack bone and bust scales. Unfortunately, the salamander had the strength of an ox and size of a horse. It shook its head from side to side, dragging Zaxis along like a rag doll. Even through all that, Zaxis just gritted his teeth and punched again.

"*Filthy beast*," Zaxis hissed. "You fought the wrong damn arcanist!"

Zaxis punched again, this time shattering the salamander's fangs.

I cursed at myself as I evoked terrors. The salamander released its hold on Zaxis's arm and opened its mouth wide. Only laughter emanated from its maw—accompanied by tears that streamed from its dead fish eyes.

Zaxis leapt away, his arm mangled, but healing fast.

The salamander wasn't held by my terrors long. It took a breath, shook its head, and then turned its attention to a nearby building. I couldn't allow it to burn anything else. I lunged forward and slashed— but the monster leaned away at the last moment, moving quicker than I had imagined. His throat bulged, similar to a frog, and I knew it would breathe its flame at any moment.

Thankfully, Zaxis rushed in while the salamander had its focus on me. He punched the beast on the temple with a cross-hook strike, his form perfect. The salamander's head caved inward, and that was all the opening I needed.

I slashed my sword—careful to avoid Zaxis—and cut the monster's throat. Then I pulled the blade upward and sliced its head clean in half, up the middle.

If the salamander had breathed its flame on me, I would've been in terrible trouble, but now it would never use its fire ever again.

The smoke and debris normally would've been a major problem, but the island winds swept most of it toward the ocean. The constant breeze kept the road clear enough to see the destruction. Not only had the schoolhouse been decimated, but Zaxis was...

Zaxis gulped down air. Then he ran a shaky hand down his bloody arm. After a long minute, the fang injuries healed, but we both knew better. The arcane plague couldn't be healed by his phoenix magic.

"I'm going to find the other blackhearts," Zaxis said, never looking at me. "I'll handle them. You help the townsfolk."

"You should return to the guild," I said.

He shot me a glare. "I can't, *fool*. Not like this."

"You can. Just tell Master Zelfree and the grand apothecary. Don't throw your life away."

Zaxis clenched his jaw. The nearby buildings crackled with heat. Walls collapsed, and embers wafted into the sky. We didn't have much time.

"I won't abandon you," I stated.

I stepped closer to Zaxis and placed a hand on his shoulder. He turned his green eyes to me, though I knew he couldn't see my face. His gaze was unfocused as he searched the front of my helmet.

I tightened my grip on his shoulder.

"What're you doing?" Zaxis asked.

I didn't answer—I just dragged him with me when I went into the shadows. I needed to speak to the guildmaster, and I hoped she was already at the docks. If not, I'd take Zaxis to the guild manor myself.

I wasn't about to let Zaxis kill himself on the enemy's guns and blades.

BATTLE FOR THE ISLE OF RUMA

*Z*axis and I emerged from the shadows on the docks of Ruma. He gasped for breath, and I readied myself for his tirade and protest, but they never came. Instead, Zaxis shook slightly, his expression hardening into something pensive. I knew the look well.

"Now isn't the time to dwell on it," I said, my double-voice confident. "The Frith Guild needs you. Our home island needs you."

"But, I..." Zaxis gritted his teeth.

"The arcanists of legend never stopped until their goals were complete."

That was all he needed to hear. Zaxis glanced up, his eyes unable to see mine, but still—he met my gaze.

"You're right," he said. Then he offered a half-smirk. *"Perseverance. Without it, we invite despair."*

Although it was a simple quote from the steps of the Pillar, it invigorated me. We *would* persevere.

The waning smoke and embers rising from the city drew my attention. Had the other members of the Second Ascension been dealt with? I hadn't seen Hexa, Illia, Adelgis, or Fain in the chaos, but I knew they had to be out helping, perhaps aiding the citizens of Ruma.

Among the wreckage and throngs of fleeing people, I spotted the telltale signs of atlas turtle magic. Guildmaster Eventide could evoke powerful shields, and they glittered with intense magic, even if they were mostly translucent. Twiçe I spotted fire spewing down the main street, but both times a magical barrier prevented the flames from touching the nearby buildings.

"The guildmaster," Zaxis said, pointing in the same direction I had been staring.

"We have to warn her," I said.

The terrible effects of the requiem aura remained. Akiva was still here, physically empowering himself with the death and carnage all around us. Had he found Guildmaster Eventide? Had their battle begun?

In the next second, the sky lit up with an explosion of light so bright, it momentarily rivalled the sun. I glanced upward, confused and with my sword at the ready.

It was the *Sun Chaser*.

Fire billowed out a portside window. Bits of glass rained down into the ocean, light glinting on the sharp edges.

"*They're under attack*," Zaxis shouted. Then he ran two shaky hands through his red hair. "How did the enemy even reach them?"

The *Sun Chaser* soared the sky hundreds of feet above us. I quickly glanced around, just as baffled as Zaxis. How *had* the Second Ascension reached the airship? Harpies, perhaps? It didn't really matter, though. All that mattered now was that we did something.

"My father is up there," I whispered.

And so were Biyu, and the rest of the non-arcanist crew.

Not only did the Second Ascension have the gall to attack the island of my birth, but now they were attempting to kill my friends and family? I couldn't allow that. Not now—not ever. The guildmaster would be safe on her own... hopefully. At least until I dealt with the menace on the airship.

I wanted my cape to transform back into wings, but the sting of the salamander fire on my skin, coupled with the glare of the sun, made the task difficult. My cape separated into two, and my armor attempted to create the bones required, but it was too much. The darkness creaked and cracked, like popping joints. I couldn't form the wings I needed to fly up to the burning *Sun Chaser*.

"Forsythe!" Zaxis cried out.

His phoenix swooped by us and then went straight into the sky. A moment later, fire burst from his body, exploding out beyond the feathers as though they had originated from his heart and shooting out in every direction. It reminded me of a firework.

Mesos sailed out from around the *Sun Chaser* and flew toward the ball of fire that Forsythe had created. The two mystical birds flew close together, and then Mesos tilted her massive roc-wings and dove straight for us. She shot through pillars of smoke, and when she flapped her wings to slow her speed, she kicked up embers near the docks. The gust of wind fluttered my cape as she hit the ground.

"Come," she said. "Quickly."

I had never heard Mesos speak before, and I was struck with how deep and confident her tone was.

Before Zaxis or I could reply, the winds in the area whipped into a powerful tornado, swirling upward with enough force that it swept me off my feet. Despite the sudden ascent, the wind kept control, guiding Zaxis and me toward the airship. Mesos took to the sky and managed to beat us to the vessel with several powerful flaps of her wings.

Her ability to manipulate the wind impressed me, and for the few short seconds it took to fly from the ground and up into the sky, I reveled in amazement. When we neared the deck of the damaged airship, I caught sight of the culprit: a third magma salamander.

But how? Salamanders couldn't fly. How had it gotten to the deck of the ship?

Captain Devlin fired a pistol, striking the beast in the eye with pinpoint accuracy. The wind had guided his bullet, ensuring the perfect strike, but the monster didn't even seem to mind.

"All the world... *is darkness*," it said with a giggle.

Although Captain Devlin was a master roc arcanist, he kept his distance from the magma salamander, never getting close enough to have the tainted blood anywhere near him. It wasn't the way to win a fight with any sort of haste.

Look there, my arcanist, Luthair telepathically spoke.

Despite the fact he couldn't point independently from me, his mental urging came with a direction he wanted me to stare. I glanced toward the quarterdeck as my feet hit the main deck of the airship. A scrawny man in a full robe and hood stood within a fresh blaze. A deranged rizzel perched on his shoulder.

No... not just deranged. It was plague-ridden. A *dread form* rizzel. It had the white and silver ferret body of a rizzel, but it also had a second head—one that appeared dead, so thoroughly disgusting that parts seemed rotted and touched with gangrene. The dread form rizzel cackled with laughter and even breathed white flames onto the *Sun Chaser*, breaking it apart with teleporting disintegration. Flakes of wood flew everywhere.

I stepped into the shadows and reemerged on the quarterdeck. The salamander wasn't as important—the rizzel was the one teleporting the enemy into place. *This* creature needed to be stopped no matter what.

I slashed wide with Retribution, but the craven rizzel and scrawny arcanist blinked so fast that I missed entirely. I spotted the pair a moment later on the main deck, outside the destructive path of the salamander, and a good fifty feet from my location.

"Rhys," the rizzel said with a glint of amusement in its bright red eyes. "A knightmare arcanist has come for our lives! We should show him how the Second Ascension deals with *delusional* meatbags. I want a cape made of darkness, cut from its very form!" The tiny beast laughed with both heads—especially the dead one.

The scrawny man nodded, and his movements had a jittery energy. I recognized the man. He served directly under the Autarch, the very leader of the Second Ascension.

He must be brought to justice, Luthair telepathically communicated.

I leapt off the quarterdeck and onto the main deck of the *Sun Chaser* just in time to see Zaxis handle the magma salamander arcanist. Instead of fighting him in a drawn-out battle, Zaxis grabbed him by the collar, fell backward, and then kicked up into the man's gut, hurling the villain over the railing of the airship with the skill of a master grappler. The plague-ridden man tumbled through the air to the ocean below.

Captain Devlin used his wind manipulation to help the airship head toward the water and to also snuff out the fires. It was clear from the sweat running down his face and getting tangled in his chinstrap beard that he was struggling to keep the massive vessel afloat in the sky.

The salamander then turned its attention on Zaxis, but I wasn't too concerned. Zaxis was already a carrier of the plague, but more importantly, he was immune to fire. It was only a matter of time before he would win the fight.

Forsythe swooped around the salamander's face, attempting to take the creature's eyes with his talons.

"So long, *knightmare*," the dread form rizzel said. "Say *hello* to the sun for me!"

The creature lifted up a paw, and my whole body felt lighter. I floated off the deck, and the sensation reminded me of Mesos's tornado, only this time it wasn't the wind. It was gravity. Or the lack thereof.

No longer tethered to the ground, I would float away from the airship and then, once I was over the ocean, the rizzel would likely drop his gravity manipulation and allow me to plummet to my death.

Instead of letting that happen, I manipulated the shadows and made a tendril of darkness reach up and grab my leg. With the shadows as my hooks, rope, and anchor, I yanked myself onto the *Sun Chaser*.

Then I let go of my sword and tossed it to the shadows. Crafting some darkness into a tentacle, I managed to catch Retribution and then slash at the rizzel and Rhys a second time. They teleported again, and I attempted to manipulate the shadows to grab them beforehand, but I failed.

A sharp pain pierced my lower back.

With gritted teeth, I slid into the darkness and then stepped out a few feet away. Rhys and the rizzel had appeared behind me—and Rhys had stabbed me with a dagger coated in blood.

"You'll carry the taint now, Meatbag," the rizzel shouted with a smile.

How had the dagger penetrated my armor? I yanked it from my flesh and almost gasped. The blade appeared black, much like Retribution. It wasn't crafted as well—and it was short—but it was the black bone of the apoch dragon that had allowed the weapon to cut through magic like it were air.

"Get away from him!" someone shouted.

A blast of white disintegrating flame washed over the deck. It hadn't come from the dread form rizzel—it had come from Nicholin!

He and Illia had appeared on the *Sun Chaser* in a puff of white glitter, both of them tense and ready for battle. Nicholin's surprise attack had amounted to little, but I was thankful nonetheless.

"What a disgusting copycat," the dread form rizzel said, his red eyes glaring at Nicholin. "You're half the creature I am." It patted its undead head. "*Literally.*"

Nicholin arched his back and hissed, his white fur standing on end. "Fight me one on one, *fool*! I'll show you who's half of what!"

Then Rhys and his dread rizzel teleported away, but that just gave Illia time to help Zaxis deal with the magma salamander. She teleported next to it, touched its scaly hide, and then forcibly teleported him ten feet to the left—and right off the side of the airship.

Zaxis offered her an amused smirk, but when she attempted to rush to his side, he shook his head with a curt motion.

"Are you okay?" Nicholin asked. "You have to be okay! We can't have another repeat of Volke! Illia won't handle losing someone else important to her."

Zaxis gritted his teeth, his expression twisted and pained.

The *Sun Chaser* lurched downward, interrupting the conversation.

I whipped around and glanced over the starboard railing. The *Sun Chaser* descended at a rapid rate, but gale force winds rushed upward to slow its fall. Captain Devlin continued to struggle—even if he was a master arcanist, this airship had to weigh thousands of tons. Keeping it in the sky with just his power would be a difficult task.

Determined to help everyone I could, I stepped into the shadows and slithered down into the hold. The crew ran through the corridors with buckets of sand, attempting to snuff out flames and embers. I used my power over the darkness to direct them to the top deck. If all else failed, Illia would be able to save a few people with her teleportation. They had to be close to her for it to work, however.

I immediately headed for my father's quarters. Sure enough, he and his blue phoenix, Tine, were there. He had gathered his star shards and important papers.

"Volke," he said the moment he laid eyes on me. "How did you—"

I grabbed him and slid into the darkness, not bothering with conversations. He couldn't walk correctly, not with his bum leg. I had to get him out of the airship as fast as possible. Once we reached the deck, I released him from the shadows and then returned to the hold. With each and every crewmember I found, I made sure I indicated they should go up, including Biyu.

The airship lurched a second time as I grabbed the last of the crew members. I almost hit the ceiling from the force of the jolt, but I managed to use the darkness to my advantage and stay on my feet.

When I returned topside, I realized we were thirty feet from the ocean, perhaps less. The *Sun Chaser* was tilted downward, creating a steep slant, and I had to grab on to the railing in order not to slip. Everyone else did the same, including Captain Devlin, even though he was engaged in deep concentration.

Right before we hit the waves, Devlin clenched his jaw and swung his arm outward. The winds buffered our landing, preventing a crash. Instead, we hit the water and then shook violently as the vessel eased itself into the island current. The *Sun Chaser* had once been a regular sailing ship, so she floated just fine, but I did worry the ship wouldn't hold together.

"Where did the enemy rizzel go?" Illia asked as she turned to face me.

I shook my head.

"We need to find them," Nicholin added. "That dastard is giving all rizzels a bad name!"

My arcanist, now that the Sun Chaser *has been dealt with, we must find Guildmaster Eventide,* Luthair spoke telepathically.

"I understand," I said aloud.

Although Zaxis's problem hadn't been dealt with, and the *Sun Chaser* was now dead in the water, there were no other immediate threats. I had to leave them—I had to get to Guildmaster Eventide before Akiva did.

I manipulated the shadows and retrieved my sword from the far end of the main deck.

"Illia," I said. "Please take me back to land."

My double voice got everyone's attention, but I ignored them to focus on my mission. Illia ran to my side, communicated in a curt nod, and then touched my liquid-shadow armor. We both teleported with a puff of white glittery magic and then reappeared on the beach of Ruma, the ocean water up to our knees.

Although Illia had vastly improved with her teleportation, it was clear she didn't quite have the range needed. Yet.

"Give me a moment," Illia breathed.

Nicholin, perched on her shoulder, wrapped his body close to her neck, his blue eyes locked on the water.

Once she caught her breath, Illia teleported us a second time, managing to take us all the way to the docks of Ruma. I wished I had strength to spare, but I knew I couldn't hold out much longer. The rumbling of the island didn't help matters, and I wondered what other terrible things were in store for us.

Nicholin perked up, his tiny ears erect. "Illia! There they are!"

Illia and I both glanced around. It didn't take long for me to notice what Nicholin was talking about.

Guildmaster Eventide and Akiva were locked in a fight to the death.

27

ROOFTOP DUEL

Akiva moved with the swiftness of lightning and the power of a hurricane. He leapt from one building to the next, careful not to jump too high, lest he lose speed. When he landed, he cracked stone and splintered wood, his strength on a whole new level thanks to his requiem aura. All the dead citizens of Ruma were nothing more than tools for his physical power.

Guildmaster Eventide stood in the middle of the road, her stance wide and her knees slightly bent. She had taken up a defensible position, much like an actual turtle. Each time Akiva lunged for her, another magical barrier appeared to fend off his attack. And not only was she shielding herself, Eventide was also protecting nearby buildings with people inside. When flames from a magma salamander rushed down the cobblestone road, she blocked that, too.

I recognized the tactic our enemy was using. They had used the same strategy to kill the Grandmaster Inquisitor. They were trying to overwhelm Eventide—distract her and drain her energy while Akiva continued to grow stronger and stronger—until she finally made a fatal mistake.

When Akiva hit the roof of the bakery and came to a momentary rest, I managed to get a good look at the man. He wore armor so finely tailored to his muscular body that it appeared more like skin than clothing. The entire thing had been crafted from gray scales and thick pieces of bone. The scales had the sleekness of a barracuda, and his pauldron seemed as though it had been fashioned from a single dragon's claw. It didn't clink or rustle when Akiva turned around and faced the main street. His entire suit of armor flowed with him, never impeding his movement.

His short, copper hair fluttered in the breeze, and his tanned skin reminded me of someone who had grown up on a sun-soaked beach. King basilisks were said to live on islands, after all. Perhaps, if Akiva weren't an assassin for the enemy, we would've been fellow isle arcanists—but that wasn't the case.

Now I had to kill him.

My arcanist, Luthair said, his mental tone one of panic. *We shouldn't engage this enemy. One wrong move and Akiva's king basilisk venom will end us instantly!*

When the Grandmaster Inquisitor had fought Akiva, I had done nothing. I had just... watched. I had watched as he had died fighting to protect all of Thronehold. Was I going to repeat that here? Was I going to watch Guildmaster Eventide die fighting to protect the Isle of Ruma?

I stepped into the shadows and emerged on the roof of the building next to the bakery. My artifact shield, Forfend, could defend me against the king basilisk venom, and my sword would effortlessly cut through Akiva's armor. In theory, I could win this.

In theory.

I will not let you throw your life away, Luthair continued, his telepathic voice echoing in my thoughts. *I lost my first arcanist to a madman, and I cannot see it happen again.*

Against my will, I took a step backward, almost sliding into the darkness and disappearing from the fight altogether, but I prevented Luthair from taking full control. We remained on the roof of the building, though my body trembled from the raging inner war.

"We won't run," I said, defiance in my tone.

We must.

"I refuse!"

Akiva spun around, his hawk-like gaze landing on me. He arced his hand outward in a fast and violent motion, simultaneously evoking venom. Thick liquid emanated from his palm and splattered across the nearby rooftops, killing anything it touched. I almost didn't have enough time to lift my shield and defend against his sudden attack. Forefend was made with one of the world serpent's scales—it wouldn't be damaged by the likes of the venom—and I blocked every bit of venom that came my way.

But that one assault made me realize I couldn't fight him standing toe-to-toe.

Akiva was too fast. Too deadly. We hadn't even started the fight and already I was on the ropes and questioning my determination...

I had to be clever. I had to outwit him. Out-magic him. *Something.*

I gritted my teeth and held up a hand to evoke terrors. I poured as much strength as I could into my magic, hoping to cripple him for just a few seconds. To my shock—and horror—Akiva didn't react to my evocation. He didn't get emotional. He didn't collapse to his knees. He just stared.

And then Akiva leapt toward me, unaffected by the tormenting magic. Was he somehow immune?

With my breath held, I stepped into the darkness, narrowly avoiding Akiva's touch. Not only could he kill people with his venom, but if he managed to touch someone, he could also turn them to stone. Both options spelled certain death.

I emerged out of the darkness and onto the cobblestone road, my heart fluttering and beating out of rhythm. Akiva didn't continue to search for me. He returned his attention to Eventide, and in my gut, I knew it was only a matter of time before her magic waned from fatigue. Akiva would be ready then.

"Volke!" a familiar voice said. "There you are."

Master Zelfree ran toward me, closing the distance between us in a matter of seconds. The arcanist mark on his forehead had the symbol of a phoenix, but when he neared, it shifted and transformed into a cape and sword—the mark of a knightmare.

The shadows stirred around Zelfree's feet as he turned his gaze to the roofs.

"Create an eclipse aura," Zelfree commanded, anger lacing his words.

"I don't sense a trinket or artifact on Akiva that'll allow him to see through the darkness, and with the empowerment to knightmare arcanists from the eclipse aura, we might be able to subdue him."

Exhaustion haunted me like a second shadow. I was still injured and currently weakened by the sun. How could Zelfree even consider me creating an aura while I was in this shape?

Master Zelfree placed a hand on my armored shoulder, his grip tight. "The guild needs you. Focus."

I held my breath, my chest tight. "Very well," I intoned—more Luthair's voice than my own.

Creating an aura required concentration, and I closed my eyes to help block out irrelevant thoughts. The burns across my body seemed more prominent when I couldn't see, but I pushed those concerns from my head. With Luthair's cold magic coursing through my veins, I knew I was capable of anything, but the added pressure of trying to save Eventide ate away at my ability to concentrate.

An odd sensation filled my being. It started from my chest and spread to the end of my extremities, causing my skin to tingle with power. A magical aura was an outward expression of power—like filling a cup with water, but continuing until the water spilled over the rim and poured onto the table. Even though it hurt to force magic into my body and then outward, I pressed through it.

My father had said I needed to be relaxed to create a perfect magical aura, but I didn't have time to *relax*, not with Akiva a few hundred feet from me.

The sun's rays stopped shining on the Isle of Ruma.

I snapped my eyes open and glanced upward. A black orb of inky void blocked out the sun, casting the entire area in darkness. It was my eclipse aura taking on a visible manifestation. But I knew I had done it wrong the moment the black orb began to break apart and weep shadows. I hadn't been tranquil enough to control the magic, and now it required all of my concentration and willpower to maintain.

If I had done everything correctly, the aura wouldn't have needed me to maintain it—it would just *exist*.

"Good enough," Master Zelfree stated with a sardonic smirk.

The thick darkness added to my magic, and Zelfree's as well, now that he was mimicking my knightmare. He stepped into the shadows and then appeared on the top of the bakery, ready for a fight. Although it pained me to do so, I also shadow-stepped to the roof.

My arcanist, I implore you to reconsider, Luthair spoke telepathically. But I ignored him. I had to do this.

Zelfree lifted his hand and controlled the shadows—dozens of tendrils lifted up and lashed out at Akiva. They tried to grab the king basilisk arcanist, but Akiva was too strong. A few latched on to his arms, but he broke free without much effort.

I lifted my hand and attempted to help. Instead of creating tendrils, or chains, or some sort of tether, the darkness lifted like the tide. In the streets, in the alleyway, all around the building—a wave of inky shadows swept over the area. The shadowy water didn't damage everything, however. It only struck out against those I wanted it to—and it didn't matter how fast or strong Akiva was then. The moment the darkness touched his feet, he became trapped in it, as if in tar, and unable to flee.

My true form knightmare magic was just more powerful than Zelfree's, but now my concentration was split in two. Maintaining the aura and this trap was almost too much. Instead of dropping anything, I turned to Zelfree.

"Finish him," I shouted as I tossed over Retribution.

Zelfree caught my blade by the hilt and then lunged through the darkness and emerged next to Akiva. He slashed wide and cut upward, slicing through Akiva's gut and chest. Akiva's armor offered no protection against Retribution, and I knew why. Retribution cut through anything magical, and Akiva's king basilisk armor was no match.

With narrowed eyes and a furrowed brow, Akiva stared down at the blood gushing down his armor and onto his greaves. He struggled harder to break away from my dark tide, but with the eclipse aura—even a broken one—I had the power to keep him in place.

Zelfree stabbed forward with Retribution, and he would've pierced Akiva's heart had the other man not moved at the last second. Although Akiva couldn't step away, he ducked and tilted, resulting in a much weaker strike to his ribs.

"Damn," Akiva hissed through gritted teeth.

He reached out—his movements supernaturally fast—and attempted to grab Zelfree.

In a moment of pure instinct, I used the shadows to yank Zelfree out of the way. Doing so caused me to lose my focus, however. The eclipse aura broke apart, and the shadows in the area drained away, but at least Master Zelfree hadn't been turned to stone by Akiva's king basilisk magic.

When the sun's brilliance shone down on us again, Akiva got a better look at his gruesome injury. The fastenings of his armor were the only things keeping his intestines inside his body. Crimson cascaded down the gray scales, and with a shaky hand, Akiva wrapped an arm tightly over his injured gut.

His requiem aura had yet to drop. With speed and unrivaled strength, he leapt off the building and retreated. A few streets down, a pop of white and glitter signaled the teleporting of a rizzel. Instead of Illia appearing to help, it was Rhys and his doubled-headed plague rizzel. Once Rhys appeared, Akiva rushed toward him.

I held out my hand, wanting to prevent Akiva from escaping, but the sun burned the shadows and made me weak. *Curse the abyssal hells!* Anger strengthened my magic, and I almost grabbed him with a black tendril, but he was too quick.

The moment Akiva reached Rhys, they disappeared in another burst of white sparkles.

I clenched my jaw, my whole body trembling from fatigue and rage.

How could I let them get away?

Master Zelfree shadow-stepped to my side and placed a hand on my upper arm. "We should stay close to the guildmaster. Come."

I shook my head and then swayed on my feet.

My arcanist, Luthair spoke. *We're at our limit. We cannot continue.*

Zelfree must have seen my exhaustion. "Never mind," he said. "Return to the atlas turtle. Help anyone you can escape the flames, but *don't* engage the enemy in combat. Do you hear me?" He tightened his grip on my arm. "You're spent. Fighting is sheer suicide in your state."

Smoke and embers continued to rise into the sky.

"Gravekeeper William," I said, my voice half-separating as I spoke, as though Luthair were struggling to stay merged with me.

"I'll make sure he's okay," Zelfree stated. "You can't take to the streets in your current condition."

We need to rest, my arcanist.

Unable to maintain my current state, Luthair and I unmerged. The instant the shadows melted from my body, my vision blurred and then tunneled. I leaned backward, but there was nothing there, so I kept going. Zelfree reached out to catch me, but I didn't know if he was successful.

Everything went black, and I slipped into unconsciousness.

28

RECOVERY

I awoke in the guild manor house. I didn't recognize the room or surroundings, but I knew it was the guild because of the smell, oddly enough. Everything on the atlas turtle had a faint smell of fresh rain and soil. The pleasant aroma created a tranquility that I hadn't realized I had missed until that moment.

After a deep breath, I forced myself into a sitting position. My lower back flared in agony, and I clenched my jaw as I gently ran a hand over the bandages. It was the knife wound from Rhys. With all of the fighting and turmoil, I had forgotten I had been injured. No wonder Luthair was so concerned—and why I so desperately needed to rest.

Sunlight poured into the room through the one giant window on the far wall. Four beds were positioned near each corner, and small tables with pitchers of water were next to each. My white sheets had a clean and soft feel against my bare skin. When I took a moment to look over the rest of my body, I noticed my burns had also been bandaged. I had wrappings over my forearms, shoulder, chest, and neck.

Someone else was in the room with me. The red hair poking out from under the blankets was a dead giveaway. Zaxis was sound asleep.

"Luthair?" I whispered.

No one answered.

His absence hurt more than the sting of the knife wound. It was childish—I knew that—but ever since he had become true form, I worried when he didn't answer my summons. We were safe in the guild now, and no doubt under the protection of Guildmaster Eventide's powerful barriers, but I couldn't help imagining the worst scenarios. Becoming true form had brought us closer together, which meant his absence was more profound.

The shadows in the room moved, and I held my breath, relief and happiness mixing in equal parts throughout my system. Evianna stepped out of the darkness, along with her knightmare, Layshl. While I didn't mind seeing them, I glanced around for Luthair, but he never emerged.

Evianna took a moment to stare at the single door in and out of the room. Her white hair had been tied back in a tight braid, and she wore no boots. With quiet movements, she tiptoed deeper into the room, her attention still on the door. She made her way to the foot of my bed before she turned around and spotted me.

"Ah!" Evianna said with a gasp.

Her knightmare—nothing more than a floating empty suit of leather and scale armor—held up a gloved hand. "Quiet, my arcanist," Layshl whispered.

Evianna smoothed her fine clothing. "Volke. I didn't know you were awake."

"I just woke," I muttered under my breath, trying not to wake Zaxis. "Why are you sneaking around?"

"I was told not to enter the room," Evianna said matter-of-factly. "But I'm not worried about the risks. I just want to see you."

"Risks?"

"Zaxis is plague-ridden."

The statement caught me off guard. The information wasn't new, but the reality hit me in that moment. What would we do to help him? I stared at the white sheets in my lap, my eyebrows knitted. I had escaped the cruel clutches of the arcane plague through a fluke. I didn't know where to begin to help Zaxis achieve his phoenix's true form.

"Don't fret," Evianna said with half a smile. "Everyone in the guild is already talking about ways to help him. I think they'll find a solution."

She waved her hand and manipulated the shadows to grab a chair that had been tucked away on the other side of my bed. Without scraping it against the floor, the shadows brought the piece of furniture over. After patting the seat clean, Evianna sat down next to me, her posture straight and her hands on her lap.

"How do you feel?" she whispered.

I rubbed at the back of my neck. "Sore."

"Can I get you anything?"

"I just need time to heal my injuries."

Evianna nodded along with my words. "I see. Well, you're in luck." She swished her white braid over her shoulder. "Thanks to my *improved* shadow-stepping abilities, I made it past the door guard, so now you have company. We can have glorious conversations while your body repairs itself."

"*Glorious* conversations?" I muttered, one eyebrow lifted.

"Of course." Evianna crossed her arms over her chest. "We only have so much time together, after all. Which means we can't talk about the mundane. We need to discuss meaningful things. So our conversations must be glorious and insightful."

"Okay..."

It wasn't a terrible idea.

But Evianna took a long moment to continue the conversation. She tilted her head to one side then the other. Did she have any questions prepared? Or was this all off the cuff?

Her knightmare waited nearby, imitating a statue. I didn't mind. I enjoyed the company of knightmares, even if they had no face or eyes and were difficult to read.

"What's one thing you can't live without?" Evianna asked.

I glanced over to make sure Zaxis was still asleep. Sure enough, the blankets lifted and fell in an even pattern. Still sleeping.

"Can't live without, huh?" I murmured, more to myself than to Evianna. "I guess I would say... my friends and family."

Evianna lifted both eyebrows. "Really?"

"Yeah."

"Okay. Next question." She held up a single finger. "Why do you have two fathers? Were they once intended for each other, but they separated?"

I stifled a chuckle. "You mean Jozé and Gravekeeper William?"

She nodded, her bluish-purple eyes never leaving me.

"Well, Jozé is my actual father, and William is my adopted father. They technically knew each other, once upon a time, but never romantically. Jozé and my mother..."

The thought of my mother stopped me from continuing the conversation. I had thought of her a few times recently, and I silently cursed the abyssal hells when I realized I knew next to nothing about her.

Seemingly satisfied with my half-answer, Evianna said, "Next question." She grabbed at the edge of my sheets and lifted a small portion. "Are you nude?"

Heat flooded my face as I slammed down the sheets to keep myself decent. "*Evianna.* That's, not, well—*it's inappropriate.*" I found it difficult to get all the words out in a proper order without yelling so loud, I'd wake Zaxis.

She leaned back in the wooden chair, strands of her white hair catching the light and practically glittering. "I was hoping to see the injury on your back. Atty was helping to heal it earlier, but they said I had to leave."

I ran a hand across the bandages covering my injury. It had already been healed, and it still felt this bad? What kind of knife wound had it been? Or was the damage due to the blade being made from the bones of the apoch dragon?

"Next time, ask before you check for yourself," I said, my cheeks and ears still bright red. "I could've told you I had no clothes."

"Do you want me to fetch some for you?"

"No. I'm fine. Just... let's not speak of this."

Evianna replied with a single nod. Then she asked, "Were you the one who created the eclipse aura?"

I nodded. "Yes."

"You did it incorrectly," she stated.

I narrowed my eyes. Although she was right, I found it strange that she was lecturing me on knightmare magic. "How do you know the difference between a proper one and an improper one?"

"I saw a perfect eclipse aura the night my brother took over the Argo

Empire with his disgusting coup," Evianna said, hate in her words. "That night will forever be burned into my memory." She hugged herself, her hands gripping her upper arms. Then she stared at my bedding. "I... I had been in the basement, mourning my sister. That's when you arrived and fought those dastards from the Second Ascension."

I, too, remembered that night with startling clarity. Even though it had been chaotic and frantic... I could still smell the blood and gunpowder.

"You... you carried me," Evianna said, her voice slowly falling below a whisper with each syllable. She never glanced up at me—she just stared downward, lost in her memories. "You fought off those sea serpents, and then the attackers, and then held me close as we ascended the grand staircase to the upper floors. That's when I first saw it. *Really* saw it."

Lost in her retelling, I tilted my head. "Saw what?"

She lifted her gaze to meet mine. "The eclipse aura. The one made by the Grandmaster Inquisitor. Somehow, you had given me the ability to see in the dark, so... so I could see the knightmare magic blotting out the moon, creating a night so inky, it was as if all of Thronehold had been dipped in tar."

"I remember," I murmured.

"You saved me that night as well," Layshl said, her voice soft, yet dark. "The eclipse aura gave you added strength to continue, even when a normal man would've faltered."

The recounting of my heroism left me feeling strange. I wasn't used to people being so complimentary. I fidgeted with the edge of the blanket and shrugged. "Yes, well, hopefully, I'll have the skill to create the eclipse aura without problems in the future. However, I'm not quite there yet. I've made a proper one once, but I need more practice."

"I was still empowered by your weak one," Evianna said, somehow sitting a bit straighter. "And I even saved an entire family from one of the salamander arcanists, I'll have you know. All by myself and everything."

"Hm?" Layshl added.

Evianna grimaced. "With *you*, of course. Always with you."

After a quick nod, Layshl returned to her silence.

I wanted to comment on Evianna's training and ask about her bond with her knightmare, but before even a single word could escape my lips, the door to the room burst open and slammed against the wall. The resulting bang echoed between the walls and even rattled the window glass.

Zaxis snorted.

Then he rolled to his other side and pulled the blankets close.

Still asleep.

What kind of sorcery allowed him to sleep like the dead? I was halfway impressed.

I listened for a long while, trying to hear the beat of corruption that I had come to hear in plague-ridden individuals. I heard the thunderbird when it drew near to the airship, and I felt it from the salamanders around Ruma. But I didn't hear Zaxis's corruption or feel a terrible bloodlust. Was it because he was newly infected? Did I only feel the pulse of corruption once it had firmly taken hold on someone? Perhaps when they were no longer curable?

"What are you doin', lass?"

I recognized the voice of Captain Devlin straightaway. He had a distinct annoyance to his speech that never seemed to clear away.

Vethica stormed into the room, followed by her scarab-like eldrin. Her pixie-cut hair, just as red as Zaxis's, fluttered a bit as she charged forward. The hard-edged look she gave me was almost enough to get me worried. Had she barged in to get me?

Captain Devlin followed behind her, his thicker leather boots clunking hard on the wood floor. He picked up his pace in order to slam a large hand down on Vethica's shoulder. "You shouldn't be in here!"

She shoved his hand off. "I need to try my khepera magic before it's too late. This is the only way."

"The guildmaster hasn't made up her damn mind yet."

"Now isn't the time for guild *dithering*," Vethica snapped. "Why are you trying to stop me? You know this is for the best. Didn't you originally create the *Sun Chaser* just to get away from all this guild nonsense?"

"We agreed to play by their rules," Devlin said as he stroked his thin beard. With a sigh, he removed his tricorn cap, ran his fingers through his sweat-laced hair, and then returned the hat to his head. "And the boy is plague ridden. I'd rather not have you... Well..."

Vethica rounded on him, pivoting on her heel so fast I almost thought she would slap him. "You'd rather not have *what*? You don't want my eldrin to get infected again, is that it? You think I'm going to be reckless?"

Her khepera, Akhet, buzzed with his insect wings. "I will be fine, Captain. Vethica and I will care for the young arcanist as though he were a member of the *Sun Chaser*."

The conversation quieted into a tense silence.

I exchanged a quick glance with Evianna. She sat, unmoving, her eyes wide. I suspected she didn't want to get involved—because neither did I. This seemed like an age-old argument between Vethica and Devlin, and as long as I didn't make any sudden movements, I hoped they would leave me out of it.

However, I was intrigued by the talk of Vethica's khepera magic.

Vethica panned her gaze around the room—looking over me and Evianna, but not stopping—until she caught sight of Zaxis. Then she strode over with purpose.

"Get up," she said as she yanked the blankets down to expose his upper body.

Like me, Zaxis didn't appear to have any clothing on, not even his fancy salamander armor. Unlike me, he didn't appear injured. No bandages. No scars. He was in perfect condition—on the outside. Too bad a sickness ran through his veins.

Zaxis shivered and then forced himself into a sitting position. He growled something I couldn't discern and then offered a cold glower to Vethica. "What're you doing?"

"Don't take that attitude with me," she barked. "*I'm here to help you.*"

While some might've been intimidated by Vethica's loud voice and demanding attitude, Zaxis just scoffed. Then he ripped the blanket out of her hand and pulled it up over most of his chest. "There's nothing you can do for me. Just stay away. As far away as possible."

Vethica walked around to the side of his bed, defiance in her stride.

After a long sigh, Captain Devlin stepped closer to the situation. "Vethica, I know you don't got any respect for what's goin' on here, but I'll be damned if I'll allow you to do this alone. I'll stay till you're done with your *treatment*."

"I'm beyond help," Zaxis stated, his glower still set in place. "Get out of here, woman."

"Hush." Vethica placed a hand on his broad shoulder. "I'm a khepera arcanist."

"So?" Zaxis hissed.

"So, I have the power of *renewal*." She narrowed her eyes into a glare. "That means, if you'll just cooperate, I might be able to renew you. As in, clear away the arcane plague and make you brand new. Do you understand?"

At first, Zaxis just stared. It took a whole sixty seconds before he finally offered a weak nod. "Oh. Khepera are those rare mystical creatures only found in—"

"It doesn't matter." Vethica tightened her grip on Zaxis's shoulder. "Just. Stop. Talking. And close your eyes. I need... no distractions."

"You're going to heal me right now?" Zaxis asked, ignoring Vethica's orders. "But I thought—"

"My renewal power allows me to reset time. The longer we wait for me to treat you, the harder it'll be for me to use my ability. I have to use it *now*. This is the shortest amount of time from when you were infected, so I have to take advantage of that."

"And this will work?" Zaxis asked—not to Vethica, but to me.

I was caught off guard by his question being aimed in my direction. I scrambled to gather my thoughts and then replied with, "Adelgis seemed to think the khepera had the power to cure the plague. That's why we ventured into the Grotto Labyrinth. For this exact reason."

I had never been as thankful to Adelgis as I was in that moment. If Vethica really *could* cure the plague, the Second Ascension would easily crumble.

Vethica clenched her jaw. "Everyone be quiet. I need to concentrate."

29

RENEWAL

Z axis turned his gaze down to the bed, his eyebrows knitted. "What if... using your magic somehow gets you infected?"

"She'll be fine," I said. "The arcane plague only spreads through blood." I shook my head. "Let her help you."

There was no way using magical powers on Zaxis would allow for contraction—unless the power somehow involved cutting him open. Vethica could attempt her renewal power without fear of infection.

Zaxis replied with a click of his tongue. "*Tsk*. Fine."

He glanced away from Vethica, his cold glare on the window. I had known Zaxis for my entire life, and he had always been haughty. But he wasn't the same. His shoulders shuddered with his breaths, and he had no snarky comments.

Perhaps the others couldn't see it, but I had never known Zaxis to be so afraid.

Vethica closed her eyes. Akhet buzzed down onto her shoulder, his six insect legs clinging to her sailing jacket. The iridescent sheen of his exoskeleton glittered, giving him an eldritch appearance.

Captain Devlin crossed his arms and observed the whole event with a stern expression. I understood his concern for Vethica, but I wondered if his hovering would somehow distract her.

The air in the room swirled at an ever-increasing rate. I glanced around, wondering if this was roc magic, but that was when I noticed something peculiar. The sheets looked... cleaner. The wood of the floor became a bit shinier. A slight crack in the glass of the window shrunk in size.

I held my breath, uncertain of whether or not I was being affected by the current phenomenon. Was this the augmentation power of the khepera? Or perhaps an evocation? I wasn't entirely sure, all I knew was the objects in the room seemed to be... freshening up? Or perhaps returning to their most sturdy state of existence?

Was this time manipulation? Wouldn't the worked material in the room come undone? The planks of wood would become trees, the glass would revert back to sand, and the lanterns would warp into raw metal? I shook my head. Vethica couldn't go back that far—she had already explained that.

"Wow," Evianna said under her breath. She tilted her head back, her mouth agape. "Are you seeing this, Volke?"

"Yeah. It's incredible."

"I bet khepera are the only mystical creatures capable of *this*. Nowhere else in the world has something so wondrous. I bet not even in the abyssal hells."

I agreed—which was probably why Theasin Venrover and the Second Ascension had gone out of their way to kill them all. Well, almost all of them.

Vethica scrunched her eyes and tightened her grip on Zaxis. He kept his gaze on the window, too stubborn to face her. Her nails dug into his flesh, but he didn't seem to care. I worried for a brief moment. What if she punctured his skin and drew blood?

But the thought left me when I realized she wasn't holding him that tightly and with the next breath I took I felt... better. My lower back didn't hurt anymore, and I fidgeted a bit with newfound energy. I ran a hand over my bandages, surprised by the lack of agony. There wasn't even a stinging sensation—I just felt normal.

I would've gotten out of bed and walked around if I had been provided any clothes, but since I didn't want to subject everyone in the room to my nakedness, I remained seated.

Evianna tugged on her white-haired braid, her gaze on her lap. "What's happening?"

"We're being rejuvenated," Layshl replied with an authoritative tone.

"Interesting. Is this a form of healing?"

"I would say it's circumstantial healing. It would only truly work if the injuries were recent, but it seems broader than phoenix or caladrius magic."

Evianna slowly nodded. "Fascinating."

Before I could ask questions about the process, Vethica gasped and staggered away from Zaxis. Her short hair had become drenched in sweat, and her khepera lay on her shoulder, barely able to cling to her jacket any longer. Captain Devlin rushed over and offered Vethica a hand. He helped steady her while she caught her breath.

The air stopped swirling, and the visual effects of Vethica's magic ceased. Everything remained in a newer condition, however, which indicated this might be a permanent change.

"There," Vethica said between deep breaths. "I think... you're okay."

Zaxis snapped his attention to her. "That's it?"

She nodded.

"I don't need to do anything else?"

"What part of *I think you're okay* was unclear to you?" Vethica growled, her teeth practically clenched for the entire question.

Zaxis rotated his shoulders. Then he wrapped the blankets around his waist and leapt from bed with a surprising amount of energy. He waited for a moment, shifting his weight from one foot to the other. "I... don't know how to tell if I'm cured or not." He glanced over his own bare chest and stomach.

Evianna covered her eyes with one of her hands. "So rude," she murmured under her breath. "Doesn't he know he's in the presence of a princess? Must he be a barbarian?"

Her words drifted in one ear and out the other. All I could think about was the situation at hand. Was Zaxis cured? And if he was, how would we know for certain? Was there a test? Or did we have to wait to see if he'd lose himself to the madness?

For the past few encounters, I had felt individuals who carried the plague. Their hearts beat so loud in my ears, I could sense them from hundreds of feet away. But those dastards had been infected for a long time—most of which were incurable. Was that the reason I felt them? Was that the reason I couldn't feel Zaxis? He hadn't been infected long enough?

"Calm down, boy," Captain Devlin said. "Take a seat right back on that bed."

Zaxis furrowed his brow. "Why?"

"Because we won't know you're cured until we find ourselves some plague hunters. Those arcanists have recently crafted a trinket that detects individuals who are infected. If we find someone from the Huntsman Guild, we'll be able to tell if you're gonna be okay."

I smiled, both relieved and anxious at the same time. How long until we ran into someone from the Huntsman Guild? I knew they practiced their trade all through the island nations and the mainland, but weren't we heading away from all that?

Zaxis slowly sat on the edge of the bed. "All right. I can wait." He tightened his grip on the blankets around his waist. "But would you mind calling for Illia and Forsythe? I want to speak with them."

"I don't think it's wise to interact with other arcanists."

Vethica stomped one foot. Her eldrin buzzed off her shoulder in shock.

"He's *fixed*," she said. "He won't be infecting anyone else. He can have all the visitors he wants."

"We don't know that for sure," Devlin growled. "This is a precaution."

"I can't believe you doubt me."

"Don't be sassing me. *I'm still your captain.*" Devlin released a long sigh. "Even if my damn ship is a pile of wreckage floating in the ocean."

Vethica huffed and then turned on her heel. She strode over to the door, her khepera flying to keep up with her quick pace.

"Where are you goin'?" Devlin called out as he went to follow.

"To tell the Grand Apothecary what I've done," Vethica replied as she opened the door and then exited into the hall. "I'm sure she'll want to know."

After a second sigh, Captain Devlin gave me, Evianna, and Zaxis a curt nod before leaving. Once the door clicked shut, silence descended around us. I couldn't help but look over at Zaxis. Was he okay? What was on his mind? He just stared at the blankets in his lap, unblinking.

"Are you okay?" I asked.

Zaxis glanced over with a narrowed glare. "Take a wild guess."

"I think you'll be okay," Evianna chimed in. She moved to the edge of her seat. "That magic was impressive."

"Heh. Maybe."

When he returned to his vacant staring, I cleared my throat, regaining his attention.

"Aren't you happy that you might be cured already?" I asked. "This is a fortunate turn of events. We won't have to fear the Second Ascension."

Zaxis twisted his grip on the sheets, his jaw clenched. "I suppose this is... for the best."

"Are you sure you're okay?"

"I'll be fine," he replied, terse. But before I could ask another question, he took in a short breath and continued, "Why is it that everything you do is *noteworthy* and *amazing*, but when the same damn things happen to me, it's a mere footnote in comparison?" He laughed for a moment and then shrugged, his posture loosening. "A small part of me thought I'd have to get a true form of my eldrin as well to get through this, and then everyone would see I was just as capable. But here I am... cured by someone else mere moments after I wake with the plague. I didn't even have a *chance* to prove myself."

I wanted to say something—to reassure him of his capability or help him understand I wasn't *trying* to show him up—but the words never came. I sat in awkward silence, uncertain how to articulate my feelings on the matter.

Then Zaxis turned to me, more relaxed than before. "I just realized something. Vethica only has her khepera eldrin because of you. So, in some small way, you not only cured yourself of the arcane plague... you also cured me, too. And probably hundreds of others." Again, Zaxis laughed, but this time, it seemed sheepish. His gaze fell to the floor, yet he retained his smile. "I would get so upset when Illia spoke about how selfless and heroic you are. But... maybe she's right, and this is why I haven't been able to compare. Why do you have to be this way all the time, *dammit.*"

Evianna glanced between me and Zaxis, her eyes wide, her posture stiff. She never contributed, but she eventually settled on just staring at me, as though I had done something worth paying close attention to.

"I'm flattered you think so highly of me," I muttered. "But you were the one who risked your life and sanity to save a small island town. You knew the risks, but that didn't stop you. How is that not selfless and heroic?"

"Well..."

Zaxis couldn't seem to finish his sentence. He tightened his grip on the blankets and kept his eyes downward, never looking up at me.

"Thank you," he finally said.

And that was it. But that was all that was needed between us.

ISLAND FAREWELLS

The *Sun Chaser*—the airship we had worked so hard to repair—was sinking to the bottom of the ocean.

The Isle of Ruma—my childhood home—was a smoking wreck of half-demolished buildings.

And Zaxis wasn't the only one who had been infected with the plague. Eight other arcanists from the Frith Guild had been afflicted. Vethica said she would cure them all, but we had yet to determine if her renewal magic was actually working. Until then, everyone who had been touched by the corrupted magic had been quarantined away in a large room beyond the guild's library. All of them, including Zaxis, would have to wait there until we found someone from the Huntsman Guild.

Now that my injury was healed, I returned to my room on the third story of the guild manor house. To my surprise, I found Luthair standing in the corner of the room, his helmet facing the open window. His star-lined cape fluttered with the gentle breeze that wafted over the sill. Although imposing, his liquid-shadow armor struck me as majestic.

Luthair faced his closed helmet in my direction as I stepped into the room. "My arcanist."

"Luthair? Are you okay?" I glanced around. "Why are you just waiting in here?"

"Illia wished to speak with me. She's come and gone several times, and I suspect she will soon return."

"Why did Illia want to speak with you?" I asked as I crossed the room. My bed appeared comforting, but I ignored it in favor of the dresser. I had been given my soiled clothing that I wore during the fight, and now I wanted some that were clean. I withdrew a pair of trousers and a clean shirt.

"Illia has been concerned for both you and Zaxis, but she was forbidden from entering the infirmary."

"And she listened?" I quipped.

Luthair gave a curt nod. "Indeed."

I reflected on that fact while I removed my old clothing and my bandages. Illia never cared much for rules or regulations, and if they ever truly conflicted with her desires, she often ignored them completely. Why was now any different?

I pulled on my fresh pair of trousers and secured them in place with my belt. The worn leather had been softened by time and use, and I appreciated having a small pouch of supplies always on my hip. I never went anywhere without my belt.

Luthair returned his "gaze" to the open window. "Illia has come a long way. She's a mature woman who understands the importance of organizations, hierarchy, and the trust forged by those who give deference to rules."

A piece of me wondered how Luthair knew my line of thoughts. "She *wanted* to follow the rules?" I asked.

"She trusted that you would be cared for and didn't want to set a poor example for the new apprentices in the guild. Such a decision—considering the future and impact it has on others—is the hallmark of maturity."

I pulled on my shirt as I recalled our adventure aboard the Dread Pirate Calisto's ship, the *Third Abyss*. Illia had been so determined to get revenge that she had disregarded all regulations—and her own safety—just to satisfy her wants and desires. It was only afterward that she had admitted she had been in the wrong. I half-expected her to return to her ways, but perhaps that was foolish of me. Illia learned from her mistakes. She wouldn't go back on her word.

As if summoned by my mere thoughts, a soft pop echoed throughout my room, heralding Illia's arrival via teleportation. I whirled around, my breath held. She stood in the middle of the room, Nicholin on her shoulder, his white and silver fur sparkling in the sunlight. I hadn't realized until then, but Illia's wavy hair had gotten longer—past her shoulders—and she now kept it tied back in a loose ponytail.

Illia's eyes widened when she spotted me. "Volke?"

"Yeah," I said. "They let me out of—"

Before I could finish my sentence, Illia teleported to my side and wrapped her arms around me in one swift and fluid motion. I returned her embrace, happy to see her so energetic. I had feared she had been injured during the fighting, but I should've known she'd be all right. Rizzel magic allowed for all sorts of crafty escapes.

Nicholin nuzzled himself between us, as though the hug were meant solely for him. "We missed you, Volke! And we were so worried!" He poked his wet nose against the bottom of my chin. "Did you see Zaxis? Was he all right? He wasn't lonely, was he?"

"Zaxis is fine," I muttered. "Vethica healed him and the others already."

Illia ended the embrace, but kept her hands on my shoulders and held me at arm's length. When her determined eye locked on mine, I couldn't help but notice her intensity. "Is Zaxis cured?" she asked. "For certain? The khepera can do that?"

"We're not sure yet. I'm sorry."

She exhaled, and then her gaze fell to her boots. She never let me go, opting instead to just tighten her hold on my shirt sleeves. I waited, unsure of what to say. Illia had always been capable, but I knew this situation would trouble her until the very end. No one wanted to feel powerless to help the ones they loved.

A tapping at the door drew everyone's attention. Illia released me, and I walked over to answer, uncertain who it could be.

To my pleasant surprise, Fain stood in the hallway, his hands casually pushed into his trouser pockets as he leaned on one shoulder against the wall.

"Volke," he said, his voice soft—almost too quiet. "The guildmaster wants you to meet her on the docks of the island."

"Why?" I asked.

Fain shrugged. "Apparently, the townspeople want to formally thank the Frith Guild, and your presence was requested."

"Interesting."

I glanced over my shoulder. Illia smiled and then walked over to join me. When I gave Luthair a quick look, he melted into the darkness—disappearing from sight and no doubt accompanying me, even if I couldn't see him.

"All right," I said. "Lead the way."

The Isle of Ruma only had one port. Now it didn't even have that. It had *half* a port, at best. Fire had destroyed buildings and piers, and it seemed as though magic had been used to devastate part of the city's defenses, including the city wall. I hated seeing my home island in such disarray, but there was little I could do about it.

Illia, Fain, and I hopped out of the dinghy and tied it to one of the few piers remaining. The aroma of sea salt from the ocean washed away the suffocating smell of smoke and ash. There were no gulls in the sky, no doubt because of the fighting that had taken place yesterday, and it gave the docks an eerie silence that didn't sit well with me. The Isle of Ruma had always been bustling with life.

"Where is everyone?" I asked as I panned my gaze over the mostly abandoned stalls and storehouses.

"I don't know," Fain muttered. He ran a frostbitten hand through his brown hair—strands of which glinted gold in the midmorning sun. "The guildmaster said she would be here."

"Look there," Nicholin said, his statement punctuated by a soft squeak. He pointed to the main road that led into the city. "I see people!"

Sure enough, a crowd gathered on the widest street of the city. As a group, we walked over, but I made sure Retribution was close at hand.

Fortunately, I didn't need it. The crowd consisted of a few hundred island denizens and a handful of arcanists from the Frith Guild, including Master Zelfree, Atty, and Guildmaster Eventide. They addressed the Ruma citizens, offering bows to everyone they spoke to.

"I'll leave some gold leafs to help with the rebuilding," Eventide stated. "Everett, before we go, can you use atlas turtle magic to help some of the vegetables and fruits to grow? As well as some wood so that they don't need to import so many goods?"

Zelfree nodded. "I'll get on that right away."

"Atty," the guildmaster said. "Would your family be willing to help in the reconstruction?"

"I will speak to my mother straightaway," Atty said.

"Thank you."

The people of Ruma whispered in surprised and hopeful tones as Atty hurried down the street. The Frith Guild had no obligation to help. Guildmaster Eventide could turn and walk away, and she'd have every right to do so. But instead, she had stayed and provided resources, both magical and mundane. A true heroic arcanist, on and off the battlefield.

"By the abyssal hells!" someone in the crowd shouted. "It's Volke Savan!"

I straightened my posture and squared my shoulders, half-expecting someone to throw something at me. I was supposed to be in exile, after all. When no rocks or fruit sailed my way, I glanced around, one eyebrow lifted. Everyone stared at me, their eyes wide.

"He saved me," someone in the crowd said.

"Me, too," a kid shouted. "The schoolhouse was on fire!"

I held my breath, both shocked and uncertain of how to respond. "Uh," I began.

"Isn't he supposed to be in exile?" someone murmured, their voice distinct. I probably knew them, but I couldn't identify the exact person.

"He rescued my daughter from the villains who attacked," a woman called out from deep in the crowd. "He's a savior!"

Another person chimed in with more doubt. "Weren't his parents criminals?"

"He's a gravedigger."

"But he did so much for us."

"The children wouldn't be here if not for William's boy. To the abyssal hells with his exile!"

The arguments from the crowd mixed together like a multi-fish stew. It became increasingly difficult to distinguish what anyone was saying, and the longer it went on, the stiffer I became. Would this turn violent? If it did, I'd just slip away into the shadows. I refused to fight the non-magical citizens of Ruma, no matter how poorly they thought of me.

Illia placed a hand on my upper arm. Nicholin gave me a sharp nod, and I knew they would both stand by me no matter what. When I glanced to my other side, I noticed Fain had disappeared. That wasn't a bad thing—I was certain he lingered nearby, ready to help me should anything turn too violent.

"Volke," Guildmaster Eventide said, her authoritative voice silencing the bickering of the crowd in an instant. "Please join me."

I did as the guildmaster wanted. Illia shadowed my steps, her one eye glaring at the island citizens as we went. With her other hand, she gently rubbed at her eye patch.

"Schoolmaster Tyms was the one who originally requested that you join us," Eventide said as I drew near. "He has an announcement to make." She swept out her arm and ushered Tyms forward.

The older man walked with dignity as he emerged from the sea of people. He wore fresh robes—a brilliant white that clashed horribly with the destruction around us—and kept his head high. When he approached, he offered all the arcanists a slow bow of his head. Today Tyms wore a cap that covered his skin down to his eyebrows.

"I would like to make an announcement," Tyms said, his voice loud enough to carry down the street, though it was completely lacking in the authority that Eventide displayed. "Volke Savan—gravedigger, son of criminals, and knightmare arcanist—was the one who... who risked his life to save the children of this island."

"He fought alongside me," Guildmaster Eventide stated. "As a journeyman arcanist, Volke has time and time again demonstrated the talent and wherewithal of a seasoned veteran."

"He's someone whom I can rely on," Master Zelfree added.

Eventide nodded. "I agree. A noble arcanist, if there ever was one."

Tyms cleared his throat. At some level, I suspected he disliked being upstaged by arcanists, but he retained his forced smile and instead said, "Which is why... I want to officially revoke Volke's exile." He said the words like they pained him to utter. "It was under my urging that the island keep him away, *but*—" Tyms held up a single finger, "—Volke has more than atoned for his earlier sins."

Earlier sins? I almost laughed, but I stifled it. Tyms and I had a different memory of what had happened several years ago.

I braced for the crowd's anger as the silence continued for a dozen seconds. But that didn't happen. Instead, a round of applause started at the edge of the street and then grew in intensity as more people joined in.

They were clapping?

I nervously chuckled and rubbed at the back of my neck. My face heated, and Illia gave me a sideways glance, smirking the entire time.

"Thank you," Nicholin said to the crowd. "I am, in fact, his best friend. I've helped him become what he is today, yes." He held up his little front paws. "I will be your new island mascot, of course."

Illia placed her hand over his face, muffling his amusing speech.

But I wasn't feeling this cheer. Why were they clapping? Arcanists were *supposed* to protect. They were a guiding light and a shepherd of humanity. I didn't deserve praise for doing my job. I hadn't even caught Akiva. I didn't deserve praise.

Master Zelfree must've sensed my doubt, because he placed a hand on my shoulder. "Arcanists like you give people hope," he muttered under his breath. The clapping almost drowned out his words completely, but I managed to hear them. "Hope that they can change their places in life. Hope that when there's trouble, someone will step up to meet it. Hope that not everyone is corrupted by their life circumstances, or power, or revenge."

"You think so?" I whispered, my brow furrowed.

"I know so. Which is why you shouldn't sulk. If you really want to continue helping them—be the hope they need. Hold your head high. And with pride."

Zelfree had a way with words. He always knew what to say to really get through to me. Although I didn't want this type of praise for my actions this time, I knew he was right. I had to accept, if only to show my tiny island home that fate isn't set in stone. Gravediggers can be more than they first appear. Anyone could rise above circumstance.

I held my head high and waved to the people of Ruma. The clapping intensified. Even Guildmaster Eventide and Zelfree joined in.

Despite that, my stomach still twisted in knots. And although I loved my home island, all I could think about was my failure to catch Akiva. He would strike again, especially now that we knew the Second Ascension was nearby.

RYKER'S REQUEST

The moment Guildmaster Eventide returned to giving instructions to the citizens of Ruma, I slipped away from the crowd. Illia and Fain followed close behind, though I only knew of Fain's presence because he accidently ran into a stone fish on the edge of a fence and knocked it over. Instead of turning to head for the docks, I went straight for my childhood home: the old cottage on the edge of the graveyard. I still hadn't seen Gravekeeper William since we had arrived, and an anxious dread had been building in me ever since the fighting had broken out. It wouldn't leave me until I knew he was safe.

Technically, Zelfree had assured me that William would be all right, and while I trusted Zelfree to come through for me, my gut didn't seem to believe that. My insides twisted as I walked along the stone path leading up to the front door.

"What is this?" Fain asked, still invisible. "Why aren't we heading back to the guild?"

"It's our home," Illia said.

Fain replied with a quiet *hmm* and said nothing else on the matter.

To my relief, everything was as it should have been. The graveyard was around back, untouched, the two-story cottage still had moss growing on one side, and the woodshed had plenty of logs and kindling.

William stood inside at the front window, his hands in a washbowl, his gaze down. He was easy to spot—he was a tall man, even taller than me, and his whole body could easily be described as *thick* and *sturdy*. Black peppery stubble covered his chin, which was odd. He had kept his face clean since his time as a naval officer. When had he stopped shaving every day?

I stepped forward, ready to shout his name, but Illia placed a hand on my shoulder. I glanced back. Her eyebrows knitted.

"We shouldn't," she whispered. "Not this time."

"Why?"

William was right there! Why wouldn't we talk to him and make sure everything was okay?

Illia shook her head. "We don't have time. Guildmaster Eventide wants us to leave the island as soon as possible. The longer we're here, the more we put all of Ruma in danger. I know you wanted to check on him, but…"

"We came all this way," Fain interjected. Then he motioned with blackened fingers. "You might not get the chance to see him again. You both should go."

Before we could debate the merits of either action, the cottage door flew open. Illia and I snapped our attention to our adopted father as he strode out of his home and headed straight for us. He smiled the entire way, clearly unable to contain himself.

"There you both are," Gravekeeper William said. He pulled Illia into his chest for a tight hug and then yanked me over by my shoulder, his grip strong, but not as strong as his embrace. "I knew you both were here, and I couldn't stop worryin'. By the abyssal hells—I thought I'd never be able to sleep again."

"We're fine," Illia said with a strained exhale. The three of us were crushed together in the type of hug that restricted airflow. "We came to check on you, actually."

Nicholin, half-smushed between my shoulder and William's, teleported with a pop of air and glitter. He reappeared on top of Fain's head, nestled in his dark hair.

"I know I'm everyone's favorite, but you have to give me a warning before squeezing me," Nicholin stated. "I'll make unfortunate noises if I'm not prepared."

I wrapped my arms around Illia and William, surprised by the differences from my memory. Illia and I seemed firmer—stronger—and William felt softer, slower. We had grown, and things were changing, but William's affection never faded. He held tight with all he had, tears at the corners of his eyes.

"You can't stay here too long," William murmured. "I know you both have to return to your guild. But thank you. Thank you for coming to see me before you two head out."

"Of course," I said.

"You're always welcome here."

"I know. Thank you. Illia and I... we've missed you."

William somehow managed to squeeze even tighter. "Aye. I've missed the two of you as well. But I know you need to go. There are villains afoot, and you're involved." He released me and Illia, but held us both at arm's length. "Just stay safe for me. Understand? Come back, no matter what."

"We'll try," Illia said as she rubbed at her one good eye. "I promise."

I nodded. "My goal is to make sure we all come back together."

Gravekeeper William pulled us in for one last good hug. It lasted several minutes before he finally said, "Someday we'll have a family dinner where you explain everything that's been happening."

A part of me loved that we managed to say goodbye to Gravekeeper William, but another part of me hurt because of the pain in his eyes. I didn't stop thinking about the event until I was on Gentel, and even then, it was a struggle. I tied the dinghy to the atlas turtle's dock in silence, my mind on past memories when William had offered advice in times of hardship. Would he have had advice for me in this situation? Maybe. But at some point, I'd have to discover my own wisdom.

Illia and Fain waited while I secured everything. To my surprise, Fain had dropped his invisibility the moment we had returned to the guild's giant turtle.

He slipped his frostbitten hands into the pockets of his trousers. "It was a nice city. And William seemed like an honorable man. I can see why you missed this island."

Nicholin swished his tail. "I love this isle. It's where I met Illia, so it'll always have a special place in my heart."

"That was an amazing day," Illia said as she petted his head. "I feel like... that's the day my life truly began."

"D'aww," Nicholin said with a squeak. "I feel the same way!"

I sighed as I finished the last of the knot and then turned and headed for the guild manor house. I ascended the stairs that led to the main pathway, but stopped once I realized Master Zelfree was standing at the top. He had his arms crossed over his chest, and his mimic circled around his legs in an eight-shaped pattern like only a cat could.

Clouds drifted by overhead, creating patches of shadows that moved across the ground like silent waves. Zelfree stood in one, wearing nothing but black. It made for effective camouflage up until the cloud moved away with the wind.

"Volke," he said. "I need to speak with you."

"How did you beat us here?" Fain interjected. He motioned to the island in the distance with a look of mild disbelief. "We went to the graveyard for a minute, and somehow you made it back here in that time?"

Traces offered a loud purr. "I'm a mimic. Why travel on a dinghy when we can soar with roc magic? Or swim with the ability of an atlas turtle? So many faster possibilities."

Fain opened his mouth as though he would continue the argument, but then just closed it and said nothing.

"Volke," Zelfree said again, my name laced with irritation. "I have an assignment for you."

I lifted an eyebrow. "Okay. What is it?"

"I need you to watch over Ryker, in addition to helping Evianna train with her knightmare magic. Do you think you can handle that?"

"Where *is* Ryker?" I asked, glancing around as though I might spot him nearby.

"He's in the guild house, on the first floor near the master arcanist quarters. It's the largest guest room."

I nodded along with his words, familiar enough with the layout of the guild to remember the guest area. "How long should I watch him for?"

"Until he bonds with the world serpent."

Illia, Fain, and Nicholin all glanced over at me, their faces marked with concern.

"Shouldn't the master arcanists be protecting him?" Illia asked before I could voice my own questions. "Surely, they would be better suited."

"I've already been assigned to it," Zelfree said. "But I don't want to take any chances. The Second Ascension will eventually figure out why he's here, and I want someone with Ryker at all times."

"I can teleport." Illia stepped forward. "I can get Ryker out of danger far faster than Volke. Let *me* watch over him."

Why was Illia so concerned? Did she think I couldn't handle the assignment?

Master Zelfree shook his head. "If I wanted, I could mimic your rizzel magic. That's not the point. Volke has his artifact sword and shield, and he's fought these villains before. Not only that, but his knightmare magic allows him to travel through the shadows, which is almost as effective as teleportation."

"But, I—"

"I've made my decision," Zelfree growled, cutting Illia off. Then he turned on his heel and headed for the guild house. "And I don't have time for arguments like this. We're leaving port, so make sure you have everything."

Traces leapt from the ground to Zelfree's shoulder. Mid-leap, she transformed from her gray-cat self into a beautiful white-and-silver rizzel. When her paws landed on Zelfree's shoulder, they both disappeared in a pop of white, glittery magic. I had sometimes wondered if Traces preferred style and panache, and in that moment, I was certain the answer was *yes*.

"I think we could've done an amazing job protecting Ryker," Nicholin said as he gently patted Illia's shoulder. "Don't worry. Maybe we can prove to Master Zelfree that we're capable."

Illia didn't respond. She just stared at the distance and caressed her eye patch. That was the look she made when she was worried—the one she wore when she couldn't see an easy solution. I would've asked her thoughts, but I didn't know if she felt comfortable discussing such matters in front of Fain. Although it appeared they had been getting along, I feared Illia still held a grudge about Fain being a part of Calisto's pirate crew.

I turned my attention to the Isle of Ruma. It looked worse from a distance, and I couldn't help but frown.

"Everything okay?" Fain asked.

"I wonder if Atty has come back," I muttered. "I haven't seen her yet."

Illia pulled her buccaneer coat tight around her shoulders. "Atty is probably with her mother. That's what she always does when she returns to the island."

The temper in her voice surprised me.

"You know Atty's mother?" I asked.

Illia offered a sarcastic glower. "Yeah. She's a controlling woman who places a huge burden on her children to be perfect. She needs her family resurrected, after all."

"How did you know all that?"

Fain's eyebrows shot to his hairline. "Wait, she's not making the resurrection part up?"

"I snuck into the Trixibelle House from time to time," Illia said with a shrug. "Atty adores her mother—thinks her mother has given her a *noble cause*, rather than thinking her mother is treating her like a tool."

"Who does that?" Fain murmured.

Illia chuckled as she headed for the guild manor house. "I never understood why you pined after her, Volke." She dismissively waved her hand, not even bothering to glance back at me. "She doesn't have an adventurer's spirit, like you and me."

That last statement both irritated me and gave me pause. I wanted to ask Illia what she meant, but she, too, disappeared in a puff of glitter.

An adventurer's spirit? Of course Atty had an adventurer's spirit. She was part of the Frith Guild, after all. And she had accompanied us on all our quests, including to the pirate city of Port Crown. What more did Illia think someone needed to do to prove their inner adventurer?

I shook my head, dispelling the thoughts.

Perhaps Illia was jealous?

"Would a parent really expect the impossible from a child?" Fain continued, seemingly lost in his own conversation. "My older brother never did anything like that..."

"We should head in," I said, never acknowledging his comments. "I'm sure the guild will want to make sure everyone is accounted for before leaving."

———

Ryker's room wasn't difficult to find. It was right were Master Zelfree had said it would be—and there was already someone watching the entrance. Journeyman Reo and his giant ogata toad stood watch, both eldrin and arcanist wide awake. Reo wasn't intimidating—he was a thin man with a stutter, after all—but ogata toads were highly poisonous. If someone came for Ryker, they would be in for a not-so-pleasant surprise.

"E-evening," Reo said as I walked by.

"Good evening," I muttered.

The sun had set only thirty minutes ago, but already the manor house felt dark and unwelcoming. A lantern hung outside Ryker's door, and it shook when I knocked, disturbing the shadows all around us.

No one answered.

"I could enter and speak with him," Luthair said from the shadows at my feet.

I shook my head. "I don't want to be rude."

"He's still a-awake," Reo said as he smoothed his robes. "But he sometimes takes a while to answer his door."

As if Ryker were listening to the conversation, the door finally swung open.

Ryker stood on the other side, his honeyed complexion pale and his hair unkempt. He looked like a man who hadn't slept in days. He had no lantern burning in his room, however, and he stayed in the darkness, practically shielding himself with the door. Did anyone know how rundown he appeared to be? Or was he hiding from everyone?

"Can I help you?" Ryker asked, his voice soft.

"I came to speak with you," I said. "Do you mind if I come in?"

"I... Well, all right."

Ryker stepped back and allowed me into his private quarters. I walked inside and took a quick moment to examine the place. There wasn't much to it. A bed, a dresser, a bookshelf, a washing basin—everything someone would need to have a comfy living arrangement. But it was devoid of any personal effects. It was a stranger's room, not Ryker's.

Ryker shut the door and then felt his way over to the lantern hanging from a chain in the corner of the room. The oil and flint allowed it to be lit without the use of outside materials, but it still took Ryker a good forty-five seconds to figure everything out in the dark.

I could've given him the ability to see through the darkness, but I had been so distracted that I hadn't thought of it until a moment before the light flooded the room. Ryker closed the lantern's shutters halfway, dimming the light to a comfortable glow.

"There," Ryker said. Then he ran a hand though his black hair. "What can I do for you, Sir Arcanist?"

"Just call me *Volke*." Silence passed between us before I motioned to his quarters. "How do you like the Frith Guild so far? Are you sleeping well?"

"Quite well," Ryker replied.

A twinge of pain shot through my chest after his statement. It was enough that it startled me, and I flinched.

Ryker lifted an eyebrow. "Are you okay?"

"Uh, yes. Sorry." I rubbed at my neck, wondering if that was my new power acting up—the one that seemed to detect someone's lies.

But I didn't need my newfound ability to tell that Ryker was lying. It was apparent from the bags under his eyes. And why would he want to deceive me?

"You don't look like you've been sleeping well," I said. "You seem ragged."

Ryker stared, and I once again took note of his height. Damn near the same as me.

And he wore thick leathers, even so close to bedtime. A heavy coat, boots, and thick trousers. Why wasn't he prepared for sleeping? Had he been wearing this all day?

"I'm sorry," Ryker eventually said with a long sigh. "I haven't slept well."

"Well, I'm going to be one of the arcanists watching you from now on. If you need anything—or if there's any way I can reassure you so that you're comfortable enough to rest—just let me know."

Ryker shook his head. "I'm comfortable. The Frith Guild has been more than accommodating."

"The Grand Apothecary is just down the hall," I said, motioning to the door. "I'm sure she could give you something to help you sleep."

Again, he shook his head. "*No.* No—I don't want to sleep. Thank you, though." Before I could ask why, he turned away and fiddled with the first drawer of the dresser. "If you simply came to introduce yourself as another one of my bodyguards, consider your mission complete. You're Volke. The Knightmare Arcanist. I understand that you'll protect me."

"That's correct. However—"

"If you want me to sleep, perhaps you should wait outside," Ryker interjected. "I have enough problems as it is."

He didn't look at me. He just continued to pull and adjust the drawer, no purpose to his actions other than to occupy his hands. He trembled slightly—was that from lack of sleep or nervousness? I couldn't tell. But something was wrong. That, I knew for certain.

I stepped toward the door. "You know, we have an ethereal whelk arcanist here," I said. "He can manipulate dreams with surprising finesse. If you suffer from any unpleasant nightmares, Adelgis can take them away."

Ryker stopped fidgeting. Then he turned around to face me. The bags under his eyes seemed worse in the low light of his dimmed lantern. "Really?"

I nodded.

"And he wouldn't mind altering my dreams?"

"I'll ask him, if you want." I shrugged. "I think there's a high likelihood he is willing."

When Ryker turned pensive, I just waited. A long minute passed, and his gaze fell to the floor. "It won't help, though. Thank you for the offer. It was generous."

I lifted an eyebrow. "If you have nightmares, Adelgis can definitely help."

"I do have nightmares," Ryker whispered. "But they aren't the kind I suffer from while sleeping. So, I doubt an ethereal whelk arcanist can help me."

He had nightmares... while awake?

"What do you mean?" I asked.

"I mean I'm haunted by... everything that's been happening to me." Ryker exhaled, his breath unsteady. He combed back his hair with both hands and then ambled over to the side of his bed. "There were so many people who died today. The Isle of Ruma will never be the same. And I... I contributed to that."

"*No*," I stated, more forceful than I had intended, but I still got my point across. "You don't need to blame yourself for this. The Second Ascension came here to assassinate Guildmaster Eventide, not you. This would've happened regardless of whether or not you were here."

Ryker remained quiet, and his expression never changed. Was he not swayed by the argument?

"I'm telling the truth," I said.

"I believe you," Ryker replied in a soft tone. "But my presence here cost the Isle of Ruma many lives. And now I have that guilt, and I don't know how to get rid of it."

I stepped closer. "Explain, then."

"Master Zelfree knew that a king basilisk arcanist was approaching," Ryker continued in the same melancholy tone. "But instead of leaving the atlas turtle with Eventide, the two of them stayed here to shelter me away. *They were delayed because of me*—they didn't start fighting the Second Ascension until I was someplace safe."

Ryker took a deep breath as he slowly turned around. He seemed paler than before. Or perhaps more exhausted.

"I wanted them to confront the enemy straightaway, but they stayed regardless," Ryker said, confusion mixing into his words. "Don't you see? If I hadn't been here, Guildmaster Eventide and Master Zelfree would've been able to save more innocent people, but... but because I'm here..."

He laughed, but it was forced and dark.

"They say it's because I'm *too important to risk*, but is that even right? What if they're wrong and... and all those people lost their lives for nothing?"

The heaviness of his words filled the room with dread and

uncertainty. I hadn't thought Ryker would be so concerned about others, but now that I knew he was, I could see why the sybil arcanists said he would be the perfect world serpent arcanist.

Which was why I couldn't allow him to suffer alone in this room.

"Is there anything I can do for you?" I asked.

Ryker exhaled. "I doubt you can do much, Sir Arcanist."

"Volke. It's just *Volke*." I walked up next to him and placed my hand on his shoulder. Ryker's attention snapped to the point of contact. I continued, "Listen. You don't have to do this alone. The whole Frith Guild is here to help you." I smiled as much as I genuinely could and added, "And if you need more support—if you need anything at all—you can ask me. I'll try to make it happen."

I meant every word. If Ryker needed the blood from my veins, I wanted to give it to him. The world serpent was too important—its role would shape the course of history. Ryker *had* to be healthy enough to bond with it.

Ryker slowly made eye contact. "You seem like an honest person," he muttered. "So... what I really want is... I don't want anyone else to die for me. Not directly or indirectly. I just... don't want that guilt. It's killing me inside."

"What do you mean?" I asked, my brow furrowed.

"Don't let anyone die just to protect me," Ryker stated, louder than before. "Can you do that, *Volke*? Can you promise me that you won't let your fellow arcanists die just so that I live? On the off chance that I'll become a fantastic world serpent arcanist? If you can, that would be wonderful." He pulled away from my grip and shook his head. "Maybe then I could get some sleep. Maybe then I... I wouldn't have these doubts."

I didn't know how to respond.

Ryker didn't want me to protect him? Because he feared it would take my attention away from protecting other people?

"That's my one request," Ryker said in an icy, serious tone. "Please, protect the others first. I just... I can't stand the thought of innocent people paying the price for my power."

32

GUARD DUTY

"I don't think you understand," I said, slow and careful in an attempt to pick the right words. "Villains of the highest order are trying to bond with the world serpent. If they do, thousands of people will have their lives ruined—or worse. Tyranny will reign supreme."

Ryker listened, but his despondent expression remained.

"If you really want to save people, you'll bond with the world serpent and prevent those villains from bonding with other god-creatures," I said as I straightened my posture. "That's how you can honor the people of Ruma who died today. You have to stay the course—until the bitter end. Or else their deaths really will be in vain."

"But I'm not *someone*," Ryker said, an odd emphasis on the word. He gritted his teeth, ran both hands through his hair like a nervous tic, and then faced the wall, his shoulders bunched. "I'm not a famous swashbuckler or skilled soldier or a talented officer—*there had to be a mistake*. The sybil arcanists who predicted my bonding must have been wrong... or perhaps they... overlooked someone..."

His voice grew quieter and more distant until I eventually couldn't hear it at all.

The shadows around the lantern flickered. Luthair shifted so that I could eventually see his faint outline in the darkness at the foot of the bed.

"My arcanist," he whispered.

But Luthair didn't need to say anything else. I knew what he was suggesting.

"Ryker," I said, crossing my arms. "If you had to describe the person who would become the world serpent arcanist, what kinds of qualities would they have?'

"They'd be capable, and determined, and honorable," Ryker replied immediately. He turned back to face me, a sigh at the edge of his breath. "They'd be experienced and trustworthy and willing to do whatever it takes."

"You're still young."

"That's the problem," he snapped.

I shook my head. "You don't understand. You're young enough that you still have time to write your life story. *You* can be all those things. You just need time and tenacity."

"But the world serpent arcanist has to fight the Second Ascension!" Ryker waved an arm in dramatic fashion. "That's not me. It never has been."

"The Frith Guild will remain by your side. If you want, you can become everything you just described. But again, you must stay the course. You have to be strong when it seems impossible."

I didn't know if I sounded like Master Zelfree or Gravekeeper William, but they were the ones I pictured when I imagined the words in my head. They always had wisdom when I needed it, and if Ryker needed advice, I had to be there for him. The fate of the world could depend on how determined Ryker was in a single moment of adversity, and I couldn't allow him to falter.

"You're right," Ryker muttered. He exhaled and then took a seat on the side of his bed, his body tense, his hands unsteady. "It's too late to turn back now. I have to... bond with the world serpent no matter what."

I nodded.

Ryker glanced up at me, his dark eyes practically a mirror of my own. "But please don't abandon innocents for me. They need arcanists to help them."

"I'll try," I said. "I promise."

"You're a good man, Volke. Thank you. I appreciate you taking the time to speak with me."

I nervously chuckled, unsure of how to reply. "Think nothing of it."

Ryker rubbed at his eyes. "I think I might finally be able to get a few hours of rest."

"I'll go get Adelgis right away. He'll help you rest. Trust me."

Without another word between us, I headed for the door. Ryker had pulled off his boots and kicked his feet up onto the bed by the time I exited. His fatigue was as blatant as the sun at noon.

The hallway remained lit with a single lantern. Instead of Reo and his ogata toad standing guard, I spotted Zelfree leaning against the nearby wall. He had one foot hooked on the ankle of the other and one hand in the pocket of his coat. Although he appeared tired, he met me with a sharp look in his eyes.

His arcanist mark—normally just a blank star—was now in the shape of an ethereal whelk, a seasnail-looking creature of mystical dream powers. I didn't see Traces anywhere, but if she had transformed into an ethereal whelk, that meant she'd be able to hide in the very light itself.

"What're you doing here?" I asked. "What happened to Journeyman Reo?"

"I relieved him." Zelfree motioned to Ryker's door with a jerk of his head. "And I came to see what you would talk about with our world serpent arcanist."

"You came... to *spy* on me?" I muttered, half in shock.

"That's right."

"But why?"

Zelfree pushed away from the wall and stood in front of me. "I knew you wouldn't disappoint."

I shook my head. "Disappoint *how*?"

"Ryker has been having doubts for days. If I had sent anyone *but* you in there, I suspect they either would've made the situation worse—or they would've agreed with Ryker and helped him flee to the farthest island he could reach."

"But I was different?" I asked.

Zelfree nodded once. "You went in there and told him what needs to be done. And in no uncertain terms."

"Is that why you didn't allow Illia to take my place as Ryker's guard?"

"Exactly." Zelfree patted me on the upper arm. "And I know you won't let me down, either. You're one of the few apprentices—excuse me, *journeymen*—whom I've come to depend on. I need your help in this matter, Volke. I need someone to watch Ryker and to give him advice as a peer, not a mentor."

This wasn't the first time Master Zelfree had asked me to help him, but never before had he made his plea with such emotion. He really wanted my help in this matter, and hearing him ask me—not as his student, but as a fellow arcanist—filled my chest with an overwhelming sense of warmth and lightness.

I stood a bit taller and took in a quick breath before saying, "Of course. I'll be there for Ryker. I won't let you or the Frith Guild down."

Zelfree nodded. "I know you won't."

***

I enjoyed the evening. The quiet stillness of the dark had become a favorite of mine. I stood outside Ryker's room, remaining ever vigilant until the dawn. Master Zelfree had said this would be better—as a knightmare arcanist, my powers were enhanced at night. Not only that, but I could shadow-step away with Ryker and warn the master arcanists the moment anything out of the ordinary happened.

The creaking of floorboards drew my attention to Ryker's door.

Adelgis was inside, helping our future world serpent arcanist to rest. He had been in there for an hour already, and I wondered what would take Adelgis so long. He could force people to sleep with a single touch. What more was there to do?

The door opened, the hinges silent, and Adelgis slipped out of the room with the stealth of a light breeze. He shut the door behind him with a soft click.

His long black hair hung as a loose ponytail over one shoulder. His lean frame, dark robes, and heavy cloak allowed him to blend into the darkness. Even viewed through my enhanced sight, Adelgis mixed well with the gloomy surroundings.

"Ryker is sleeping," he whispered. "I spoke with him for a long while, trying to determine what he liked and what brought him joy."

"Can't you hear thoughts?" I asked. "Couldn't you just hear that all immediately?"

"I still need to ask questions. Most people don't usually dwell on their favorite people and things. And Ryker was in a dark place until we spoke, which hindered my investigation. That's why it took so long, but I eventually discovered useful information."

I crossed my arms, my eyes narrowed. "What brings him joy?"

"His mother," Adelgis replied. "His hometown. His childhood friends."

My anxiety melted away from my thoughts. Those were good answers. They would've been mine if someone had asked me before I had bonded with Luthair.

"He wished he knew his father," Adelgis continued, his voice low. "Ryker never met him, and the memories where he had searched for his father across several islands are some of Ryker's worst recollections."

"I can understand," I murmured. "I was adopted, and sometimes I wondered where my birth parents were."

Adelgis held up a finger. "You found your father, though."

"But I still know the feeling of looking and feeling like it'll never matter." Then I shook my head. "Is there anything I can do for Ryker?"

Adelgis smoothed his ponytail, combing his slender fingers through the inky locks. His gaze fell to the floor as he mulled over the question. "I think you already have. You see, Ryker is apprehensive of taking on so much power and responsibility as the world serpent arcanist, but after speaking with you, he feels he has no choice but to go through with it— if only to honor the people who died on the Isle of Ruma."

While I was glad Ryker would help us, I wished it hadn't come to this. Why had people needed to die for him to accept his destiny? Most people would've been elated to bond with a god-creature, but Ryker wasn't most people.

"Well, it is late," Adelgis said, his gaze lifting to meet mine. "If you have nothing else for me..."

For a long moment, I held my breath. Was there something else I wished to speak to Adelgis about? A part of me wanted to ask about Atty. Where was she? Was she okay? Was she... thinking about me? But I couldn't leave my post the first night I stood guard at Ryker's door.

Adelgis lifted an eyebrow with startling precision. "That's odd. Your thoughts aren't usually like this."

My face heated, and I focused my attention to the opposite wall. "I'm sorry." I kept forgetting that Adelgis always knew every thought I had, no matter how tiny. "I'm concerned about Atty."

"I can tell."

My face, neck, and ears grew hotter.

Adelgis chortled for a second and then offered a smile. "Atty went to bed a while ago. She's fine, though exhausted." Then his expression returned to a neutral serious. "But she hasn't been thinking about you, no. She was thinking about her mother."

"You don't have to tell me private thoughts," I said.

"Her mother's *coffins* were damaged," Adelgis continued regardless. "I'm not sure what that means, entirely, but it has Atty preoccupied. She thinks of nothing else, and as a friend, I think it would probably be best for you to help her through this."

Ah. That was why Adelgis had continued and told me anyway.

"Thank you," I muttered.

But I didn't know what I could do to help. Was her mother worried the bodies would be damaged? Could phoenixes not repair all injuries, even ones created postmortem? And why was Atty concerned? Had her mother blamed her for taking too long to achieve a true form?

"Fascinating," Adelgis said, an eyebrow raised. "I didn't know about any of this information. No wonder she's upset."

I ran a hand down my face. "I'm sorry. Please don't mention anything to her."

"I won't." He offered a sarcastic smirk. "I know what it's like to have a family with dark secrets. Atty will want me to keep quiet, and that's what I intend to do." Then Adelgis bowed and headed down the hallway and toward the grand staircase.

My thoughts went straight to Atty's mother, Bayva. How could she do that to her own daughter? How could she put so much pressure on one person? I gritted my teeth as I thought back to Illia's statement. *Atty doesn't have the spirit of an adventurer.* Of course not! Her mother had taken that from her by placing such a heavy burden on her shoulders.

And what did it matter if she wasn't as enthusiastic about adventuring or sailing the wide-open seas? It was a noble goal to gain a true form of one's eldrin. Atty had aspirations. And grand desires. Those were probably *better* than an adventurer's spirit.

"Luthair—"

But before I could get another syllable out, Luthair cut me off with, "*My arcanist.* Please focus."

I snapped my attention to the darkest corner in the hallway. "I *am* focused."

"You forget that my first arcanist was also a young man," Luthair quipped. "I know what you're dwelling on, and now isn't the time for trysts."

"*Trysts?*" I balked. "I would never. You know that."

"T'was an exaggeration, my arcanist." Luthair chuckled—a rare occurrence—his voice dark and haunting. "But I do advise that you let this go for now. We have five weeks of travel, according to the journeymen I spoke to earlier. You should use the time wisely."

"*Five weeks?*" I had known the information, but it hadn't registered until now.

"The atlas turtle must take unusual routes to our destination. We will make our way to the eastern dock city of Millatin, so long as the Occult Compass doesn't point us in another direction before then. Once there—and safe within the heavily defended city—perhaps you can take time for romance, but focusing on it now would be foolish."

I rubbed at the back of my neck. "I'm only guarding Ryker at night. I have plenty of time during the day."

"You must hone your skills. And you must help Evianna do the same. Please, my arcanist. Consider my words carefully."

Although I wanted to tell him everything would be fine, at some level, I knew he was right. There were more pressing matters at hand. I had to improve my magic before we reached the world serpent.

Atty would understand why I had to wait.

"Let me speak with her first," I muttered.

33

TRUE LOVE

Atty's room was nestled in the middle of the girls' wing of the manor, on the third story. I had been there before, but only a handful of times. It took me a few moments to remember the exact door, and when I arrived, I had Luthair check to make sure it was correct before knocking. Although it would soon be dawn, people were still sleeping.

Atty was, too, of course, but anxiety gnawed at my thoughts. I wanted to speak with her like a fire wanted kindling.

I rapped my knuckles on the wood of the door, soft at first, and then growing louder. I stopped at five and waited. Sounds from the other side told me I had awoken her. I held my breath as the floorboards creaked ever closer.

The door opened inward a crack. Atty peered out, her blonde hair puffed on one side and flat on the other. I hadn't ever seen her like this. For some reason—even though I knew it wasn't a flattering look—I found it adorable.

"Volke?" she whispered.

"Atty?" I stepped closer, but I didn't attempt to enter. "I apologize for coming to you at this early hour. I just didn't think I could wait. Do you mind if we speak for a bit? I have some things I wish to discuss."

She nodded once and then slowly opened the door all the way. Although I hadn't expected her to invite me inside, I quickly stepped in to avoid any prying eyes. It was technically against the rules for apprentices to have intimate relationships with anyone else in the guild, and although Atty and I were journeymen arcanists now, that fear of "getting caught" still stuck with me.

Atty's room was much like my own, except for the phoenix nest made of down feathers, soot, and blankets settled at the foot of her bed. Titania slept much like a heron—curled around herself, her head tucked under a wing, and her peacock-like tail draped down to the floor. When she breathed, it sounded similar to a whistle-snore.

"Is everything okay?" Atty asked.

She wore a long robe—fluffier than her normal attire, but just as white and pristine. The fur on the collar and sleeves made it difficult to see her neck and hands, and the material was so long, it pooled at her feet.

"I just wanted to check on you," I said as I stepped close. "It's felt like an eternity since last we spoke."

Atty crossed her arms and nodded once. "A lot has happened. It's understandable."

"Is your mother okay? Adelgis said—"

"No, she's not okay." Atty's gaze fell to the floor, her shoulders tense. "She's very distraught, and she didn't want me to leave the isle."

Just hearing Atty's distress twisted my anxiety into frustration. I moved closer again, and this time, I placed a hand on her shoulder, trying to show support. "Why didn't she want you to leave?"

"Because she wanted me to *help the family*." Atty closed her eyes and then stepped away from me. "Volke, maybe now isn't the best time. I'm not... looking like myself."

"I don't mind. How you look isn't important."

"It's important to me." Atty pulled her robe up so that it half covered her fair and disheveled hair.

I eliminated the distance between us again by taking a hesitant step closer. "Are you okay?" I whispered. "You seem upset."

"I am, Volke." Atty rubbed at her face with the back of her hand, her fluffy sleeve blocking her face completely.

Her distress was too much. I wrapped my arms around her, squeezing her tight in a powerful embrace. Atty pressed her forehead on my collarbone, but she kept her arms up and hands on my chest, limiting how close I could really get.

"What's wrong?" I asked.

Atty took a long moment to mull over my question. I gently rubbed my knuckles on her back and said nothing. She didn't sound like she was crying, but she trembled for a few seconds before taking a deep breath and calming herself.

"I feel like I've lost my way," Atty murmured, her voice soft.

Despite our conversation, Titania continued to sleep, her whistle-snores the only sounds besides us.

"Lost your way?" I tightened my grip. "Don't worry. I'm here for you. What can I do to help you find your way back?"

Atty brushed her fingers over my shirt. "Volke... You're a good man. I knew you'd offer to help, but... that's the problem. I can't have you help me. I... I need to conduct myself better. I need to have Titania achieve true form."

"Because your mother wants it?"

"Because my family *needs* it," Atty corrected. Then she shook her head. "Don't you understand?"

I didn't reply. How could I? Making someone carry such a heavy burden seemed unfair—almost ludicrous. How could Atty's mother put such pressure on her to resurrect their dead family members?

"Is that what you really want?" I whispered. "You could take some time to think it over. We can talk about it."

Atty gripped my shirt. "Volke, I need to stop making excuses. My mother's right. I'm... I'm getting distracted." She pressed her forehead harder into my collarbone. "I enjoy every moment with you, but any time spent not working toward achieving Titania's true form is time wasted."

"Bayva said you were distracted?" I asked, disgust in my tone. No one worked harder than Atty. How was she distracted? "I don't think your mother knows what's going on. And sometimes rest is needed—it's a crucial step to training."

"Spending time with you isn't *resting*. It's just me being selfish." Atty released my shirt and then pushed herself out of my embrace. "And being selfish definitely won't lead to my true form phoenix."

"But—"

"I can't abandon my family," Atty interjected, her voice louder. "My mother has always been there for me, and she wants nothing but the best for the Trixibelle House." Atty turned away, her robes still pulled tightly around her elegant body. "Please, Volke. Please just understand that I need to limit all distractions in my life right now."

"I'm a distraction?"

"Yes." Atty shook her head. "I mean *no*. But also, *yes*." Her shoulders bunched at the base of her neck. "The fact of the matter is—I can't focus my magic when you're around. I just can't. At least, not like how I want."

"Well, but, can't we help each other? Isn't that the ideal solution? I'd help you to help your family? Like a united partnership, and—"

"Maybe some other time," Atty said. "But not now. This is my own struggle."

I opened my mouth to say something, but stopped before the words came out. I couldn't argue with her. If she needed time and rest, that was for the best—I could do the things Luthair wanted me to focus on while Atty came to terms with the pressures of her family.

I just... didn't understand. The pressure her mother shouldered her with seemed ridiculous—or at least damaging. But Atty carried the weight regardless. Was it out of duty? Or love? Or was it because she had been a child when these expectations had been thrust upon her?

I didn't know, and now wasn't the time to figure it out. And that realization stung. I wanted to make this right, but it was like holding water. What more could I do? Why was this so difficult? I thought two people intertwined in a relationship shared all their burdens with each other.

"If you ever want to talk, you know where to find me," I said.

Atty nodded once. "Thank you, Volke. You've always been dependable. If... if I need anything, I'll let you know."

I had never traveled so far east before.

In relation to the Isle of Ruma, the Argo Empire, the Shard Sea, and New Norra had been to the south. The city of Fortuna and the Isle of Landin had been to the west. And finally, Port Crown had been to the north. When I had been a child, I had assumed nothing of real interest was out east. It wasn't until I had read the more complicated tomes in Gravekeeper William's personal library that I had realized a vast body of water separated our island territories from those to the east. And supposedly, beyond the glorious port city of Millatin, there was an even greater body of water with even more lands beyond that.

It was difficult to fathom at times. Every day that I learned something new, the Isle of Ruma grew smaller.

I stared at my bedroom ceiling, my fingers laced together behind my head, creating a cushion with my palms as I sprawled out on my bed. The morning sun crept in through the window like a cautious burglar, bringing with it a pleasant increase in the temperature.

But despite the refreshing breeze, and the journey to a grand new location, my thoughts always returned to Atty. She hadn't come to see me since when I had tried to have a talk with her yesterday morning. It was true that we were both busy, but her absence made everything more worrisome. Illia's offhand comment about how we weren't compatible also rang in my ears.

Luthair was right. This worrying would consume all my time.

A soft knock at the door drew me out of my head.

I sat up and walked across the room, taking note of how slow it was when compared to shadow-stepping. When I opened the door, I couldn't help but lift both eyebrows.

"Karna," I said.

She smiled, her beauty heightened with the soft glow of morning light. Then she combed her silky blonde hair with her fingers and tilted her head. "I'm glad to see you're still awake." Karna eyed my coat and boots. "And still fully clothed." With a chuckle, she added, "Not much has changed, I see."

I opened the door wide and motioned for her to join me.

Karna took a moment to stare at me, her blue eyes searching mine, as though trying to find something. "You don't mind if I come into your room?" she whispered, her words on the edge of a purr.

"I... don't like it when you put it that way," I muttered, my chest tightening. "But no—I don't mind if you come into my room."

"I'm honored."

She slipped past me and then twirled around, practically dancing, taking in the sights of my simple living quarters. Today, she wore a long dress with a slit up one side, revealing the entirety of one sculpted leg. The azure color complemented her eyes.

Karna stopped spinning and giggled. With all the energy of a child, she bounded over to my bed and hop-sat on the very middle. "My, my. So humble for an arcanist with a true form knightmare. You'd think they'd upgrade your quarters to better suit your new status."

"This is fine," I said as I shut the door. "Is there something I can do for you, Karna?"

"I heard you were guarding the future world serpent arcanist," she replied, crossing her leg and then smoothing the skirt of her dress to ensure her decency.

"I am guarding him, yes."

"Tell me all about it."

"Right now?" I asked.

"You're awake, aren't you?" Karna leaned back. "It's difficult to get time with someone as important as you. I shouldn't waste this opportunity with idle chatter."

After a deep exhale, I ambled over to the bed and slowly took a seat on the edge. "Well, Ryker is a fine man, and—"

"Wait," Karna said. She sat up straight and placed a hand on my shoulder. "What's wrong?"

"Huh?" I stared at the spot where she touched me. "What do you mean?"

"You're not feeling well. You're upset."

It took a long moment for Karna's words to sink in. By the abyssal hells—she could tell my mood from just a couple of words? I narrowed my eyes and stared into hers. "I... Well, it's complicated."

Without a moment's hesitation, Karna scooted to the edge of the bed and leaned against my arm, her soft body pressed against me, her arms wrapping around my elbow. If it had been anyone else, I would've been startled and probably uncomfortable. But I knew Karna. This was just how she operated.

"Tell me about it," she said.

I glanced at her arcanist mark while I tried to sort my feelings. The human-shaped creature on her star represented her doppelgänger eldrin. A small piece of me was thankful she hadn't tried to use her powers of deception on me. Now that I had this new knightmare ability to sense lies, it probably wouldn't work anyway, but that wasn't the point. I appreciated that Karna was coming to me as herself and not someone else. Perhaps it wasn't a bad idea to trust her as well.

"I'm having problems," I finally stated.

"Obviously." Karna caressed my elbow. "What about?"

I gritted my teeth for a few seconds. Then I said, "About... things related to romance."

Karna grew tense and quiet, but after a handful of seconds, she relaxed. "You and the phoenix arcanist."

"Yes. Her name is Atty."

She placed the side of her head on my shoulder. "Tell me about it."

Despite her casual tone, I could sense the strain in her words. Karna had made it clear she cared about me on a certain level. Was this the right conversation to have? Especially after a long night and little sleep? I didn't want to upset Karna with such dealings, but at the same time, I felt disoriented—like a traveler who suddenly realized they had lost the trail in the fog.

"I'm not sure what I'm doing," I whispered. "Atty and I had gotten close—closer than we ever had been before—but for some reason, I'm having doubts. Is that normal in a relationship? Shouldn't true love... feel right all the time? No matter what?"

Silence.

Was my question too difficult? Or perhaps too awkward?

Then Karna snorted back a laugh. She sat away from me, covered her mouth with the back of her hand, and continued to struggle with stifling her mirth.

"What?" I barked.

"*True love?*" she replied, half-chuckling. "Oh, Volke." Karna shook her head and offered a wary smile. "This is why you're not like other men I've known. This very conversation encapsulates everything about you."

She brought a hand up to the side of my head and then ran her fingers through my black hair. I didn't pull away. Instead, I kept eye contact, searching her expression for the explanation of her odd response to my question.

"There's no such thing as true love," Karna whispered, a slight frown on the corner of her lips. "I'm sorry I have to be the one to tell you, but everyone has problems. There isn't a love so pure that it kills all conflict."

"We aren't having a *conflict*," I said. "I'm just... I'm just worried."

"That's a conflict, sweetheart."

I didn't appreciate the sarcastic tone of her voice, but instead of arguing, I let it go. "We're fine. This might just all be in my head."

"What did she say that caused you to worry?" Karna asked.

"That she needed time to focus on her magic. That I'm... a distraction."

With a chuckle, Karna said, "I keep forgetting she's seventeen. It's an age prone to all sorts of *interesting* decisions."

I mulled over the comment for a long moment before asking, "How old are you?"

As a doppelgänger arcanist, she could change her appearance at will. Currently she seemed young—early twenties at the most—and arcanists lived extended lives of youth and vigor. An arcanist's physical age wasn't directly indicative of their real age.

"A girl must keep some mysteries," she said as she touched her lower lip with her pointer finger. "But I'll tell you this—I'm not a seventeen-year-old girl anymore. I can see the mistakes your phoenix arcanist friend is making, because that's common for young women her age."

"She's not making any mistakes." I shook my head. "Atty just needs time."

Karna leaned away from me. She said nothing as she rested against my pillow and then lay down fully on the bed. With gentle motions, she wrapped herself in my sheets. Then Karna turned her attention to the window. "Volke," she said. "I don't think I'm the right person to have this conversation with."

"Why's that?"

"Because I have everything to gain and nothing to lose if you and your phoenix arcanist friend decide to part ways."

I rubbed at my neck. "I told you. We're not having a problem."

"Why don't you speak to others about the matter?" Karna asked. "Other men, perhaps."

"I tried speaking to Master Zelfree, but he almost shattered his knees in an attempt to jump out a window as fast as possible."

Karna lifted her head to better stare at me in disbelief. "Seriously?"

"He was being sarcastic," I muttered. "But it basically happened."

She lay back down. "Perhaps the other men, then. Just get some perspective. See what they have to say. If they agree you're not having any conflict, perhaps this *is* all in your head, and your *true love* will flourish without delay."

Karna still retained her harsh edge of sarcasm.

"Maybe I will," I said.

She shrugged. "It'll be interesting to hear the advice you gather."

I stood from the bed. "Well, I'll come tell you about it once I'm done."

"Sounds like a deal," Karna said with a soft chuckle.

TRAVELING EAST

The first week of guard duty went by without incident.

Each night, Adelgis arrived to help Ryker sleep. It reminded me of Master Zelfree—and myself, to be honest. Adelgis's ethereal whelk magic had come in handy more times than I could count and in interesting ways I had never expected. The inability to sleep could damage a person far worse than a sword or a pistol.

On the seventh night, Adelgis came out of Ryker's room, quietly shut the door, and then said, "I crafted him dreams of his home, but this time he desired to be a bird. He wanted the ability to fly and see everything from overhead."

"You made him into a bird?" I whispered, fearful I would wake Ryker, even though I knew in my gut that Adelgis's magic put individuals into a *deep* sleep.

"That's right."

"You can make people into *animals*?"

"I gave you dreams where you were someone else." Adelgis shrugged. "But I never knew I could make people animals until Ryker started asking for all kinds. First a horse, then a salmon, and now, like I said, a bird."

"Interesting."

I didn't know why, but my mind immediately went back to Atty. Could I have a dream from her perspective? Perhaps then I could understand her better—maybe see her rationale for wanting to distance herself from me when all I wanted was to help.

Adelgis lifted an eyebrow. "Volke... You continue to have new, and somewhat fascinating, thoughts."

I swear my face grew so hot, it almost caught fire. Holding my breath, I pivoted and faced away from him, even though I knew that wouldn't conceal my thoughts.

"I'm sorry," I muttered. "I just..." I swept a hand through my hair in one quick motion. "I think I need some advice."

"Regarding?"

"Atty." Clenching my jaw, I turned back to face him. "But you can hear my thoughts. You knew that already, didn't you?"

"I've been trying to pretend that I don't hear people's thoughts," Adelgis muttered. He sighed and stared at the floor. "I ask questions, even if I already know the answer, or engage people in mundane conversation, all in an attempt to seem more... *normal*."

"Why?" I asked. "You don't need to pretend around us."

"Most people avoid me. Well, except for you and Fain."

I crossed my arms and narrowed my eyes. Why would anyone avoid Adelgis? I knew the answer before I was finished with the thought. Reading someone's thoughts was a violation of their privacy, and I was certain most people didn't appreciate it. It pained me to hear their solution was simply to avoid him.

"I heard from your thoughts that you want to ask people for advice regarding relationships," Adelgis said as he brought his gaze up to meet mine. "But I was hoping you'd give me advice for appearing personable."

"Me?" I balked. "Why?"

"Most people around the guild have positive thoughts about you."

"Uh..."

I tried to think of positive moments and interactions—or any reason why the other arcanists would think fondly of me—but I found it difficult to concentrate when I had so much on my mind. Couldn't Adelgis hear my thoughts? Surely, he already knew my advice, or at least my experiences.

"Should I smile more?" Adelgis asked. He rubbed at his thin cheeks. "People think I'm creepy when I smile."

When Adelgis smiled, it came across as forced and without passion or mirth. *Creepy* was the perfect word—it was the smile of someone who was about to murder you and then eat your organs raw.

Adelgis's smile melted into a frown. "That was harsh," he muttered. "*Murderer* is hardly the look I'm going for."

"I'm sorry," I said, sheepish in all regards. "But perhaps you should just stick with what you're good at: information. People will come to you if they think you're a wellspring of knowledge. And you are."

He rubbed at his smooth chin. "You think so?"

"Yeah. You're the son of Theasin Venrover, one of the most famous artificers of all time, even if he is a snake in the grass. You've always had answers and wisdom for me in the past. I think if you provide that to people, you'll find yourself approached by all sorts of individuals."

Adelgis mulled over my comment for a long moment. Then he replied, "Thank you, Volke. I think that's a fantastic suggestion."

"No problem."

Then, with all the awkwardness of a blind man searching through a glass maker's shop, Adelgis placed a hand on my shoulder and squeezed. "I'm sorry. I don't have any romantic advice. I've never been intimate with anyone."

"Uh... that's fine."

Adelgis half-smiled—more natural than his forced version. "Perhaps you should ask Captain Devlin. I hear he's quite talented with the ladies."

On the tenth day of our trip, I awoke early to do my training.

Still, Atty hadn't wanted to see me.

When not guarding Ryker, I spent most of my days with Illia, Hexa, or Evianna, and sometimes even a combination of the three. I had wanted to master my eclipse aura, but I couldn't focus on that when I was with Evianna. She insisted on training for every second of the day, and she wanted me there to make sure she mastered the proper technique.

With Illia, I practiced my manipulation. While I used the shadows in small and dexterous amounts, Illia used her rizzel magic to manipulate gravity. Floating and pinning things to the ground seemed a useful ability, but Illia's problem came from using her power at a distance. With her missing eye, Illia had difficulty with depth perception, so anything more than fifty feet away was a struggle for her.

The only time I had to train on my aura was with Hexa, surprisingly enough. She had taken to physical training in the morning and spiritual training in the afternoon. I had never known her to be an individual of great focus, but she had taken it upon herself to hone her thoughts by sitting in quiet places around the shell of the atlas turtle, her hydra eldrin by her side at all times.

I sat in the shade of the sole tree next to the pond. White blossoms occasionally wafted away on the wind, creating a tranquil scene. It helped me control my inner thoughts and emotions. I wanted to recreate the feeling I'd had when I had created a perfect eclipse aura while fighting the Second Ascension—that moment Luthair had become true form—but it was difficult to even articulate that feeling of overwhelming potential and power.

Raisen's four heads slept in a curled-up position, his necks wrapped around his fat body. When they inhaled, it sounded like four tiny whistles. When they exhaled, it was a hiss. It created an odd symphony of sleep.

Hexa exhaled, drawing me out of my own meditation.

"Are you okay?" I asked.

Hexa swept back her curly mane of cinnamon hair. "This isn't working. I'm just getting tired." She glared at her hydra eldrin. "Raisen gets to sleep. Why can't I?"

"You have to focus on your magic overflowing out of you," I said.

"Yeah, I got it." Hexa rolled her eyes. "It's just difficult not to have my *consciousness* overflow out of me."

I glanced at her hydra and then back to her. "What kind of aura do you create?"

"Hydra arcanists create an *immortality* aura," Hexa said, her words a mix of matter-of-fact and pride. "The arcanist and their eldrin can live so long as the other does, and all injuries regenerate five times faster than in most magical creatures. And, if Raisen were to lose any of his heads, they would grow right back!"

I lifted an eyebrow. "That sounds amazingly useful."

"It is... So long as your eldrin is nearby." Hexa slumped her shoulders. "Raisen is almost too big for me to be carrying around. I'm going to have to start leaving him at the guild or something. And if he's too far away, my magic will be weaker, and I won't be able to create my aura."

"I see," I muttered. Then I turned my gaze to the grass, wondering if my current mental state was preventing me from achieving the perfect eclipse aura.

"Why aren't you training with Atty?" Hexa asked me out of nowhere. "Not even the abyssal hells would keep me from a cute girl who wanted to be mine. Whatever problems you two have, you should get over them."

Everyone knew—of course they did. No problems remained personal in the Frith Guild, not when everyone worked, trained, and spoke to everyone else.

"It's not a problem," I said through gritted teeth. "She just wants time to herself to focus on her magic."

"You mean... like we're doing right now?" Hexa motioned to the immediate area. "This *focusing* we're doing *together*?"

I sighed. "Look, I don't know what to say. Atty made it clear she didn't want me around."

"Hey," Hexa said. Then she placed a hand on my shoulder and squeezed. She had a surprisingly strong grip. "You've always been there for me, Volke. Even though you're an islander, and I'm from the mainland, and despite the fact that you're kinda rigid and not as fun as others... You've always been there for me. Offering advice. Helping me out of problems."

"Okay," I muttered. "Well, I appreciate—"

"Let me give you some advice," Hexa interjected as she held up a single finger. "Just keep spending time with her. Don't take no for an answer. Wear her down and win her through the sheer force of your will."

"Uh..." I rubbed at the back of my neck. "Listen. I think you might be confusing advice for combat with advice for romance."

"Pfft." Hexa dismissively waved away my comment. "Combat and romance *are* the same thing, don't you know? You have to press forward no matter what." She flexed her scarred arms. "That's how you bond with a hydra, by the way. Impressing them with your grit! I'm sure Atty will appreciate your assertiveness."

Although Hexa meant well, I didn't agree with her plan of action. Additionally, I didn't like the idea of *wearing someone down* just so they would spend time with me. None of the tales of ancient arcanists involved them forcing their company onto someone else. And not only that, but I could never imagine Gravekeeper William—my standard for proper behavior—doing such a thing. He would find it rude and inappropriate.

"I'll think about it," I said, opting to avoid telling Hexa I outright disagreed. She was just trying to help—no need to get into an argument about it.

Hexa nodded and then glared at the grass swaying all around us. "I need to follow my own advice so that I learn this aura faster."

35

ADVICE

Sixteen days into the trek and my routine had solidified.
In the morning, I slept. In the afternoon, I trained. In the evening, I guarded Ryker. Very little deterred me from this schedule, but occasionally, I took a small chunk of time to deviate to something else.

Today, I decided to see Zaxis and the others affected by the arcane plague. While other arcanists were forbidden to interact with them, my true form eldrin prevented me from contracting the plague, so there was no need to fear.

When I entered the library, the first thing I noticed was the many piles of soot that had been swept into the corners. It took me a short moment to catch the culprit—Forsythe sat on top of a nearby bookshelf, his flame body flickering under his feathers. Whenever he moved, even to just scratch at his leg, more soot wafted to the floor.

A young woman walked by and quickly swept it away.

Forsythe turned his heron-like head in my direction the moment I headed for the back of the library.

"Volke," he said as he half-spread his wings. "You came to visit!"

I nodded. "Why are you here, though? Shouldn't you be far away from Zaxis?"

If an arcanist's eldrin caught the plague, it was only a matter of days

—perhaps hours—before they lost themselves to the madness permanently.

"I can't leave Zaxis," Forsythe replied, his wings drooping. "I can't see him, either... but I want him to know I never left his side. We're in this together, no matter what."

"I'm sure he appreciates it," I said.

Then I continued on my way, my thoughts dwelling on Forsythe's dedication. Once I had passed several bookshelves, I glanced at the shadows between books.

"Luthair, what if Zaxis isn't all right?" I whispered. "What do you think Forsythe will do?"

"Kill himself to save his arcanist," Luthair replied, his tone cold and serious.

"Even if Zaxis told him not to?"

"Phoenixes are noble creatures of healing and fire. I am certain that Forsythe will take action before he allows his arcanist to come to harm."

That was what I had feared. Few things were worse than an arcanist losing their eldrin, and I could only imagine how Zaxis would take that.

I reached the door at the far end of the library and opened it without knocking. Originally, it had been a room for studying and unfurling large scrolls. A gigantic table ran the length of the rectangular room, accompanied by chairs. At least fifty people could sit at that table, but it had been pushed up against the wall to make room for cots. The plague-tainted arcanists had spent the last sixteen days making this space their home. Some cots were even "decorated" with utensils and plates from the guild kitchen.

And while some of the arcanists sat around, their shoulders slumped and their heads hung, Zaxis was too busy training to be woebegone. He stood near the door, his fists up, his gaze intensely focused on the wall. He threw shadow punches, practicing his breathing and form. For each strike he threw, he followed up with another in a swift and fluid motion, much like a powerful river torrent.

Sweat flecked off his arms and dappled his salamander-scale armor. He practically lived in that outfit. It wouldn't hurt him to leave it off for extended periods of time.

I waited on the sidelines, watching his punches with a keen eye. It didn't take long for Zaxis to notice my presence, and when he did, he stopped mid-throw and then slowly turned his head to face me. His red hair, weighed down by sweat, had been slicked back.

"What're you doing here?" Zaxis asked, gruff.

I sarcastically panned my gaze over the room. "Well, I came to check on a few friends of mine. Specifically, Left Chair, Right Chair, and Long John the Table. I wanted to make sure they hadn't gotten scuffed."

Zaxis lowered his hands and then faced me fully, his scale armor glistening. "You know nothing has happened to us since they locked us in this room. And the plague takes way longer to affect an arcanist—we still have time, *if* we're still infected. You don't have to check in on anyone."

"Doesn't mean I don't worry," I said with a shrug. "About the furniture, obviously."

"Everything here is fine." He turned away and huffed.

"Illia also asked me to check on things since she's not allowed in here."

Although Zaxis was already pink in the face from training, he grew slightly redder. "Yeah, well, tell her that Long John the Table is sick of being cooped up in this room." He gave me an irritated sideways glance. "And tell her that Right Chair and Left Chair miss her. And Nicholin, too, dammit."

I couldn't help but chuckle. Then I slipped my hands in my pockets. "Are you okay? Really? You seem stressed. We're almost to Millatin."

Zaxis let out a long exhale and then sauntered over to the wall in order to lean against it. His phoenix healing magic allowed him to recover from training far easier and faster than other arcanists, but he still needed *some* sort of rest.

"I'm fine," he said, curt. Then he motioned to the others. "Better than these guys. Maybe you should quote them the Pillar. Something about optimism, or not giving up, or some phrase like that."

I nodded. "Maybe I will."

"And I do miss Illia."

"She doesn't like to admit it, but I can tell she's really worried about you," I said, shoving my hands into my trouser pockets. "Which, uh, reminds me. Do you mind if I ask you a question?"

Zaxis slowly narrowed his eyes into a suspicious glower. "What's this about?"

"Well..."

I didn't know why, but the thought of asking Zaxis about romance struck me as more awkward and terrible than asking anyone else. We were the same age and from the same island—whatever he knew, I should have known. Asking him was admitting a weakness, at a certain level. I had somehow fallen behind.

"Out with it," Zaxis growled. "The chairs and I have a lot of practicing to get done."

"Have you and Illia had any, uh, disagreements or anything?" I asked, my words coming out painfully deliberate. "Something you had to work through?"

Zaxis pushed away from the wall and stepped close. He grabbed the collar of my shirt, his grip twisting into the fabric. I hadn't been prepared to fight, but my whole body tensed in an instant.

"Is this about the night on the *Sun Chaser*?" Zaxis whispered. "Because I told Illia that was a fluke—it's never happened to me before or after."

"W-what?" I stammered as I jerked out of his grip. "*No!* I have no idea what you're talking about—and I don't want to know, either. I just meant, that, well—I need advice! Atty has been distancing herself from me lately."

Zaxis stared for a long moment, his glare shifting into a bemused expression. "Wait, *you're* having problems?"

"Yeah," I murmured, glancing around. "Well, *maybe*. I'm not sure."

"You're the one who helped me get with Illia."

"Getting together with someone isn't my problem, trust me."

Somehow, even though I had never intended it, four women had all indicated they were interested in my affection. It wasn't finding someone interested that was the problem—it was the part that all the fairy tales glossed over. What happened during the course of the relationship? Should I push to change things? Let Atty do as she pleased? Help her like I think a couple should help each other? I didn't know. And why didn't anyone else?

Zaxis crossed his arms over his scaled chest plate. "What's the problem?"

"Atty said I'm a distraction," I muttered. "She wants me to stay away. What do you think I should do?"

"Do whatever she says," Zaxis replied without a second's hesitation. Then he shrugged. "She'll eventually come back around, once she's done with whatever she needs to do."

"Why do you say that?"

"Because you *are* a distraction," Zaxis quipped. "An irritating one at times, too."

I smacked myself in the face with my own palm and then dragged it over my nose and mouth, silently cursing the abyssal hells for all the bad luck they had bestowed on me in my life. I had known asking Zaxis was a terrible idea, yet I had done it anyway. What had possessed me to do this?

"You're no help," I said as I turned on my heel. "Forget I even came here."

Zaxis grabbed my shoulder and held me back, his strength startling. "Wait."

"What?" I barked.

He turned me half around and glowered. "You really came here just to ask my advice?"

"Unfortunately," I muttered. "Clearly I had a lapse in judgment."

The other arcanists in the room never attempted to join our conversation. They remained off to the side, low on energy and willpower, sitting on the floor and murmuring to each other as though they were planning a funeral.

Zaxis kept his hand on my shoulder. He exhaled and then said, "Look, I've known Atty for a long time. She likes you. If she said you're a distraction, it's probably because she's concerned about her family. That's the only other thing she ever really talks about. So, you shouldn't be too worried, got it? She wants to be with you."

"I wasn't worried about her not wanting to be with me." I moved Zaxis's hand off my shoulder. "I was worried that I wasn't being a supportive partner. Or that she doesn't trust me. Or that perhaps she doesn't think she can rely on me."

The words seemed to take a minute to sink into Zaxis's head. When he finished mulling over it all, he rubbed the side of his nose with his thumb. "Huh. Right. Well, I don't know about any of that."

"That's it?" I asked, lifting an eyebrow.

"Yeah. I don't know." Zaxis relaxed a bit. "And I'm sorry about that. I wanted to help you—to make up for you helping me so many times—but I'm not the man for this. I like to punch problems into submission, both literally and metaphorically."

I snorted back a laugh. "Ah. That makes sense." And it was shockingly honest for someone like Zaxis. "I appreciate your attempting to help."

"Sorry I couldn't do more." Zaxis patted me on the elbow. "But I'm pretty sure she'll come around."

Twenty days into our trek.

In fifteen more days, we'd arrive at our destination.

Atlas turtles swam through rough ocean waves with little difficulty, and when I trained outside, a small piece of me kept an eye on the waters. Living on an island, it was important to keep track of the weather. Storms could arise in a few short hours, and the vastness of the ocean meant tsunami waves could wash ashore at any time.

But Gentel didn't need to worry about that. If waves ever got near her turtle shell—and the guild manor house—a barrier of magic appeared around her entire body. Even on days when only the winds were rough, Gentel would use her magic to make sure the trek was pleasant for all the arcanists living on her back.

Evianna and I trained near the pond. She insisted on practicing with a blade first then adding magic to the equation.

"Lyvia said people need to master the fundamentals," Evianna stated. "She said amateurs were the people who thought they were above *menial* training."

She thrust the practice blade ten times, making sure to keep her footwork proper and her arm up. I watched with a critical eye, ready to point out anything questionable, but the time to do so never came.

Evianna had her eyebrows knitted in deep concentration and only seemed to relax between practice sessions.

Using the back of her arm, Evianna wiped the sweat from her brow. "How was that?"

"Good," I said. "Nice form."

Evianna pivoted on her heel in order to face me. "And?"

"And what?" I asked.

"And *what else*? What should I do to improve?"

"Uh, well, your technique was perfect as far as I could tell."

Evianna swished back her white braid and then held her head high. "Volke, as the arcanist responsible for my training, I need you to improve your pedagogical skills."

I placed my hands on my hips, verging on baffled. "Why do you say that?"

"Because having a *nice form* and *perfect technique* on some practice thrusts doesn't make me a master swordswoman." She held up her practice blade—the heavy wood dulled on the edges, but polished smooth—and then stared at the tip. "You need to give me more instruction to help me achieve that goal. Should I do more thrusts? Should I try on a practice dummy now? Should I spar with a partner? Should I hone my body through exercise so that I can wield a heavier weapon?"

"I..."

"You're clearly talented with a sword," Evianna continued, lowering her practice weapon. "So I have no doubt you have the capability to help me improve, but the ability to instruct others is a completely different skillset."

Although Evianna was younger and less experienced than me when it came to combat, she brought up several crucial points I hadn't yet considered when it came to her training. Typically, I relied on Master Zelfree to tell me where I needed to improve, and I clearly had to step into that role if I was going to be there for Evianna. Why hadn't I been doing that from the beginning?

On the other hand, Master Zelfree only wanted my help when it came to the knightmare side of Evianna's training. He had said he would handle the rest—but ever since the attack on the Isle of Ruma, he had been preoccupied with Ryker's safety. It was an understandable deviation, so I couldn't fault him, but at the same time, I hadn't even mentally prepared myself for being Evianna's sole teacher in *all* things.

But our enemies didn't care about our excuses or what obstacles we have to face. I couldn't explain to the Second Ascension that they needed to go easier on Evianna because she hadn't been trained properly yet. I just had to make sure this was done. I had to rise to the challenge—my own training *and* Evianna's. There was no other choice.

"I apologize, Princess Evianna," I said as I offered her a formal bow. "I'll strive to improve as an instructor."

Her cheeks flushed, and then she pursed her lips. "Hm. Well, given your knightly status, and many heroic deeds, I'll deign to forget this. But just this once."

I straightened my posture and smirked. "Too kind."

She fidgeted with the hilt of her practice blade, her flustered expression shifting into awkward glances around the grassy hill that made up the shell of the atlas turtle. Her gaze landed on Mesos and her giant roc wings that were outstretched. The golden feathers caught the afternoon sun just right, shimmering like polished metal.

"What is that airship captain doing?" Evianna asked, pointing to a man under Mesos's wing.

It was Captain Devlin—and he was doing *something* under his roc eldrin. But what? I couldn't make it out, not at our distance some 300 feet away. He moved around with some energy, but Mesos's wing was so large it could hide a small dinghy with ease.

"I'll go ask," I said.

"I'll go with you." Evianna leapt to my side. "Just in case." She tucked her practice blade into her belt, hanging it on her side by the hilt.

Her shadow shifted around her feet as the two of us walked across the emerald grass, toward Captain Devlin. Mesos kept her eyes closed as her arcanist shuffled around under her wings. She lifted her head and tilted it back, her sharp beak as visible as the azure sky.

When Evianna and I drew close, Mesos snapped open her eyes and stared at me with an unnerving focus. I tensed as I took the last few steps, hoping I wasn't interrupting anything important.

"Captain Devlin?" I asked.

"Yeah?" he called out, his hands in Mesos's chest feathers, his attention locked onto his work. "What is it, lad?"

"Do you need help with anything?"

He glanced over his shoulder and narrowed his eyes. He had the face of a hardened sailor, unafraid of storms and monsters. "Help me with anything? *Help me?* No. No one can help you when fate herself decides she wants your damn airship." He huffed and returned his attention to his roc eldrin. "She came for it *twice.* Not once. Twice. First with a blasted thunderbird, and now *this?* Hmpf." He muttered a few more curses under his breath before ending with, "Why did I even bother rebuilding the damn thing in the first place? Why even bother?"

"Volke meant to ask *what're you doing*," Evianna said, her tone matter-of-fact. "He understands you're upset about your airship."

Mesos tilted her head to the side like only a bird could. Captain Devlin, on the other hand, just chortled. "I'm helping my roc preen herself, lass. These feathers are massive and get dirty with ease. Mesos needs help cleaning them, so here I am. Plus, any feathers I collect I can use for trinket creation in the future, ya see." He patted a pouch hanging from his belt. Gold feathers stuck out from the top.

"Why aren't you trying to rebuild the airship instead?" Evianna demanded. "You can't let the Second Ascension win by giving up."

I almost grabbed her by the arm and dragged her away from the roc out of sheer embarrassment. Why would she ever say such a thing?

Captain Devlin belted out a quick, but boisterous, laugh. He rubbed his face with the back of his arm and then returned to sifting through Mesos's feathers, untangling some and cleaning others. "I need star shards, lass. And material. Most of the *Sun Chaser* sunk to the depths, so now I have to wait till we reach Millatin before any repairs can be made."

The remains of the ship—or what could be salvaged, at least—were being dragged behind Gentel, tossing and swaying in the wake of her giant turtle body. We still had the majority of a ship, but it wouldn't fly or even sail without major repairs.

"We understand," I said. "Crafting an airship is a difficult undertaking."

"Hm. It is—but I intend to rebuild her." Devlin finished with Mesos's chest and then shifted his focus to her fluffed-up neck. "No one keeps

Devlin grounded. Mesos and I are born to soar through the sky, and there aren't any dastards or guilds that can stop us."

He spoke each word as though it were a promise to a longtime friend.

"And who's helping you?" Evianna asked. Then she crossed her arms. "Don't you have several arcanists in your crew? Where are they?"

"Busy," Devlin replied, curt.

"What about your lover? Your significant other should be here with you, helping."

Mesos chuckled, her breaths coming out as bird-like whistles.

"Enough from you," Devlin hissed to his eldrin.

His roc quieted herself without elaborating, though a glint of amusement still shone in her eyes.

"You have no one?" Evianna asked, undeterred from her path to pester Devlin.

Unable to take this anymore, I turned to her. "Evianna, would you mind finding Biyu? She's Devlin's cabin girl. Her book has details on the *Sun Chaser*, and perhaps some of your knightmare training can involve finding components for the airship."

Technically, Master Zelfree had had us find apples when I had been an apprentice. It had been an attempt to help us master our magic for non-combat purposes, and I still thought fondly of the event from time to time. Perhaps Evianna could learn some essential skills from locating mystical parts or star shards.

"Very well," Evianna said, her bluish-purple eyes hardening with determination. "I will find Cabin Girl Biyu and return at once." Without another word, Evianna stepped into the shadows and disappeared into the darkness.

Devlin let out a long exhale as Evianna's shadow traveled straight for the guild manor house.

"That lass is a handful," he muttered. "I'm surprised you train with her day in and day out without needing a rest."

"I find her resolve invigorating," I said.

"Is that right?" Captain Devlin stroked his chinstrap beard. *"Resolve* is a nice way of puttin' it."

Ocean winds whipped by, rustling the leaves of the sole tree and creating a chorus through the grass across the field. Mesos puffed her feathers and then relaxed. I suspected she missed being in the air with the wind as her constant companion.

"Uh," I said, breaking the silence between us. I stared at the ground, unable to find the words for my question.

"What is it, lad?" Devlin asked. "You got somethin' in your throat?"

"I was wondering if I could ask your advice on something."

Both of Devlin's eyebrows lifted toward his tricorn hat. "Oh? Aren't you Zelfree's apprentice? You aren't askin' him?"

"Well, I'm a journeyman now... and I *did* try asking him, but he's had terrible luck with relationships."

Mesos cried out another laugh, her eagle-voice piercing. I didn't know why, but she definitely found the whole exchange amusing.

Captain Devlin did not, however. He frowned deep and just glowered at me. Even his posture stiffened, as though he were preparing to throw a punch.

"Listen," he said, his teeth gritted. "Zelfree isn't the only one who's had a rough time, got it? I don't need no young arcanists comin' up to me, askin' me question about things that aren't any of their damn business."

I nervously chuckled. "Uh, yeah, well, I wasn't planning on asking about *your* relationships. I meant, I wanted advice on how to tell someone that you want to help them, even though they think you're a distraction."

Devlin scoffed and rolled his eyes. After a long moment of silent contemplation, he finally softened a bit and then placed a hand on my shoulder. He tightened his grip as he spoke. "By the abyssal hells—no one can help you in these waters, lad. You have to navigate them with trust and rely on tenacity as your first mate. No route is the same, and no boat has the same problems as the last, no matter how similar they may sound. You either stay here and sink, or you keep moving forward to the port city of paradise."

His words sunk in deep, and for a second, I didn't know how to respond.

"Uh," I murmured. "Thank you. That was... poetic and insightful. I hadn't thought of things that way."

Devlin released my shoulder. "Don't bother thanking me. That's the standard advice I give everyone, no matter the problem." Then he shrugged, blasé about everything. "People read into it whatever they want to see. You're your own best adviser."

Somehow, even though he had admitted his previous advice had been uninspired, his explanation left me once again dwelling on the wisdom.

"Still," I muttered. "Thank you for this."

"Don't worry about it." He pointed to the guild house. "You can make it up to me by making sure your little white-haired harpy doesn't come over asking about my *lovers* anymore, understand me?"

THE GREAT CITY-STATE OF MILLATIN

D ay thirty of our journey.
We only had five days left before we reached our destination.
At night, while most of the guild slept, I spent my time guarding Ryker's room and also reading a book about the dock city, Millatin. I had found it in the guild library and was shocked to see the history stretched back to its very founding. It was more flowery and poetic than a standard historical recounting, but it fascinated me nonetheless.

It read:

Millenia ago, when the first men bonded with mystical creatures, there existed an island of rock. This island housed a beautiful, and legendary, freshwater spring. So pure were its contents that whoever sipped of the water would shed away all fatigue.

After the sky shattered, and star shards rained to the ground, the island was forever changed. A god-creature was born from those pure waters—so gorgeous and radiant that some found it difficult to look upon her.

. . .

I stopped reading for a moment and recalled my time in the Argo Empire. God-creatures were only born during the *turning of an age*— which was just a fancy term for when a new fundamental change in magic occurred. Star shards raining from the sky had been the first age. And now the arcane plague was the second. The god-creatures and their powerful arcanists were destined to usher humanity through the turbulent times, and once the problems were solved, they were all to be destroyed by the devastating apoch dragon.

I flipped the page and continued reading.

The god-creature was none other than the scylla waters, a powerful naiad—a water nymph without equal or compare. She called herself Millatin de Viennois and would only bond with a hero who possessed both the appropriate runestone and the courage to face the depths of her spring.

It excited me to learn that Millatin was a city named after the god-creature herself. From what I could remember of old fairy tales, the scylla waters was such a powerful nymph that she could control all other nymphs, regardless of their type or abilities.

Still interested to learn the rest of the history, I turned the page.

On the day of bonding, Millatin de Viennois rewarded her new god-arcanist by blessing the island. She created a natural port in the form of a bay, lifted the rocks around the edge of the island for defenses, and made the land fertile enough for habitation. Her freshwater spring, once untouched, became the heart of the entire area, flowing with magic that fed into the island and transformed it into the city-state that it has now become.

Then the prelude ended, and a more detailed account of modern history began. It made me curious—so little was known about the previous god-creatures. Even this segment of the book was only three pages of information, and none of it mentioned anything important, like who had bonded with the scylla waters or where they had gone after the founding of Millatin the city.

I closed the book and held it close, wondering where the new scylla waters would appear. Would it be the same place? Would it be a different spring entirely? If I found the location of one god-creature in this random history book, could I find others? Had Guildmaster Eventide found this information yet?

"Are you okay?" someone asked.

I pushed off the wall and tensed, my chest twisting into a knot of dread when I saw no one in the hallway with me. I was supposed to be watching Ryker! I couldn't afford to let my mind wander like that.

Fain appeared from thin air as his invisibility dropped. His wendigo, Wraith, also appeared, his sleek, gray wolf fur shimmering in the lantern light. The skull over Wraith's face didn't look quite as elegant, however. Dark shadows created from the odd angle of the lantern created a scary visage—which was justified, considering that wendigo were man-eaters who craved the flesh of others.

I let out a long exhale. "I'm fine. Just... preoccupied."

"I've been watching you for the last two weeks," Fain said, his voice low. He tucked his frostbitten hands into the pockets of his trousers. "You keep yourself inordinately busy."

"I have to. There's too much riding on this."

Fain replied with a curt nod. "I've been training whenever there's a spare moment, but I've also been keeping an eye on you and Evianna."

I opened my mouth to say something, but then stopped midway. After a moment of confusion, I asked, "Why me and Evianna?"

For a long while, Fain didn't say anything.

I turned my attention to Wraith. The wendigo sat down and twitched his canine ears. But he also said nothing.

"Has something happened?" I asked, my voice low.

"I'm a wendigo arcanist," Fain muttered as he reached up with one of his blackened fingers and touched the mark on his forehead. The wendigo laced around the star made for a menacing image. "Wendigo arcanists can... I don't know how to describe this... They feel death?"

"What do you mean?"

Wraith shook his head. "It means our magic can sometimes sense those with strong auras of death. Either they kill people—or perhaps they, themselves, are close to death."

From what I could remember, wendigo were mystical creatures who lived in the snow to the north. They waited for travelers to lose their way before stalking them into the cold unknowns and slowly killing them over the course of several days. Wendigo were agents of death, at a certain level, but I never knew they could sense it.

"I'm not sure if I'm even sensing death," Fain said with a shrug. "I just know that... I sense something about you. Something that wasn't there before. Same with Evianna. I'm... concerned."

"Luthair," I said.

The shadows of the hall stirred at the sound of my voice. A moment later, Luthair rose from the darkness, his star-marked cape catching the light and sparkling. His inky armor practically spilled to the floor, but it never made a mess—it just flowed like a never-ending black waterfall.

"Yes, my arcanist?" Luthair asked, his voice echoing inside the empty helmet of his body.

"My ability to sense lies... Is that similar to Fain's death sense?"

"No." Luthair motioned to the full plate of his body. "From what I can determine, our newfound ability to detect falsehoods has been born of my true form. Wendigo of a certain age always have the ability to sense death and rot—it is in their magics and nature."

"You know about that?"

Luthair slowly nodded. "Mathis hunted down a few dastard wendigo arcanists. He lured one out of their hidden lair by using the dying body of the other."

I wanted to question Luthair regarding this ability, but I couldn't bring myself to stop dwelling on the situation. If Fain *could* sense death, why did he sense it with me and Evianna? I touched my chest, pressed hard through my shirt, and felt no pain. Then I proceeded to pat myself down, fearing I had some sort of unknown injury or sickness.

"Do you know how someone will die?" I asked, my brow furrowed.

Fain shook his head. "No. It's not like that. Think of it more like... a smell. I smell death about you. Maybe it's yours. Maybe it's someone else's. But it's there."

"So, this isn't necessarily a bad thing?"

Fain shrugged. "Like I said—I've just been concerned. That's why I'm keeping an eye on you two. I asked Moonbeam to do the same."

I snorted back a laugh. I sometimes forgot Adelgis's nickname.

"Thank you," I said. "I really appreciate it."

Although Fain and I didn't share many moments together, he replied with a half-smile and nod, and it reminded me of the time he had agreed to stay by my side, even while I had been infected with the plague. Even now, when I hadn't realized anything was wrong, he had been watching out and protecting me—a true friend, vigilant, even without acknowledgement.

Day thirty-three of thirty-five.

While Evianna trained with her practice sword, I continued to read about the city-state of Millatin. Apparently, the massive rocky island was home to nests of mermen and mermaids, as well as the breeding grounds for many nymphs.

Most people didn't know, but mermaids and nymphs were similar in many ways. They both had the lower bodies of aquatic creatures, complete with scales and fins. They both had the upper bodies of young women, though their skin often shimmered with an inner sheen. And they both had hair that flowed and rippled like thick kelp caught in a rough current.

Their differences were few. Mermaids lived in saltwater, whereas nymphs lived in fresh water. Mermaids created nests and raised young, but nymphs were fable born—springing to life whenever a body of fresh water went 100 days without being disturbed. It sounded simple, but apparently even a tiny insect could interfere with the magic that called a nymph into existence.

I flipped through the pages of the book, fascinated by the many drawings of the city and surrounding territory. Depictions of mermen swimming through the waves caught my eye. While mermaids were women, mermen were male, but they also had horns made of coral reef. Everyone from the islands knew coral was as sharp as shattered glass, and I wondered if the horns of a merman were just as painful.

"There it is! *There it is!*"

The random shouting drew my attention away from the book. Evianna stopped her practice and stared out across the glittering ocean.

"Look there," she said with a gasp. Then she waved at the shadows. "Layshl! You look, too!"

The shadows swirled and coalesced into the partial armor of Layshl, complete with wing-like cape. The dragon details on the body reminded me of the late queen of the Argo Empire.

I didn't pay attention long, however. The city-state of Millatin dominated the horizon with its jagged cliff faces and giant port bay. Massive steel chains hung from both sides of the bay mouth, ready to be lifted should there be an invasion of ships. Each link of the chains was larger than most carriages, horses included, and I knew only an arcanist could create such colossal objects.

It was difficult to see the city proper—it was all tucked away behind the stoneface defenses. The city had to be huge, however. There were at least three dozen ships in the bay, which meant Millatin was likely equipped to handle the influx of individuals.

If three dozen ships had arrived on the Isle of Ruma, all the food would have vanished, and there wouldn't have been room for half the sailors to sleep anywhere.

"It's so amazing," Evianna said as she placed a hand on her eldrin's cape. "Can't you just imagine all the—"

She caught her breath and stopped speaking.

I waited a few moments, wondering if she would ever pick up her thought, but the time never came. I glanced over, one eyebrow raised.

"Evianna?" I asked. "Is everything okay?"

She ran to my side, gripped my elbow, and then pointed. I followed the tip of her finger to a specific boat floating in the bay. It was a massive galleon, complete with three masts and eight sails. Three nautical flags waved from the center mast. Every ship had to have three flags for communication—one was for the ship's nation, one signified if they had arcanists aboard, and the last one was to communicate the state of emergency, if any.

The galleon that Evianna pointed at flew a flag with a red rose and black dragon intertwined, which meant it hailed from the Argo Empire.

The arcanist flag fluttered a bright gold, which meant there were, in fact, arcanists aboard the ship.

And finally, the last flag was a dull gray, indicating no emergency.

"That's the *Black Throne*," Evianna whispered. "It's the ship the royal family uses whenever they must travel across the ocean." Her hand trembled slightly, and I knew what she was trying to imply.

That wasn't a random ship from the Argo Empire.

That was her brother's personal ship.

The murderer and traitor, Prince Rishan, was in the city-state of Millatin.

37

KING RISHAN

R age boiled in my chest, threatening to consume my rational thoughts.

Prince Rishan—*King* Rishan now—was a man with no moral fiber in his being. He had killed Evianna's sister, then murdered the queen of the Argo Empire, and helped the Second Ascension gain tremendous power. I had been there when he had bonded with his eldrin, the legendary sovereign dragon.

And like Guildmaster Eventide and me, King Rishan had achieved his eldrin's true form.

There were few people in this world whom I thought beyond redemption, and King Rishan was one of them. When Evianna tightened her grip on my elbow, I knew she felt the same. But the sane part of me said it was a mistake to hunt King Rishan down while in Millatin. We weren't here for revenge. We were here to continue our journey to the world serpent.

Then it hit me.

Rishan and the Second Ascension were here for the same reason.

"But how?" I murmured aloud, lost in my own thoughts, unable to hear things around me as my focus tunneled. "How did they know to come here?"

Evianna shook my arm, drawing me out of my personal darkness. "Volke, look there. It's the Argo Empire elite naval forces."

She pointed to a grouping of three sailing ships. Two were *clippers*—fast vessels meant to maneuver around larger ships. The last was a *ship-of-the-line*—a massive ship with nearly a 100 cannons, meant to devastate the enemy by defeating them in a single run. All three boats had dragons carved into the sides, and on the bow—each made of ebony wood, black and frightening, marking them as distinctly different than all the other ships in the bay.

"Those are the ships meant to protect the *Black Throne*," Evianna whispered, her gaze never leaving the naval vessels. "Does that mean... Rishan intends to fight people while he's here?" After a long moment, she finally glanced up at me. "Do you think he knows where the world serpent is?"

"I don't know," I said, trying not to allow my dread to slip out with my words. "But even if he does, we have the jade runestone. He won't be able to get to it."

Evianna nodded along with my words. Then she took in a deep breath and squared her shoulders. "That's right. We'll stop him no matter what."

"And I will be by your side," Layshl said, her voice echoing from the darkness around Evianna's feet.

When I glanced to my own shadow, Luthair made himself visible by shifting the edges, fluttering them like the wings of crows. "We stand as one, my arcanist."

Luthair's reassurance quelled some of my rage. Although Rishan had a true form sovereign dragon, he had bonded with his eldrin after I had. I had the advantage of experience, but at the same time, dragons were mystical creatures beyond compare. They were stronger than knightmares, which meant Rishan's magic would have a lethal potency I couldn't ignore.

For several minutes, Evianna and I just stood and watched as our atlas turtle vessel drew closer and closer to the massive gates into the bay. The chains would stop ships, but I suspected Gentel could rip her way through them, if she so wanted. Although atlas turtles were not known for their offense, I suspected her barriers would hold against the chains, and her body was so massive there would be no stopping her momentum.

But she didn't attempt to enter the bay. Instead, Gentel slowed her speed and turned toward the massive cliff face. I wondered how the guild arcanists would make it to the city, but my confusion didn't last long. Small hopper ships left port and headed in our direction, no doubt to ferry individuals into the city. Were they friends of Eventide's? Or was this common practice for the city of Millatin?

Hopper ships were smaller and quick, and it didn't take long for the four city vessels to attach themselves to Gentel's fin. I didn't approach the sailing ships. I just watched from afar as Journeyman Reo and three other guild arcanists met with the hopper captains.

In theory, Captain Devlin could use his roc magic to control the winds and carry us over to Millatin, but I knew that would be risky. Millatin wasn't a single city in a nation of many—it was a *city-state*, meaning it maintained its own power and autonomy and answered to no one. The laws of Millatin were unique, and from what I had read, they didn't care for individuals who entered the city through unofficial means.

"Shall we head to the ships?" Evianna whispered, her gaze distant.

"Stay with me while we're in the city," I said. "Guildmaster Eventide said we need to find someone from the Huntsman Guild, and then afterward we'll use the Occult Compass to determine the best route toward our destination. This shouldn't take long."

And although she didn't respond for a long moment, Evianna eventually replied, "That's probably for the best."

The hopper ships were, in fact, official ferries for the city. Apparently, it was common for oversized vessels to stop outside the bay. Sailing ships and massive eldrin from the other side of the vast ocean would rest in Millatin before heading out, and the city now maintained the hoppers to carry crewmen and arcanists from these massive vessels all the way to port. It kept the bay clear of giant obstacles and allowed the city more control on who entered and when.

Unlike other cities I had entered, Millatin had a receiving area where everyone entering had to give their name, age, and occupation—it was a dark building with tiny windows and thick shutters. Counters lined both walls, and people were funneled between, creating a natural line where the city officials could ask questions. Arcanists were dealt with separately from the rest, and each one had to describe their eldrin, including their name.

When it came time for me to answer the questions, a short, elderly woman with bronze skin and black hair was the one to greet me from behind the counter.

"Name, sir arcanist?" she asked, her attention on her small book, her ink quill poised to write.

"Volke Savan," I said.

The woman wrote it down as fast as I could say it.

"Age?" she asked.

"Seventeen."

"Hm."

I didn't know why, but she wrote more down for my age than my name. I couldn't glimpse the notes she wrote, but I could see they were off to the margins.

"Occupation?" she asked.

"I'm an arcanist with the Frith Guild."

"And your eldrin?"

"A knightmare by the name of Luthair."

"Oh?" The woman glanced up, her black eyes half-glazed with age. "A knightmare arcanist hasn't come to port in over twelve years. So rare."

That was when she finally noticed my glowing arcanist mark. Her eyes went wide, and she furrowed her brow in shock. Unlike others, she didn't say anything. She just stared. Awkwardly.

I rubbed at the back of my neck. "Uh, well, if we're done here..."

"O-oh. Of course, sir arcanist. Welcome to the great city-state of Millatin." The woman bowed her head slightly, like most islanders, and I returned the gesture.

Before I could reunite with Evianna and keep her out of trouble while we were here, I heard the pop of teleportation. Illia and Nicholin appeared next to me. Perhaps on a different day, I wouldn't have been startled, but ever since I had laid eyes on the *Black Throne*, I hadn't been able to relax. The moment Illia and Nicholin appeared, I tensed and placed my hand on the hilt of my blade.

Nicholin perked up, his ears erect. "Did you see who was in the bay?" he asked. "I recognized the flags straight away."

"Are you okay, Volke?" Illia asked me. She placed a hand on my shoulder and squeezed tight. "You're not going to do anything rash, are you?"

I shook my head. "Now isn't the time for that. We have to protect Ryker, and we need to make it to..." I glanced around and opted for secrecy. "Our destination is too important."

Illia smirked. "I knew you'd stay focused." She ran a hand over her eye patch, and for a brief moment, I wondered if she was contemplating her own past rashness.

"I bet Illia you would charge the *Black Throne* under the darkness of your eclipse aura," Nicholin said with a sigh. "Now I've lost two gold leafs."

I smiled, though it was short-lived. Nicholin's levity always brightened my mood, but now wasn't the time. My smile died as fast as it had appeared.

"What was that?" someone said, their voice filled with shock.

"You heard me," Evianna said, her voice so distinct and haughty that I could recognize it in a crowd of thousands. "I will not repeat myself."

I turned around and caught sight of her with a Millatin official. She was being questioned, like all the other arcanists from the Frith Guild, but the man helping her was now standing close and hastily scratching notes in his tiny book.

"You're Evianna *Velleta?*" the man asked. "Sister to Rishan Velleta?"

Evianna didn't reply. She pursed her lips and then shot me a glance from across the room. Although I hadn't known her long, she was the type of person who wore her emotions for the world to see. She was worried—I could tell by her knitted eyebrows and the slight twitch of her lips.

Without waiting for an invitation, I walked through the crowd until I made it to her side. The closer I got, the more confident Evianna became. When I reached her side, her posture was just as straight as ever.

"I didn't arrive with my brother," Evianna stated. "And I'd prefer he not be informed of my presence."

The official—a non-arcanist man in his early sixties—brushed back his thinning white hair and nodded. "Of course. These are for official records only. I just assumed you were here for his wedding."

I caught my breath.

"Wedding?" Evianna asked, heat in her question. "Who is Rishan marrying?"

"Councilor Chandra Tavvin. It's been the talk of the city for weeks now. I assumed King Rishan's relatives would come pouring in from the four corners of the world, but so far there have been few guests to arrive..."

"A councilor?" I asked. "What kind of title is that?"

The Millatin official scowled in my general direction, but he didn't keep his eyes on me long. He returned his attention to Evianna as he replied, "Millatin is ruled by five councilors. Councilor Chandra is the youngest, but she's extremely talented. It doesn't surprise me she won the admiration of a *king*."

From what I knew about Rishan, he wasn't a man to love anything other than himself and power. Which meant this was more than likely a step in the Second Ascension's schemes. If they gained control of the council in Millatin, then the Second Ascension would have yet *another* location under their influence.

But again, I couldn't worry about that. The world serpent took top priority.

"May I go now?" Evianna asked.

"One moment," the man said. "I need your age and occupation."

"Fifteen, and I'm a knightmare arcanist of the Frith Guild."

"You're fourteen," I interjected.

Evianna clenched her jaw. "I'll be *fifteen* in four weeks."

"That means you're still fourteen for four more weeks."

The official ignored Evianna's icy glare and wrote the information down without further comment. Then he gave us both a quick bow of his head and moved on to the next arcanist. He continued to glance back at Evianna, however, even when we walked away to rejoin Illia.

Instead of waiting around in the dark office building, Illia tugged on my sleeve and then headed for the door. I followed, and Evianna chased after until we had passed through the heavy double doors and emerged inside the city, bathed in bright island light. The afternoon sun had never felt so good.

The city-state of Millatin stole my breath a moment later. The streets were massive—wider than in Thronehold, the capital of the Argo Empire. The cobblestone they used for the streets had been smoothed and fashioned into bricks, creating a uniform appearance, even if the colors of each stone were all a slightly different shade of gray.

The buildings were taller than most I had seen—some even seven stories tall! They cast long and harsh shadows, blocking out the island light, preventing some plants from growing around the buildings. The mood within the darkness was drearier than most.

And it wasn't just the dark shadows that gave the place its dour feel. Most buildings were made with dark woods, black stones, and blood-red roofs. The windowpanes were thick, greenish glass, adding to the gloomy and somewhat sickly atmosphere. The stench of the city wasn't as bad as I thought it would've been, probably thanks to the island winds, but the farther I walked into Millatin, the more I realized the streets were lined with grime and sewage.

The people were almost worse than the infrastructure. In Thronehold, the streets were patrolled by unicorn and pegasus arcanists. In Millatin... I wasn't sure who was a guard and who wasn't. Most people wore long coats and dark hats slung low, obscuring their forehead. Who was an arcanist and who wasn't? It was difficult to tell.

As I stepped out onto the street, a horse-drawn carriage raced by, kicking up sludge and splashing it on a man who had been standing to the side. Both the driver of the carriage and the man covered in muck yelled curses at each other.

"What a pleasant place," Illia muttered.

Evianna scrunched her nose. "Putrid. Who would live in such squalor?"

I panned my gaze over the tops of the buildings. Several places in the distance caught my eye, including a cathedral so massive, it practically pierced the clouds with its pointed roofs. Just the sight of it reminded me of Gregory Ruma—and his undead wife. I suspected I would never see cathedrals in the same way ever again.

Another carriage raced by. Were they in a hurry? This one splattered grime across a small grouping of individuals, two of whom were women, and both became rowdy and agitated.

"Let's escape this," Illia said, a hard look in her one eye.

She placed a hand on my shoulder and then Evianna's. Although it took Illia some hard concentration, the three of us popped out of existence and then reappeared a half second later. My feet didn't land straight, and I almost tumbled, but I managed to remain upright. Once I got my bearings, I realized the problem—we were on a roof overlooking the city. Not what I had been expecting. The slant and tiles of the roof made it difficult to stand straight.

"We probably won't be here long," Illia said as she squinted. "So we might as well get all our sightseeing in now."

Smoke rose from the smelting district of the city. Again, unlike Thronehold, and even New Norra, the city-state of Millatin wasn't well organized. The roads seemed to have no rhyme or reason, the buildings fluctuated wildly in height, and many parts of the city appeared cramped, as though too much had sprouted up at once there, even though there were plenty of other spaces they could've moved to.

While Illia and I examined our surroundings and enjoyed the sights, Evianna only had eyes for the bay port. She stared at the *Black Throne*, her focus unwavering. I wanted to tell her to let it go—to forget about it —but I knew that was impossible. It would've been like asking me to forget that the Dread Pirate Calisto had taken Illia's eye. It just wouldn't happen.

But then I got caught up in the watching as well. Something was happening on the *Black Throne*. A crowd had gathered in the port, and the pier where the galleon berthed was filled with individuals all throwing rice, paper, and shiny bits of pottery—most of which caught the sunlight and glinted.

"What's going on?" I asked.

"They're celebrating his engagement," Evianna murmured, her glare intense. "He must be with her right now."

"Well, as much as I hate to say this to you, I think it'd be best if—"

Before I could even finish my statement, Evianna stepped forward and disappeared into the shadows. Then she slithered away as a shade, straight off the roof of the building and straight for the docks with the *Black Throne*.

"Evianna!" I held out my hand.

But it was too late. She was already shadow-stepping across the rooftops to confront her brother.

38

THE GRIM REAPER ARCANIST

I gritted my teeth and leapt off the roof. Illia's one eye widened as I sailed down to the ground, and for a split second, I felt guilty for making her worry. I never hit the ground, however. With the fluidity of water, I dove into the darkness, disappearing from sight and using the shadows to travel across the roads and walkways of Millatin in the blink of an eye.

The tall buildings blotted out the light, which helped with my shadow travel. In a matter of seconds, I slithered all the way to the edge of the port, beyond the market and the stable for carriages. When I emerged, I took a deep breath—and then immediately regretted it. The pungent odor of rotting meat clogged my throat and threatened to choke me. Where and what was it? I glanced around, but the answer wasn't apparent. I blamed that on the crowds. It was too difficult to see anything, even the stones of the road.

Hundreds of people—perhaps thousands—swarmed the docks, all pushing and shoving their way closer to the pier with the *Black Throne*. They clumped together, like a river of human bodies, and spoke in excited tones. Most wanted to see the new king of the Argo Empire, but a fair number of people claimed they were here specifically to see Councilor Chandra.

I didn't know why, but the terrible smell didn't seem to bother the denizens of Millatin. None of them held back gags or covered their mouths and noses, like I had to. Were they used to this stench? Where was it coming from?

I shook the thought from my head. "Luthair. I need your help."

"Whatever you need, my arcanist," he said, his dark voice rising from the ground, strong enough to pierce through the commotion.

"Find Evianna. Stop her—bring her back."

"As you command."

Although I couldn't see him, I somehow knew Luthair had left.

With what little time I had, I pushed my way through the crowd, scanning the tops of people's heads, searching for any trace of Evianna's white hair. She wasn't tall—around five feet, five inches—but no one in the crowd had anything close to her unique and striking features. Most citizens of Millatin had shiny black hair, while a few had copper tresses so rust-red it looked like neglected metal.

"So exciting," someone said as I squeezed past.

"I can't believe the king of the Argo Empire would come here," another muttered.

"I heard he's handsome!"

"Councilor Chandra should count herself lucky."

Their fawning twisted my insides and made me sick. Did they know whom they were praising? Rishan was the worst kind of villain— someone who hid his black heart from the world and lived behind a veil of lawfulness. Such dastards were the worst to uproot. Everyone in the crowd thought him a hero, when in reality he'd willingly kill them all if it meant it would further his goals.

A wave of silence rippled through the crowd.

I tensed and turned in the direction they were staring. The *Black Throne* lowered a wide gangplank, and two unicorn arcanists—and their beautiful eldrin—walked down to the pier. The unicorn arcanists, both men with plate armor, didn't ride their unicorns, but instead walked at their side. The golden horns, as well as their hooves, glinted in the sunlight.

King Rishan was the next to walk down the gangplank, and I held my breath along with the denizens of Millatin.

Every time I had seen him in the past, it had been during extreme circumstances. Either he had been in a death match with his own sister, Lyvia, or he had been actively killing his kin in the throne room of his family's castle. In both instances, I had never really paid much attention to his appearance and expression, but now I couldn't help but notice every detail.

Rishan walked down the gangplank with a barely restrained smirk on his clean-shaven face. He walked with such power and confidence that I could almost feel the challenge he issued with each step. He wore half-plate armor—enough that he was combat ready, but the plate didn't cover him completely, allowing for some mobility. It was fashioned with the Argo Empire's symbol of a dragon and a rose and done in the colors of black and gold. His muscular frame, and the way he carried himself, betrayed his serious commitment to combat.

His white hair, cut short, caught the light and shimmered as he stepped onto the pier. His bluish-purple eyes matched Evianna's in color, but they were cold and focused, his brow hard set.

None of that compared to his forehead, however. His arcanist mark was like mine—it glowed a soft white, indicating he had a true form eldrin.

And that was when I saw it. The sovereign dragon that Rishan had bonded with over six months ago...

It leapt off the *Black Throne* and spread its wings, eliciting gasps from the crowd. The sovereign dragon, while young, was still the size of an adult elephant. When it hit the pier, the structure shook, causing a few nearby people to lose their footing.

Sovereign dragons always impressed me. Their black scales—and red scaled underbellies—gave them menacing appearances. But that didn't compare to the true form of a sovereign dragon. Rishan's eldrin had a second set of wings, albeit smaller than the first. And instead of horns that angled forward, this sovereign dragon had gold horns that were twisted together to resemble a crown. The beast flexed its muscles as it lifted its head to observe the crowd, its fangs visible as it glared out across the city's residents.

The unicorn arcanists, Rishan's personal guards, marched forward, clearing a path for Rishan and his sovereign dragon. The people of

Millatin didn't mind. They happily leapt from the path—curious to see the dragon, but unwilling to get too close to the beast.

Instead of walking into the city, Rishan waited for a moment, his attention turning to the *Black Throne*. "It's time we head out, my love," he said.

I would never forget his voice. It was the same cruel tone he had when he had spoken to Queen Velleta in Thronehold. Hearing it caused me to tense. I placed my hand on the hilt of my blade, wondering if striking him down in front of everyone was worth the price I'd pay.

Again, the crowd seemed to collectively hold their breath.

I glanced back at the gangplank. To my shock, a woman strode off the ship, a long cloak flowing behind her as she moved with purpose. Her black hair had been braided and woven into a tight bun on the top of her head, exposing her slender neck and delicate features. With eyes larger than most, she stared across the grouping of Millatin citizens. And unlike Rishan, who hadn't paid them much attention, this woman offered a small wave, as though acknowledging adoring fans.

And they cheered. The crowds actually cheered.

They clapped and threw more bits of rice and colored cloth—a symbol of the engagement, apparently.

Was that Councilor Chandra?

She walked the rest of way down the gangplank, her head held high, her posture straight. Although I was in the crowd, and a good twenty feet away, I could see the details of her arcanist mark. The star on her forehead was intertwined with a double-sided axe and a cowl. At first, I wasn't sure what that meant, but once I saw her eldrin exit the ship, everything came together.

An empty suit of clothing walked off the *Black Throne*. Like Luthair, the clothing hung as though draped over an invisible man. Unlike Luthair, who was armor made of shadows, this creature was nothing more than an executioner's cowl—only eye holes cut into the black cloth —a dark cloak with bloodstains, a pair of rough leather pants, tall boots, and a thick belt.

Well, and the giant executioner's axe that floated in the air around the creature. It was so massive that the handle was over six feet long, and the blade itself had to have been three feet wide. Skulls decorated the weapon, from the tip to the bottom.

This creature was none other than a *grim reaper.*

Councilor Chandra was a grim reaper arcanist—that explained her mark and her eldrin. But I almost couldn't believe it. Grim reapers were some of the most enigmatic mystical creatures I had ever read about. Normal reapers were already rare and powerful, but *grim* reapers took it to a whole new level, the same way king basilisks were deadlier versions of normal basilisks.

"Three cheers for Councilor Chandra!" people from the crowd shouted.

The compliance half-frightened me. The cheering happened instantly—three hoorays, all enthusiastic—and Councilor Chandra went along with it, smiling wide and waving again. She had an elegant beauty about her, the type that was effortless and timeless. Her olive skin carried a healthy glow, and her smile seemed genuine.

Her grim reaper walked like a normal man down the gangplank. Instead of taking a position by her side, it stopped next to the sovereign dragon, its giant skull-marked axe floating behind it, always within arm's reach, as though the creature might need to use it at a moment's notice.

Normal reapers carried scythes and weren't a complete set of clothing, but the grim reaper folded its arms over its "chest," and I realized then it had a black tunic and thick leather gloves—the fingers stained crimson.

"Thank you all for the glorious welcome," Chandra said to the people, her voice polite to the point of political. "It's such a pleasure to be home on our island fortress."

Then she took her place at Rishan's side and gently wrapped a hand around his elbow, holding him with a delicate touch. Her affection for him only helped me make a few quick conclusions—Chandra wasn't to be trusted, and she was likely aiding the Second Ascension.

For a brief moment, I had almost forgotten why I had come to the docks, but that was when Evianna finally appeared. She didn't emerge in the crowd or even by my side. She emerged from the shadows only ten feet in front of her brother—in the path the unicorn arcanists had created for his trek into the city.

Rishan and Chandra stopped in their tracks as Evianna stepped from the darkness and out into the full view of the city. The hair on the back of my neck stood on end when I realized what she was doing.

"How dare you," Evianna said, her words shaky at the end. "*How dare you.*"

The island citizens didn't seem to understand, and their agitation quickly became apparent. Murmurs sifted through the ranks, but no one would interfere.

Rishan took a single step forward, his smirk a permanent feature of his face. "Well, well, well. If it isn't my youngest sister. This is a good day —I thought we had lost you."

Of course he had to say that. His assassination of the old queen was a secret. No one here knew of his betrayal and treachery.

"You can lie to everyone here, Rishan," Evianna barked, her confidence building with every shout. "But you can't lie to me. I know what you've done! *I know all the people you've killed!*"

"Evianna," Rishan drawled, his arms still wide. He took another step forward. "You're distraught. Come, come. Give your brother a hug, and I'll take you home. It's been forever since we've been able to speak."

Evianna shook her head, her white braid flying back and forth from the force of her rejection. "You're a wicked man. How could you hurt Lyvia like that? Our sister... Our own flesh and blood."

"*Enough,*" Rishan growled through gritted teeth. "That's not true, *little sister.* You don't have the facts correct. Come with me, or you might regret what you're about to do."

The crowd around the docks didn't offer much commentary. People shifted to get better views, and some men and teenage boys even climbed up a building so that they could sit on the third-story roof. It wasn't a bad idea if I wanted to watch, but I figured if fighting broke out, I'd have to be the one to stop it.

"*Layshl,*" Evianna shouted.

The shadows around her feet coalesced into dragon-like armor that formed up around her. Gasps, shouts, and mild panic went through the citizens of Millatin, to the point that I could feel the anxiety from the people pressed up against my shoulders. My heart pounded against my ribs once I realized that Evianna fully intended to fight her brother, right here, right now.

CRIMTHAND THE SOVEREIGN DRAGON

"Crimthand!" King Rishan shouted.

Rishan's true form sovereign dragon lifted its head, the crown-horns glittering gold in the afternoon sun. With a snort and flared nostrils, the dragon—Crimthand—leapt to his arcanist's side, its mighty fangs on display. Each step caused the docks to shake, and I suspected the dragon weighed at least three tons. At least. And despite his impressive size and intimidating presence, he was still considered a hatchling—a dragon less than three years in age.

Gasps erupted from the citizens of Millatin. Some fled the docks, but most remained, their wide eyes locked on the conflict, no hint of hesitation or fear on their faces.

When the two unicorn arcanists rushed forward, unsheathing their swords for combat, Rishan waved them away, a smirk at the corner of his lips. His personal guards slowed, bowed their heads slightly, and then stepped back, allowing their king to do whatever he pleased.

During the commotion, shadows in the nearby area flickered, and I knew them to be Luthair—he had a way of signaling to me when he didn't want anyone else to know. He was nearby, and the fluttering at the edge of the darkness was his way of saying he'd help with any conflict.

"You dare threaten the king of the Argo Empire?" Crimthand asked

Evianna, his deep voice laced with a powerful growl. "The punishment is death. Your flesh will be fuel for my fire."

Rishan and his eldrin didn't even give Evianna a chance to apologize or recant. Crimthand stepped forward and inhaled, his scaled body expanding slightly with the air. In a moment of desperation and panic, I shadow-stepped out of the crowd and into the fray, between Evianna and the sovereign dragon. Although Luthair didn't have time to merge with me, he tossed my shield, Forfend, from the shadows, and I caught it in time to block the torrent of flames that ushered from Crimthand's mouth.

In the past, my shield had reflected magic back at the attacker. Now that I had fixed the shield with additional star shards, nothing reflected back, much to my confusion. Instead, the flames hit the heater shield and were sucked into it, similar to water sucked down a hole. I thought my artifact shield would grow hot afterward, but that wasn't the case, either. It glowed a slight white and red, but then the colors faded, and Forfend returned to its original black coloration.

Sovereign dragon fire was intense—the nearby area became hotter just for having it around. If the flames had touched Evianna or me, our shadows would not only falter, but so would our bodies.

In the next moment, darkness sprang up around my feet and covered me in inky blackness. Luthair's shadow armor formed a complete suit from head to toe, and once he was merged with me, I couldn't help but revel in the newfound power.

"It's a Steel Thorn Inquisitor!" someone from the crowd yelled.

The ensuing commotion created a blanket of buzzing that almost drowned out the dragon's next words.

"*Pathetic peons,*" Crimthand growled. He lumbered forward, his claws unsheathing and digging into the planks of wood that made up the majority of the docks. "You don't know what it's like to face the might of a dragon."

Before I could deescalate the situation, Evianna—wrapped in her own knightmare—held up a hand and evoked terrors. As a knightmare arcanist myself, I was unaffected by the power, but both Crimthand and Rishan shook their heads and shouted profanities.

But because Evianna hadn't yet mastered her powers, her terrors affected *everyone* in the nearby area. Hundreds of Millatin citizens screamed and held their heads. Some even wept.

Councilor Chandra and her grim reaper didn't move. They didn't engage in the fight, nor were they gripped by the terrors. They simply watched from afar, never taking their gazes off the spectacle, though the grim reaper didn't even really have eyes. Still, it watched, its bloodlust palpable.

The moment Crimthand shook free of Evianna's power, he lunged at for us, the full weight of his elephant-sized body enough to tear up a part of the docks with his every movement. He flapped all four wings, gaining force and speed in the blink of an eye.

All dragons, no matter the type, were far more powerful than other mystical creatures. Their scales were thick and resistant to magic, and their raw abilities were just better than others. I had no doubt that this true form sovereign dragon, even though he was a child, could give me an actual fight—which was why I unsheathed Retribution and then slashed wide.

It didn't stop Crimthand's momentum. He collided with me, regardless of my sword strike, and the two of us slammed to the ground, the dragon on top of me. The weight might have crushed some, but I slipped into the darkness, becoming as thin as a shadow, and escaped his pin with the effortlessness of water. When I finally staggered to my feet, I realized I had struck Crimthand across the face, slicing open his mouth until it reached the corner of his eye. Retribution cut through magic without resistance, and the attack had happened so quickly, it wasn't until then that I understood the injury I had created.

Crimthand struggled to stand as blood gushed from his mouth, cheek, and face. The rivulets of crimson dripped off his scales and splattered across the docks. Onlookers who weren't stricken with Evianna's terrors moved away, most shouting and pointing and calling for help.

"The king of the Argo Empire is in trouble!" someone yelled.

Another added, "Summon the guards! Call the councilors!"

"*Enough*," I said, my double voice with Luthair nearly perfectly mixed. "We must end this, and—"

Despite his wounded face, Crimthand vomited flame so white hot, it was almost blinding. I barely got my shield up in time, and even then, it wasn't large enough to protect my entire body. Flames splashed around the sides, striking my shoulders, shins, and feet. I gritted my teeth, holding back a cry of anguish. The fire could've melted brick, that was how hot it felt licking at my body, even through the knightmare armor.

My arcanist! Luthair warned me in my thoughts, his panic like a bolt of lightning to my spine.

The inky waterfalls of my armor hardened in an attempt to dampen the damage of the sovereign dragon flames, but it was too much. Luthair broke away in places, resulting in my skin burning to a crisp in an instant in the few areas the flames managed to touch.

I couldn't escape the fire—not because of inability, but because the strength and speed of the attack meant that it could strike innocent people, perhaps even Evianna herself. I had to protect them. I had to deal with the situation, not just run away.

"My sister is clearly a traitor to the Argo Empire," Rishan declared with an amused smile. He swept back his short, white hair. "*Kill her, Crimthand. Show them the might of a king and his eldrin.*"

The sovereign dragon stopped its fire and leapt for me a second time. Although I was injured, I shadow-stepped and dodged, but just barely. The dragon's flames had left me drained, and I was surprised at how sluggish I had become. Even when I emerged from the darkness, it took most of my focus just to breathe and remain on my feet. The smell of burnt meat hung in the air.

Evianna manipulated the shadows and grabbed the dragon by his legs, holding him in place. Crimthand was too strong, however. He ripped free from her restraints and then roared, the force of his frustration and anger enough to be heard throughout most of Millatin. More blood wept from the sword wound on Crimthand's face, despite the fact that he was in the process of healing.

"My dearest," Councilor Chandra called out, her regal voice laced with a warning. "This is *my* city. You will do well to respect that."

King Rishan exhaled with a scoff and then snapped his fingers. His true form dragon flared his scales, but otherwise refrained from spewing fire a third time.

Exhausted and panting, I wasn't entirely sure what would happen if the fight continued. The nearby denizens of Millatin had moved away a fair amount, but they weren't gone—many remained too close for comfort.

Evianna took her place at my side, and I debated the best method of escape. Did I have the strength necessary to shadow-step the both of us away from the docks? It had taken a considerable amount of effort just to avoid Crimthand's last attack.

Thankfully, I didn't need to test my luck. A pop of air and sparkles heralded the arrival of Illia. She appeared between Evianna and me, and with a light touch of her fingertips, she teleported all three of us away from Rishan and his killer dragon. Technically, individuals could reject her magic—Illia wasn't skilled enough to force me to teleport long distances—and I feared that Evianna would opt to stay and try to finish the fight she had started.

The teleport lasted a fraction of a second. When we arrived, I staggered for a moment, my vision shaky and blurry. I managed to focus on my feet and gulp down air, which allowed me to regain my bearings.

We had appeared in an alleyway. The rank odor of fish and rotted bread permeated the area, sinking into the stone. The tall buildings blotted out the light, creating an artificial gloom. None of this bothered me—not even the smell—it just reminded me of our terrible circumstances. We were on an unfamiliar isle, one that wasn't friendly, and the governing structure was in league with the enemy. Councilor Chandra and King Rishan were individuals I'd have to watch out for.

"Volke, are you okay?" Illia asked. She reached out to me with a shaky hand, but she never made contact.

Although I had been burned by the salamanders on the Isle of Ruma, I knew this was worse, even without looking. The urge to sink into the shadows and stay there as long as possible was strong. The shadows had a cold comfort that hid the burning sensation left behind by the sovereign dragon's flame.

Nicholin popped his head over the edge of the nearby roof and stared down at me with bright blue eyes. "You don't look so good..." Then he teleported to the ground at my feet. He rubbed at his face and frowned. "Are you trying to take Zaxis's spot as the person we have to constantly look out for? Because you're doing a good job of it!"

If I unmerged from Luthair, I wouldn't be able to speak. Instead, I remained with him and turned on my heel to face Evianna. She was still merged with her knightmare—the scale leather armor covered her chest, arms, and most of her legs. Her cape and cowl obfuscated most of her form, and I couldn't make out her expression when she kept her gaze down at the ground.

"What were you thinking?" I barked, unable to hold back the anger in my tone. "You can't just fight your brother. *You know that.* You're lucky the other arcanists weren't called in. That grim reaper could've ended us in a heartbeat."

"I can't let him get away with it," Evianna replied with no hesitation, her voice a mix of her own and Layshl's.

"And now the *Second Ascension* knows you're here. You realize that, don't you?"

Evianna snapped her attention up to me, her eyes glassy with water, but her expression determined. "I want everyone to know what he did!" She balled her fists and gritted her teeth. "I want him to know that I'll never forgive him! *That he'll regret everything he's ever done!*"

Her shouting was enough that it echoed throughout the dank alleyway. I didn't try to stop her or to tell her to lower her voice. I just listened.

"He killed our sister," Evianna continued, tears streaming down her cheeks, even though she didn't allow sobbing to enter her voice. "*My* sister. He killed Oma. *He tried to kill me.* Doesn't he... doesn't he remember when we were younger? When we'd have dinner together? Or play hide and seek on the castle grounds? We were siblings!"

I didn't say anything. All I could think about was my time with Illia. Could I ever forgive her if she betrayed me as thoroughly as Rishan had betrayed Evianna?

But Illia didn't feel the same. She stepped closer to Evianna and placed a firm hand on her shoulder. With a hard yank, she forced Evianna to stare at her. Then Evianna grew silent.

"We know," Illia said, her voice slow and quiet. "Because you talk about it—*obsess* about it—*all the time.* There isn't a day that goes by where you *aren't* talking about the revenge you'll seek or how your brother wronged you."

I lifted a hand to interject, but Illia gave me a curt and dismissive wave. I held my tongue, fearful that Illia would harm Evianna's emotional state, but at the same time, this was probably something she needed to hear.

"I know what you're going through," Illia said, still firm. "I know what it's like to never let go of a grudge—to have someone wrong you, and you want nothing more than to make them pay. But sometimes you have to let your personal hatred go for the better good. This isn't just about *you*. Stop pretending it is."

Nicholin teleported onto her shoulder and nodded the entire time. "You should listen. My arcanist learned the hard way."

Without acknowledging her eldrin, Illia continued, "Think about what your sister would want. You think she wants you to die on the pier of Millatin seeking revenge? Or do you think she wants you to help us find the world serpent and stop your brother once and for all?"

While Illia made logical arguments, Evianna didn't seem receptive. Evianna ripped her shoulder out of Illia's grasp and then wiped the silent tears from her face. When she went to speak, the air caught in her throat, threatening to break her composure. Instead of risking an outburst, Evianna turned away from us, her shoulders bunched at the base of her neck.

Then she stepped into the shadows and disappeared from the alley.

Would she listen to Illia and heed her advice? I didn't know.

But as long as Evianna didn't rush straight back to fight her brother, we'd likely make it through the city. I hoped.

Left alone with Illia and Nicholin, I let out a long exhale. "Being an instructor is difficult."

Nicholin nodded along with my words. "Tell me about it. The really frustrating part is when no one listens." He patted his little chest. "I know so many answers to so many problems, but no one ever takes my advice. Can you believe that?"

I managed a chuckle, but my whole body hurt, and it grew worse with each passing second. My adrenaline from the situation wore away, leaving me more sensitive to aches and pains. The fire burned some of my feeling, however, meaning I wouldn't feel much until I healed a decent portion of my body.

"I'm sorry," Illia whispered. She rubbed at her eye patch. "She is your pupil. I should've allowed you to speak with her."

"Did you mean everything you said?" I asked, ignoring her statements.

Illia brightened red a small shade. "Of course."

"Then you were the right person to tell her." I shifted the weight on my feet, the agony of the burns slowly sinking to my bones. It required most of my willpower to remain standing. "You two are similar in a lot of ways," I continued, determined to say my piece. "Any heartfelt advice you offer will likely resonate with Evianna."

"You really think so?" Illia asked, one eyebrow raised.

"Definitely. It'll be genuine when it comes from you."

40

THE HUNT FOR THE WORLD
SERPENT

I sat in a small room next to the library, my shirt on the nearest chair, my whole body tense, and my shoulders tingling. The Grand Apothecary and master caladrius arcanist, Gillie, moved around the room with a surprising amount of energy. Her ivory parrot-like eldrin, the legendary caladrius, could heal almost anything, but apparently Gillie wanted some sort of ointment to take effect first before she mended my flesh.

"How does it feel?" she asked with a smile.

I couldn't bring myself to shrug. "I'll be okay."

Gillie smiled enough for ten people. Her golden hair had been pulled back in a tight ponytail—it was longer than I remembered, past her shoulders now—and that made it easy to see the merriment lines on the side of her eyes. She wore a robe of sun-kissed yellow, an odd choice for anyone but her.

"It's almost time for the healing." Gillie shuffled over to my side and brought her face close to my burned shoulders. "But dragon fire is unlike others. It can distort and warp magic itself. You must be extra careful when it comes to wounds from dragons. Even their claws can be unusually destructive."

"I'll keep that in mind," I muttered.

Gillie wasn't particularly tall—not even five and a half feet—and she had to make a show of moving about to examine one side of my body, and then the other. My legs tingled from the ointment, but less than my shoulders and the outer edges of my arms. I still couldn't believe how powerful the blast of flame had been. Normally, my shield protected me, but the attack had been too much.

"Where is your knightmare?" Gillie asked, looking around.

I glanced at the darkness. Without a word between us, Luthair rose out of the shadows as a full suit of plate armor, the inky blackness running like water across his entire visage. Although he had no visible damage, I detected the hesitation in his movements and the heaviness in his steps when he moved closer to Gillie.

Alana, Gillie's caladrius eldrin, bobbed her head up and down, the type of excited gesture only birds could muster. Her beak glistened with the luster of gold, and her blue eyes sparkled with interest. "Luthair— I've never seen a true form knightmare before. You look so dashing!"

"Indeed," Luthair replied, his tone emotionless.

Gillie withdrew a jar of ointment from her yellow robes and proceeded to smear it into the water-like ink of Luthair's armor.

"You'll feel better soon," Gillie said matter-of-factly. "But you must promise me not to fight with a sovereign dragon in the future. Knightmares are not mystical creatures capable of dealing with flames."

I held my breath and said nothing.

As if trying to deter me through fear, Gillie continued with, "Although sovereign dragons aren't the most combat-oriented of the dragon species, they are stubborn, and typically fight to the death with little provocation. They're also cruel. Decades ago, when the Argo Empire had been fighting a war with some nation or another, the sovereign dragon arcanists made a point of allowing their eldrin to eat the insides of their enemies while they were still alive. Barbaric."

"Such actions were deemed unacceptable by all nation's leaders," Luthair interjected. "The Steel Thorn Inquisitors were given orders to stop such a practice if observed."

Gillie slowly shook her head. "*If observed*. Trust me when I say—I saw the bodies. Animals don't hollow out their prey like an avocado."

The vicious imagery left me nauseous. I stared at the wood floor, my brow furrowed. Had Rishan allowed his dragon to feast on the insides of his enemies? It wouldn't have surprised me.

"You must be careful," Gillie concluded. "And take great care not to fight with the sovereign dragon again, understood?"

I couldn't agree to what she wanted. In my gut, I knew conflict with Rishan was inevitable. Someday, we would have to fight him, and that day was looking closer by the moment. He was here to help the Second Ascension find the world serpent, that much I knew for certain.

Gillie grazed her fingers across the burns on my shoulders. Her healing magic bled into my skin, down to my muscles, and eased the aching in my bones. It had only taken a moment, but in that brief time, I had felt so refreshed, it was as if I had slept for ten years and awoken from a beautiful and pleasant dream.

"Remember that the Frith Guild needs you," Gillie said, her tone now serious. Did she know I couldn't promise her that I'd avoid Rishan? "There will be time for personal vendettas later."

The Frith Guild remained on edge.

Some arcanists were searching for members of the Huntsman Guild, others were gathering supplies for the trek east, and some were gathering information, like Master Zelfree. I walked the halls with my attention inward, barely seeing my surroundings. I preferred the dark halls to the ones bathed in light, if only because the shadows gave me comfort.

When I finally reached Evianna's room, my thoughts came to an abrupt halt. I needed to speak with her about her brother—about our plans for the future. Illia said she would say something, but I felt it important that I also have a conversation with Evianna.

I had promised her sister, Lyvia, that I would look out for Evianna. I wouldn't fail to keep that promise, not so long as I had blood in my veins and strength in my body.

With a forced exhale, I knocked on the door.

Half a moment later, as though she had been standing on the other side and waiting, Evianna swung the door wide. She stood on the other side, looking older than her years, her hair unbraided and wavy, hanging down to her waist. She gave me the once over, her eyebrows knitted.

"Volke?" she asked. "What're you doing here?"

"I came to speak to you." Then I motioned to her room. "May I come in?"

Evianna replied with a *hmpf* and then stepped out into the hall. With a quick and forceful motion, she shut her door with a harsh *click* and then turned to face me with her full attention. The hallway we found ourselves in didn't have any lit lanterns, but that wasn't a problem for knightmare arcanists.

"Are you okay?" I asked, keeping my voice down just in case there were other arcanists down the adjoining halls. "After everything that happened with your brother, I mean."

Evianna pursed her lips as she mulled over my question, her gaze falling to the floor. "Of course. It'll take more than my brother's visage to deter me from my path."

"His presence obviously bothered you. And you acted on that. I need to make sure that doesn't happen again, especially since we'll likely be running into him in the future."

Her shoulders bunched at the base of her neck. Then she turned a glower in my direction. I thought she'd go off on a tirade, tell me about her *plans for revenge* or how she *has to do what her heart tells her*, but after a prolonged moment of staring, her expression softened into more of a neutral—perhaps melancholy—gaze.

Evianna relaxed, her shoulders loosening. "You're right. And you don't have to worry. I won't do it again." Although such a change felt sudden, her tone rang sincere. Even my new ability to sense lies didn't warn me when she made her declarations.

"Really?" I asked. "You already came to that conclusion?"

She nodded. "Yes. I realized something when I thought over the event."

"What did you realize?"

"That... I should listen to you more often." Evianna sighed as her gaze fell to the floor again. "You really do... remind me of my sister. And like her, I feel like you're a compass."

I lifted an eyebrow. "What do you mean?"

Evianna tensed again, but this time it seemed more from certainty than frustration. "You always point true north, Volke. I know now—you won't lead me astray."

The words hit me a little hard, and for a moment, I didn't know what to say. I just rubbed at the back of my neck, my breath held and my chest tight. No one had ever said something like that to me before...

A compass? A guiding force in the world? It was high praise. Probably more than I deserved.

"I, uh, think that your brother will be sending soldiers to search for us," I muttered, forcing myself to get to the next topic I wanted to discuss with her. "I don't know if he's aware we're part of the Frith Guild, so he might not send them here, but they'll definitely be in the city."

Evianna nodded. "You're probably right."

"I think you should stay on the atlas turtle for the time being, then."

"If that's what you think is best." Evianna took in a deep breath and matched my gaze. "I'll stay here and make sure Ryker is guarded." She ended the statement with a tight smile.

"I... really appreciate that, Evianna."

Then, without warning, she stepped forward and wrapped her arms around my torso. The embrace wasn't new—she had done this before—so I relaxed a bit and returned the hug. For a minute or two, we said nothing. Evianna eventually ended the moment, her resolution apparent.

"Don't worry about a thing," she said. "I'm here to help the Frith Guild no matter what."

***

The Huntsman Guild was one of the largest guilds that sailed across the high oceans. They specialized in tracking down individuals—specifically criminals—but sometimes others. Many nations, and sometimes wealthy individuals, hired them for their skills when it came to locating particularly dangerous arcanists.

Recently, they had become known for their ability to track plague-ridden people and creatures. They tracked them down no matter where they ran—to the edge of the Shard Sea, to the frost of the Diamondsaw

Mountains—and collected the bounties that nations would place on individuals who spread the awful disease.

Which was why I figured we'd be able to find individuals from that guild here in Millatin, even if this port city was five weeks away from my home isle. I hoped we wouldn't meet anyone I knew from the Huntsman Guild—like Jevel Balestier, the reaper arcanist. He had come to kill me in New Norra, and I wanted to avoid unnecessary conflict.

"How will we know we've found someone from the Huntsman Guild?" Fain asked as we walked one of the narrow streets of Millatin.

"Their guild pendants are marked with a bow and arrow," I said. "Most are equipped for combat and carry themselves accordingly."

"Oh, there they are again." Fain pointed to the sky. "More pegasus arcanists..."

Unicorn and pegasus arcanists from the Argo Empire were crawling through the city, just like I knew they would be. I kept myself swaddled in a heavy cloak and hood, hiding my glowing arcanist mark from the world. King Rishan had seen my unusual arcanist mark on the dock, and there was no doubt in my mind that those arcanist soldiers were looking for anyone with a knightmare mark on their forehead. I also suspected the Argo Empire was allowed to roam the streets with impunity thanks to Rishan's betrothed. The council of Millatin was on his side.

Fain wore his standard sailor's coat, trousers, and thick boots, but he also had a tricorn cap to half-shield his arcanist mark and keep his gaze hidden. He walked with his hands in his pockets, though he strode down the street with a tense gait.

And I knew why.

Millatin wasn't a city someone came to relax in. Every alleyway was dark, every smell was rancid, and every man or woman with a cloak looked like a cutthroat. People watched the movements of others with keen eyes and fidgety hands, and twice someone moved too close to me for comfort. Fortunately, they realized I wasn't an easy target because the moment we made eye contact, they darted away like a cat spooked by a loud noise.

"It's hard to see anyone's pendant in this mire of a city," Fain murmured, his eyes narrowed on each person we passed.

I shook my head and stuck close to him. "They'll have a crimson bracelet on their wrist."

"Bracelet? Some sort of trinket?"

"That's right. It glows red when there are plague-ridden arcanists nearby."

Fain's eyebrows lifted. "Ah. Like in New Norra. That was how the hunters tracked you down."

I nodded. "They should be easy to spot."

Fain kept close as we rounded a corner, his eyes not on the people, but the side of the building. I followed his gaze, mildly confused, and when he glanced at me, I lifted an eyebrow.

"Sometimes pickpockets like to reach out windows," Fain whispered as he eyed a couple of thick-paned windows. "It's real quick and subtle, but they can take a few coins from you and disappear in the next instant. And since people don't know we're arcanists, I'm sure a few of these sticky-fingered kids will try something."

"I never knew people reached out windows…" I glanced at our surroundings more thoroughly. There were plenty of windows around. So many opportunities to steal something.

"I used to nick things from people all the time," Fain said with a shrug. "Back before I had joined Calisto's crew." As if unconsciously checking, Fain reached up and touched the ascot around his neck. It hid the pirate tattoo on his neck, and I wondered if he thought of it often.

Fain gave me a sideways glance.

"Everything okay?" I asked.

He shook his head.

"You seem off."

Fain clenched his jaw for a moment. "I sometimes worry you'll think less of me when you hear these stories."

"On the contrary," I said. "I admire your determination to change yourself. Not many can say they've traveled through the abyss and somehow pulled themselves out of it."

"Hm." Fain sarcastically chuckled. "You're too naïve sometimes, you know that?"

I wanted to contradict him a second time, but a man with a shaky hand grabbed my shoulder. I snapped my attention to him, still on edge from everything that had been happening, but I relaxed when I realized he carried no weapons. He barely carried his pants, in all reality—they hung half on his hip, secured only with a ratty belt. His tunic was in terrible shape, with holes and stains from a million bar fights.

"Are you two looking for work?" the man asked, his breath laced with booze. "There's a payin' job in the square. Ships are hirin' young lads to help with somethin' big. Mystical creatures are up for grabs."

The man leaned on me more than necessary.

"What're you doing?" I asked. "Why even bother telling us this?"

With a drunken chuckle, the man swept back his black hair. "They paid me. Not much. But still. I'm deliverin' the message to everyone I meet."

Fain shoved him off me and then motioned to the people around us. "Tell someone else," he growled. "We don't have time for this."

Although I didn't agree with his gruff tone and attitude, I did want the half-drunken man to leave. Thankfully, that was exactly what he did. He walked over to the next group of people and said the same damn thing—there was work in "the square" and that it paid. I didn't think it was the most enticing pitch, but I was intrigued. Mystic hunters were typically the individuals people wanted to hire if someone wanted specific mystical creatures caught.

"Let's check this out," I said, tapping Fain on the shoulder.

"You sure?" he asked. "I thought we only had a limited amount of time."

"It'll only take a moment."

The city square wasn't far from our location, and I swear the closer we got, the more pungent the odor. Still, no matter how bad it got, I never saw the source. Were there rotting corpses hidden in every building? I wouldn't be surprised if there were.

The smell grew worse. I wrinkled my nose in disgust, unsure of how to handle the foul scent. Even Fain, who normally didn't complain, sneered as we continued on our way.

"Reminds me of my time in the hold of a ship," he muttered.

I shook my head. "It's worse."

A low whining noise seemingly came from nowhere, but I knew it was Wraith, Fain's wendigo eldrin. The poor wolf-like creature probably had a better sense of smell than both Fain and me. Was this place torture for him?

When we finally reached the square, I stopped in my tracks and took everything in. Nearly a hundred people were gathered around a giant freshwater spring. It was the type of natural stone formation that involved a pool and a geyser of water and shot liquid into the air. Unfortunately, the waters that spewed forth from the spring wasn't clear and enticing.

The water was heinous and disgusting—filled with unidentifiable chunks and a foul color of brown. It was most definitely the source of the rotten smell that soaked into the nearby area. But why? I had never known a spring to run so rotten.

Despite that, the many people in the square didn't seem to notice or care. Fain and I did, however. Both of us covered our noses and mouths, our facial expressions twisted in a mild amount of disgust.

I grabbed a nearby citizen and then motioned to the spring. "What happened here?"

The woman shrugged. "That's the Millatin Spring. It's always been like that."

"I thought the Millatin Spring was the source of the island's magic and power? I thought... it was supposed to be pure?"

With a laugh, the woman continued on her way. "Old tales of times long past. The spring has never been pure, not in my entire life."

A part of me wanted to weep. The legend of the spring made it seem like the most beautiful thing on the island. But when I gazed upon it now, the spring resembled the backwash of a swamp. A god-creature had been born from this? Impossible.

Before I could ask any further questions, a man shouted over the crowd.

"Ladies and gentlemen," he said, though I couldn't see him though the small crowd of people gathered around. "I'm here today to offer you jobs. I have plenty of coin, and I need a few dozen strong and strapping individuals." He spoke with a semi-regal accent. Upper crust upbringing, perhaps? And definitely not from the island. His words were too... precise.

The interest from the citizens of Millatin remained high. They whispered amongst themselves and pointed forward, all gathering closer to the putrid spring.

The job-giver continued with, "It's a dangerous mission, but I'll pay handsomely. You see, we need mystical creatures. Well, just *one*. But it's a big one. Bigger than any you have ever seen."

Then the man stood up on the edge of the dirty spring to get a better look at the crowd. Although I didn't know the man's name, I did recognize him. He was the gentleman arcanist I had seen on the Isle of Ruma—the one who had been wielded a rapier. Just like then, he wore a long coat, had his blond hair slicked back, and kept his face clean-shaven. Much cleaner than the crowds around him.

"Who here is interested?" the gentleman asked.

And my chest immediately tightened into knots. The Second Ascension was hiring strong men to help him with a single mystical creature?

"It's the world serpent," Fain murmured, parroting my inner thoughts. "They know where it is."

41

THE SHALE RUNESTONE

I kept my head down, careful to keep my cloak in place. The gentleman arcanist smiled with perfect teeth, his salamander arcanist mark plain to see on his forehead. As if to accentuate his magic, the shirt he wore was a bright red, and the sash around his waist was a burnt gold, all of which evoked an imagery of flames.

Where were Atty and Zaxis when I needed them? Both were immune to the ravages of heat.

"They don't know where the world serpent is," I said to Fain, my gaze locked on the man with the rapier. "They don't have an Occult Compass like we do."

Fain motioned to the man with his blackened fingers. "He's gathering people to help. He *must* know."

Perhaps Fain was right. The thought got me pensive. "Follow him," I commanded. "He'll finish recruiting people here eventually. See where he goes next."

Fain replied with a curt nod and then shrouded himself in invisibility. "I can do that."

I waited around the square with the vile spring, loitering near alleyways and pretending to be a vagabond. The water that shot into the air created a fine mist that sprinkled down onto everything nearby. It wasn't a large square, and those who drove carriages or rode horses took a large quantity of odiferous water with them. It was no wonder the stench filled the streets from here to the docks.

"Luthair," I whispered. "Why do you think the spring is like that?"

The shadows twisted at the alley. "It stinks of corruption, my arcanist. The magic here has been damaged."

"How can you tell that?"

"Mystic creatures are made solely of magic. It is in our very nature to be more susceptible to change and disturbances, which is why the arcane plague affects us faster than it does arcanists. Trust me when I say —something is wrong with this spring. I can sense the sickness."

"Yeah, and I can smell it," I quipped.

I leaned against the wall to better help with the wait. The sun set in the west, beyond the stone cliffs that surrounded the island city, and the scarlet hue of the sky added another layer of uncertainty to my surroundings. I hadn't realized it until then, but there weren't many arcanists roaming the streets of Millatin. When I had been in Thronehold, knight arcanists had kept the peace. Their presence had been a deterrent against criminal activity. But here, it seemed like there wasn't a watchful eye representing the governing forces.

All the people here openly wore knives, swords, and pistols, much like spiders wore bright red symbols on their abdomens—as a warning. Individuals were their own forms of justice and deterrent.

Someone gripped my shoulder, and I whirled around on my heel. In the next instant, Retribution was in my hand, pulled from the sheath I kept hanging on my side. I didn't see anyone, however.

"It's just me," Fain mumbled from his invisibility. "You can relax."

I quickly tucked away my black blade and sighed. "Next time, say something before touching me."

"I apologize, but I have news. That salamander arcanist who was recruiting people is named Fazri. He led me straight to the Second Ascension's hiding place."

My heart pounded faster in excitement. I almost tripped over my words as I asked, "Where are they?"

"On the *Black Throne*."

My heart stopped for a moment, caught in my throat and stealing my ability to breathe. That was the one place in the whole damn city we wouldn't be able to catch them. We could petition the Millatin council to allow us to search the ship, but knowing that Councilor Chandra was King Rishan's betrothed meant that would probably never work. And if we attacked the ship while it was docked here in Millatin, we would have to contend with the military might of the fortress island.

"They're clearly gathering people to make up a search party," Fain said, his tone low. "I think, given Fazri's instructions, that they're planning on scouring a large area in an attempt to stumble upon the world serpent."

"Probably," I muttered.

"He told them all they had to be on the lookout for a large tree."

I nodded along with the words. "That's right. The world serpent will be born under that tree. The roots are what keep it hidden and protected. Only someone with the jade runestone can gain access."

Fain allowed his invisibility to drop. One eyebrow was already lifted. "How do you know all that?"

"I learned about it in Thronehold," I said with a shrug. "So don't worry. We still have the advantage."

"They *do* have a runestone with them, though."

The statement took me by surprise, and instead of asking anything, I just furrowed my brow and waited. They didn't have the world serpent runestone. I knew that. But they did have six of the twelve runestones—which one had they brought with them?

"It was gray," Fain said. He made a motion with his hand, showing me the rough size—about a palm. "I think it was made of shale. And it had a picture of a wolf on it." Fain swept back his chestnut hair. "I liked it. Reminded me of Wraith."

"That's the runestone for the fenris wolf." Although I wasn't an expert on the god-creatures, I had memorized all thirteen and the order in which they had appeared. "The fenris wolf is said to spawn third, after the world serpent and the soul forge."

Another round of panic hit me hard.

The world serpent was already in existence, and so was the soul forge —I had heard the Second Ascension say so myself. Was it possible then... that they weren't looking for the world serpent after all? Were they looking for the fenris wolf?

"We need to get that runestone," I whispered, my gaze on the dirty cobblestone around my feet.

"I agree," Luthair said from the shadows.

"So do I," Fain said. "But what're we going to do about the *Black Throne*? It's heavily guarded."

I shook my head. "You made it aboard, right?"

"Yeah."

"Then we'll just have to do it again." I snapped my fingers. "Luthair, return to the guild, tell them what we're doing, and then ask Karna for help."

"By your command, my arcanist," Luthair said, his dark voice becoming distant as he shifted out of the alley.

"Why her?" Fain asked.

I glanced around and lowered my voice. "Karna's doppelgänger magic will be useful in this situation. She might even be able to steal the runestone herself without much problem."

"But weren't we looking for an arcanist from the Huntsman Guild? Should we really go out of our way to potentially provoke the Second Ascension?"

"We need that runestone," I said, my tone heated. "And someone else from the Frith Guild will no doubt find an arcanist from the Huntsman Guild. Now isn't the time to dither."

It took a long moment for Fain to mull over the rationale. With a resigned sigh, he said, "Very well. I'll follow your lead on this."

I had wanted to avoid the *Black Throne* at all costs, especially after my confrontation with Rishan on the docks. Yet here I was. Facing it.

It was a massive galleon-style ship with multi-stories, gigantic sails, and enough storage space in the hold for long voyages. The *Black Throne* was decorated in carved dragons and roses, symbolizing the Argo Empire. Because sovereign dragons had prosperity auras—magic that increased the wealth and health of the nation's citizens—the Argo Empire was one of the wealthiest around, and it showed in the quality of the ships.

Other ships docked on nearby piers didn't have anywhere near the craftsmanship of the *Black Throne*. The type of wood used alone was expensive and kept the water rot at bay. I also imagined the *Black Throne* had magic imbued into it, considering the numerous guards standing watch on the deck and at the end of the gangplank, many of whom were unicorn arcanists.

Fain, Karna, and I stood on the next pier over, sneaking quick glances when we could to determine the number of arcanists and the changing of the guard positions. It was night—and the dock offered poor lighting —but with my knightmare augmentation magic, I gave both Fain and Karna the ability to see through any level of darkness. Hexa had agreed to watch Ryker for the evening, allowing me to run this operation under the watchful gaze of the moon.

Despite the midnight hour, the docks crawled with individuals. Seedy individuals, but still—they lingered around, maintained conversations, and occasionally gave us sideways glances. We hid our guild pendants under our clothes and wore tricorn hats that covered most of our foreheads. I had to wear an extra bandana, to hide the glow, but we had made it work.

Karna had disguised herself as an older man—some sailor who had to retire due to a bum leg. The guise helped us blend in, even if the residents of Millatin were suspicious. She wore a dark red handkerchief around her neck, one that almost seemed soaked in blood. Such clothing choice was common for sailors who wanted to avoid the sun. They used them over their head or face when the weather became too harsh.

Luthair had returned from the Frith Guild an hour ago, bringing little news. Apparently, most arcanists had been out exploring the city, either gathering supplies or looking for crucial individuals. If we wanted this operation to be over with quickly, I'd have to act without the permission or guidance of Master Zelfree. I had already come to terms with that.

"They're changing again," Fain whispered as he motioned with his eyes.

Sailor-Karna tucked her hands into her coat pockets. When she spoke, it was with a man's gruff voice, which was unfamiliar. "That's once an hour. We have the pattern now."

"Where do you think they'll be hiding the shale runestone?"

"In the captain's quarters," Sailor-Karna replied, no hesitation. "Captains usually have a lockbox handy for special cargo."

That made sense. Most captains kept important documents and coin tightly locked down. Could my knightmare magic destroy a heavy metal box? Probably not. Retribution cut through magic and mystical creatures with no resistance, but a solid metal container wasn't an option. Neither Fain nor Karna had the magics necessary to help in this situation. We would probably need a key.

Sailor-Karna gave me a sideways glance and smirked. "I'm so happy you decided to ask me to help you with this. It's been awhile since we were on an adventure like this."

I rubbed at the back of neck. Fain forced himself to pay attention to something far off in the distance.

"Yeah, it has been a while," I said, the words coming out slow and awkward. "But your skillset is perfect for this type of mission. Atty's healing and fire aren't really suited for, uh, *this*."

Sailor-Karna narrowed her eyes as she said, "Did you find the answers you were looking for?"

I crossed my arms and then uncrossed them, the question sinking deep into my gut. "Well, if I listen to my friends, my options are *do nothing, force my desires,* or *jump out a window to avoid the situation.* I'm leaning toward the latter."

"Most men do," she quipped as she rolled her eyes.

Fain scoffed. "I'm not sure what you're talking about, but my advice is *trust your gut.*" He snapped his blackened fingers. "No, wait. I got a good one. *Kill it with fire.* That was what my brother used to say."

I pinched the bridge of my nose. How was this simple issue resulting in such preposterous responses? "Thank you," I muttered. "Much appreciated."

"No problem. I hope it helps."

Not wanting to continue the absurd conversation, I asked, "How did you see the shale runestone?" The chill in the evening air caused me to shiver.

Fain, unbothered by cold, exhaled a line of visible breath. "King Rishan, Councilor Chandra, and Fazri were all examining it. They kept trying to look at it with a piece of paper—whatever that was about—but when nothing happened, they got frustrated and started yelling. I left shortly afterward. The sovereign dragon arcanist was getting violent..."

I nodded. "Well, I have a plan. Maybe—"

The click of boots on wooden planks interrupted my thought process. Fain, Karna, and I collectively turned and spotted a young woman wearing a striped skirt with a slit up to her hip. Her blouse had a stain and a few holes, but it was difficult to focus on anything other than her long, bare leg.

"Evening, boys," she said with a giggle. "You look bored."

Fain gave me a nervous glance, and I returned the look with a frown. "We're busy," I muttered. "I apologize."

The harlot sauntered closer, her arms crossed in such a way to prop up her bosom. "Oh? I think you might have a few extra moments. And coins."

Fain shook his head. "No. Not us."

"C'mon. Don't be that way."

What would we do if she persisted? Throw her into the water? We couldn't use any of our magic, and I didn't want the guards paying any more attention to us than necessary.

Sailor-Karna stepped forward, and I feared she would make a scene. Instead, she offered the woman a half-smile. When she grinned, it was with the mouth of a drunkard man, all teeth out of place and yellow from years of abuse. Sailor-Karna tapped the side of her head. "Oh, you know what? I was wondering where I knew you from, but you just look like a lady I once knew."

The harlot woman perked up and forced another giggle. "Hopefully, it was a lady you enjoyed?" She fluttered her eyelashes.

"Yeah," Karna said. "She was the best horse I ever had."

My eyebrows shot for the hairline, but I didn't say a word. The woman grew red in the face, her mouth slightly open as she slowly came to terms with the comment.

"I see," she spat. "You're *those* type of men. Well, I'm going to let all the girls in town know you're not welcome."

"Be my guest," Sailor-Karna quipped as she stroked the stubble on her disguise chin.

The woman turned and flounced away, her striped skirt fluttering behind her as she went. While I disliked insulting her, I was mildly impressed with Karna's quick handling of the matter. The conversation had been over and done within a matter of moments.

"You're terrible sometimes, doppelgänger," a low voice said from a nearby coil of rope. Wraith, Fain's wendigo, allowed his invisibility to drop, showcasing his wolf-like form lounging happily on the ropes. "That young woman was just trying to do her job." Wraith softly chuckled at his own joke.

Fain shifted his footing and moved away from the rope, his gaze darting to the *Black* Throne and then away. He remained tensed as he inched his way closer to me.

"What's wrong?" I asked.

"I have a bad feeling about this," Fain replied, his voice low. Then he leaned in close and shifted his tone to a whisper. "I still get that death feeling around you. What if this is the place? What if something happens here?"

"It'll be fine."

Fain furrowed his brow. "What if we run into trouble?"

"Then I use my knightmare magic to get us out of there. You don't have to worry about that."

THE BLACK THRONE

W endigo arcanists, in theory, had the ability to augment objects and shroud them in invisibility. They also had the ability to manipulate flesh, which could come in handy if we got into a fight, but I hoped it wouldn't come to that.

"Can you make us both invisible?" I asked Fain as I motioned to myself and Sailor-Karna.

He shook his head. "I'm not... talented... with my magic."

"What do you mean?"

"I mean—I've never learned how. And I'm not sure if I'm capable."

For a split second, I almost opened my mouth and gave a speech about how *every* arcanist could use their magic to augment people and objects, but I swallowed the words before they left me. Evianna had said I had to increase my *pedological skills*, which meant I needed to take opportunities to teach others.

"Augmenting other things isn't difficult," I said. "You just have to will your magic into an object."

Fain lifted an eyebrow. "But how?"

"Through focus and conviction. Like pushing air out of your lungs or tightening your grip on something until it explodes." I motioned to myself. "Try it with me. I'm sure you'll pick it up in no time."

Although it probably wasn't the best time for a lesson, Sailor-Karna didn't interject or comment on the task at hand. She just watched from the sidelines, her arms crossed over her burly form. Sometimes, when I glanced over for a brief second, I forgot it *was* Karna and then spooked myself thinking we were being watched by a random man. I felt silly afterward.

When Fain didn't move, I grabbed his wrist and brought his hand over to my shoulder. Fain's blackened fingers had an icy twinge to them, and the moment they grazed my neck, I shivered.

"Go on," I said.

Despite the dangers of practicing in this location, I opted to continue. Fain was older than most apprentices in the Frith Guild, and he was far behind in terms of magical understanding. He needed to improve himself, not just for his self-esteem, but because we needed competent allies.

Fain scrunched his eyes closed and squeezed my shoulder. I recognized the struggle. Almost a year ago, I'd had the same damn problem.

I wasn't wrapped in invisibility.

And after thirty seconds, Fain released my shoulder. "I can't do it."

"Yes, you can," Sailor-Karna said. She placed Fain's hand back on my shoulder. "I've seen lowlife arcanists in Thronehold who can augment objects. If *they* can do it, *you* can do it. Trust me."

Lowlife arcanists?

I didn't question it or ask for the story. And neither did Fain. He just gripped my shoulder with a harsher conviction, and I held my breath, hoping this would work. Fain's eyebrows knitted together as he glared at his hand, as though angry that the magic just hadn't flowed outward yet.

Seconds went by.

Then a minute.

I lost count after four minutes.

"Don't think about the object you're affecting," I murmured in a soft tone that only Fain could hear. "Think of it as though you're altering something ethereal. Like sunshine. You're altering the *intangible* qualities about me, not the physical."

"Sunshine?" Fain whispered.

"Like sunshine streaming through a window. Your magic is the ray of light that illuminates a room."

Sailor-Karna glanced at me and lifted an eyebrow. I gave her a half-shrug, careful not to move Fain's hand. The sunshine analogy had worked for me. Why wouldn't it work for Fain?

"You can do it, my arcanist," Wraith said from his own shroud of invisibility. It was amusing to hear his dark and gruff voice give encouragement, but I didn't comment.

Then, as I was starting to get nervous, Fain's wendigo magic wrapped over me, blocking my whole body from sight. I chuckled, and Fain opened his eyes, his expression shifting to delight.

"I did it," he murmured.

Sailor-Karna offered a silent round of applause, no doubt to keep us inconspicuous. I joined in for a moment, but then I realized no one could see me. My face grew hot with embarrassment as I clasped Fain on the shoulder to show my encouragement.

"Okay, here's the plan," Sailor-Karna said, ending the celebrations. She tucked her hands into her coat pockets. "You two will remain invisible while I assume the appearance of the first gangplank guard to shift positions. We'll walk onto the *Black Throne*, and I'll shift to whatever appearance I need in order to gain access to the captain's quarters— specifically, to get his keys. I'll also gather information while you two search any and all rooms you deem important. Perhaps we can find more than just the shale runestone. Star shards would be nice."

"Do you think it's wise for the three of us to be on the ship without a disguise?" Fain asked. "I mean, I know we'll be invisible, but what if something goes wrong?"

Sailor-Karna waved her hand. "Trust me. It won't."

"Still..." Fain sighed and then glanced at the pier next to his feet. "Wraith—if we don't return in an hour, inform an arcanist from the Frith Guild, understood?"

"Of course," Wraith replied, a happy tone to his voice.

Not wanting to prolong this mission any longer, I shook my head. "This is a fine plan. But we shouldn't wait any longer. The gangplank guards are changing."

Sailor-Karna replied with a curt nod. Then she stepped behind a dock and knelt down, as if finding something shiny at her feet. In an instant, her appearance shifted and altered, rearranging itself to form yet another guise.

When Karna stood, she was now the gangplank guard—just in her same clothes as before, including the crimson handkerchief. She pulled it off her neck and tucked it into her coat pocket so that it hung out slightly, and I knew that was our signal. Karna would be the one with the handkerchief in her pocket. We would always know her from the others.

"What're we going to do about that?" Fain asked, motioning to the rest of her sailing outfit.

She ran a male hand through her thick, brown curls. "Interesting form... and I'll just find a similar coat and wear that. Don't worry about me, though. You'll be invisible, so sneaking on shouldn't be a problem for you."

Fain let out a long exhale and then nodded. With the ease of donning a coat, Fain became invisible. Before I gave the command to leave, he added, "Careful when aboard the ship. Most of it is made from wood that has been cured in nullstone."

I caught my breath, my chest tightening.

Nullstone.

I had seen it in Thronehold. The Argo Empire was famous for the stones that negated magic, and I had seen several buildings, objects, and even chests that were made out of wood that had been cured in nullstone, giving it the *resistant to magic* quality.

"The whole ship?" I asked.

"Yes."

Curse the abyssal hells! Nullstone would make everything difficult. It meant that using my magic to bypass doors and other minor obstacles would be impossible.

I reached out and groped around for something tangible. When I found Fain's shoulder, I tightened my hold. "We'll deal with all that as we come to it. But we should go. Karna will join us."

"Okay," Fain whispered.

The two of us hustled off our pier and over to the next. Even though I couldn't see my body, I was sure enough of myself that I didn't need to. When we reached the pier for the *Black Throne*, Fain and I both slowed our pace to a crawl to avoid any unnecessary noise. It was probably pointless, though. Even at night, the ambient sounds of the ocean concealed most movement. The waves crashed against the docks, and the creaking of the wood created a soft chorus that never ceased.

The only thing missing at night was the squawking of the gulls.

When we reached the gangplank, I realized there was another guard standing on the ship, watching the plank with a dull expression on his wide face. That didn't matter much. With slow and cautious steps, I made my way up, followed closely by Fain. He kept a hand on me at all times, and we ambled past the guard without incident. We never made a sound.

Once aboard the *Black Throne*, the rocking of the ship put me at ease. I had grown up on and around boats my entire life. The gentle sway and creak of a vessel on the waves always managed to calm my nerves.

Even if I was surrounded by enemies.

Everywhere we looked, there were sailors, soldiers from the Argo Empire, or shady arcanists who didn't look *all there*. Although it was night, several deckhands were up and about, checking the ropes, rigging, and bundled sails. The unicorn and pegasus arcanists stood on the quarterdeck—an elevated platform on the ship meant for officers—and they observed everyone with narrowed eyes. Even their unicorns and pegasi stood vigilant and in their armor, as though prepared for full-blown combat at a moment's notice. The night's breeze ruffled their perfectly groomed manes.

I turned my attention to the physical construction of the galleon ship. Just as Fain had said—the entire ship had been constructed out of a dark wood, the type soaked in nullstone and made magically resistant. I knelt for a moment and brushed the grooves and grains with the tips of my fingers. The anti-magic quality left a terrible sensation on my skin, and I had to stand to rid myself of it.

I wouldn't be able to shadow-step here or even manipulate the darkness unless on non-nullstone surfaces. Ongoing effects wouldn't be terminated—like Fain's invisibility—but he wouldn't be able to activate it again once we were in the thick of it. Evoking terrors would likely work, but my combat options were limited. And I knew from experience that I could remove my sword and shield from the shadows, but I wouldn't be able to put anything back. The same went for Luthair—once he lifted out of the darkness, he would be with us the entire time.

With Fain still holding on to my shoulder, I crossed the deck of the ship, searching for a way to the officer's quarters.

Fain tightened his grip on me. I couldn't see him, so it resulted in an awkward glance.

"Hm?" I whispered, trying my best not to utter anything too loud.

"Left," was all Fain replied.

I stopped and turned. My heart beat so painfully, it echoed in my ears.

King Rishan and his lady, Councilor Chandra, stood near the mizzenmast, engaged in conversation. They spoke softly and occasionally chuckled, so I assumed it was a pleasant chat, but the lap of gentle waves and the howl of the night air made it difficult to discern anything else. That didn't matter, though—what mattered was we got what we had come for and then flee. Everything else was a distraction.

Councilor Chandra's grim reaper stood nearby, his arms crossed and his executioner's cowl hung in a glare-like position. The double-edged axe that circled him had a crimson stain along one blade. The dreadful creature looked as though it belonged next to the gallows, not on the deck of a royal galleon, and every deckhand gave the beast terrified glances, their eyes wide and their hands shaky.

Again, Fain tightened his grip.

"Under the quarterdeck," he whispered.

I turned away from Rishan and Chandra, only to smile to myself. The captain's room was labeled as such and was located under the main walkway up to the quarterdeck. We wouldn't need to explore the belly of the ship to find what we wanted—hopefully.

Fain and I hustled our way over, careful not to disturb the deckhands or do anything to draw the suspicion of the Argo Empire soldiers. When we reached the door, Fain held on tight. Were we to wait for Karna? Had she even come aboard? I hadn't seen her distinct outfit or even the guard she was supposed to be impersonating, but perhaps it was best to do this right.

Fain and I stood under the stairs to the quarterdeck, out of the way so that no one could have a chance to stumble into our invisible bodies.

When standing still, I could feel Fain's cold breath on my upper arm. It came out shallow, and I knew the man was on edge.

Luckily, we didn't have to wait long. Plank-Guard-Karna walked onto the ship with purpose, and the other guards only offered nods as she walked by. I held my breath as she crossed the deck and then made her way down into the hold. She only glanced at King Rishan once, and I was impressed with her ability to maintain a straight and confident composure.

"What now?" Fain whispered, the ice of his voice leaving goosebumps on my neck.

I shrugged. "We wait."

"How long?"

"Relax."

The more we spoke, the more chances we gave the enemy to catch us. We didn't need that. I offered nothing else in terms of conversation, and Fain seemed to understand. The groans and creaks of the massive galleon ship added to the tense atmosphere, and occasionally, the conversations of the crew wafted over.

"They say the city isn't safe at night, ya know," one man muttered, his words filled with his uncertainty.

"Lots of thefts," another replied. "I heard because they're so separated from everything out here, they get away with everything, too."

"Yeah."

"The dockmaster is a nymph arcanist, and the deputy dockmaster is a grootslang arcanist, and they can be paid off to look the other way for all sorts of things."

"Is that right?"

I didn't find their conversation comforting. Millatin already felt like a city forgotten—even the lustrous history of the god-creature creating a perfect island seemed tainted by the present-day reality.

Soldiers from the quarterdeck stepped down the stairs, their heavy boots creating more noise than the deckhands exchanging rumors. When the unicorns and pegasi moved, their hooves shook the deck. They were essentially horses wearing heavy armor, so I wasn't surprised by the amount of noise they created by merely shifting around.

My anxiety built with each passing moment, and the knots forming in my gut and chest refused to lessen. I stared at the ladder leading down to the hold, hoping Karna would soon return with whatever we needed.

To my relief, she emerged from the depths of the ship, but this time, her appearance was slightly altered, including her clothing choice. I only recognized her because of the handkerchief in the pocket.

But she didn't head for the captain's room. Instead, she shuffled toward the gangplank, one hand on the side of her head the entire time. She wobbled like someone who'd had one too many to drink—was she acting? She had to be. Of course she wouldn't be drinking at a time like this.

Karna rubbed at her temple as she stumbled off the ship.

She was leaving? Why? Had something gone wrong? Or was she just done with this?

My thoughts buzzed in my head. Should I get off the ship and see what's wrong with her? Or stay and retrieve the runestone?

"Did Karna leave?" Fain whispered. "Why?"

I shook my head. "I don't know."

"What're we going to do?"

My heart hammered against my ribs. The runestones were too important to abandon. Much too important.

"We're going to continue without her," I said, keeping my voice low.

Fain squeezed my shoulder so tight, I felt his nails digging into my skin. "We have no keys."

"Luthair," I whispered. "Slip under the door and unlock it from the other side."

"I won't be able to dive back into the shadows, my arcanist."

"I understand. Fain can make you invisible."

The shadows shifted around under the staircase of the quarterdeck. "As you wish, my arcanist."

43

LIFE & DEATH SENSE

A few seconds later, the door to the captain's room opened outward, revealing Luthair, his liquid darkness armor both comforting and imposing. He stood half a foot taller than me, and I was already over six feet. It was rare for me to realize the difference in our heights, and I wondered if his true form had given him a few extra inches.

Fain and I slipped into the captain's room and shut the door as soon as possible. Although I wanted to drop the invisibility, I knew it wasn't wise.

"My arcanist," Luthair said, his helmet never moving, even if the voice emanated from within. "We should merge. Fain's wendigo magic will transfer to me then."

I nodded.

And I then remembered he couldn't see me.

"Okay," I said aloud.

Luthair couldn't dive back into the shadows because the nullstone wood, and instead took a step toward my voice, preparing to merge with me in an unusual way. His armor split open down the center like a sideways mouth, peeling back in a matter of seconds and revealing his hollow insides. I stepped forward. The shadows reached with hundreds of tiny thread-like tendrils until the shadows of Luthair's armor had hooked themselves onto my body. In the next instant, Luthair melded across me, forming in places around the vital organs and covering my head with his helmet.

Sure enough, once merged, we were both invisible.

"That was interesting," Fain murmured from the corner of the room. "I've never seen a knightmare merge with *nothing* before. You were invisible the whole time."

"Don't bother thinking about that right now," I said in my new merged voice. "We need to find the lockbox."

"Right."

The two of us shifted around the room. There was a desk, four chairs, three bookshelves, a chest of drawers, a cabinet of compasses, and several paintings of a city I was unfamiliar with. I figured it had to be Thronehold, given it was the capital of the Argo Empire, but the city was located near the ocean, which wasn't true about Thronehold.

There were three windows, but each had been constructed with opaque stained glass, preventing me from seeing out to the dock. I suspected it was also intended to dull the sunshine, since it could glare off the waters while sailing across the ocean.

But my mind could barely focus. I continued to dwell on Karna. What had she been thinking? Why leave? My inability to concentrate hindered my search. I barely saw the things I touched and moved aside.

"Volke," Fain whispered. "I think I found it. It's here—under the desk."

I tried to shadow-step over to his voice, but the sting of the nullstone wood prevented me. I cursed under my breath, hating every moment I was on the *Black Throne*, and instead walked over to Fain to better see what he was talking about.

The captain's desk was uncluttered and tidy. No papers. No maps. No quills or ink or wax for letters. I had never seen a captain's space so barren and lifeless. Did anyone actually use the desk or was it all for show?

Fain, still invisible, dragged a chest out from under the table—the chest was made of steel and looked as though it were scooting itself across the wooden floor. The scraping that echoed throughout the room put me on edge.

It was a decent sized lockbox, rectangular in shape and weighing at least 150 pounds, perhaps more. Was the shale runestone truly inside? What else would we discover?

"This is why we need a key," Fain whispered. "Without Karna's assistance, I don't know if we can do this."

"Hm."

I dwelled on the situation, the creaking of the boat our only other companion.

A minute passed and I couldn't stop shifting my weight from one foot to the other. Although Luthair was now merged with me, it felt claustrophobic to be with him, and I paced back and forth, my legs shaky, my hands unsteady. What were we going to do?

Karna had left in what appeared to be pain. Perhaps she had become ill? I shook my head. I couldn't think of that. I had to focus on the situation. I scrunched my eyes closed, trying to picture the lockbox, but all I returned to was Karna. Technically, doppelgänger arcanists could manipulate people—if she had been in trouble, why hadn't she controlled someone?

My arcanist, Luthair spoke, his telepathic voice ripping me from my thoughts. *This line of thoughts will get you killed. Leave it for now. Instead, use our shadow manipulation.*

I gave the lockbox a long stare. It was sturdily constructed—completely metal, with interior hinges, a small keyhole, and sharp corners. It would sink to the depths of the ocean if it were thrown overboard, and it'd probably keep the contents completely saltwater free.

"I can't break this," I mumbled under my breath.

But it also wasn't made from the nullstone wood, like the rest of the ship. Magic could be used on it, theoretically. It was still a steel container, but some magical abilities really didn't care what kind of material had been used in the construction.

Destruction is not always the answer. Now is the time for finesse. You practiced your smaller manipulation for this very reason.

I couldn't help but smile to myself. I *had* practiced using the shadows to craft smaller objects, but nothing as exact or important as a key before. Perhaps this was the moment everything came together.

"Fain, step aside," I said. "I'm going to try picking the lock."

"Do you know how?"

I grimaced at the comment. "Well... No. But I'll try."

"We need tools. My brother always had a leather pouch with hooks and small hammers."

"Don't worry about that. I can make my own."

Fain shuffled away, and although I couldn't see him, I could picture his baffled expression in my mind's eye.

Due to the nullstone wood of the ship, I couldn't manipulate the shadows on the floor or wall—they just wouldn't answer my commands. Instead, I tugged at the small amount of darkness on the empty desk. I couldn't get much, but I didn't need much, either. The keyhole was small, and as long as I could release the locking mechanism, we'd obtain the contents.

With a great deal of concentration, I focused on the darkness and manipulated it as a tendril into the keyhole. Then I knelt close to the box and listened. Then I forced the shadows to spin and fork out, creating even smaller tendrils that acted as the teeth to a key, I paid careful attention to when my shadows touched anything or caused the lockbox to make a noise.

"Are you really picking the lock?" Fain asked.

"Shh," I replied, unable to carry on a conversation while I worked.

Fain didn't say anything else. He quieted himself and remained unseen, though I knew he was close by. Occasionally, I'd feel the warmth of his breath on my shoulder, or his odd gunpowder scent whenever he stood too close for too long.

Although the keyhole was small, it seemed deep. It took many tries—frustratingly turning one way and then the opposite—to feel the pins of the lock and move them so that the lid would open.

The hardest part was maintaining the shadows. They constantly threatened to collapse, and I gritted my teeth, closed my eyes, and focused on making sure that didn't happen.

When the last of the mechanism sprung loose, I nearly shouted and patted Fain on the shoulder. I held back, since we were in enemy territory, but the relief in my heart was enough to warrant ten celebrations once we returned to the atlas turtle.

"Let's see what we've got," Fain whispered as he threw open the lid.

Much to my disappointment, the first thing we saw was a pile of fabric. Without dropping his invisible state, Fain lifted a gray cloth out of the box and examined it. Gold stitching formed an intricate picture on both sides.

"Odd," I whispered. "What is this?"

"It's a nautical flag..."

"For what?"

"Well, this flag here has a distinct pattern. See the compass shape made from weapons? That's Calisto's sign. Any flags that display this will be given mercy and passage by the *Third Abyss*."

"That's not surprising," I said in a sardonic tone. "Calisto is deep within the Second Ascension. He even—"

The door to the captain's room opened.

The slow creak of the hinges was like the yolk of an egg slowly sliding down my back. All my thoughts came to a halt as my heart seized inside my chest. Without thinking, I glanced over, hoping beyond reason it wasn't Rishan and his dragon. This whole boat would burn if we found ourselves in combat.

But the moment I saw who it was, my panic doubled. It wasn't Rishan, or one of his guards, or even his fiancée, Chandra...

It was her grim reaper.

The floating suit of executioners clothing ambled into the room, the hollow cowl glancing around. I froze—I didn't even breathe—and the grim reaper never stared at me or Fain, even though it could see the lockbox had been moved and the lid was still open.

"Intruders," the grim reaper said.

His voice was a thing of terrors—deep and unforgiving. It had a tone belonging to what all children imagined was under the bed. A creature of hate and scorn. A creature of death.

"Show yourself," the monster continued.

Fain and I did nothing.

The grim reaper's axe floated along behind it, but then the empty beast turned and grabbed it midair. With an effortless twirl, he spun the axe around, and the blade whistled—both sharp and weighty.

"Don't think you can hide from me," the grim reaper stated. "I am Demise, a creature far beyond your years and capable of sensing life itself. I can feel your heat—your heartbeats—and if you reveal yourselves now, I'll allow you to live."

A terrible feeling ripped through my whole being.

This grim reaper—*Demise*—was lying. He had no intention of allowing us to live. None whatsoever. He had said whatever he thought he needed to in order to get us to reveal ourselves—which meant that while he could sense us, he couldn't *pinpoint* us.

I placed a gauntleted hand on Fain's shoulder. "Keep searching," I whispered, though it was barely audible. "I'll handle this."

"We can fight together," he whispered back.

Was that truly the best course of action? We still hadn't found the runestone.

Demise turned his cowled head in our direction. I thought he would give us another warning, or perhaps he'd make a statement of some sort...

That wasn't the case.

Instead, he swung the axe with such intensity, I almost didn't have time to react. Demise used an overhead strike, and it was difficult to see the strain in his "muscles" when he barely "wore" anything. He cleaved the desk in two, right down the center, as though he thought we were underneath, hiding from his view. Splinters flew everywhere as a cacophony of destruction echoed throughout the room.

Fain and I leapt away, but neither of us shouted or yelped in surprise, maintaining our hidden state. I had to stop myself from breathing deeply, lest I give away my position.

With a grunt, Demise yanked his axe blade out of the severed desk and swung it over his shoulder.

The nullstone boat prevented me from shadow-stepping around the room, but it didn't prevent me from using my blade. With my pulse high, I unsheathed Retribution and held Forfend on my other arm, ready to make this a quick fight.

Then Fain gripped my arm, his icy touch intense. "Don't," he said through gritted teeth. "I swear I sense death about you. If you fight this reaper... I think..."

He didn't need to finish the statement. I knew what this would result in, especially since reapers were such dangerous opponents. This grim reaper had instant death abilities—I was certain that if the axe blade nicked me, it would all be over.

And even if I managed to defeat the grim reaper in combat, I would still die due to the *king's revenge*—the signature trait possessed by all reapers. Killing a reaper resulted in an instant death for whoever landed the final blow. It was divine punishment—a terrible curse—and I knew that limited everything I could do to fight this monster.

"We need to run," Fain whispered as Demise stepped forward, splintering wood under his executioner's boots.

"Keep searching the lockbox," I commanded. "I said I'd handle this."

"Come out and face me," Demise stated, loud enough that it filled the whole room. "I'm going to enjoy painting the walls with your blood."

44

DECOY

I couldn't evoke my terrors. I remembered how the grim reaper had ignored me the last time, which meant this would be a technical fight. Demise couldn't use his abilities, and neither could I. Our weapons would solve this conflict.

"I'm here," I said, my invisibility still shrouding me from view. "And you don't frighten me."

Demise didn't need any more taunts. Again, he swung heavy and overhand—his axe blade coming down with such force that I could tell it would rip through the floor and bust down to the deck below if it hit the wood. Parrying an attack typically hurt the attacker's arm, but I wouldn't be able to tell with a grim reaper. They were basically invisible themselves—just a suit of clothing with nothing inside—so when I blocked with Forfend and slammed the axe blade to the side, I couldn't tell if I had managed to hurt Demise in the process.

And to my frustration, my own arm ached after the effort. Demise's strike had been more brutal than I had anticipated, and a burning sensation tore across my shoulder. Adrenaline spiked through my bloodstream, dulling the agony, but I knew I wouldn't be able to block that kind of strike a second time.

Careful, Luthair spoke telepathically. *This isn't a time for recklessness!*

While Demise hefted his blade, I slashed outward in a horizontal arc. I sliced through some of the grim reaper's executioner's shirt, tearing through the fabric and creating a hole. The monster growled something dark and hate-filled, but I couldn't tell what. Then it kicked with its boot and hit me in the chest. The shadow armor hardened and protected me, dampening the blow, but I still stumbled backward and hit the bookshelf.

The slam of dozens of hooves on the quarterdeck rumbled the whole ship.

Where was Karna? If she were here, perhaps she could've distracted the others!

When I pushed away from the bookshelf, I realized my invisibility had vanished. Was it because of the hit? Or because Fain had failed to maintain his focus? I didn't know, and I didn't have time to figure it out. All I knew for certain was that I still couldn't see Fain—at some level, his invisibility persisted.

"A knightmare arcanist," Demise said, a drawl to his dark voice. "The same one who came to the aid of that wretch, Princess Evianna. Your true form is impressive." He held the double-bladed axe with a strong grip as he widened his stance. "Your death will fuel my growth—make me stronger. I can't wait to taste the difference your true form magic brings me."

We should escape while we can, my arcanist.

I ignored Luthair's pleading. Anger tainted my vision, darkening the edges. Even though my shield arm throbbed with a dull pain, I could sense something else from Forfend, like it was answering my deepest desires. The face of the shield glowed a terrible white, bright enough to light up the room. In the next instant, flames erupted forth.

But not just any flames. Sovereign dragon fire—the very breath attack that Crimthand had used against me on the docks. Forfend had stored the destructive power and was now unleashing it upon rage-filled command.

The flames lashed out, washing over Demise and then across most of the room. The temperature rose, my armor faded a bit, and the grim reaper screamed in both agony and shock. The white fire contrasted harshly with the dark wood of the *Black Throne*.

Panic seized my chest a second time. What if I killed the beast?

My arcanist! Luthair's alarm caused even more anxiety. *Don't kill the reaper! The king's revenge will kill you in turn!*

"Volke!" Fain shouted as he dropped his invisibility. "I have it!" He held up the palm-sized runestone. The gray shale shone in the light of the flames.

That was all we needed. Instead of waiting to see if Demise would survive my attack, I rushed for the nearest stained-glass window. The design was a black dragon on a field of red roses, its wings outstretched. Instead of admiring the craftsmanship, I did the exact opposite—I smashed the glass with the hilt of my sword, shattering it outward and creating an impromptu opening.

"*Fain,*" I shouted in my perfect double voice. "To me!"

He ran to the window, and I used Forfend to break away a few shards around the sill in order to easily escape. Fain didn't need any further commands. He leapt out head-first and then dove the twenty feet to the waters below.

The door to the captain's room opened, but the flames and smoke made it difficult to really tell who was there. I didn't spend time staring, either.

"You'll rue this day," Demise growled, the terrible tone of his voice like a nightmare's promise. "Soon, your magic will be mine."

I followed behind Fain, leaping out the window and plummeting to the waters below. My inky armor smoothed itself to help with the impact with the water. I had made jumps like this many times as a child, and it didn't frighten me to sink so far beneath the waves afterward. To my surprise, my cape ripped apart and became fin-like appendages that helped me swim faster, guiding me through the current and allowing me to escape the *Black Throne* with ease.

Fortunately, I found Fain in the darkness of the depths as I made my way away from the galleon. He swam without heading toward the surface, and I could see why—lines of air pierced the surface of the water and shot downward from the force of bullets raining all around us. The flintlock pistols could only shoot one at a time, which limited the barrage we faced, but it still meant we couldn't surface until under the pier.

When I grabbed Fain, he allowed me and my fish-like suit of armor to help him swim faster through the waters around the dock. Although my hearing was distorted while underwater, it didn't prevent me from distinguishing the harsh break of the waves when people jumped in after us. And, thanks to my ability to see through darkness, the murky depths of the bay didn't prevent me from identifying our pursuers.

To my horror, one of them was Demise himself.

I dragged Fain up to get air once under the pier, and he gulped it down the moment he could. Then I rushed toward the shore, my heart racing. The double-sided executioner's axe slammed into the wood of the dock as though someone with the strength of ten men had thrown it. The blade had narrowly avoided my head, passing by close enough that I felt the concussive force of the blow. The splintered wood and explosion of damage told me my head would've reacted much like a watermelon if the axe had actually struck it.

Fain gripped me tighter, but then he jerked his attention to the grim reaper swimming toward us, his empty clothing clinging to his unseen body, as though worn by a ghost with a physical form. Fain held up his hand and evoked frost over the water. I thought his magic would be too weak, but his ice created a solid mass that managed to slow Demise.

Once I reached land, I yanked Fain up the steep bank and right onto the dock. My cape and my armor shifted to its normal state, returning to shadowy plate armor. Fain struggled to move with haste when his clothing hung heavy with saltwater, but that didn't matter. I held onto his shoulder and dove into the shadows. My body hurt—an odd drained feeling lingered throughout me—so I didn't take us far. I emerged from the darkness only fifty feet down the road.

Again, Fain emerged gasping for air.

"Let me... catch my... breath," he said through huffs.

I pulled us down one of the narrow alleyways, hoping it was enough to throw the enemies off our trail. But we didn't have much time to ourselves. Something else smashed through the dock, and I chanced a glance around the corner of the alley. Demise walked out of the water, his massive axe in hand. And unlike the dockhands and sailors with rifles, Demise wasn't confused by our disappearance. He strode straight for the alleyway where I had us hidden.

But how did he know?

His life sense, Luthair spoke telepathically. *Grim reapers can sense the subtle tug of life. He will be able to follow us until we're dead.*

I held my breath. My teeth gritted hard enough that it hurt. What was I going to do? Continue to fight this beast? We weren't trapped by nullstone wood, but this wasn't going to go well. Grim reapers were too deadly. One hit from that axe... And I couldn't paralyze him with my terrors—I had seen his immunity on the docks.

I also couldn't lead him to the Frith Guild. But I couldn't hide, either. Wait—couldn't I?

"What're we going to do?" Fain asked.

"Hold your breath," I commanded.

"Again? But—"

I grabbed Fain's arm and then dove into the shadows before he could finish his thought. We emerged at the other end of the alleyway and then I continued toward the city's center. Perhaps I could do something to hide from the grim reaper's life sense...

The moment the rank odor of the corrupted fountain reached my nose, I knew I was on the right track.

My arcanist?

"I know what I'm doing," I said aloud.

Fain huffed as he continued to struggle with keeping my pace. "That's good."

Despite my fatigue, I shadow-stepped until we arrived near the Millatin spring. The disgusting water gushed up from the twisted geyser, creating a mist of foul scents. Luthair had said that mystical creatures were more affected by the corruption—they felt it stronger, they fell to the arcane plague faster—and I figured it was the only safe place in the city.

With a deep and ragged breath, I stepped through the darkness and emerged in the sludge-filled water of the spring. Fain emerged with me, his eyes wide with incredulous disbelief.

"*Are you serious?*" he barked, the spring water up to his waist.

The geyser rained water onto us, and it was chunkier than I thought it would be. I wondered if the stench would ever come out of my star-lined cape, but I shook that idea from my mind.

To make sure we weren't found, I moved Fain around the other side of the spring, keeping to the waist-high water. Thankfully, shadow-stepping into the spring prevented the handful of Millatin citizens from seeing us enter the spring, and when Demise walked into the city's center, none of the vagabonds or urchins could give him directions.

With an empty cowl, Demise walked around, his boots echoing between the shabby buildings. My theory had been correct: he couldn't sense us beyond the powerful corruption. Or smell. Which meant he had no idea where we had gone.

Instead of wandering aimlessly through the streets, Demise muttered a curse under his breath and then stormed from the city center, his giant axe floating behind him as he went.

Although we reeked of slime and sewage, we had managed to avoid the agents of the Second Ascension, the city of Millatin, and the Argo Empire.

Returning to the atlas turtle had never felt so comforting.

The first rays of dawn shone down on Gentel's shell, highlighting the emerald green of her grass and reflecting off the pond in such a way that it created a mirror-like image of the pinkish sky. It could only be described as glorious.

For the second time in recent memory, I returned to the Frith Guild with aches and pains so deep, it was difficult to make it to the infirmary. I couldn't unmerge with Luthair or I would collapse, and every step had me gritting my teeth in determination.

The terrible smell didn't help, either.

Once in the safety of Gillie's care, and cleaned from the corrupted spring, I rested on the far bed, satisfied that Fain and I had accomplished something worthwhile.

Gillie's healing lulled me into a quiet sleep, but not before Luthair finally shed himself from my body and disappeared into the shadows in the corner of the room.

If I had dreams, I couldn't recall them. I awoke with the sun high in the sky—a short ways beyond noon—while a chorus of gulls sung the day's praises. I stared out the window, admiring the blue of the world, until a sense of tranquility overcame me. Then I turned my attention to the rest of the room and caught my breath.

Illia sat in a chair next to my bed. Nicholin lay asleep in her lap, curled into a tight O-shape. She wore a long coat, high boots, and a bright white tunic. It wasn't like her to wear anything that wasn't dark in coloration, and for whatever reason, it made her seem more jovial, though I knew color choice for clothing had little to do with that.

"What're you doing here?" I asked as I sat up.

Only then did I realize I didn't have on any clothes. I clutched the blankets and held them close, careful never to be indecent. How many times would I interact with women while nude? It was starting to get ridiculous.

"Good morning to you, too," Illia quipped.

"Sorry," I said as I rubbed the back of my neck. "I just didn't expect you here."

"You're my brother. Of course I'd come to see you."

"Fair enough." I relaxed a bit, calmed by Illia's demeanor and presence. "You seem happier than last we spoke."

She touched her eye patch and smiled. "We found people from the Huntsman Guild. They checked all the arcanists of the Frith Guild for signs of the arcane plague."

"And?" I asked.

"And none of them are infected. Vethica cured them with her khepera magic."

I almost gasped aloud. Relief and elation soared through my body in equal parts, mixing together to become genuine excitement. Illia smiled wider and then leaned forward for a hug. I embraced her tightly, thankful that I wouldn't have to worry about anyone else contracting this terrible disease ever again.

"*Hey, hey, hey,*" Nicholin shouted, his voice muffled and his body squirming between us. "I was sleeping here!"

Illia and I broke apart, both of us chuckling—either from the good news or Nicholin's puffed-out fur, I wasn't sure.

"I can't believe it," I said with a smile that wouldn't fade. "That's such a relief."

"Zaxis is thrilled as well." Illia ran her hands through her wavy brown hair, her cheeks a slight shade of pink. "He said he's never felt so good."

While the current news and situation had me happy for the future, I couldn't help but dwell on everything else I had just experienced. "Illia," I said. "Has Karna returned to the guild house?"

She shook her head. "She went out last night, according to the other journeymen and she hasn't returned."

My eyebrows knitted together. "At all?"

"No one has seen her."

"She *is* a doppelgänger arcanist. Maybe she's here?"

Illia shook her head. "Perhaps. But she hasn't made her presence known, let's say that." Then she frowned and furrowed her brow. "Master Zelfree left last night as well. No one has seen him, though I'm a lot less concerned if he manages to find trouble."

Both Karna *and* Master Zelfree? I bit my thumbnail, my gaze unfocused as I mulled over the situation. It was odd for either of them to leave without saying a word, and even odder that Karna would just abandon Fain and me in the middle of an operation.

"What about the shale runestone?" I asked. "Did Fain manage to bring it to Guildmaster Eventide?"

Illia shook her head. "I'm sorry, Volke. According to Eventide, the runestone you brought back was a fake. She suspected the real one is with Rishan at all times, and this was just a decoy for would-be thieves."

My heart sank into my gut. *Damn them.* They had known people would come for the runestone, and they had tricked us. How was I supposed to know the one in the lockbox had been a fake? How did Eventide even know? I would have to ask her at some point.

After a long yawn, Nicholin stretched and then arched his back. "Okay. I'm awake. The real work and conversations can begin." He glanced between Illia and me. "Are we heading to the world serpent yet?"

"Almost." Illia stroked his elegant white and silver fur. "First, we have to wait for Master Zelfree and Karna to return."

"We're leaving already?" I asked.

Illia nodded. "Eventide has all the supplies and materials she needs, and she's gathered star shards and a handful of mercenary arcanists to help us on the last leg of this trek. We can go at any time."

We had only been in Millatin for a short time, but I understood the need for urgency. We couldn't stay here, not when the *Black Throne* was in the port and our enemies were all around. Still, my pulse ran fast as I realized we were coming to the crescendo of our journey.

"Is Ryker okay?" I asked.

Illia nodded. "He is. And he said he's finally ready to bond with the world serpent."

"So, when will Zelfree and Karna return, do you think?"

"No one knows where they went," Illia muttered. "It's really odd. If they're gone for much longer, we might have to search for them."

A FAVOR OWED

M illatin wasn't an island that grew on me. The longer I wandered the dank streets and seedy alleyways, the more I longed for the quaint peace of Ruma and the grand elegance of Thronehold. The corrupted spring in the center of the city acted like the beat of a black heart. Its foul stench and disgusting visage only reminded me that the core of Millatin wasn't pure. It was twisted—no longer glorious and legendary.

The shops of Millatin didn't endear me to the city either. Unlike on my island nation, the vendors here conducted themselves as though they would happily rob me if they could get away with it. The haggling was aggressive, and they seemed to know I was a foreigner. They'd try to take advantage of that fact—tell me they were giving me a good price for the area, even though I could tell they were lying.

That was the biggest problem.

Everything was a lie.

One of the main councilors was in bed with the Second Ascension, yet no one knew. The thieves on the streets conducted themselves as merchants. Millatin was a place of heroic beginnings, yet there was nothing of honor or nobility here.

"I don't like the city much, either," Adelgis said, clearly listening to my thoughts as we walked a side road that connected the docks to the city's warehouses. "The thoughts here are basting in unsavory imaginings. An unusually high number of individuals took note of our lack of armor."

I touched my button-up shirt, and I realized that—besides our arcanist marks—Adelgis and I *did* look like casual wanderers. Even then, I still kept myself swaddled in my cloak and hood, hiding my mark from the world, thus making myself more of a target.

Adelgis wore long, black robes with deep pockets and a cloth sash, and I wore sailing trousers, a long coat, and thick boots, with no visible firearm or armor of any kind. My belt had several pouches, most of which were filled with medical supplies, but the denizens of Millatin didn't know that. I could be carrying a year's worth of coin from my time as a sailor on a ship for all they knew.

"We'll be fine," I said. "If anyone attacks us, it'll be one of the greatest mistakes of their life."

Adelgis tapped his fingertips together. "I'd prefer not to get involved with unnecessary violence."

"Don't worry. *I'll* be the one doling out the violence."

"Still. I think it would be in everyone's best interest if we just avoided these hooligans. We could return to the Frith Guild and allow others to handle this. Or perhaps arm ourselves with blatant weapons to act as a deterrent."

"We don't have time for that," I muttered. "Just keep searching for the thoughts of Master Zelfree and Karna."

"I am."

"And you're sure you can detect them? Even though there are thousands of people around?"

"I know Master Zelfree and Karna extremely well," Adelgis said with a smug chuckle. "There is no way I won't recognize them in this sea of mediocrity."

I nodded along with his words, hoping he was correct. I didn't have any sort of mind-reading ability, so I didn't know how difficult it would be to locate two individuals in a group of people, but I trusted Adelgis enough that I figured he knew what he was talking about.

What worried me was that *I* knew both Master Zelfree and Karna very well. Neither of them would just *up and disappear* into the city without a valid reason. And why both of them? They had so little in common. The fact that no one seemed to know where they were was also disturbing—why wouldn't they say anything to anyone?

The dirt and sewage on the side of the road had become thick enough that I had to take note of it. Insects made their lair in the piles of decomposing garbage. How many bugs were there? How many types? They writhed together as though in sync.

"Please," Adelgis said as he held a hand up to his mouth. "You don't *also* need to think about it..." Then he caught his breath and came to an abrupt halt. "Wait. Something... isn't right."

"What do you mean?" I asked as I slowed and then turned around.

"Someone's thoughts... They're jumbled."

I examined our surroundings with a keen eye, though nothing stood out as noteworthy. A man on the corner begged for food. A small boy stood on the opposite corner, selling scraps of paper with crude maps to any of the sailors walking by. And then there was the foot traffic—dozens of individuals moving about, going from one destination to the next. How was I supposed to tell who had messed-up thoughts?

"It's not a person," Adelgis whispered, his dark eyes on the sky, like he was searching for something otherworldly. "It's a mystical creature."

"Does it have the plague?" I asked.

Then I held out my hand. Retribution flew upward from the shadows, as though Luthair had tossed it to me from the depths of the darkness. A few individuals gasped and hustled away, but I suspected they weren't aware of my transgressions against King Rishan—they were just afraid of my magic and weapon.

"No," Adelgis said, his voice distant. "It's not plague-ridden. It's just... unlike anything I've sensed before. And it's thinking about Karna and Zelfree."

"Really?" I practically gasped. "But why? And is it hurting them? Are they okay?"

"It's too difficult for me to tell."

"Can you lead me to it? Maybe it'll know where Karna and Zelfree are."

"I think I can take us to it." Adelgis ran a hand through his long, silky, black hair. "People's thoughts become louder and more prominent the closer I get."

I motioned to the scummy cobblestone road. "Lead the way."

It didn't take us long once we realized we had to circle around a building and head for the dock warehouses. I thanked whatever lucky stars were watching over us that the docks and the nearby areas weren't as filthy as some of the streets in town. It made the hunt for the strange *mystical creature* less irritating.

"The creature admires Karna and Zelfree," Adelgis said as we ambled toward the entrance of the warehouse. "It considers them family, somehow."

"Family?" I asked, more to myself than to Adelgis.

"Yes. It's an odd thought. I'm not sure why…"

The sign on the side of the warehouse read, "*Dried Goods and Storage.*" The dockhands around the place weren't particularly vigilant, but there was a lock on the main entrance, and the windows were closed tight. Fortunately, there was a gap between the door and the ground.

I took hold of Adelgis's shoulder. "Hold your breath," I commanded.

He probably already knew what I was going to do, but I gave Adelgis a second to comply before diving into the darkness and slithering my way into the warehouse. The dockhands were none the wiser, and I emerged on the other side, shrouded in darkness.

Adelgis gasped and then exhaled. He glanced about, his eyes straining for light. I was about to augment him to allow dark-sight, but Adelgis held up a hand and evoked an orb of light instead. With the intensity of three lanterns, it created enough illumination to see the dozens of crates scattered around the long, rectangular room.

Rats scurried from us in all directions, fleeing to the harsh shadows created by Adelgis's magical light. They hissed and squeaked, but none of them approached. They fled as fast as possible, their fur matted and slick with some sort of sticky liquid.

"It knows," Adelgis muttered under his breath. "And it seems… interested that you're here, Volke."

"Me specifically?" I asked.

Adelgis nodded. "It knows your name."

In that moment, everything fell into place. I knew what was here—and why Karna and Master Zelfree had been mysteriously drawn to it. The creature was unlike any other, and one of vast magical power. But why was it here?

I stepped forward and took a deep breath. *"Mother of Shapeshifters,"* I called out. "It's me, Volke. Show yourself."

The only thing that answered me was the squeaking of the rats.

"She knows who you are," Adelgis said, almost like he was an interpreter. "She... apparently owes you a favor."

I nodded once, my thoughts dwelling on the time I had met her. The Mother of Shapeshifters had been imprisoned by the Second Ascension, and I had freed her before they could cut apart her body and use the pieces for trinket and artifact creation. We had every reason to hate the same enemy, and I was glad to hear she was in Millatin, even if I didn't understand why.

"She wants to know what you're doing here," Adelgis said.

"I'm looking for Karna and Zelfree," I said, loud enough my voice carried throughout the warehouse. "Do you know where they are?"

More squeaks. More hissing. The movement of rats created a white noise of scratching paws and angry growling.

"She says they came to visit her," Adelgis said. He patted my upper shoulder. "And that she's glad you also came, even though she doesn't have the power to summon you. She wants... to help you locate the world serpent."

"She does?" I asked, one eyebrow raised.

"Like I said. She owes you a favor."

A part of me wondered how the Mother of Shapeshifters even knew about the world serpent, but another part of me remembered she was a child of a god-creature from the first era of gods. Perhaps she knew I was chasing them? Or perhaps she knew the Frith Guild was in possession of a few runestones.

"Please, show yourself," I called out. "I mean you no harm."

Nothing replied.

I continued with, "I've seen your natural appearance. I want to speak with you face-to-face."

For a long while, nothing happened.

Then the rats gathered at the edge of Adelgis's light, hiding in the darkness just beyond its reach. One by one, the rats went from normal creatures to a thing of night terrors. Their eyes shifted to a bright red, and they piled on top of each other until they created mountains of fur and flesh, their hundreds of red eyes twinkling in the darkness.

"Salutations," a deep rumble of a voice said, echoing throughout the warehouse. "Volke. My savior. The true form knightmare arcanist."

It was as if the many rats were speaking in a chorus of voices, mixing together to become a single entity.

But the Mother of Shapeshifters never left the safety of the darkness, even though I could see her many rats without difficulty. I stepped forward, no hesitation in my actions. Even if some people feared her, I knew the Mother of Shapeshifters would never harm me.

"Where are Karna and Zelfree?" I asked. "Can you summon them back here? Tell them I need to see them?"

"They will return to the guild," the Mother of Shapeshifters said.

"And you can help me find the world serpent?"

"A favor is owed. I will fulfill this request, if so desired."

"Well, the Frith Guild knows how to find the god-creature. What we need is help getting to it. Will you please help us beat the Second Ascension to the creature's location?"

The rats skittered and squeaked, all in merriment and delight.

"It would be an honor," she said, her dark many-voices more ominous than before.

I nervously chuckled. "Thank you." Then I pointed to the warehouse doors. "We'll be leaving on the atlas turtle as soon as Master Zelfree and Karna return. You can join us."

"I'm old enough to know the pathways of the ancient world. I will make my own way there."

"O-okay," I muttered. "Thank you again." I turned toward the door, intent on shadow-stepping outside with Adelgis, when a low rumble filled the warehouse. I glanced back and saw the rats shifting about until a single one leapt from a massive pile.

No. It wasn't a rat.

It was a mouse.

The adorable little creature scurried across the open portion of the warehouse, straight to my boot. Then it hopped onto the toes, grabbed my trousers, and then climbed up to my coat pocket. It squeezed itself inside, playfully squeaking the entire time. Its glowing red eyes stared up at me from the depths of my coat pocket, but I found it rather adorable, not frightening in the least bit.

"I will watch over you," the Mother of Shapeshifters stated. "Safe travels, Volke. May the good winds keep you and your companions safe."

HEADING EAST

The compass room of the Frith manor house was once again packed with arcanists and guild attendants. The excited buzz of anticipation pulsed through everyone, myself included.

Guildmaster Eventide stood at the head of the map table, her expression somewhat tired, but the fire of determination still alight in her eyes. She panned her gaze over everyone and then motioned to the topographical map of the surrounding area. Millatin was as clear as day —a fortress island with tall walls in the middle of the ocean. Then Eventide pointed farther east, to the empty waves that stretched all the way to the table's end. Technically, the map table only showed the surrounding area around Gentel, so the edge of the ocean wasn't the end of the world. Unfortunately, that meant we didn't know what was beyond the vast open waters.

We would have to find out ourselves.

"I have some good news, and I have some bad news," Guildmaster Eventide said, her tone serious, her attention on the peaks of the map. "The good news is that Vethica the Khepera Arcanist has the ability to cure individuals of the arcane plague so long as she can reach them with her magic before too much time passes."

The cheering and applauding that erupted was enough to hurt my ears. I cringed and scooted closer to the wall, fearful the celebrations would last long enough to cause a ringing noise deep in my eardrum. Some voices were louder than others—like Nicholin, who shouted and teleported around the room as though caught in an invisible hurricane.

Eventide held up a hand.

The room quieted quickly. Even Nicholin popped and teleported onto Illia's shoulder without further fuss.

"The bad news," Eventide drawled, her voice lowering, "is that the city of Millatin is being picked clean for the Second Ascension."

The statement garnered confused glances and bemused stares. The guildmaster took a deep breath before continuing.

"I searched for mercenary arcanists to help us on our quest," Eventide said. "But we didn't find many. Most are now in the employ of the Argo Empire. Specifically, King Rishan." Then she pointed to the east part of the map. "To make matters worse, the Occult Compass continues to direct us eastward, into the Elgan Ocean. It hasn't changed more northern or more southern, meaning our trek will be a long one. So long, in fact, I cannot give you an accurate prediction on timeframes."

The news settled like a rock that had fallen on top of a cake. No one spoke. No one made a noise. No one even moved. The terrible reality was: we didn't know *exactly* where we were going, and we didn't know how long it would take before that information became apparent. If we continued, we were taking a leap of faith.

"There's one more piece of disturbing news," Guildmaster Eventide said, her voice the only one in the map room. "The Second Ascension has in their possession six of the twelve runestones. The shale runestone for the fenris wolf has been seen in Millatin, meaning the enemy is out looking for other god-creatures even as we speak—some of which have already come into existence and are waiting for worthy individuals to bond with."

Somber nods and muttered concerns filtered through the guild arcanists.

I briefly wondered who would bond with the fenris wolf, but I shook the thought from my head. We still hadn't concluded the matter of the world serpent. I'd have time to worry about other god-creatures once this ordeal had finally been settled.

"We have supplies enough for three months of travel," Eventide said, pulling me from my tangent. "And starting today, we'll be heading east as quickly as Gentel can take us."

I stood watch at Ryker's door, the sole lantern above it the only light in the hallway. Although it was a lonely assignment, I still had Luthair—and my troubled thoughts—to keep me company. Thankfully, the darkness in the guild manor house also meant I could practice my fine shadow manipulation. Using the shadows to create a key to a lockbox had been satisfying, and I wanted the option to do more with the power in the future.

As I waved my hand and crafted tiny objects from the far corner, a soft squeaking emanated from my coat pocket. My concentration broke, and I glanced downward, startled by the strange noise. The mouse from the Mother of Shapeshifters stared up at me, its nose twitching.

"Hey, little guy," I muttered. "Are you... hungry?"

It squeaked again.

I glanced up and down the hallway, curious to see if anyone was watching.

Then I stared at my lantern-cast shadow. "Luthair—what do you think this thing eats?"

"Forgive me, my arcanist, but I don't know. If I had to guess, I would say it didn't, since the Mother of Shapeshifters is beyond most normal magics."

"It seems hungry."

"What do mice normally eat?"

My mind drew a blank. Didn't mice eat human food? Scraps from the table? Garbage on the roads? But then I remembered all the memories I had that involved the Mother of Shapeshifters. What did *she* eat? Wasn't it... people?

It hadn't occurred to me until then, but was she a man-eater? A type of mystical creature that mostly consumed flesh?

More out of morbid curiosity than anything else, I manipulated the darkness to create a tendril up to my hand. Then, using the fine control I had worked on, I created a needle-like point and touched my finger against it, breaking skin enough that a droplet of blood bloomed from my flesh.

"Here you go," I whispered as I lowered my finger into my coat pocket.

The red eyes of the freakish mouse grew wide, and it lapped up the blood on my finger in an instant. I feared the creature would accidentally bite me in its feeding frenzy, but I should've known better. This wasn't an actual animal. It gently took the blood I offered and left the rest of my hand untouched.

Then I patted its little head, taking note of its soft fur, and withdrew my hand from my coat pocket. As an arcanist, my flesh naturally healed itself far faster than the average man's, and by the time I had my arm back by my side, the pinprick had healed completely. There was no trace I had ever been injured.

"The Mother of Shapeshifters is with you now?" someone asked, their gruff voice enough to get me on edge and reaching for my sword.

But I relaxed the moment I realized it was Master Zelfree. He stood at the end of the hall, leaning on his shoulder against the wall. His black hair, dark clothing, and still stance made him blend in with the surroundings. I almost didn't notice him, even when looking around.

"I, uh, have this mouse," I said. "So, *yes*. She's with me."

Zelfree pushed away from the wall and walked over. He wasn't wearing boots, just a pair of sailing socks meant to dry quickly if ever wet. They were dark, nearly black, just like his trousers, shirt, and long coat. They dampened the sound of his footsteps.

"She's interested in you," Zelfree said. "She said as much when she summoned me."

"How *did* she summon you? I didn't know that was in her capability."

"Neither did I."

Without warning, Traces leapt from the pocket of Zelfree's coat and up to his shoulder. Had she been a pair of bangles inside his clothing? Probably. I hadn't been expecting her sudden appearance, however.

"She's worried about a great many things," Traces said with a purr. "And she wants to meet the god-creatures."

"All of them?" I asked.

Traces shook her head. "She's a child of the progenitor behemoth—the first one that died at the claws of the first apoch dragon. The Mother of Shapeshifters believes these god-creatures will be reincarnations of the old ones. She believes the behemoth will recognize her."

I nodded along with her words, intrigued by the concept. But then my eyebrows knitted in concentration as I recalled the great many legends about mystical creatures. "But they don't have souls. What's being reincarnated?"

Traces tilted her head from one side to the next. "They have the souls of their old arcanists."

Interesting. I hadn't thought about that angle. The god-arcanists would be people of extraordinary talent and force of will. They were the individuals who helped shape the world, after all. Perhaps they would be reincarnated in the bodies of their powerful eldrin. Anything with these god-creatures seemed within the realm of possibility.

"Regardless, the Mother of Shapeshifters said she wanted me to look after you," Master Zelfree stated. "And she told me she would be here to help stop the Second Ascension from claiming the world serpent." He narrowed his eyes and cast a glower down the hallway. "I don't have any proof of this, but I suspect she's here on this atlas turtle, sailing east with us in the form of insects or rats."

"Probably," I muttered as I patted the head of the little mouse again.

It gave a soft *squee* of appreciation.

I met Zelfree's gaze. "What did the Mother of Shapeshifters want with you and Karna?"

"She wants help with locating the progenitor behemoth. She realizes it won't come into existence anytime soon, but she's asked all her *children* to help her with this goal."

"Uh... how many children does she have?"

"I'm not sure. But from the way she spoke, I'd at least say there are dozens, if not hundreds." He offered a sarcastic smirk. "She mothered *all* shapeshifters, as far as I know."

I had never met another doppelgänger or mimic arcanist, and as far as I knew, they were rare. So rare, in fact, there were myths that there was only *one* doppelgänger arcanist and that they singlehandedly were the arcanist in all other stories, just in a different shape.

"It would be interesting to meet another mimic arcanist," I said.

Zelfree shrugged. "You probably will." Then he motioned to Ryker's door. "But don't worry about any of that—not even the behemoth—until after this is finished, understand? We're close now. The last leg of this journey."

I nodded. "I understand. And I won't lose focus."

"Good. Because I'm counting on you."

I slept in the mornings, after my shift watching Ryker had ended. I couldn't rest too long, though, not when I had to train with Evianna and the others. I hustled to my room, my feet sore and my mind buzzing with odd existential questions I wouldn't ever get the answers to.

The hall to my room was quieter than normal. It got me on edge, and I remained tense as I opened the door. To my shock, *I* was already in the room. I stood near the window, wearing a simple white tunic, dark trousers, and a pair of rough-worn boots. The *other me* turned to meet my gaze, and for a moment I remained confused, but the obvious answer came to me half a second after.

"Karna," I muttered.

The Volke-Karna smirked. "You finally arrived. I've been waiting."

It was... *odd*... to hear my own voice spoken back to me. I shuddered and then rubbed at my neck, my hand unsteady. "Uh, are you okay? You disappeared from the *Black Throne* and Master Zelfree said the Mother of Shapeshifters had summoned you."

Volke-Karna stepped away from the window and crossed the room. When she stopped a few feet from me, I couldn't help but stare. It was rare to meet people my height—Master Zelfree and Ryker were the only ones in the guild who were as tall—and it bordered on surreal to see my own facial expressions done to me.

My black hair was so disheveled it appeared more like a rat that had been struck by lightning than something fashionable. Fortunately, I had the physique of a fighter, and the hardened face of an adult, rather than the soft roundness of a child coming of age.

"I wanted to let you know I'm okay," Volke-Karna said. "The Mother of Shapeshifters has never summoned me before, but now that I know she wants to locate one of the god-creatures, I'm intrigued."

"She's the child of the progenitor behemoth," I said. "Well, the *first* progenitor behemoth... I understand why she might be interested in finding the new one that's born."

Volke-Karna limited the distance between us and then placed a hand on my shoulder. I wasn't entirely sure how I felt about her appearance. I couldn't stop dwelling on it.

"This just means I'll probably be with the Frith Guild for some time," Volke-Karna said, my stolen voice a rough whisper.

Had I ever spoken like that before?

"Okay," I muttered. "You're a valuable ally."

She lifted an eyebrow, and I almost chuckled at how playful my own expression could be. "Just keep it in mind," she said. "I don't mind waiting. Obviously, you're young and you don't yet know what you want from a partner in life. I understand. But you should also understand that I'm interested in you—and only you."

"What does that mean?"

"Many men and women have tried to woo me—but they all came up short." Volke-Karna slid her hand from my shoulder to the base of my neck. I recognized the feel of my own calloused palm. "You've made your position clear. You're with the phoenix arcanist, Atty. But time has a way of changing things."

I took a step backward, breaking her contact. "I don't know," I said. "I don't... want you to wait. It makes this..." I motioned between us. "It makes this strained."

She giggled, but my voice wasn't really the type to pull it off. Then she smiled. "Don't worry. I won't make things awkward for you in the meantime."

"That seems unlikely," I quipped.

"It won't make it *public*, how about that?" Volke-Karna walked over, patted my shoulder, got dangerously close to kissing me on the cheek, and then continued toward the door. "But I've been around the block several times, Volke. Young romances are the ones with the highest likelihood for regret. Mark my words."

I hadn't seen much of my father, Jozé, during the trek, so when he ambled out to the field during the day, I always took special note. His blue phoenix eldrin gave him away every time—she glittered with a sapphire majesty that couldn't be ignored.

"I think you should pay more attention when we're training." Evianna curled her white braid into a tight bun and then secured it in place with a pin. "What if I hit you with this practice sword? It could still hurt."

"I'll be fine," I said, my attention still half on my father.

Jozé never came to visit me. He always made his way over to Captain Devlin and Mesos and spent the afternoon discussing things with them. It made sense. They had been on an airship together for years. Both had bird-like eldrin. Both were older men who had seen a lot over their lives —to the point I would describe them both as *jaded*.

My father and I had little in common. Well, outside of magic and self-improvement. My father obviously loved creating trinkets and artifacts and would happily discuss that from here to the abyssal hells and back, but other than that, what did we have?

Evianna struck fast and low, aiming for my hip. Out of instinct, I manipulated the shadows to grab her wooden practice blade, preventing her from striking me.

"Hey," she said. "That's against the rules. You're not supposed to be using your magic."

I shook my head. "Sorry. I wasn't even thinking." I returned my full focus to her. "Let's go again."

She lifted an eyebrow as she ripped her sword from my shadow-grip. "Very well."

I widened my stance and attempted to pay attention to Evianna's grip and form. When she swung, I blocked in the most predictable manner so that she could familiarize herself with the standard methods of swordplay.

To my surprise, something struck me from behind. I whirled around to find the shadows had been manipulated to create a claw-like tendril. It hadn't been sharp enough to even pierce my clothing, but it had been pointed enough that I felt it.

And while my back was turned, Evianna whacked me on the hip.

"Gotcha," she said with a laugh.

I waved my hand, controlled all the shadows in the nearby area, including the one Evianna had created, and then turned back around, my eyes narrowed in a sardonic glower. I rubbed at my hip as I said, "No magic, remember?"

"Well, you used the shadows to block my attack," she said, playfully wagging a finger. "So I thought it was only fair if I got to use them once, too."

It was my turn to laugh. I shook my head in an attempt to dispel my mirth, but it was no use. She was right. And it had been a good move. If her shadow tendril had been more of a weapon, it would've been a great tactic.

"I'm surprised you have the concentration to both fight with a sword and manipulate the darkness like that," I said. "It's impressive." I tended to get distracted—or I focused too much on the opponent in front of me.

Evianna lifted her head just a little higher. "I know people don't like it when I say this, but I *am* talented. And I'm training under a true form knightmare arcanist, after all. Of course I should step up my skills and rise to meet the challenges of my circumstances."

I released my magic on the surrounding shadows and returned to my starting stance. "You've improved quite a bit. But that doesn't mean you should get cocky."

"Oh, I won't." She took her stance a few feet from me, her sword at the ready. "I'm not nearly strong enough to do all the things I need to do. Which is why I have to get even better. I'm hoping we can train all the way until sundown."

"That can be arranged."

COMING OF AGE

The Elgan Ocean was the largest body of water in the world, as far as I knew. It was 15,000 miles from one coast to the next, at least according to Gravekeeper William. He had never been to the other side, but all naval officers had to know the distance across the great ocean.

Each night, I watched over Ryker's room. Each morning, I snuck in my rest. And each afternoon and evening, I worked with Evianna and the others on their combat and magic. Fain, Hexa, and Evianna made the fastest improvements. Fain with his augmentation and ice evocation, Hexa with her aim and weapons, and Evianna just made general strides in all areas—she desperately wanted to catch up with the rest of the apprentices of the guild, even though she was the youngest and technically not of age.

But not for much longer. She reminded me of that fact every day.

"Twenty days until I come of age," she had said last week.

I had nodded each time—I hadn't wanted to focus on it much—and then went straight into our training.

The most disturbing thing that happened during our trek east, however, was the constant sign of ships on the horizon. It meant we were being followed. Someone, perhaps King Rishan himself, was sailing in our wake, keeping out of range and pursuing us at the same speed.

It had to be an arcanist, perhaps more than one. Gentel didn't need favorable winds to travel east. She had giant atlas turtle fins that propelled us toward our goal at a steady and even rate—but the ships matched our pace regardless. If I had to bet, I would've said there was an arcanist with wind magic aboard one of the ships, similar to Captain Devlin and his roc eldrin.

Guildmaster Eventide didn't seem concerned. No matter how many people pointed out the ships on the horizon, she pressed forward, following the guidance of the Occult Compass. We would eventually find the world serpent. Eventually.

I just worried that we were leading the enemy straight to it as well. At the same time, I didn't know what to do about the villains. Should we stop and fight them? They could get away. They could hurt Gentel or other arcanists in the guild. Or worse yet—they could capture or kill Ryker, and then our whole plan would be for naught.

So, like most other worries I had recently, I pushed it from my mind. I focused on helping Evianna and the others—and on improving my own magic—for impending, and likely unavoidable, conflict.

I awoke most mornings after a series of pleasant dreams. Today was no different. I had been dreaming of quiet white sand beaches, similar to those found on the Isle of Ruma. The dreams were too vivid and real to be normal... It had to be Adelgis's doing.

Was he helping me rest? That seemed like him. He always went out of his way to aid everyone else, even in subtle ways that may not have garnered him recognition. Adelgis gave for the group, and I appreciated his assistance, though I did worry for him. His father, Theasin Venrover, was one of the higher-ranking members of the Second Ascension and would no doubt be our enemy. Would Adelgis stand against him in the final confrontation? Or would he stand back and watch as everyone else engaged in a fight to the death?

I didn't care to think about it.

Once dressed for the day, and after I had laced up my boots, I headed for the door of my guild room. The creaking of floorboards on the other side signified someone was waiting for me, but who could it be? Evianna was always waiting for me on the field—she trained in the morning while I slept—and the others typically joined us closer to the evening.

I opened the door, half-expecting Master Zelfree or Karna, but instead found Atty and her eldrin, Titania, waiting for me. I caught my breath, shocked by Atty's bright smile.

"Uh, er, *Atty*," I said, somewhat awkwardly and foolishly. "What're you doing here?"

"Volke, I did it," she said with a single clap of her hands. Her tone was far giddier than I had ever heard it previously, even when we had been kids.

I waited, hoping she would elaborate, but she never did. I stepped out into the hall and shut my bedroom door behind me. "What have you done?"

"My fire! It's just like I said it would be! I can evoke flames that also transfer my healing augmentation." She spoke with haste, almost tripping over her words. "Don't you want to see? Come with me."

She took my hand and rushed down the hall, her long, white tunic and loose ivory trousers fluttering with her every movement. I admired the way her blonde hair caught the afternoon sunlight streaming through the windows—the stray strands glinted with the inner glory of gold. It matched the glitter of her phoenix, who hop-ran beside us, her peacock tailfeathers spiraling with the rush of movement.

We made our way down the grand staircase and then out to the manor house courtyard. Atty glanced back at me a few times, her enthusiasm never waning. Curiously, she had bags under her eyes—dark marks of sleepless nights—but that didn't seem to lessen her excitement. After we passed the fountain, we hustled along the main path and then veered off to the grassy field that covered most of Gentel's shell.

Sure enough, Evianna was already there training. Captain Devlin and his roc sat on the edge of the shell, near Gentel's head, overlooking our current path. My father and his blue phoenix accompanied them. Otherwise, there was no one outside—the cool ocean breeze kept most apprentices and journeymen inside.

"Stand there," Atty said as she pointed to an open spot of grass.

I did as she had instructed. Titania fluttered her wings, dropping soot on the grass and watching me with eyes that resembled liquid gold. Although it was harder to read the emotions on a creature with a heron-like head, I could tell Titania was excited as well.

Atty stepped close, her smile never fading. She grazed her fingers along my forearm. "I'm going to burn you. Is that okay?"

Although I didn't want to be burned, per se, I knew she could always heal me afterward, so I nodded. "That's fine."

She hesitated for a moment, her brow furrowed, as though the thought of hurting me was an anathema. Regardless, she evoked fire from her fingertips and scorched the skin just above my wrist.

Despite the fact that I had known it had been coming, I jerked my arm away and sucked in air through my teeth. The fire gnawed at my red and waxy skin, digging deep and causing me to shudder from the sting.

"Volke!"

In an instant, Evianna shadow-stepped to my side, her bluish-purple eyes wide with concern.

"I'm fine," I said as quickly as I could.

"*You*." Evianna whirled on her heel toward Atty, her expression set in a cold glare. "How dare you." The shadows of the field fluttered with an uncontrolled rage. "As a princess of the Argo Empire, I will—"

"Whoa, whoa," I said, stepping between them and holding up my good hand. "Everything is fine. Atty is demonstrating something. I allowed her to hurt me."

Evianna's expression softened, and the shadows around us seemed to calm. Then she patted the side of her trousers and frowned. "Well, you could've started with that. I wasn't sure what was going on."

"Don't fret." I stood closer to Atty. "Watch this. She's going to show us something no one has ever seen before." I held my injured arm up for Atty to examine. The salty winds stung my injury, but I gritted my teeth and tried to ignore the agony.

Atty hesitantly returned her fingertips to my arm. When she evoked her fire again, this time, it was a golden color the likes of which I had never seen. The shine of the flames took me by surprise, and I held my breath as the amber gold flowed over my skin.

There was heat—a warmth that was hard to describe—but it never hurt. If anything, it was the exact opposite. It felt like a gentle caressing, almost like the fire was licking my skin with the care of a sleepy puppy.

Evianna leaned in closer, her eyes practically saucers, the flames reflected across her irises.

Little by little, the fire healed my previous injury. The burn disappeared beneath the golden flames, leaving my skin pristine and new. When Atty's fire disappeared, the world seemed darker and my arm didn't feel quite as pleasant.

I looked everything over. I had been completely healed.

"That's amazing," I muttered.

Atty smiled wide. "Isn't it?" Then she touched my upper hand, her hand shaky. "So, what's next?"

"Next?" I asked, half-smiling from confusion. "What do you mean?"

"To have my eldrin become true form. What did you do next? I mastered this healing fire, so it should happen any day now, right?"

I slowly lifted an eyebrow. "Uh, well, I don't know. I said that already. Each mystical creature is different. When Luthair became true form for me, it was immediate. I didn't even know it was going to happen... It just *did.*"

Although Atty had been excited and filled with energy a moment ago, it all seemed to drain from her at once, like a barrel that had suddenly lost its bottom. I wasn't sure what to say, so I reached out and pulled her into a slow embrace, trying to let her know I'd be there for her, and everything would be all right, but she yanked out of my hold and turned away from me.

"Volke, now isn't the time for that," Atty stated. "I have to... focus. Clearly, I need to do more studying."

Her phoenix flapped her wings and leapt to Atty's side. "Everything will be fine, my arcanist. We just need to try harder. We'll achieve this. We will."

"We have more important issues to focus on," I said. "Like Ryker and the world serpent. Should you really focus on the true form of your eldrin when it's not crucial to our overall goals?"

Atty lowered her head, her blonde hair spilling forward, blocking her expression. She took a deep breath and forced a smile. "Achieving this *will* help us, don't you see? What if I can learn what it takes, and then I can instruct all phoenix arcanists to follow in my footsteps? What if I change the world?" She shook her head and took a step toward the guild house. "What if things like *death* become less meaningful? Matters like the world serpent will look trivial after that."

I held my breath, uncertain of how to counter all that. Was Atty's end goal to change the entire world with her phoenix magic? Surely, that couldn't happen overnight. Why was she pushing herself so hard when the enemy was around the corner?

"I think you'll exhaust yourself." I rubbed at my neck. "What if the Second Ascension attacks? You have to be ready."

"I'll be ready," Atty said, more edge in her voice than normal. "Come, Titania. We can't be bothered with any more distractions."

Before I could voice an objection, Atty stormed off the field, away from me and Evianna. Titania gave me a look and then followed her arcanist, her trail of soot becoming lost in the emerald blades of grass.

"Only five days until I come of age," Evianna said as she stared at the setting sun.

The ocean winds had been relentless today, and I'd had to continually comb at my black hair to keep it out of my eyes. No matter what I did, my hair grew in disheveled, but I felt like I looked like a homeless vagabond after the salty breeze tangled my hair further.

I motioned to the shadows around our feet. "You should focus more on your current progress. Your age progress isn't as important."

"Isn't it?" she whispered. Then Evianna turned to face me, a slight frown on her face. "I keep thinking... *what if we find the world serpent before my birthday*? I dread that outcome."

"Why?" I asked.

"What if I die before I'm an adult?"

The question caught me off guard. The winds whipped at my hair again, and I had to pat everything back into place, so I took the time to mull over Evianna's statement.

"You won't die," I said.

"You don't know that," she muttered, her gaze down. "And the wendigo arcanist told me about his death-sensing ability... about how *I* have the scent of death around me at all times. What if... I'm going to die at the birthplace of the world serpent? What if that's my destiny?"

Evianna never met my gaze. She just stared at the horizon, the dying light highlighting her emotionless face.

"You won't die," I stated again, this time firmer. "I won't let that happen."

That was when she glanced over with a glower. "You can't know that."

"I made a promise to Lyvia. I told her I'd protect you, and that's what I'm going to do."

"Well, what if we *both* die?" Evianna said, defiant. "What if that's why your wendigo friend keeps having these senses? Because you die protecting me."

"Nothing is written in stone," I said. "Not even Ryker bonding with the world serpent. There are just *likely* futures and outcomes." I stepped forward and breathed deep. "I won't let you die at the birthplace of the world serpent. And I definitely won't let you die before you come of age."

Although it took a prolonged moment of staring, Evianna's glower eventually cracked. She smiled, slowly at first, but then all the way. Her eyes glazed over, and I thought she might cry, but the look was gone in the next instant. Perhaps I had been imagining it?

"Thank you," she said. Then Evianna lifted her hand to return to her shadow manipulation. "But since you have the death sense about you, I'm also going to protect you. We'll be watching each other's backs, no matter what."

48

A BLACK SKY

I had worried about Evianna's prediction—that she wouldn't make it to her coming-of-age—but the moment the sun rose on her fifteenth birthday and we still hadn't discovered the world serpent, I breathed a sigh of relief. Her fears hadn't come to pass, and she would finally be an adult.

Now all I had to do was make sure nothing happened to her once we reached the world serpent itself.

Ryker's door creaked open, and I tensed as I whirled around. He stood in the doorway, his expression distant, his eyebrows knitted in concern. His ebony hair, unruly from a long night of sleep, puffed out on one side.

"Are you okay?" I asked. "Should I go get the guildmaster?"

He shook his head. "No. I'll... be fine."

A loud squeaking interrupted our conversation. I glanced about, confused and unsure of what was happening.

"The mouse, my arcanist," Luthair said from the darkness.

I chuckled to myself and then smiled. "Oh, right." I reached into my pocket and pulled out the strange rodent. It never left my coat—except when I picked it up—and it never ran off or hurried for a door, but it did like to fidget restlessly.

"I dreamt about mice last night," Ryker muttered as he watched me prick my finger and feed the creature. "Or maybe they were rats..."

"Hm." Once fed, I tucked the mouse back in my pocket. "I see. Strange."

Hadn't Adelgis been crafting Ryker's dreams? Why would he include some sort of narrative with mice and rats? Seemed odd. And out of character. Or maybe this had been one of those nights where Adelgis had gone out of his way to be adventurous with his storytelling?

"I think we're close," Ryker whispered.

I softly patted my pocket to make sure the little mouse was tucked in safe. Then I lifted an eyebrow. "What makes you think that?"

"It's hard to describe." He motioned to his gut. "But my insides feel twisted. It has gotten worse the farther we've traveled. I think... it's reaching an end point."

A part of me wanted to tell him he was making things up, but I had felt it, too. Each day brought with it a bit more tension and anxiety. Something was close, and it wasn't like with the plague-ridden monsters, where I felt their malice and heartbeat. This was intense. Something that reached into my core and told me this would be different than anything I had ever faced before.

"Do you mind if I accompany you?" Ryker asked as he stepped out of his room.

He wore a pair of neat trousers and a white tunic. He seemed plain, though tall and gentlemanly. I offered him a smile and then a slight bow of my head.

"Well, this is typically when I sleep."

"Uh, I see..."

The hesitation in his voice gave me pause. Was he just anxious? "I can change my plans," I said. "Evianna tends to start her training at dawn. I can meet her now and sleep later, if you'd rather accompany me to that."

Ryker smiled. "Perfect. I'd rather be surrounded by people than allow this feeling to consume me."

I thought the sentiment wise, and together we walked out of the hall, into the front room of the guild house, and then outside. Although anxiety was high, it felt calming to be in Ryker's presence. He kept quiet the entire time, almost pensive, and I retreated to my own thoughts as well.

When we stepped outside, I took a deep breath, enjoying the ocean scent and the warm glow of the rising sun. Ryker exhaled, a contented expression on his face. I would've asked him what his ultimate goals for the day were, but something happened.

I caught my breath as the sky went dark.

And not the kind of darkness where a cloud moved in front of the sun—or like my eclipse aura, when something physical got in the way—but the type of darkness only brought about by the night. By the *absence* of the sun.

"What's going on?" Ryker asked.

I ignored him and stared up at the sky, watching as the sun just... *disappeared...* as if it faded into the sky itself. The utter blackness left over sent gasps and shouting throughout the guild, but I wasn't blinded like everyone else.

"I don't know what's happening," I muttered. "Luthair?"

"I've never seen anything like this before, my arcanist," Luthair said.

There was nothing to see. Even though the sky had gone dark, there was nothing and no one to pin it on. Not even a mysterious creature flying through the clouds—I had no way to explain the phenomenon.

Before I could voice my lack of findings, I was caught off guard.

A bright—and intense—beam of rose-pink light shot up into the sky. It was on the horizon, far from us, but it was still visible, even hundreds of miles away. What was it? I had no idea, but the beam of light went all the way up, disappearing into the clouds, but continuing until I couldn't see it any higher.

Everyone gasped and pointed. Something shuddered, and the windows of the guild house were slammed shut.

What was going on?

The mouse in my pocket thrashed about so violently, I almost thought I was under attack. I jerked my attention down to my pocket. The mouse squeaked and clawed and kicked. I manipulated the shadows to grab and restrain the beast, confused by its sudden berserker rage.

And then as quickly as it had appeared, the beam disappeared. The light vanished, and then the sun reappeared in the sky, returning the world to normal, as though nothing bizarre had ever happened.

The mouse calmed itself. No more clawing and biting. Its glowing red eyes just stared up at me as though lost. I released the creature from my shadows, and it returned to hiding in my pocket.

"Something has happened," Ryker muttered. "Something terrible..."

A shiver ran the length of my spine. Although I didn't know what had happened exactly, I knew in my gut that Ryker had to be right. The Mother of Shapeshifters wouldn't have reacted that way if it had been *nothing.*

Master Zelfree dashed out of the guild manor house, his trousers half-secured by a loose belt and his button-up shirt only half buttoned. When he rushed over, I could see the scars on his body left over from Calisto's torture session. The twisted and gnarled knife wounds always inflicted empathetic twinges of pain across my skin.

Zelfree fastened the rest of his shirt closed, his gaze on the location where the rose-pink beam had been. "Dammit," he whispered.

"What's wrong?" I asked. "Do you know what that was?"

With his jaw clenched, Zelfree shook his head. "The master arcanists and the guildmaster will need to discuss this. Gather everyone else up and bring them into the guild house. Stay inside until told otherwise, understand?"

I nodded once. "Okay."

The Frith Guild had expanded since our time in Thronehold. Guildmaster Eventide had done what she had set out to do: bring us more arcanists and like-minded individuals. It was a shame we hadn't gotten many more from Millatin, but I was thankful for whom we did have. Ryker, Hexa, Illia, Fain, Adelgis, Zaxis, Vethica—seeing them all together and mingling was pleasant, but there was an impending sense of dread that still loomed over us all.

Most individuals looked exhausted—Evianna and I weren't the only ones training daily.

Well, everyone except for Zaxis. He smelled of sweat, but he always had a lively aura about him. Even now, while everyone waited in the dining hall, he seemed to be the sole individual with enough energy to leap over benches and tables as he made his way over to me. He even dodged around other arcanists and eldrin with the grace of a dancer.

"Did you see that light?" he asked as he neared me, his eyebrows knitted. "Only half the people said they managed to see it."

"The beam lasted a few seconds." I shrugged. "If you weren't outside, or by a window, it would've been easy to miss. Fortunately, Ryker and I were outside the entire time. It was distinct—obviously magical in nature."

Zaxis smacked me on the shoulder. "What do you think it was?"

I shook my head. "I'm not certain." Then I patted the pocket with the strange mouse. "But it was important."

His phoenix rested atop one of the many rafters, along with Atty's phoenix, though Atty hadn't left her room. I suspected she had sent her eldrin to the dining hall to see if we would discuss anything important; that way, she didn't have to stop her own personal training.

"Did Atty tell you about her healing fire? How she evokes and augments at the same time?"

Zaxis replied with a curt nod. "Yeah, but from what I can tell, it requires a lot of concentration and energy. I've seen her use it twice, and she's ragged afterward. It's interesting because what if your shadows could have terrors inside of them, ya know? Or what if a wendigo arcanist's ice could rend flesh, but if it requires *that* much from an arcanist, and months of training ahead of time to barely do it, is it worth it when we have a fight coming up?"

"I'm not sure."

"Exactly." Zaxis rotated his head, his neck issuing a few loud *cracks*. "I don't want to see the abyssal hells anytime soon, you understand? I've heard stories of the gatekeeping Death Lords that consume souls, and that's not going to be me. *I'm* going to send the Second Ascension there."

"Listen up, everyone!"

The shout interrupted all conversations in the dining hall. I turned to see Hexa standing on one of the tables, her cinnamon hair bunched up and puffy, adding another three inches to her height. She placed her hands on her hips and smiled.

"Today is Evianna's coming-of-age," Hexa said, her voice boisterous enough to echo throughout the dining hall. "That means we're going to have a celebration!"

People around the room exchanged questioning glances. Typically, individuals weren't allowed to join guilds until they were already of age, so I understood the confusion. On the other hand, I could see some of the other people here weren't of age, either.

To my surprise, I recognized one of the younger individuals in the crowd.

"Grant?" I said. "Is that you?"

He was a young man, only about thirteen, with a mole on his cheek and short, muddy brown hair. He wore a cloak with griffin feathers on the shoulder—a prize from the Isle of Landin for having passed the griffin's trial of worth. The cloak had the same amber brown coloration of an adult griffin, and it hung past the boy's ankles, as it was clearly designed for a grown man.

Grant turned to face me, and a smile erupted across his face. "Volke? Is that you?"

Although he had been still and quiet a moment before, he leapt through the crowd and then threw his arms around me the moment he could. I chuckled and returned the embrace, though I found it a tad harder to breathe.

"You joined the Frith Guild?" I asked.

Grant held me a moment longer. Then he broke the hug and pulled a guild pendant out of his tunic. It was bronze. He was, in fact, an apprentice with the Frith Guild.

"I had to join," Grant said. "Both me and my brother just had to!"

Then Grant turned his excitement to Zaxis. With another leaping hug, Grant wrapped his arms around Zaxis's muscular torso and squeezed as hard as he could. Zaxis frowned slightly, but didn't push the kid away. Instead, he patted Grant's back twice.

"Okay, that's enough," Zaxis growled. "This isn't a funeral."

Grant rubbed at his chubby face. He still had baby fat about him, but the mark on his forehead was as clear as anyone else's. It had the seven-pointed arcanist star along with a griffin wrapped around the points. Because the griffin had the head of a lion, I knew it was male, though I would've known anyway, considering I had been there when Grant had bonded with his griffin eldrin, Bedivere.

"Everyone, we're going to prepare a feast," Hexa said, her voice cutting through all other conversations. "Tonight will be a wonderful party, but everyone has to play their part!"

Although the idea of cooking and setting up festivities was far from people's mind, Hexa's command seemed to resonate with some. It wasn't a bad idea to lighten the mood, and it *was* Evianna's coming-of-age, so it seemed appropriate.

"I can't wait," Grant said, his smile never fading. "This way, I'll know what to look forward to when I come of age."

The festivities weren't elaborate.

We had simply prepared fish, soup, and hard biscuits. That probably would've been good enough, but Hexa and Zaxis had demanded that some of the rum be opened up for the occasion, so two barrels were rolled out into the dining hall for general consumption. I wasn't a fan of drinking—mostly because Gravekeeper William always abstained—and I maintained that stance, even while everyone else was filling their tin cups. Everyone but Atty, that was. She still hadn't exited her room.

It was amusing to see some people let their guard down when awash in enough alcohol, but it was more entertaining to watch a few eldrin take part in the drinking.

Nicholin didn't hold his liquor well, but I wasn't worried. There was no malice to his mischief—even if he had *a lot* of mischief.

"I could be a god-creature," Nicholin proclaimed loudly from atop the rum barrel. He waved a tiny ferret paw back and forth. "That's what I'll be when I achieve my true form, thank you very much."

Illia motioned for him to come down and get back on her shoulder, but Nicholin kept his nose high and his paw in the air.

"And, like, maybe I could cure the arcane plague with *gravity*. You all don't know!"

He waved to the nearby crowd, and individuals began to lift off their feet. Fortunately, in all the festivities and jovialness, no one seemed to mind. Laughter filled the hall as a drunken Nicholin levitated people a few seconds at a time.

Two people vomited, but even that was met with more laughter.

"You're all *weak* to my powers," Nicholin shouted as he pointed to the vomit. "*Weeeaaakkk!*"

While he lorded his newfound abilities to cause drunken people to puke, I turned my attention to Adelgis and Fain. For whatever reason—because no one else had bothered to dress overly fancy—Adelgis wore his old shoulder cape, his shiniest black boots, and a set of dark robes that fit him perfectly from his shoulders to his ankles. He spoke with Fain in the corner of the room, but it wasn't a large environment. I could hear them when I concentrated on their location.

"What do you think of the celebrations?" Adelgis asked.

"Don't you know what I'm thinking about all the time?" Fain asked as he took a swig of rum, one eyebrow lifted.

"Well, I've, uh, learned how to control my abilities better." Adelgis brushed back his long, black hair. "So, now I would like to know your opinions. With your words."

Fain lowered his cup and frowned. "Life might change, but you'll always be an awkward moonbeam, won't you?"

"You think so? That wasn't me acting normal and striking up a casual conversation?" Adelgis's eyebrows knit together. "Should I have inquired about the weather more?"

"No."

"Do you need a more interesting subject of conversation? How about —whom would you like to take to bed this evening?"

In the blink of an eye, Fain's face brightened to a shade of scarlet. "Moonbeam, what in the abyssal hells is wrong with you? I swear you keep trying the same, but slightly different, tactic, and it's not going to work."

"We're on the precipice of war and change. Death is nearby—your thoughts are filled with your *death sense*. I thought it was appropriate to speak about the opposite. Which would be intimacy and love and—"

"*Enough*," Fain growled as he pinched the bridge of his nose. "I meant we've known each other for a while now. You don't need to *act casual* with me. Enough with the bizarre questions. I don't give a damn if you read my mind."

Adelgis exhaled. "I know. I can hear your thoughts. I apologize." Then his shoulders slumped. "I just wanted to practice my charisma and charm."

"You have plenty." Fain took another swig of rum. Then he half-smiled. "I associated with pirates for years, and none of them had an ounce of charisma. You don't have to do much to keep me entertained."

"But you wish *you* had more charisma so that you could mingle more with the others," Adelgis said matter-of-factly. "I thought if we practiced together, we both could benefit." He smoothed his fancier outfit.

"Eh. I'm not so sure."

"How about I tell you one of my secrets, then? That way, you can get insight into *my* thoughts?"

Fain scratched at the stubble on his chin. He mulled over the offer for a long moment before he said, "Okay. Tell me."

"Ah, well, I promised my sister when I left home that I would keep a charm she gave me, but I dropped it during the long ride to Fortuna, and... well... I haven't written to tell her the news yet." Adelgis sighed. "It weighs on me. But I trust you'll keep my secret?"

Fain took a long swig of his rum, his eyes half-lidded. "Moonbeam, your secret is safe with my lack of giving a damn."

"Oh, perfect. That's such a relief."

"Just... go back to talking about the party."

"Very well," Adelgis said. "I can tell from the thoughts of those nearby that some individuals think we're handsome."

Fain's eyebrows shot to his hair, and his face remained slightly red. "Oh, yeah? Who?"

"Well, that woman there. And also Vethica." Adelgis stealthily motioned to them in the crowd. "A few individuals think we're weird. Like him." He made a hand gesture to a guy against the far wall. "Volke thinks we're entertaining, and has been listening for a while, and also suspects we might be a couple, but we're just not telling anyone. Hexa *definitely* thinks we're soulmates."

It was my turn to get red in the face. I turned away, ashamed I had been listening for as long as I had.

"I thought you said people's thoughts were their own private musings?" Fain said, slightly indignant and loud enough that I heard, even with my back turned to them.

"It's a party," Adelgis responded. "I think I've had a bit too much to drink…"

I walked away, trying to distance myself as much as possible. I made my way around the edge of the dining hall, avoiding eye contact with most individuals, attempting to be as covert as necessary.

That was when I almost ran into Vethica. I had to stutter-stop to a halt an inch from her. She shot me a quick glare before relaxing. Her khepera eldrin sat on her shoulder, his iridescent scarab shell glittering in the lantern light.

"Good evening," Vethica muttered. She sipped a cup of rum and then returned her attention to the corner of the room—the same one with Adelgis and Fain.

"Enjoying the party?" I asked as I stepped around to the other side of her.

I had intended to only make small talk before heading on my way, but Vethica replied with a genuine sigh. "I don't know these guild arcanists very well."

"They're generally friendly," I said, taking up a position on the opposite side of her.

"I know. But still. They're all comfortable with each other… and I'm…" Vethica clicked her tongue in disapproval. "What does it matter? I'm not part of the guild, anyway. Even if we *are* helping each other."

"Why do you hate guilds so much?" I asked. It was a question I had never gotten around to asking, even though I had always wanted to.

"Their rules and regulations make it difficult for arcanists," she spat. "Plus, they're so large and organized that it's difficult to compete with them unless you're *also* a guild. And every guild arcanist I've ever dealt with—except you and your friends, granted—have been rather pompous and insufferable."

"Right," I said as I rubbed the back of my neck. "Well, most people here aren't like that. So, I think you're safe to mingle."

Before she could respond, the loudest and most boisterous person in the whole room sauntered over. Zaxis combed his red hair back with one hand and then approached Vethica with a confident smile.

"Good evening," he said. Then he glanced over at me. "Volke."

I nodded. "Zaxis."

Vethica huffed and crossed her arms. "Can I help you?" Her tone was anything but friendly.

"I came over to thank you," Zaxis said, his smile waning. "Not to bother anyone. I mean, I owe you my life, basically. So, well, I thought that deserved some significant acknowledgement."

Vethica held her breath for a moment, obviously confused. She hadn't expected that from Zaxis. Neither had I. Zaxis tended to get... *weird*... when he drank.

"You're welcome," Vethica finally said. "But it was nothing. I'm just glad I'm able to help."

"Yeah, well, is there anything I can help you with right now?" Zaxis asked.

"No. I appreciate the offer, though." Vethica glanced into her empty cup and then forced half a smile. "Excuse me." She broke away and headed straight for the rum barrel with Nicholin on top.

Zaxis exhaled and then shot me a glare. "What were *you* talking to her about?"

Instead of engaging him in petty arguments, I simply motioned to Adelgis and Fain. "Hey, if you really want to thank her, you should bring Adelgis and Fain over here. Apparently, she thinks they're handsome. Or, well, maybe one of them. I'm not sure which."

For a long moment, Zaxis glowered at me. Then, in a sardonic tone, he said, "So, she saves my life... and I'm going to repay her by playing matchmaker? Is that it?"

"Do you have a better idea, mister *I'll saunter over here and just make statements without any sort of real plan because who needs those*?"

"Tsk." Zaxis shrugged. "You're such a smartass sometimes, you know that, right?" Then he shot Adelgis and Fain an odd look. "And there's no helping those two. One's a renegade pirate and the other is... well... *kooky*. For lack of a better word. Vethica won't be interested."

"You don't know that," I said, lowering my voice and motioning for him to do the same. "She thinks they look handsome."

Zaxis sardonically frowned. "Adelgis? Seriously? I've seen more meat on lettuce."

"Just help her out, okay? She's having problems interacting with people, and they're both nice enough. It's the least you can do for her."

Zaxis returned his attention to me, his expression so sarcastic, I almost laughed. "Damn you, Volke. Damn you."

I couldn't help but smile. "Thank you, Zaxis." Then I patted his arm and continued on my way, leaving him to the interactions. Hopefully, it would all work out. I had my doubts, but I decided to remain optimistic.

After walking half a loop around the room, I managed to observe most of everything happening.

While the party was enjoyable and distracting, two things disturbed me. First, the master arcanists had yet to come out of their talks. All day, they had been discussing the beam of light and dark sky, yet they had no conclusions they wished to share.

Second, it worried me that Evianna wasn't herself. She walked from arcanist to arcanist, giving thanks and smiling, but I had come to know her rather well over the last few months. She wasn't happy. This was her fake smile and forced laugh. Nothing about her attitude was genuine.

"Are you feeling well, my arcanist?" Luthair asked.

I nodded. "Yes. I'm just worried Evianna isn't enjoying herself."

"It's foolish to worry about matters you can't affect. It's even more foolish to worry about matters you can't affect right now."

His words stung with an edge of truth. After exhaling, I put my plate of fish down on the nearest table and decided to walk over to Evianna and engage her in conversation. For some reason, everyone who noticed me cleared a path immediately, all with smiles and slight bows of their head. It made me a little nervous—mostly because I wasn't one for attention—but the reactions were pleasant enough that I shook it from my thoughts.

When I approached Evianna, she stopped her conversation mid-sentence and then turned to face me.

"Volke?" she asked.

The female apprentice next to Evianna offered a nervous chuckle and then pointed to the barrel of rum. "My cup is empty," she said. "I think I'll get another drink."

Once the lady arcanist had gone, Evianna smiled up at me with genuine happiness. "There you are! I was wondering when you'd come to congratulate me. It's not nice to leave a princess waiting, you know."

I half-smiled as I cocked an eyebrow. "I thought knights didn't mingle with royalty at fancy soirées?"

Evianna's cheeks grew pink. She had allowed her white hair to hang down for the party, and she brushed some of the locks over her shoulder. "You clearly haven't been to many social gatherings with royalty. They love to have their knight arcanists in attendance. It's a sign of prestige and power."

"Oh, so I should've been by your side this entire time, acting as a manservant?" I offered a formal and sarcastic bow and then presented my elbow. "*Princess*," I said, attempting a poor upper-crust accent.

Evianna smacked my arm and—with her face now bright red—crossed her arms tightly over her chest. "You're incorrigible."

"Indubitably," I drawled, maintaining the same pompous accent.

But that was when a smile crept in at the corner of her lips. She snickered, unable to hold back, her irritation cracking under the playfulness of it all. I laughed and then motioned her to one of the nearby tables.

"Maybe we should sit down and see if there's any honey left for the biscuits," I said. "It makes for a fine dessert."

Evianna pointed to the door to the garden trails around the side of the guild house. "I think we should go outside and get some fresh air. It's so,"—she glanced at someone tripping over their own feet and then crashing into a nearby table, and then to Zaxis yanking Adelgis out of the corner of the room—"*rowdy* in here."

The roaring laughter that followed surprised me, but only for a short bit. Even if that arcanist had been hurt, he could eventually heal himself, or perhaps even be healed by Gillie.

As I followed Evianna to the far door, I noticed that Illia was staring at me with her one eye. She had somehow managed to wrangle Nicholin and take him to the corner of the room, where he was obviously unconscious and draped over her shoulder like a terrible scarf. She didn't say anything, though—it was a look of sadness when I went, though perhaps I was seeing things.

I dispelled the thoughts from my mind as I stepped out into the cool evening air. I preferred the slight chill to the warm excitement of the dining hall. The garden around the side of the guild wasn't large, but it did have tall hedges, flower bushes, and a couple of trees whose leaves changed colors with all the seasons. The pleasant aromas helped me forget our many troubles.

Evianna and I walked only ten feet or so from the door when she stopped and turned to me. Her ivory hair glowed in the moonlight, and her strangely colored eyes seeming darker when not exposed to direct light.

"I've never actually knighted you," she said. "I think, now that I'm of age, we need to correct that."

"I'm pretty sure you need to actually be the ruler of a territory to knight people," I said.

Evianna narrowed her eyes into a playful glare. "Once my brother is dethroned, I'll be returning to the Argo Empire, thank you. So, until we oust that traitor, I will have to work with what I've got."

She waved her hand around and manipulated the shadows to create a crude shadow sword. It wasn't that sharp, and it moved around at the edges as though not held together tightly with magic, but it would work for a simple knighting.

"Kneel, please," Evianna said.

Although I felt it mildly silly, I decided to play along. I went down on one knee, so that I wasn't taller than she was and then bowed my head, awaiting my new imaginary title as her knight.

In a soft voice, barely above a whisper, Evianna said, "You know, you're more than just a knight to me." She took a deep breath. "You're my mentor, my savior... my friend. Someone who has helped me in all aspects of life."

Her words seemed heavier than they needed to be, and my breath caught in my throat as I waited for her to finish.

"So, I can't knight you," she muttered. "It's not right."

Slightly baffled, I lifted my head. "This isn't a real knighting, it's—"

Evianna delicately took hold of my chin and then leaned down, bringing her soft lips to mine. Shock paralyzed me, and my heart hammered in my chest. Evianna kept her eyes closed as she deepened the kiss, pressing harder against me, her hand sliding down the length of my jaw and onto my neck.

I didn't move. Not even when Evianna finally pulled away and opened her eyes.

"Volke?" she whispered.

It was difficult to breathe. For a prolonged moment, I didn't know what to say.

49

A DISTANT TREE

"Evianna," I said.

She stared at me, her body stiff, her breath caught. I knew of her feelings for me, but I hadn't expected something like this. It felt more... *personal* and *real* than Evianna had ever been with me in the past.

I stood faster than I had wanted to, and somewhat to Evianna's surprise. She took half a step back, but then she straightened her posture.

"I know you said we couldn't be together because I wasn't yet an adult," she said before I could get a word in edge-wise. "But now I am. And... well... I'm not confused about what I want." She took a deep breath and spoke again a moment later, her voice soaked in conviction. "I want us to go on life's adventures together."

Still, I couldn't find the words. My mind buzzed like a hive of bees, and my heart refused to control itself. There was too much to think about outside this moment for me to fully grasp the significance of the words.

"Volke?" Evianna said again, her voice losing its strength. "Do you... have anything to say?"

I took a deep breath, my gaze fixed on her. "Evianna," I muttered. "I'm not sure. Atty... She and I..."

Evianna turned away from me in one sharp movement. "Of course. I've been foolish. Forget this ever happened."

"Wait!" I grabbed her shoulder before she could shadow-step away. "I meant to say that she and I have never had something like this. Something... different. Special. This is the first I've ever... experienced it."

With wide eyes, Evianna slowly turned around. Her brow furrowed, her body shook, and she brought her hands together in front of her. "You mean that?" she whispered.

The situation was awkward, and I found it difficult to articulate, but this a feeling I didn't want to lose. And it was surreal—I *had* thought of Evianna as a child because she conducted herself as one, but the last few times we interacted, she had been... different. Things between us had changed. I just... hadn't been paying attention.

She was beautiful, her feelings genuine, and her intent pure. Why couldn't I say these things to her? What was holding me back?

As if the universe had a cruel sense of humor, a harsh shriek filled the night sky. It was the cry of a roc—I had become familiar with the sound when riding on the *Sun Chaser*. I glanced upward, confused and curious. Sure enough, I spotted Mesos soaring toward the atlas turtle. Her glorious golden wings would have been difficult to spot at night, but my knightmare powers made that irrelevant.

"It's Mesos," I said.

Evianna replied with a curt nod. "What do you think's going on?"

"That's the screech she makes when she's spotted something important. She's probably returning to Captain Devlin to report."

"We should be there when she lands," Evianna said as she grabbed the sleeve of my shirt. Then she fluffed her white hair. "You can finish your speech about our special and unique relationship once this is all over."

Mesos arrived on the atlas turtle about the same time that Evianna and I found Captain Devlin. He was standing near the edge of the turtle shell with Master Zelfree, Guildmaster Eventide, Gillie, and my father, Jozé.

The giant roc landed on the grass, her wings spread wide. She turned her bird-like gaze to Devlin and then huffed.

"It's a giant tree," Mesos said, deep and regal. "We're heading for a tree growing out of the ocean, its trunk the diameter of ten battleships lined up stern to bow."

"A *tree*?" Devlin barked. "Growing out of the *ocean*?"

"It defies the saltwater."

"That's our destination," Guildmaster Eventide said. She glanced over at Evianna and me, but then returned her gaze to the others. "It's the birthplace of the world serpent. It'll be entangled in the roots."

"How can you be so certain?" Gillie asked, her white bird eldrin sitting on her shoulder. "What if the tree is another god-creature?"

"It's not," Eventide stated.

She reached into her jacket pocket and withdrew the jade runestone —a rectangular piece of stone that fit perfectly in her hand. On one side, it had the imprint of a giant serpent with wings made of foliage. But then she flipped it over. On the other side was the imprint of a massive tree, its branches reaching for the sky...

"The world serpent's haven is that tree," Evianna continued. "That's where we need to bring the jade runestone."

Master Zelfree stroked the stubble on his chin. "I see. And how fast can Gentel swim?"

"I've already asked her to pick up the pace." Eventide turned to face the distant horizon. "According to Mesos, we should be there before high noon tomorrow."

"How has no one else found this tree?" Jozé asked. He leaned heavily on his good leg as he pinched the bridge of his nose. "If it's so massive, it should've been found by now, yeah?"

The guildmaster held the edge of her hat and frowned. "I'm certain individuals have run across the tree, but that doesn't mean they knew what it was or what do to with it. Without the jade runestone, they aren't getting into the world serpent's haven, and without knowledge of the tree's purpose, why would they dwell on it? This life is filled with mysteries. What's one more to the pile of unanswered questions?"

Zelfree exhaled, his frustration plain in his voice. Then he glanced over to me. "Volke. I know you're all celebrating for the evening." He shot a glance to Evianna. "Congratulations. You didn't die a child." Then he returned his attention to me. "But you need to inform everyone they have less than fifteen hours before all their training and skills will be tested."

He said each word with deadly certainty.

I replied with a nod. "I'll do so."

Evianna stood close to me, her head high. "I'll aid in the efforts."

"Very well," Zelfree muttered. "We'll need all the help we can get to avoid a fate at the depths of the abyssal hells."

Although I should've been sleeping, I never found the ability to do so.

I waited out on the field of the atlas turtle, Luthair my constant companion. Knightmares didn't need to sleep, after all, and he stayed out of the darkness the entire time. His inky-liquid armor was interesting to watch, but his cape caught everyone's attention. The twinkling stars in the lining of the material mimicked the night sky. I stared at it from time to time, remembering how the stars maintained their positions in the sky, even if they never received recognition.

That was what I needed to be.

As I watched the silhouette of a massive tree emerge through the fog of the horizon, I knew that this would be the time I had to stand strong. The tree was in front of us, but the ships of our enemies were on the opposite horizon, following us at a distance with their force of cutthroats and villains.

We couldn't allow anyone else to bond with the world serpent. I would help take Ryker deep into the haven, and that would be when he bonded. Then we would have a god-arcanist on our side. We could win this war.

Hopefully.

As if summoned by my thoughts, Ryker exited the guild manor house and strode across the field. I greeted him with a reverse nod—just a jut of my chin—and he smiled in return.

"We're almost there," Ryker said, motioning to the tree.

The thick trunk had no branches except for at the very top. The leaves that grew reminded me of an oak, but they were such a strange rectangular shape that it was difficult to say what kind of tree it was, exactly. The tree's canopy cast a giant shadow across the waves, especially since the sun was almost directly overhead. The dark patch gave me hope, especially as Gentel swam through the curtain of darkness. My magic would be more effective here.

"Are you nervous?" I asked Ryker.

He shook his head. "I have confidence, but I doubt it will do much against the Argo Empire."

I snapped my attention to him. "What do you mean?"

Ryker pointed to the enemy ships in the opposite direction. "Mesos attempted to gather information on our pursuers, but it seems she's no match for the plague-ridden beast that is helping the *Black Throne* chase us down."

"The *Black Throne* is one of the ships?" I asked, glancing over my shoulder.

"It has a unique coloration," Ryker drawled. "There can be no mistake. The king of the Argo Empire, along with his soldier arcanists, has an interest in the world serpent."

The fights between Crimthand and Demise flashed through my mind. They were just two of our enemies—not even the arcanists themselves—and already, they had proven to be substantial challenges. I gritted my teeth, preparing myself for the worst.

Ryker and I stood in silence as Gentel continued toward our ultimate destination. The closer we drew to the mighty tree, the more I realized the trunk was a series of gnarled bark twisted tightly together, creating grooves and ridges all the way to the branches. The leaves were the size of ships, each a bright green, damn near close to glittering emerald. When the leaves crashed against one another, the rustle blasted down to the waves, echoing off the ocean and rumbling the air.

The roots lifted out of the water at various points, so spun together and knotted that they looked like knees. Some were spiraled together, some were tied, some appeared damaged—but they were larger than Gentel herself. When she swam between two, I couldn't help but crane my head back, my jaw slack.

Apprentices and journeymen rushed out of the guild house to get a better look at our surroundings. The roots appeared at least a mile away from the trunk, sticking out of the water at odd angles. We passed two more, Gentel swimming under an arch. We would've been cast in a shadow, but the canopy prevented the sunshine from creating any others. The closer we drew to the tree, the darker it became, and I knew that once we reached the trunk, the others might not be able to see.

"We should augment the others," Luthair said.

I nodded. "You read my mind."

We headed for the other arcanists and eldrin, and we took the time to touch each and every one. My augmentation abilities allowed me to pass on my dark sight, and I didn't need to explain this as I went from person to person. Everyone in the Frith Guild knew of my powers, and they weren't confused. Each one thanked me and mumbled appreciation as I went.

Once everyone had been granted my ability temporarily, I felt a twinge of fatigue. There were a lot of individuals, and I had to maintain the power—something that required a bit of willpower.

Luthair helped, but it was still an ordeal. Evianna wasn't quite strong enough to pass her ability to dozens of individuals yet, but perhaps she would be sometime in the future.

"Volke!"

Fain emerged from thin air—dropping his invisibility as he made his way to me—and his wendigo, Wraith, ran at his side. He looked me up and down, examining my person as though unsure if I actually existed.

"Are you okay?" he asked.

I nodded. "Of course."

"It's just... I keep getting that feeling. You radiate death... It just seems like... something terrible will happen to you at any moment."

The information didn't help and only added to my agitation. I gritted my teeth. "Fain—I can't focus on that. I have to do this. *I have to.*"

He slowly nodded and calmed himself with a deep breath. "Right. Sorry. I'm just... concerned for your safety." Then he turned around and pointed to a spot on the trunk of the massive tree. "Look there. It appears to be an entrance."

I followed the tip of his blackened finger to a portion of the trunk with a knotted hole. The entrance to the tree was small—person-sized—

and I might've missed it had it not been for the tiny dots fluttering around the location.

Wait.

They were creatures, not dots.

Birds of some kind.

What were they? But I didn't have to wait long for the answer. A terrible heartbeat began to echo in my ears. I felt the pressure of awful corruption. And it grew. We were half a mile away, but still... there were so many. Each one a shock. Each one a vibration. Each bird creature a monster that was far beyond saving.

How many were there? Twenty? Thirty?

When I closed my eyes, I could sense each one individually. They were... filled with malice.

"Are they plague-ridden?" Ryker asked.

Fain replied with a curt nod. "They have to be... Look at their wings."

I was surprised with Fain's eyesight, but thankful because he was correct. The birds had an odd number of wings, some twisted, some small, some crippled. The plague's touch of corruption was obvious.

"So, we have plague monsters in front of us and the Argo Empire behind us?" Ryker asked, his panic growing. "We don't have enough arcanists to deal with all this."

"We have someone who can cure the plague," Fain shot back, much to my shock. He offered a glower and then motioned to the tree. "We're going forward, and there's no way those beasts are going to stop us. If we make it into the tree before the *Black Throne* can catch us, then it's all over. You just have to make sure you're ready."

Ryker hesitantly nodded. "I'm ready."

The winds whipped by, disturbing my hair. I combed it back, keeping it from my eyes.

Master Zelfree and Evianna exited the guild house, their belts lined with pouches and patches of leather armor over vital organs.

"Volke!" Zelfree shouted without even knowing where I was. "To me! It's almost time!"

50

THE ENTRANCE TO THE WORLD TREE

Luthair dove into the darkness and then reformed from my feet up to my head. The armor coated me in a cold, reassuring power—the monsters might have hearts of corruption, but my magic wouldn't falter. I pulled Retribution and held Forfend on the other arm. The other arcanists of the Frith Guild hurried to assemble their trinkets and gear as well, each rushing into the manor house to gather the last of their possessions.

Our atlas turtle vessel had to change course several times to avoid the roots. Each root became thicker as we drew closer to the trunk—some so thick they could be hollowed out and turned into mansions. Waves crashed against the wood, but they didn't yield. No amount of rage from the ocean seemed to affect the tree. For whatever reason, the turbulence of the waters became worse the closer we got, and if we had been sailing a ship, we would've been thrashed about.

Instead, magical barriers lifted up around Gentel, like an impenetrable bubble. The winds and water broke against a shimmering semi-opaque field. Atlas turtle magic had some of the sturdiest magical shields—I had seen them in action several times before, and nothing had torn through them, not even lightning itself.

The enemy ships that followed weren't as lucky. With a spyglass we could see that the ships were tossed among the waves, making their journeys difficult. One ship was even bashed against one of the roots—it shattered like a glass plate struck on the side of a brick.

It would take them at least a couple of hours to reach us. We had the advantage.

When we finally neared the trunk, Gentel lifted her massive head out of the water. She opened her maw and bit down on the wood, her turtle-beak tough enough to splinter a small portion of the tree. She had created a bridge with her neck and anchored herself to something stable. Although the trunk was mostly vertical, the twisted nature of the tree allowed for climbable paths.

Well, *climbable* was a generous term. If we'd had equipment, it would have been possible, but by hand, it would be too difficult a task.

Master Zelfree placed a hand on the shoulder of my armor. "You, Illia, Evianna, Ryker, Devlin, and I will scale the trunk," he said as he pointed to the knotted hole at least a mile above us. "The guildmaster and the others will secure the area and prevent any pursuers."

Sure enough, Guildmaster Eventide and the other arcanists were already on Gentel's neck and rushing to cover the area. The plague-ridden birds that circled the hole took notice. They dove for our location, and the moment they got close enough, I recognized what they were.

Tengu.

Tengu were a type of bird—usually ravens and hawks—that had the wings and head of a bird, but the body of a man. Unlike harpies, which were always female, tengu were always male. They flew around without modesty, unclothed and muscular, their fingers curled into claws, and their toes ending in talons. When tengu spoke, they screeched, and when they flapped their wings, it sounded as if they were cutting the air with knives.

And these tengu were worse than normal. They were plague-ridden, and the beating of their corrupted hearts dumped adrenaline into my system.

Most of these vile tengu had several wings, some growing out of their spines, some growing out of their stomachs, some jutting from the legs—none of them natural or useful, all twisted and bleeding. Their long beaks leaked crimson waterfalls, and their talons were hooked in such a way that they wouldn't easily be pulled from flesh.

Zelfree's arcanist mark shifted into that of a knightmare. Then Traces formed up as a shadowy suit of armor and wrapped herself around Zelfree's body. Once merged, Zelfree shadow-stepped over to the others of our strike force. He gathered up Illia, Evianna, and Devlin and then physically held on to Ryker as he used his mimicked shadow-moving abilities to "climb" the massive tree.

And then I understood.

Evianna, Zelfree, and I could use the shadows to quickly ascend. Illia could teleport. Devlin could fly using the winds. We were the team that could reach the knotted hole the quickest—everyone else would struggle to keep up.

Once assembled, we went across Gentel's neck. I emerged from the shadows on the base of the trunk, surprised by how slippery the wood was beneath my feet. Fortunately, my shadow-armor altered itself to accommodate my needs. Small spikes formed on my heels and the balls of my feet, clinging into the wood and giving me a solid grip.

Other arcanists from the Frith Guild crossed Gentel's neck by foot. Hexa, Fain, Atty—even Adelgis, though he wasn't much of a fighter. Even some of the apprentices crossed over to help in securing the tree, including Grant and his griffin eldrin, Bedivere. Karna was likely among the assault group, but since she changed shape, I wasn't entirely sure where she was.

And although my father wasn't capable of balancing on the trunk of the tree or roots, not with his bad leg, his blue phoenix, Tine, flew from the atlas turtle to aid in combat. Blue phoenixes could burn creature that were immune to heat, and her sparkling sapphire body added to my confidence.

"Volke!" Zelfree yelled with his new double voice.

A tengu dove for an arcanist near me. I manipulated the shadows and threw my sword—a dark tendril caught the weapon, and then I used it to slash at the monster.

It was a freakish beast with two normal arms and then three baby-like arms, each ending in a deformed black wing. It also had five eyes across its raven head, all of which bulged and jiggled. My sword sliced clean through the monster, its guts splattering across the wood of the trunk and the other arcánist. Fortunately, being infected with the plague was less of a concern. Everyone could be healed so long as Vethica and her khepera survived the fight.

The plague-ridden tengu blasted icy wind across the trunk as it slowly died from the injury I had given it. The heavy gust nearly knocked Journeyman Reo from the wood, but I once again manipulated the shadows to make sure he didn't fall. When I placed him right-side up on the trunk, Reo used his ogata toad magic to secrete acid and burn small handholds in the trunk of the tree, allowing him to hold on.

"Th-thank you, Volke," Reo stuttered.

Because the canopy of the tree provided so much darkness, there was plenty of material to manipulate—it would be easy to make giant creations and wield them against my enemies, and I started making claws and hooks for any future tengu attacks.

"We need to get to the entrance," Zelfree shouted. "As quickly as possible!"

When three more disgusting tengu shot for us, Illia used her white flames of teleporting disintegration to tear one apart. Evianna evoked her terrors, and when the tengu crashed into the tree trunk, she manipulated the darkness to catch it and squeeze—killing it through asphyxiation. The last one tried to blast more icy wind, but Devlin countered with wind manipulation of his own, and roc magic was far superior to tengu magic.

The beasts just laughed—including the one being choked, though it made no sound.

The incessant giggling, cackling, and chortling filled the area, more so than the crash of the waves. More tengu soared down, and I could still count a few dozen in the air.

"Your magic... *will add to my power*," one tengu shrieked. "*You'll be part... of me... forever.*"

I pulled back Retribution with a yank of the darkness, bringing it to my hand within half a second.

When a tengu flew for Adelgis, I caught my breath. I knew I didn't have enough time to interject, but it turned out I didn't need to. The tengu slashed with his claws, but Adelgis dodged and then gently grazed the tengu with the tips of his fingers. In the next instant, the tengu fell into a deep sleep and then tumbled down the trunk, onto the roots, and straight into the ocean.

A part of me wondered if Adelgis had given the tengu specific dreams as he had fallen to his death...

When five more tengu flew for the arcanists of the Frith Guild, they were not only met with my tendrils, but they were also met with a blast of dazzling golden flame.

Audible gasps rung throughout the assault group when the golden fire washed over everyone. Not only was Atty creating gold flames, but so was her phoenix eldrin, Titania. The beautiful blaze healed the Frith arcanists of any injuries they sustained, but also burned the tengu who got close. The double power—her evocation and augmentation—was so powerful that I wondered if she could single-handedly turn the tided of future battles.

A few of the sturdier tengu rose out of the ocean for another round, their mangled bodies weeping blood as they flew for the arcanists. Thankfully, Hexa's evocation handled the issue. She created a poisonous gas so thick and deadly that when the tengu tried to burst through, most were overcome by the substance. A few vomited, and others outright died.

Hex kept the poison floating around the waters of the ocean, away from the other arcanists of the Frith Guild. It was a clever tactic that prevented sneak attacks from the waves.

But I couldn't think about that for long.

Guildmaster Eventide leapt onto the tree trunk and evoked a powerful shield. The tengu crashed against it, as if running into a brick wall, some even breaking their necks against her magical fortification.

"Go," Eventide commanded. "The faster we get this world serpent, the faster we can leave this place."

I nodded.

Then I shadow-stepped upward, traveling with the swiftness of darkness and emerging on a "ledge" that was more than fifty feet higher than my original position. It was a tiny foothold I could barely stand on, but it was enough, and that was all that mattered.

Evianna shadow-stepped, and to my surprise, she had gone at least thirty feet—an impressive feat for someone at her skill level. She was either pushing herself to the limit, or the darkness provided by the canopy was aiding her more than I suspected.

Illia teleported to a ledge about my height, her movement heralded with a pop and a splash of glitter. Nicholin stayed perched on her shoulder, his bright blue eyes fixed on the point above us.

Master Zelfree and Ryker went up next, a little farther than Evianna and also with more skill and finesse. He shadow-stepped again and again, beyond Illia and me, and just kept going with no moment for rest or delay. I followed, my heart beating harder with each new plateau I managed to find.

The tengu tried to stop us, especially Illia and Nicholin. Rizzel had a special scent, and they were often hunted to make lures for other mystical creatures, so it didn't surprise me that they targeted Illia. And appearing and reappearing made it difficult to orientate myself when they came in for an attack, but that didn't matter. Captain Devlin used his powerful winds to blast them all away. Mesos screeched and flew with us as we traveled the height of the tree, her talons about as long as half a tengu, and when she connected, she skewered them completely.

The blood of the tengu splashed in one of her eyes and into the nose of her beak. There was panic in her cry when she flapped away from the tree, and I could feel the pain reverberating in my chest.

As long as Vethica made it through this... everything would okay.

Devlin hesitated for a moment as he rode the winds straight up alongside the trunk. He slowed his pace and glanced back at Mesos—his eldrin sailed for the ocean, and a moment later, she dove beneath the waves, no doubt to clear the blood from her body.

But it was probably too late.

With a clenched jaw, Devlin redoubled his efforts and flew faster. He even manipulated the winds to help the rest of us. Each time I emerged, I didn't need a ledge to land on. I sailed a bit upward, going higher and higher, no matter what.

The knotted hole came into view, and I shadow-stepped one last time to reach it. The tengu that had once been fluttering around were now down near the Frith Guild, attempting to eat the arcanists that had arrived. With the knotted hole clear of enemies, I stepped inside, disgusted by the amount of blood pooled at my feet. Black and brown feathers floated across the top, creating an odd moss of fluff and down.

I splashed my way through the gore, surprised to see a hallway-like tunnel.

Illia, Zelfree, Ryker, and Devlin arrived at the hole next, each still tensed and ready to go. They, too, sloshed their way into the tunnel, their gazes fixed on the straight path ahead. Evianna was the last to arrive, and when she emerged—merged with her knightmare—she had to take several deep breaths.

"Are you okay?" I asked, my smooth double voice gruff.

She nodded. "I've handled worse," she replied, her own double voice amusing.

I chuckled and then motioned her inside. Evianna shadow-stepped through the pool of blood and emerged by my side. Considering the plague-ridden nature of our surroundings, I wouldn't have been surprised if everyone was now infected, but I shook the thought from my head.

We had a cure. Although I chanted that over and over in my head, the thought of everyone going insane—especially Evianna—left me shaking.

We don't have time to dwell on those possibilities, Luthair spoke telepathically. *Focus on the task at hand. We're almost finished.*

I nodded along with his words, steeling myself to the reality.

There was no turning back now.

Evianna and I ran down the tunnel and caught up to the others. As we went, an odd sensation tickled my side. It was the mouse—the Mother of Shapeshifters—squirming under my armor. Could it breathe? I assumed so, since I could, but I didn't know for sure. Was it upset? It was also another problem I couldn't focus on right now.

I slowed my run when we reached the end of the tunnel. Before us stood a circular stone door. On the door was the image of a snake, the same one that matched the jade runestone. It was carved intricately and deeply, with such detail that I could see the scales running the length of its serpentine body.

"Let's break into this chump," Nicholin said with gusto.

"Do we have the jade runestone?" Illia asked.

Ryker removed the object from his trouser pocket. The runestone glittered a bright green for a moment, like it was reacting to the environment. Even the scales on the door responded in kind, each glowing a soft green before returning to their dull state.

But the door didn't open.

"Should I... press it against something?" Ryker asked.

Devlin shrugged. "How should we know, boy? We're just as new at this as you are."

"I... I'm not sure." He held the runestone over his head. Nothing happened. "I think it needs to go somewhere..."

"Slap it against the serpent's face," Nicholin said as he pointed to the top of the door. "Teach it who's boss."

Ryker stepped closer. The door had to be fifteen feet tall, and even though he was a tall man, there was no way he'd be able to reach the head of the carving.

"I think we need a new plan," Ryker muttered.

Nicholin shook his head. "Oh, forget this. I'll handle everything!"

He arched his back and then disappeared in a puff of sparkles. But then he reappeared, his face flat against the door, as though he had thrown himself against it. Nicholin fell, but he teleported before hitting the pool of blood. He reappeared back on Illia's shoulder.

"Drat," he said as he rubbed his little ferret nose. "I thought I could teleport past it..."

"Touch the door with the runestone," Zelfree barked. "It's the most logical solution. What's wrong with you fools?"

Ryker replied with a curt nod. Then, with an unsteady hand, he brought the runestone to the door. It glowed a brilliant green, and so did the carving of the serpent.

Then it got so bright, I had to close my eyes.

51

THE WARPED INSIDES

The entire tree rumbled.

And then the knotted hole closed behind us in a bone-shattering slam. Fortunately, the door in front of us opened inward, revealing another hall made of twisted bark and wood. Then the rumbling stopped. Illia, Devlin, Zelfree, Ryker, and Evianna stared for a prolonged moment. The air that rushed out of the hall smelled of sap and blood.

The mouse in my pocket thrashed for a moment, and then went still. A part of me thought it had died, but when I concentrated, I could feel its tiny heartbeat and breath.

"We should proceed with caution," Zelfree muttered with his knightmare double-voice. "But that doesn't mean we go slow. I'll take point. Devlin, you stay in the rear. Ryker and Volke—stay between us. Evianna and Illia will act as protectors wherever needed."

"Understood," Illia said.

Evianna nodded.

Devlin spit onto the ground. "Of course I'm in the back..."

"Wait," Ryker said as he held up a hand. "P-perhaps I should go alone."

Everyone turned to face him, and my mind immediately snapped to the conclusion. This tree was the trial of worth. Well, technically, *gathering the runestone* was the first step, but Queen Velleta had already completed that step for us. The second step to this trial of worth was navigating the tree. *Should* the rest of us be here? Would the world serpent deny Ryker if the rest of us escorted him there?

Zelfree exhaled. His mimicked knightmare wasn't true form, so his helmet had an open visor, and I could see the troubled look in his eyes. "No," he finally said. "If the world serpent wanted an individual to pass the trial of worth, then we already failed by giving you the runestone. Additionally, the sybil arcanists predicted you would become an honorable world serpent arcanist."

"That's not true," Ryker said, his voice shaking.

"What?" Captain Devlin barked. "Are you saying you're *not* the destined world serpent arcanist? You better not be pulling our legs, boy! I swear to the Death Lords that I'll—" He grabbed Ryker by the collar of his button-up shirt and yanked him close.

Zelfree grabbed Devlin's arm and separated everyone. "*Get ahold of yourself,*" he growled. "He *is* the future world serpent arcanist." Then Zelfree turned his attention to Ryker. "*Right?*"

"The sybil arcanists..." Ryker shook his head, his eyes downcast. "There is always room for doubt. And they were vague with me."

"Now isn't the time to second guess! The sybil arcanists are right the majority of the time. Get your act together and *focus.*" Zelfree pointed to the twisted hall. "Now stay close to Volke."

I held up my cape, ready and willing to keep Ryker close. But my chest tightened in anxiety. Ryker had never mentioned that he doubted the prediction of the sybil arcanists. Was it just his nerves getting the better of him? Or was that why he felt guilty over the deaths of the Ruma citizens?

After a long exhale, I shook the thoughts from my head.

No. Master Zelfree was right. I couldn't doubt now. We were locked in this mystical tree, heading for the world serpent. There was no turning back.

Ryker moved close, and I wrapped my cape over his shoulders, making sure that I always had some part of the knightmare touching him at all times. Zelfree went up ahead, taking point and checking the hallway before ushering us forward. Captain Devlin stayed in the rear, ever vigilant. I had heard that roc arcanists had heightened eyesight, and I wondered if it synergized with my augmented ability to see in the dark.

We all headed down the odd hallway, our footfalls echoing against the wooden walls. The floor eventually turned and slanted, heading downward. Was the world serpent near the roots? That would make sense. We would have to travel through the entire trunk in order to reach the god-creature slumbering beneath.

I caught my breath as I was struck with a powerful feeling. Then I stopped dead in my tracks—Illia and Evianna both did the same the moment they realized what I had done. Ryker never left my side, and he stopped with a furrowed brow.

"What's wrong?" Illia asked, curt.

My throat tightened, and my pulse quickened. Where was the source of this agitation?

The tree, Luthair spoke telepathically. *It's made purely of magic. The entire structure, from the roots to the leaves. It knows we're here.*

Devlin came to a halt behind us. "What's going on?"

Zelfree, at least three hundred feet ahead, turned on his heel and glanced back. "We don't have time for this!"

"Can the tree be infected with the arcane plague?" I asked aloud.

Doubtful, Luthair replied. *My true form is pure enough to stave off the ill effects of the plague. I'm certain this tree is the same, just as the god-creatures likely are. This feeling you're sensing is likely the tree realizing someone has come to bond with the serpent.*

I placed a gauntleted hand on my chest.

The others waited with confused glances, but no one bothered to speak.

"No, it's not just the tree," I said. "Something is wrong. It's... disturbed. Angry."

"The tree?" Illia asked in a whisper.

I nodded. "It's... being harmed."

Again, the others exchanged questioning glances.

"Okay," Evianna said as she waved her hand through the air and manipulated darkness into an impromptu sword. "Tell us what to do, Volke. What're we up against?"

"I think we should hurry," I muttered, but it wasn't fast enough.

The tree shook. Soft at first, but then more powerful and terrible as the seconds went by. Everyone braced themselves against the walls, and I kept one arm around Ryker, ready to shadow-step if needed. Air rushed up from the hall, hollowing with anger. The feeling I had—the one that the tree was upset—grew more intense, matching the rumbling. This shaking was different than when the door had opened. It felt violent and untamed.

"What the?" Devlin shouted, his voice almost drowned out by the shaking of the tree.

The wood at Devlin's feet rose up and twisted itself around his ankles. He tried to pull away, but the sturdy, bark-lined wood held fast. He used magic—blasting it with wind, knocking Illia and Nicholin over with his gale force attack—but it didn't affect the tree.

The agitated rumbling of the tree prevented me from attacking with any sort of swiftness. Instead, I barely kept my footing, and hold on Ryker, as Devlin was swarmed by the tree. The walls, ground, and ceiling of the twisted hallway grabbed and sucked him in. He disappeared into the tree like he had fallen into a sinkhole—disappearing from sight within a matter of seconds.

Then the hall returned to normal and the shaking stopped.

"Devlin!" Master Zelfree shouted.

He stepped into the darkness and moved down the hall in an attempt to follow after Devlin, but he had no luck. Zelfree emerged from the darkness, unable to find a crack with which to travel through the shadows. He felt around the ground and walls, desperately searching for some sort of hole or opening.

But there was nothing.

"Did the tree just... *eat someone*?" Nicholin asked, his white-and-silver fur standing on end. "That's a statement I never thought I'd mutter..."

Using the shadows, Zelfree created claws of darkness to strike at the ground. The claws didn't pierce the wood. They didn't damage anything.

There would be no chasing after Devlin.

Illia patted Nicholin's head with an unsteady hand. "Volke was right... we need to hurry. Before that happens to another one of us."

Evianna nodded along with her words.

I swallowed hard, uncertain of what had happened to Devlin. Had he been sucked into the tree and crushed? Or was he alive somewhere? I had no way of knowing.

With a vise-grip, Ryker grabbed onto my upper arm and held tight. I took him with me into the shadows and traveled a short distance, but the tree... the tree was so magical, it distorted my ability to move quickly through it. It was some sort of aura that made my sorcery difficult to use, even the simplest of abilities. At least I *could* shadow-step. I doubted it would work through the wood, just like Illia and Nicholin couldn't teleport to the other side of it, but at least I had *some* options for mobility.

I ran with Ryker after that, determined to move as quickly as possible. Zelfree shadow-stepped ahead and returned to his position at point.

The darkness and the length of this twisted hall crept into my mind and sowed doubts. To make matters worse, it was only a few minutes before we ran across a problem: the hallway split in four different directions. Zelfree stutter-stepped to a halt and glanced between them, his breathing heavy. Illia, Evianna, Ryker, and I arrived a short moment later, and we all waited behind Zelfree, content to allow him to make the decision.

We couldn't split up. That would defeat the purpose. We all had to get *Ryker* to the roots of the tree. And even if we all went in different directions, it would take too long to backtrack if one of us were successful, not to mention the peril of being eaten by the tree itself. We didn't have time. We *had* to hurry.

"Which way?" Evianna asked, breaking the silence.

"Let me think," Zelfree said through gritted teeth, his double voice filled with irritation.

He ran a gauntleted hand over his shadow-plate helmet, his breath more ragged than before. Technically, mimic arcanists could sense magic and the purpose of that magic. They could sense the magical abilities of mystical creatures, and they could detect trinkets. Perhaps Zelfree was using his mimic powers to help him make a decision.

The tree smelled of several trees—cedar, oak, and pine. It was an interesting combination that made me think of several forests merging into one.

"This way," Zelfree whispered as he pointed to the third tunnel. "It's... it's the one that's the most magical."

The tree began to rumble again.

Illia grazed her eye patch with trembling fingers. "Let's move!"

We all ran in the direction that Zelfree had indicated. With my darksight, it didn't matter that light wasn't reaching the inside of the tree. The grizzled and gnarled wood of the mystic tree became grainier as we entered the new hallway. Dark flakes marked the chestnut-colored wood, which reminded me of parasites. I had seen woodworms and other disgusting creatures while working as a gravedigger. We were given some of the worst wood for caskets and coffins.

The shaking of the tree worsened, but everyone either shadow-stepped or teleported to maintain their footing.

Ryker closed his eyes, held them shut, and then opened them a few seconds later. He did that several times while we ran, and I wondered if he would be okay.

We made it several minutes deep into this hall—as it turned and continued downward—when I felt another pulse of terrible energy. The rumbling stopped, but it was like the tree was holding its breath, and I could feel the building pressure beneath the wood.

"Watch out!" Zelfree shouted. He waved his hand, creating shadow tendrils. "They're all around us!"

Cracks appeared across the walls, floor, and ceiling. Squirming, writhing worm bodies appeared from the depths of the tree. They were bloodsuckers—a terrible type of parasite sometimes found in trees with nesting birds—and I had seen them on the Isle of Ruma, just smaller.

They were the type of parasite that fell off birds when they preened themselves. Tiny reddish-crimson worms with circular mouths filled with sharp teeth meant to grind through flesh and squeeze out the last of the blood, like juicing a corpse. And these worms were just as ugly and disgusting—but they were five times the size of a man and the length of a small tugboat. Their bodies undulated and shook as they squirmed their way toward us, each without eyes, and each with their circular maws wide open.

Master Zelfree used his shadow tendrils to tether some in place, but there were at least forty that came from the walls and ceilings and another twenty more from the floors. He managed to subdue a dozen or so, but it just wasn't enough.

I held up a hand and evoked my terrors, but the worms ignored my efforts, probably because they were mindless parasites, and then lunged forward, leaping at the group with fervor and insatiable hunger. I shoved Ryker behind me and slashed with Retribution, cutting up the first parasite that reached me.

It wasn't plague-infected. I didn't feel a pulse of corruption. This was just a magical construct—a monster made by the tree itself—to be a defender or an obstacle. When the parasite "died," it withered and rotted in a matter of moments, becoming a pile of dehydrated dust that melted into the wood and returned to the tree.

"Stand back!" Illia commanded as she lifted both arms above her head.

The gravity in the hallway answered her will. The worms floated upward, losing contact with the floor and walls and jiggling around in the air. Some screamed—it almost sounded human, which sent a shiver down my spine—but otherwise, they attempted to continue their relentless assault; they just couldn't move.

Evianna manipulated the shadows to cut and slice the monsters, even drilling into them with spikes of darkness.

While Illia halted the advance of the worms, Nicholin used his evocation breath to wash the monsters in white disintegrating flames. Flakes of the monsters broke away, teleported in disgusting chunks. It was effective—the second one died, it dusted instantly, merging back with the tree.

I wondered if they would just reform and come back for us, because the parasites continued to slither out of the cracks in the wall, floor, and ceiling, one after another. They clogged the way forward with their thrashing bodies, each one trying to slither over top the other.

With violent motions of my hand, I manipulated the darkness into spikes and knives and started hewing through the beasts. I killed ten at a time, cleaving through their vile bodies and watching as they pooled in ash on the floor.

We had so much darkness that Evianna, Zelfree, and I were killing the monsters faster and faster. Hope filled my chest as I imagined an end to the stream of beasts.

But a dozen came up from the hall in the opposite direction, and one managed to lunge at Illia before we had a chance to avoid the pincer attack. The giant beast managed to get her arm in its mouth, all the way to the elbow. She screamed and then teleported, but when she reappeared in a puff of sparkles, her arm was so mangled, it appeared as though she didn't have skin on half of it.

Rage gripped my heart and lungs, burning my insides.

In an instant, I didn't think. The darkness of the tree became *my* darkness. It filled the area like a water and then it filled the bodies of the monsters, suffocating them and ripping apart their insides at the same time, killing them in an instant. The darkness never harmed Evianna, Zelfree, or Ryker, however. It left them alone, perhaps even helping or empowering the other knightmare arcanists.

The parasites that weren't immediately torn apart by my shadows retreated. They squeezed themselves back into the cracks—at least the ones I wasn't killing from the inside.

That was when the tree rumbled again, shaking so harshly and suddenly, I was caught off guard. The ground and walls moved—like with Captain Devlin—threatening to suck us all in. Fortunately, Evianna, Zelfree, and I could shadow-step, and I took Ryker with me, protecting him no matter what.

But Illia wasn't as lucky.

Still cradling her mangled arm, she was pulled into the tree and disappeared into the wood within a fraction of a second. One moment she was there, and the next she wasn't.

"No!" I cried out.

Even with the tree still tossing around, I used the darkness to travel to her last known location.

Zelfree held out a hand. "Volke, stop! Not Ryker!"

I managed to regain my senses and shadow-step away from the twisting wood, preventing Ryker and me from also getting caught. That didn't help the raging headache building behind my temples, however. With each beat of my heart, I grew angrier and more vindictive.

I wanted to burn the whole tree down.

"Illia!" I shouted, hoping beyond hope that she would answer me back, just so that I would know she was safe. *"Where are you?"*

Nicholin had disappeared with her.

Then the tree stopped its shaking and rumbling, and the hall settled back to normal. I was left standing in the middle, holding Ryker with one hand, Retribution in the other. I couldn't control my breathing. I gulped down air, but it didn't help.

Captain Devlin had been... *consumed* by the tree.

And now Illia.

52

A WATERFALL OF SAP

A terrible numbness seeped into my limbs and ran down my spine. *Illia.*

I released Ryker and fell to my knees, unable to feel *anything*. Even when I took a deep breath, it didn't seem to help. My lungs burned as if I lacked oxygen. My head throbbed as though I were being choked.

What had happened to Illia? I didn't know, but what frightened me the most was that I didn't even understand how I would go about figuring it out. Should I search the whole tree? Should I abandon my mission here and seek her out right away?

I lifted Retribution up above my head and then stabbed the blade down into the wood. I hal-expected my sword to be knocked away, but to my surprise, Retribution pierced into the tree without much difficulty. Unlike other magical things, there was no resistance to the strike—it felt solid, and Retribution became half-stuck in the wood—but I could still *easily* slice the tree. Should I use it to carve my way through miles of wood and sap?

Or...

Should I... forget about Illia... and press on?

The last thought sent agony through my chest. Illia would never abandon me. Why was I even contemplating it now? I should search for her no matter what.

My arcanist, please focus, Luthair spoke telepathically. *Consider this: finding Illia would likely be a simple task for the world serpent arcanist. This tree is the beast's lair. You can ask for its assistance and grace the moment we find it—the moment Ryker bonds with it.*

The logic lifted some of the fog from my thoughts, and when I took a breath, the agony in my lungs began to fade. He was right. The world serpent and its arcanist would know how to solve this problem. They would know what had happened to Illia.

"Volke," Master Zelfree said as he grabbed my upper arm and yanked me up to my feet. "Now isn't the time to give up."

Evianna rushed to my other side, her knightmare armor sleek and lined with shadow scales. She placed a hand on my shoulder. "I understand what it's like to... lose a sister. But we can't stop to grieve now, just like I couldn't stop to grieve in the Thronehold castle."

Although a part of me wanted to protest—and rip this whole damn tree apart—I knew they were right. I couldn't give in. I had to move forward. Luthair's determination was merged with me, and his strength gave me the mental fortitude to shake away the despair. I *could* handle this. I *would* see Illia again. I had to cling to that hope and wear it as an armor around my heart.

"I'm fine," I said, my double voice filled with conviction. "Thank you, but we should press forward."

Zelfree gritted his teeth. "If you falter, it could cost us our lives. Perhaps the lives of millions more, if the Second Ascension wins."

"I won't falter."

With a curt nod, Zelfree accepted my statement. Then he motioned to the warped hallway of the massive tree. The path continued downward, closer and closer to the roots. He ran ahead, I took hold of Ryker and followed behind, and Evianna took up a vigilant position in the rear. The floor became uneven as we went, and it felt like running across rocks or gravel. It slowed our pace and kept us from recklessly charging forward.

It almost felt like the tree was messing with us.

"This is the trial of worth," Ryker said through his huffed breathing. "It's a god-creature's trial of worth…"

I glanced over as we continued, but I didn't ask any questions. The panic in his voice seemed genuine. I didn't want to add to it.

But Ryker continued speaking regardless. "Locating a runestone hidden somewhere in the world… Climbing to the entrance… Searching through a maze… Fighting through beasts…" Ryker's breaths became shallow. He held on to my arm as I half-dragged him along the hall. "Is there a mortal alive who could possibly do all these things by themselves? This trial of worth seems too extreme. Too ludicrous. No one could've done it without assistance."

"This is the trial of worth for a god-creature," I stated. "It isn't for normal mortal men and women. It's for a god-arcanist. It's for someone who will shape the world with their decisions."

I probably shouldn't have said that, since I knew Ryker suffered from the pressure of his soon-to-be station, but I couldn't help myself. Of course the world serpent would have a trial of worth far beyond anything ever seen before. It was a creature of might and power.

To my surprise, Ryker didn't buckle. He inhaled with more confidence and pressed forward, matching my pace, despite the awkward floor we ran across. "You're right… I apologize. I knew that before coming here… but after witnessing everything firsthand, I almost forgot the significance of the creature we're searching for."

Master Zelfree stopped a good fifty feet ahead of us. I stopped twenty feet behind him, worried there were more parasites to deal with. Instead, I noticed Zelfree standing on the edge of a massive ledge. It was a crack in the tree that had created a chasm. The "hole" went on forever—all the way down. The crack was only five feet across, which meant we could probably jump across. Why was Zelfree stopping?

"What's wrong?" I asked.

He motioned to the crack. "Perhaps we can bypass this whole *maze* if we leapt down."

"Wait, what?" Ryker said, his grip tightening on my arm. "As in, *jumping*?"

"Yes."

"I don't think we should cheat this trial of worth," Ryker muttered. "Surely, we can do it through normal means?"

"Normal means have cost us two talented arcanists," Zelfree snapped. He wheeled around on his heel. "Or have you forgotten that the accursed tree could take another one of us at any point?"

Ryker shook his head. "No. No, you're right. We should do whatever you think is best."

Although I didn't want to come between them, I released Ryker and walked to the edge of the chasm. Could Master Zelfree sense powerful magic down below? Was that why he wanted to go?

But when I got close to the edge, another shiver of dread rolled down my spine. I could sense the same malice I had felt before—when the parasites had struck out at us. Something about this crack and chasm didn't feel right.

"Since Luthair gained his true form, I've been able to sense things easier," I said. "I don't know why. I don't know if it's a knightmare ability, or if it's because I'm more in touch with magic, but I can *feel* intent. I can *feel* corruption. Something down there isn't right. I don't think we should take this path."

Evianna, who lingered a good sixty feet away, chimed in with, "I agree with Ryker. We shouldn't cheat the trial. What if the world serpent knows?"

"This isn't a debate," Zelfree said. But then he faced me, his knightmare armor soaked in the shadows of the lightless hall. "But I am curious about this *magic sense* you claim to have. My mimic abilities are telling me powerful magics are below us. *Directly* below us."

"They're angry," I said. "Just like the parasites. I think we should avoid this route. It's wrong. And perhaps... the parasites were a punishment for taking the wrong path to begin with."

"You think so?" Zelfree's voice seemed quiet and distant, and I wondered if he suddenly blamed himself for Illia's disappearance. Before I could say anything, he said, "You make some sound points. Very well—we'll leap over and continue on the normal path."

I nodded. "Thank you."

Then I shadow-stepped to Ryker's side and offered my arm. He took hold the moment he could, his nerves showing through his wide eyes and unsteady grip.

"You won't be harmed," I said, trying to be as reassuring as possible in my tone. "You can count on us."

Ryker didn't reply. He simply offered a forced smile, but it was fleeting and replaced a neutral expression of inward contemplation.

With our path set, Zelfree simply manipulated the shadows to carry him over the five-foot gap. He "landed" on the other side without incident. I did the same thing for Ryker and then myself. The plentiful shadows made everything effortless, and it wasn't long before Evianna joined us as well. As a group of four, we hustled down the path, following the hall as it began to turn.

Were we spiraling downward? I suspected we were. How far had we gone? I suspected not far, which added a layer of panic to my darkest of thoughts. What if the tree swallowed us all before we even made it halfway?

Fortunately, we continued down the hall without much incident. The ceiling seemed to get lower and lower, but never to the point I had to bend over to continue. It did, however, seem to be only a few inches from the top of my head when before I'd had several feet of room.

An odd roiling sound filled the hallway. It... was almost like water. But thicker. I kept Ryker closer and held Retribution at the ready. Perhaps these were more tree guardians?

Zelfree stopped up ahead and then held up a hand for us to wait. I did as I was instructed and stopped dead in my tracks. So did Evianna. We waited without moving, and I wondered what could be creating the strange noise.

Then Zelfree motioned us forward with a quick flick of his hand. I moved up, never blinking, and then caught my breath once I realized the source of the sounds. The hallway had led us to a giant "room" inside the tree. It must have been sixty feet to the ceiling, and the circular space was large enough for a small sailing ship. There still wasn't any light, but that didn't prevent me from catching all the details—like the waterfall of sap gushing from the wall on the opposite side of the room.

The sweet scent of maple overpowered the room, making it difficult to breathe. The sap was so thick, I swear it altered the air. Was the tree injured? Or was this an intentional design?

If this is a trial of worth, the sap is clearly another test. I could sense the hesitation in Luthair's words since his mind was basically merged with mine, preventing him from concealing his deepest thoughts or emotions. *I suspect the way forward is beyond the vile liquid.*

"The sap doesn't seem dangerous," I said aloud.

That is a false sense of security. There is something dubious at work here. Only the truly clever will make it through this without difficulty.

"The sap must be blocking something," Zelfree said, definitely unaware of my conversation with Luthair. "But this is a test. I can feel it."

He glanced around the area, but there was nothing here. The sap pooled in the center of the room like a thick pond of stagnant pudding, leaving us a few feet around the edge to walk without touching it. Zelfree stared at the small area, his breathing still noticeably audible. Was he uncertain?

"We'll use our shadow manipulation to create an umbrella or canopy," Zelfree finally said. "It'll prevent us from getting in the sap, and hopefully we can find the path through on the other side."

Evianna and I both nodded.

Ryker furrowed his brow. "How was a non-arcanist supposed to complete this task if the goal is not to get sap on you? I keep wondering... how anyone was ever meant to overcome all of these challenges."

"We don't have time to deal with the *fairness* of the situation or your *existential crisis* over the difficulty of this task," Zelfree growled. "Just focus. I'm sure once we reach the world serpent, there will be one final test that will make all these previous ones seem like jokes in comparison."

With a ragged breath, Ryker half bowed his head and offered no other comments.

It was obvious to me that everyone was on edge, but I wished Zelfree would be a little diplomatic. Now wasn't the time for arguments.

"We'll make it through this," I said, firm and confident, even if my heart beat at odd intervals. "And I should tell you that I was there for Vethica's trial of worth with the khepera. It was an underground labyrinth, with puzzles and traps. I technically saved her in the end, and the khepera didn't consider it a dishonorable act or even cheating the trial."

"Really?" Ryker asked.

I replied with a single nod. "Think of us as your retinue. We're here freely and willingly, and nothing about this tree or situation has indicated you need to do it alone."

My words had a visible impact on Ryker. He exhaled, and his stance and shoulders relaxed. When he returned to his calm state, he seemed to regain his determination for the process. The weight of responsibility clearly impacted him. Ryker probably blamed himself for Devlin's and Illia's disappearances. If he had done this alone, no one would have had to suffer—that had been some of his logic when it came to the deaths on the Isle of Ruma.

With everyone recentered, Zelfree, Evianna, and I manipulated the shadows in the room. Evianna created a bridge of darkness over the pool of sap. Zelfree and I created a tunnel through the waterfall, splitting it in half by creating umbrella-shaped objects to protect us from the sugary substance. We moved the umbrellas around until we found a hidden passageway behind the sticky liquid—exactly as Luthair and Zelfree had predicted.

"We should go," Zelfree said, motioning to the path.

He shadow-stepped across and then waited for us near the passageway. Evianna walked onto the shadow bridge, and I took Ryker halfway through the darkness, but I had to emerge near the end due to the pressure of magic-use in the tree. Not to mention the sap-filled air... It made breathing so difficult.

Evianna dashed forward, but once she made it halfway, the tree shook yet again. The rumble happened so quickly and intensely that it caught me by surprise. It must've been shocking for Evianna as well because the shadow bridge flickered for a moment.

"Dammit," Zelfree cursed.

He leapt into the darkness, emerged near Evianna, and used his magic to rush her across.

I ran the last of the distance while half-carrying Ryker. We didn't need this kind of stress, but it was clear the tree wasn't going to relent. This was, by far, the worst trial of worth I had ever witnessed.

Ryker and I made it to the passageway. Zelfree leapt out of the shadows and deposited Evianna safely on the other side of the sap waterfall, but then *his* magic wavered for a moment, and his half of the umbrella flickered, allowing sap to rush down. It splashed across his shoulder, arm, and side, but he managed to get in the passageway before becoming any stickier.

Then I allowed my magic to fade, closing the waterfall behind us.

A dim and haunting light filled this new passageway. As Zelfree tried —and failed—to clear the sweet sap from his person, the rumbling stopped, leaving us in the strange green glow of our new environment.

And something floated in the air. Tiny specks of dust? Pollen? They were just as vibrant green as the glow.

Again, my chest twisted in dread. But with the sap waterfall behind us, there was no direction left other than forward.

53

INVADERS

Z elfree stepped forward and glanced around. The glowing specks illuminated his shadow-plate armor, reflecting off the surface like a black mirror. Now that I was closer, I recognized the little specks—they were spores, likely from mushrooms. I waved my gauntleted hand through the air, disturbing the glowing, green spores. They swirled around in the air, and a few clung to my inky armor.

I wiped them away, and my armor changed itself to help me with that task. The inky outsides warped and shook, tossing the spores away from my person.

But Zelfree...

The sap residue on his armor worked against him. He tried to take point ahead of us, but the spores clung to him—some even moving as if attracted to the sap. When Zelfree attempted to brush it away, the sap made it impossible. The spores *clung* to the sticky substance, unable to be shaken or disturbed.

"Damn," Zelfree muttered under his breath. Then he glanced back. "Avoid the spores as much as possible. They're magical... but I can't sense what they do. So be careful."

"They're all over you," Evianna said as she pointed to his shoulder.

Sure enough, the green glowing spores had clumped on Zelfree's shoulder, like a bizarre patch of illuminated moss. Zelfree ran a hand over the clump, but the spores didn't come off.

"Don't worry about me," he said. "Let's press forward."

The four of us moved on. The mushroom spores kept the corridor lit, and that messed with my ability to use the darkness, but it wasn't too bad. The spores created a soft light that created a dream-like atmosphere. I avoided the little specks when possible, and that was easy with Zelfree in the lead. He cleared a path, his sap-covered arm gathering up spores at a fierce rate.

Was that what the sap was for? Had the previous room been a trap? The sap wasn't dangerous on its own, but when combined with the spores...

The corridor opened up again into another giant and circular room with a corridor on the opposite side wall. This one didn't have a sap waterfall like the last one, however. The entire room, from top to bottom, was covered in glowing, green mushrooms. The emerald hue that filled the area was almost blinding—the exact opposite of the spores.

"What is this?" Ryker asked as he lifted the collar of his shirt up to cover his mouth. "These can't be good..."

My knightmare armor prevented me from ever breathing in the spores, and for that I was grateful. I didn't know what these mushrooms did, but given the problems we'd had before, I knew it couldn't be good.

"Stand back," I told the others as I hefted Retribution. "I'll cull this fungus and create us a path."

Zelfree held up a hand. "Don't. We... It'll... create more spores."

He spoke every word as though exhausted, some of his syllables coming out as half-yawns. Then he shook his head and ground his teeth.

"Are you okay?" Ryker asked from behind his shirt. "Is something bothering you? Draining your strength?"

"I'll be... fine." Zelfree motioned to the mushroom room. "We should... walk through... and disturb this place... as little as possible."

I didn't know what was happening to him, but Ryker was right. Something was terribly wrong. Still, we couldn't dwell. None of us had healing magic, none of us knew what these spores did, and none of us knew what the world serpent's trial of worth required for success. We were all traveling blind, and the faster we made it out of here, the better.

When I attempted to shadow-step with Ryker, nothing happened. I caught my breath, my body tense. It wasn't because I *couldn't*. It was because the light in the room was so all-encompassing. The mushrooms were so bright and so numerous that there wasn't a path for the darkness to travel. I couldn't create shadows to travel through this fungus—I just had to walk through it all.

"I can't travel through the darkness," Evianna said, her double-voice shaky. "We'll have to do this the hard way. Should we go slow or fast?"

My second thought was to create a bridge of shadows, like we had with the sap, but if I couldn't shadow-step, I doubted I'd be able to craft enough darkness to make a walkway. There were few options for us. If only Illia were here with us...

"We'll go slow," I said. "Careful with our steps so that we don't disturb the shrooms."

Evianna nodded along with my words.

But Zelfree didn't respond. He just swayed on his feet, his shoulders slumped. I motioned for him to go first, and he just shook his head in response.

I would have to go. With a heavy sigh, I scooped Ryker up into my arms, holding him like a bride, keeping him close.

"I can walk," he said as I took a step into the garden of fungus.

"This will be easier." I stepped around a cluster of mushrooms and then onto a small patch of tiny ones. Spores puffed into the air, but because I had been gentle, they didn't get too high. "Hold your breath," I commanded.

Ryker closed his mouth and stopped breathing.

Step by step, I made my way across the room. Evianna followed my path, retracing my steps. She avoided crushing any new mushrooms, limiting the spores in the air to the few I added. As long as we went carefully, the threat seemed limited.

I made it to the other side of room, beyond the field of fungus. Evianna quickly leapt to my side, free of the mushrooms as well. The few spores that clung to us were nothing. We wiped them away.

Zelfree, on the other hand, attempted to follow us, but not on the same path. He stumbled through the mushrooms, creating his own trail and kicking up more spores in the process. The sap on his body meant that it all went straight to him and clung fast. To my surprise, he actually unmerged with Traces, separating from his mimic-knightmare as if trying to escape the spores any way possible.

Zelfree's eyes seemed unfocused. His legs almost buckled underneath him.

"Master Zelfree!" I said, trying to keep his attention on the immediate. "Just take my path!"

But it was too late. He closed his eyes and collapsed to his knees. Spores sprang up all around him in a cloud of glowing green. He took a deep breath and then fell face-first into the mushrooms. Traces, still in knightmare form, tried to reach out for him, but she, too, collapsed forward and then went face-first into the fungus.

"We should go get them," Evianna said as she grabbed the edge of my cape. "If we hurry, perhaps we can—"

The tree rumbled.

I took several steps backward, my foot unsteady due to the uneven ground. Evianna did the same, if only to avoid the spores being kicked up from the movement.

As if this were a literal nightmare made flesh, the tree opened up like a mouth underneath Master Zelfree. It swallowed him, Traces, and a cart-load of glowing mushrooms in one horrible "bite." I wanted to shadow-step out and grab him, but the shine of the room still prevented me from acting.

A part of me wanted to create my eclipse aura in an attempt to snuff out the lights, but it was too late. The tree closed a second later, preventing me from chasing after.

"No!" I yelled.

But it was futile. The tree didn't care. It was devouring each of us, one by one, until there would be no one left. Perhaps Ryker was right—no person could possibly complete this trial of worth, and it was foolish to even attempt.

I shook my head.

No. If the Second Ascension came here, they would find a way—through magical corruption or brute force or something sinister. They would stop at nothing, which meant we couldn't give up.

The tree twisted the room of mushrooms, warping it before the rumbling finally came to a halt. There were still spores in the air, but they seemed fewer and farther between. Most of the mushrooms themselves had been gobbled up by the tree, leaving the room a knotted mass.

For a prolonged moment, Ryker, Evianna, and I just stared out into room, all of us unmoving. Were these tests? Did the tree consume someone whenever a test was failed? Or was this all random? I wished I had answers.

Evianna slowly turned her head to face me. "It's just the two of us," she whispered. "We're the only ones who can get Ryker to the world serpent."

"We'll do it," I said, though with less confidence than before. "We'll succeed."

"R-right."

Although my legs felt ten times heavier than before, I turned and guided Ryker away from our latest failing. Evianna followed close, and it was probably for the best. I didn't have much of a strategy at this point beyond *survive*. Whatever happened, we would have to deal with it as a duo.

Fortunately, the corridor led deeper into the tree, and we traveled for some distance without running into another obstacle. The spores eventually disappeared completely, leaving us once again wrapped in darkness. The void helped me regain my strength. I jogged some of the distance, and Ryker kept my pace. Evianna had no trouble staying close, though from time to time, I caught her mumbling to herself.

"We'll do this," she whispered, so quiet I almost couldn't distinguish the words. "We'll do this. We have to."

When I felt recovered enough, I even shadow-stepped in short bursts, avoiding the tree as much as possible. The lumpy ground became even, and it almost seemed like we would reach the roots without another test.

But then I heard voices echoing from farther down the hall. The moment a single word wafted up, my heart leapt into my throat. Was it Illia, Devlin, and Zelfree? Had the tree just deposited them lower in the trunk and they were waiting for us?

Despite the strength it took to shadow-step great distances, I dove into the darkness and emerged a hundred feet down the corridor—one of my longest distances traveled, even outside of the tree—and I emerged to find a disturbing sight.

There was a large "room," similar to the last two, but this one was five times the size. Light poured in from the outside, creating a column of white that pierced the darkness. It was so bright that I could see dust particles floating through the sunlight, spinning and twirling, beautiful yet also concerning.

But that wasn't the worst part. There were *people* inside the tree, and I knew them all to be members of the Second Ascension.

King Rishan and his sovereign dragon eldrin, Crimthand.

Chandra and her grim reaper eldrin, Demise.

Fazri, the gentleman with the rapier, and his salamander eldrin.

And two others...

Rhys, the thin man who jittered around as he moved, and the double-headed dread rizzel—the one twisted by the arcane plague. And then a woman I hadn't seen in a long time, not since my encounter with the Second Ascension at the dig site of the dead apoch dragon.

Her name was Orwyn, and I'd recognize her anywhere. She had short, strawberry blonde hair, oversized clothing of white and silver, enough to cover her neck and the entirety of her arms. Her pants were tied snugly at her waist, but then they puffed out as they covered her legs all the way to the ground. What style of clothing was that? She didn't come from the islands or even places like New Norra or Thronehold.

But nothing was as distinct as her eldrin—the legendary and majestic kirin.

Kirin were equestrian creatures, horse-like in most regards, but delicate and magical in a way few creatures were. Its "coat" was actually silver dragon-like scales. And the kirin's cloven hooves—standard for a deer, and not a horse—had all the toughness and hard edge of real silver. The beast's tail resembled a lion's, and it had a horn on its forehead, similar to a unicorn. A kirin's horn, however, grew in twisted and jagged, and Orwyn's kirin's horn glittered with an inner power and was semi-transparent crystal.

To make matters worse, there were a dozen pegasi Sky Legionnaires —knights of the Argo Empire who served King Rishan. They were here as his retinue, no doubt, but how had they gotten here? There hadn't been a second hole in the tree before. Or perhaps we were on the other side of the trunk?

I glanced up at the beam of light. The hole of the tree was knotting closed, like a wound healing on an arcanist.

Then I realized something—all the Sky Legionnaires, and even Rishan himself, were carrying black blades, similar to Retribution. They weren't as powerful as Retribution, which I had crafted with enough star shards to make into an artifact, but they were still made of the same apoch dragon bone that was capable of cutting through magic like butter.

Had they *sliced* their way into the tree from the outside? Was that how they had beaten us to this point? That had to be the explanation. The Second Ascension was using their destructive and corrupted magic to drill straight to the world serpent and bond with it.

But who would? Everyone here seemed to have an eldrin…

Well, that wasn't entirely true.

The special quality of kirin was that they allowed their arcanist to bond with a second creature. Orwyn was here without a second eldrin.

Then I remembered another detail about my time at the dig site. The leader of the Second Ascension, a man they called *the Autarch*, had said *he* would be the one to bond with the world serpent. Which meant this was probably a team of arcanists meant to clear an easy path for the Autarch. They would find the creature and then give him the opportunity to bond.

The Autarch had to be nearby. Or perhaps that was why Rhys was here—to teleport him in whenever they were done with their investigations.

Evianna moved to my side, and I almost flinched. She was quiet, and we were both dressed in the blackest of blacks, so I suspected our enemies hadn't yet noticed us. Ryker remained on my other side, unmoving and studying the situation in this new room.

Two corridors leading downward—one no doubt toward the world serpent—were on the other side of the massive room, beyond Rishan and his grim reaper arcanist wife.

It was Evianna and I versus seventeen enemy arcanists. Plus, we had a ward to worry about. If anything happened to Ryker, we would automatically fail our mission. The terrible odds of the situation were stacked so thoroughly in the enemy's favor, I wasn't sure how we would pull a victory out of the bag.

The tree finished mending itself, casting the whole room in darkness.

I caught my breath, wondering how our enemies intended to see in this all-consuming void. In the next few moments, all the Sky Legionnaires lit lanterns and tied them to the saddles of their pegasus eldrin. The light wasn't extremely bright, but it was enough to see a few feet in all directions.

Still...

I knew this was the key to some sort of victory. Evianna and I could see in the dark. And they couldn't. I had to use this to my advantage. I had to think of a way to remove their light permanently.

"Where is this serpent?" Rishan barked. He wore plate armor and carried his apoch dragon sword in one hand, as though afraid to let go of it. "You said this is where we should enter the tree, but I don't see the beast."

Rhys stepped forward, his movements so jerky and odd that I suspected he had some sort of disease or nervous tic. "I said this was the *easiest* point to enter the tree, my king. The trunk was the thinnest here for us to enter through. From everything I've read, the world serpent will be curled up in the roots of the tree, not far from this location."

"Well?" Rishan practically yelled, his gruff voice echoing off the walls and carrying upward to the vaulted ceiling. "Which way, then? There are Frith Guild arcanists outside! We can't allow them to get to the beast first."

The double-headed rizzel motioned to the three twisted hallways that led away from the room—including the one where Evianna, Ryker, and I stood off in the shadows.

"Look at all our options!" the rizzel said with a snicker, his second head flopping around as if dead. "We'll have to tear this whole place apart!" The delight in his voice carried with every word.

"What're we going to do?" Evianna whispered.

I placed my hand on her shoulder and motioned to the two other corridors. "We're going to sneak around the edge, avoiding their lanternlight, and then we're going to shadow-step into one of the possible exits and continue on our way."

She turned her gaze to Rishan and then back to me. I knew what she wanted. Despite that, she replied with a nod. "Very well."

Before we could enact my plan, our enemies had thoughts of their own.

"We'll split up," Rishan said, curt and filled with irritation. "Fazri, Rhys—the two of you take that hallway." He gestured to one leading downward. "Chandra and I will take the other." He waved to the one next to it. "And Orwyn will cover the last. My Sky Legionnaires will act as protectors—four for each tunnel. Does everyone understand, or do I have to repeat myself?"

"I understand, King Rishan," Orwyn replied, her voice sing-song, her gaze on the surroundings and not on him at all. Her kirin moved with the grace and fluidity of water, but it said nothing—kirin never spoke to anyone but their arcanists.

Fazri grabbed the edge of his tricorn cap and bowed. "As you wish." His salamander eldrin burped flame, creating a momentary burst of extra light.

"As soon as you find the damn serpent, you're to report back here immediately," Rishan said. "Then we'll cut our way out of this abyssal tree and continue on."

This was it. Our chance. If I managed to snuff the lights out, Evianna and I could probably take *one* of these groups as we continued on our way to the world serpent.

The enemy arcanists broke into teams, each of them taking four pegasus arcanists as they headed in their designated directions.

"Come on," I whispered. "It's a race against these blackhearts, and we can't lose."

54

DETERMINATION

E vianna, Ryker, and I slipped around the edge of the room as our enemies funneled into the three corridors. Although I would've preferred to hunt down Rishan and repay him for what he had done to his sister Lyvia, I opted instead to take the corridor with Fazri and Rhys. A plague-ridden salamander, a dread form rizzel, and four knight pegasi were frightening opponents, but they weren't a true form sovereign dragon and a death-dealing grim reaper.

The clop of pegasi hooves filled the tree.

The smell of pine and cedar waned and became a mix of mangrove and brackish water. It reminded me of the Endless Mire on the Isle of Ruma. We were getting closer to the roots. We'd stumble upon them at any point now.

We entered the corridor behind Fazri and Rhys. My knightmare armor molded and shaped itself for stealth—becoming sleeker, the greaves and sabatons becoming curved and quieter with each step. Evianna's armor was slightly different than Luthair's. It was already sleek and stealthy, with scales that moved with her actions. Ryker wasn't a man of covertness, but he stuck close to me and only did as instructed, which made it easy to keep him out of trouble.

As best we could, Evianna, Ryker, and I followed the dastards into the depths of the tree. I wanted some space between us and the other members of the Second Ascension, just in case they heard our fighting and decided to rush in and turn the tides.

Fazri took the lead, his rapier on his belt, his hand on the hilt. He wore a long coat with embroidered details of flames and lizards. His neatly trimmed mustache, styled blond hair, and high-quality leather boots hinted at a life of upper-class luxury. He was a gentleman, even as he walked, with his posture straight and his shoulders squared.

His salamander walked behind him with the gait and movements of a fat alligator. Its bulging eyes jiggled with each step, and occasionally, it giggled, its voice stolen from a 10-year-old girl. The crimson scales on his back were curled, like the edges of burnt paper, and its tail was split down the middle, as if cut open. I could see its insides, and they squirmed like worms, even veins. Blood dripped onto the wood as the creature chased after its master.

Interestingly, the tree seemed to absorb the blood, cleaning the corridor as the fiends continued on their way.

"When will the Autarch be arriving?" Fazri asked, his voice dignified and refined.

Rhys flinched at the question. He wrung his hands together as he walked, his robes so long, I could barely see any skin, including his face. "You shouldn't concern yourself with that. The Autarch and his eldrin are close. As soon as we have the world serpent's exact location, I can bring him to us."

"And he knows of my contributions?" Fazri lifted his tricorn cap as he glanced over at Rhys. "I've contributed enough to have the man's ear from time to time. I want to make sure my family's holdings are secure in this *new world order* he's creating."

"You needn't concern yourself with such trivial matters," Rhys said with a half-cough, half-chuckle. "The Autarch knows of your loyalty and sacrifice."

Fazri gritted his teeth and said, "They aren't *trivial matters* to me, cretin."

"My apologies. Your family's *holdings* are clearly on par with god-creatures and the fundamental political structure of the new world. How dare I forget."

Fazri shot the man a scathing glance.

The double-headed rizzel, twisted by the plague to the point that its fur looked as if it were rotting off its body, simply punctuated the conversation with an insane laugh. Its second head—which just hung limp, completely dead most of the time—also joined in with the ludicrous chuckling. There were no eyes in the second head's skull, just a slow trickle of infected blood. Was it weeping? I didn't know.

"The Autarch has *important* matters to deal with," the dread form rizzel said with a twisted smile. "But don't worry; you have *me* to handle all your paperwork." It snickered. "I just might misplace them behind a wall or in someone's chest. The fun is in the surprise of finding it!"

The second undead head laughed again.

Fazri exhaled. "Working with you has been less than reassuring. I much prefer King Rishan's force and immediate tactics."

"Rishan has little patience and even less subtlety," Rhys said. "The Autarch has been working on his grand design for decades—close to a century. His goals and schemes are beyond the comprehension of mortal men, and his ambition and willpower will startle you if you're not paying close attention."

"Ooooh," the rizzel said in an overly sarcastic tone. "If that's how you feel, maybe you should confess your love for him."

Some of the pegasi arcanists and their eldrin chuckled. But they quieted themselves quickly.

Rhys, despite being a thin and gangly man who constantly shook his hands like he was dispelling droplets of water, changed in an instant. He became still and forceful and then glared at the rizzel. "Quiet," he commanded, his voice haunting.

From under Rhys's hood, his arcanist mark glowed a sinister red.

I had never seen something like that before...

And despite the fact that the dread form rizzel was deranged from the plague, it immediately shut both its mouths and became quiet. Was it some sort of magical compulsion? Did Rhys have control of his eldrin completely?

Actually... was the rizzel even Rhys's eldrin? What if Rhys had a different kind of eldrin I was unaware of—one that could dominate the actions of mystical creatures? But why hadn't he used that on the Isle of Ruma?

"The Autarch has made hundreds of promises to hundreds of arcanists," Fazri growled with a clenched jaw. "If he starts failing to live up to his lofty ambitions, there could be a problem. So it would help the Autarch's cause if men like *me* reported he made good on his word. Do you understand?"

"You make such a compelling argument," Rhys sarcastically muttered as he laced his fingers together and then apart. "I'll rush to tell him the moment he arrives."

"Volke," Evianna whispered. She placed a hand on my armored shoulder. "It's time."

We had traveled a considerable distance. Now was the time to rip these fools apart.

I released Ryker and pressed him against the wall. "Wait here," I commanded. "And don't move unless you're in danger, do you understand?"

Ryker simply nodded.

After a quick exchange of determined glances, Evianna and I slid into the darkness. When I emerged, I had Retribution in one hand and Forfend on the other arm. Within a matter of moments after emerging, Evianna forged herself a blade from the shadows of the lightless tree. The six enemy arcanists barely understood that there were new individuals in the corridor until it was too late.

Despite the damping effect of the tree that made my magic harder to use, I forced every ounce of my strength into my manipulation. Hate partially filled my desire to end these dastards, and the burn of my rage flowed through into my shadow creations. In one startling opening strike, I smashed all the lanterns. In the next instant, while the enemy arcanists gasped and made shocked declarations, I used the darkness to grab their legs and hold them in place.

Evianna waved her arm and manipulated the shadows as well. She grabbed for their arms and made swords and claws to slash at the arcanists at once.

I wished she hadn't, though. While she had made great strides in her training—taking everything I had said to heart—she still wasn't skilled enough to pull off so many things at once. She cut and injured the pegasi arcanists and even managed to bind their eldrin, but she wasn't able to continually manipulate more and keep track of it. She never even hurt Fazri or Rhys, and she certainly didn't get their eldrin.

"Dinner is *here*," the salamander said in a gleeful tone.

It belched flames down the corridor, lighting the place up like a bonfire. Evianna and I had to shadow-step out of the way, and I was shocked at how the monster attacked its own allies in an attempt to kill us. Fire washed over two of the Sky Legionnaires, searing the wings of the pegasi and cooking the skin of the two lady arcanists.

I leapt out of the darkness, but instead of going behind the salamander, I came at it from the side.

Evianna took the more predictable approach—she came out of the shadow behind the monster—and it seemed ready for her. Its split tail "bit" at her, but she managed to parry with her impromptu blade, though she was knocked back and staggered.

I swung with Retribution, ready to decapitate the beast, but Fazri pulled out his rapier and spun with an attack fast enough to hinder my aim. I sliced into the salamander's shoulder, opening it up and spilling blood across the corridor.

Fire continued to burn on the walls and farther down the twisted hall, and I wondered how long it would last—or if the tree would somehow deal with this itself.

Fazri held up a hand and evoked his own flames, but I had had enough.

I wouldn't allow these blackhearts another inch.

With speed that startled even me, I shadow-stepped out of the way of the fire and then evoked terrors. Everyone in the corridor except Evianna was momentarily stunned in place, clutching their heads, some screaming. While they were frozen in place, Evianna used her manipulation to stab two of the Sky Legionnaires, dealing fatal wounds to their chests.

But I took control of all the shadows. They formed and coalesced into the form of a dragon, snuffing out the fire and returning the area to utter darkness. With fangs and a maw of inky black, my creation crunched down on the plague-ridden salamander, bursting it like a grape. Then the darkness rose like a tide, drowning out the four Sky Legionnaires and their pegasi eldrin.

I would've squished Rhys and the two-headed rizzel had they not teleported at the last second, escaping my attack in a puff of sparkles.

"*Curse the abyssal hells,*" I muttered through gritted teeth.

They wouldn't escape me long, though. I could feel the heartbeat of the rizzel—and I knew where they had gone. That dastard Rhys went farther down the corridor, no doubt trying to get to the world serpent as fast as possible.

"Finish off anyone who managed to live," I commanded Evianna.

Then I slid into the shadows and traveled down the corridor at lightning speed.

Don't be reckless, my arcanist, Luthair spoke telepathically. *These enemies can be cunning, and you shouldn't allow them to draw you into a situation. Keep control. Maintain focus.*

Although I didn't reply, I took Luthair's words to heart.

When I emerged from the darkness, however, Rhys was waiting for me. He threw a pouch onto the ground, and it exploded into a cloud of bluish-black dust.

Decay dust.

It was a heinous substance crafted by the Second Ascension that eroded and destroyed magical items—specifically trinkets, and not artifacts. It was crafted from the remains of the apoch dragon and seemed to be an enemy of magic itself. The foul dust had destroyed my last sword... but it wouldn't this time.

Rhys might have thought he had dealt damage, but none of my magical items were trinkets.

The dust clung to my inky armor and attempted to attack it, but my ever-shifting knightmare rid itself of the dust in record time. Still—each tiny bit stung, like the dust wanted to destroy me as well. The pain wasn't enough to incapacitate me, though. Not even a mountain of the dust would stop me from my goal today.

Nothing would.

"*Knightmare arcanists,*" Rhys hissed as he backed away, his eyes searching, but ultimately, they didn't lock on me. "I thought we dealt with the Steel Thorn Inquisitors back in Thronehold..."

The double-headed rizzel arched its back, its blackish fur standing on end, its fangs needle-sharp and bared. With a slight smile on its ferret-like face, it said, "You're the human equivalent to a splinter. Always irritating, but ultimately *insignificant*." The undead head laughed at the joke, but I had nothing else to say.

I lifted Retribution.

And then the gravity in the corridor flipped direction. I *fell* to the ceiling, and while that would've startled most, the rizzel obviously didn't understand that knightmares couldn't fall. I "hit" the tree and immediately dove into the darkness and reemerged on my feet.

Both of the heads of the rizzel breathed white flame, illuminating the area for a brief period, but I defended with Forfend and the shield absorbed the attack. Now that I knew what the shield did, I realized I had the evocation of the dread form rizzel stored for later use. Perhaps it could come in handy another time—because I wouldn't need it for this fight.

I controlled all the shadows in the corridor and rushed them both. The black ink of the darkness grabbed them and held tight, and then I lunged. With one forceful blow, I slashed the rizzel clean in half. It didn't stand a chance. It didn't even see me coming.

Blood gushed out of both parts, most of it chunky.

The half with the functioning head hit the floor, and its red glowing eyes stared up at me, both opened as wide as they could be.

"Everyone knows you're here, you witless rag," it said, practically giggling as it sputtered out blood. "You'll die before... you reach... the serpent..."

I went to cleave Rhys, but he clicked his tongue and then teleported away. I slashed and hit the tree anyway, frustration and anger replacing all other emotions in my body. How could he still teleport? The rizzel really *wasn't* his eldrin... yet Rhys had all the powers of one...

I closed my eyes and took a deep and calming breath.

Then I stepped into the darkness and returned to Evianna, fearful for her and Ryker. I was the most trained and skilled arcanist left in the group. I was responsible. I was the one they would depend on.

When I found her, she was standing over the bodies of the four Sky Legionnaires, the plague-ridden salamander, and Fazri. I hadn't been the one to deal the killing blow to Fazri himself, so I knew she had handled it and...

It probably explained the look on her face. Evianna stared at Fazri as though trying to piece together a difficult puzzle, her eyebrows knitted, her eyes narrowed.

Taking a life was never something to celebrate, but our enemies wouldn't be stopped unless we took the ultimate step. And in Fazri's case, he had given himself and his eldrin to the plague. What more could be done?

"Everything will be okay," I said.

Evianna glanced up and nodded. "I know. As long as we're together... We can do this."

The way she said the words had my chest twisting. She had spoken with nothing but trust and determination, as though there was no doubt in her mind. It gave me hope, and it reminded me of her kiss. I found it momentarily distracting, but I shook the thought from my head.

"Let's go," I said.

I returned to the place I had left Ryker and found him faithfully waiting. When I took his arm, he sighed in relief, and the three of us continued down the corridor.

"I'm sorry I'm not more help," Ryker muttered.

I shook my head. "Once you're the world serpent arcanist, you can pay us back in spades."

The tree grew colder as we went on.

And smoother. And stiller.

We were close. Near the end. I could feel it, just like I could feel the presence of plague-ridden monsters. The world serpent was within our grasp.

The moment we exited the corridor, I found a room with a giant door —a door similar to the entrance, just ten times larger, the carving with even more detail.

It was the chamber to the world serpent. We had successfully traveled through its trial of worth, a dungeon so massive and filled with peril that half the arcanists who had entered were lost.

But the harsh clop of hooves brought me back to the reality of the situation. King Rishan, Chandra, and four Sky Legionnaires entered the chamber from another corridor, their lantern light casting harsh shadows as they shone them over the door.

"Excellent," Rishan said as he stepped forward.

His dragon lumbered at his side, his massive head held high. The crown-like horns glistened in dim lighting, and while I hated to think it, the beast was imposing and awe-inspiring.

"Where is Rhys?" Chandra asked. She pulled the hood of her robe up higher to conceal her grim reaper mark. "He said the Autarch would be able to breach this door."

I didn't want to fight them, but now I had no choice. Rhys was somewhere in the tree, and if they met up, the Autarch would arrive, and I couldn't handle that on my own.

I pulled Evianna closer, my grip tight, my resolve steeled. I had lost to both the grim reaper and the sovereign dragon when last I had fought them one-on-one, but now we had to handle them together.

"This is the final fight," I said to Evianna, keeping my voice low.

And Fain had been so adamant about warning me of my impending death...

"I've been waiting for this since Lyvia's death," Evianna replied.

We exchanged nods, and I motioned Ryker away from the chamber. Perhaps we'd have a major advantage if I started the fight out on a surprise attack...

55

PRETENDER ON THE THRONE

E vianna didn't want the element of surprise, however. She stepped out of the corridor and then to the edge of the lantern light. I held my breath and followed behind her as a third shadow. I knew what she wanted, and I couldn't deny it to her, even if I thought it foolish.

I would just have to compensate for our lack of an upper hand.

"Brother," Evianna said, calm and cold.

King Rishan turned to face us, though it was clear he couldn't quite make out the details. We were swaddled in the darkness and only silhouetted by the dim lights.

"Evianna," he muttered. Then he huffed and let out a single laugh. "You're as idiotic as you are reckless—and you're *very* reckless." He pulled a sword from its scabbard and swirled it in his hand. The black blade seemed to absorb light, not catch it. "If you had fled to the far corners of the world, I would've shown you mercy and left you to a life as a hermit. But here you are. A nuisance, like always. Something I need to cut away so that my new life can begin."

Rishan motioned his Sky Legionnaires away, and all four backed away, though they did so with confusion and hesitation.

Evianna stepped forward once, her knightmare armor striking and distinct. The dragon scale leather, the wing-like cape, and even the cowl had designs of sovereign dragons and their crown-like horns. She looked like a dark crusader—she embodied the assassination of the late queen. In the most important ways, she had matured and knew this could be her last act, but the fear didn't paralyze her.

"We'll end this now," Evianna said, still calm. "But I have one final thing to say."

Crimthand licked his lips with his long, serpentine tongue, his gold eyes fixed on Evianna's location.

Chandra and her grim reaper stood near the giant door, neither of them moving to interfere. Were they planning on sitting this out? Would this be a duel to the death between yet another brother and sister?

I couldn't allow that. More was at stake than revenge. We had to win this fight, no matter the costs. I stepped forward, making my presence and intent known. If there was a fight, I would be a participant.

"You're a coward at heart," Evianna continued.

She held her shadow swords at the ready, and I hoped she understood it would never be able to deflect Rishan's blade. His would cut through magic as though it weren't there—they had terribly mismatched weapons, all in his favor.

Before Rishan could respond, Evianna added, "You love only yourself and your power, and that will be your undoing. You stand for nothing of substance. You want nothing of meaning. Those are the qualities that make a true warrior—a true king. You're a pretender on the throne, and history books will remember you as such."

The words lingered like a stale smell.

Rishan sneered and then snapped his fingers. The Sky Legionnaires readied themselves for combat—each lady arcanist leapt to her pegsasus and then unholstered her lance. Crimthand half-growled and half-laughed as he moved forward.

The two I feared—Chandra and Demise—didn't seem eager to join in the fighting. They didn't move. They stayed close to the door, both watching the exchange with rapt attention.

Evianna held her sword at the ready, and for a brief moment, I was impressed.

A craven would've run from combat. A sycophant would've pled with me to handle the fighting. A damsel would've been immobilized by fear. But a true knight faced darkness and fought until the bitter end.

Luthair telepathically communicated to me, but this time, it felt tainted by the hard edge of concern. *You must be careful, my arcanist. These are fiends who will use whatever means to kill you both. Please never lose focus.*

With that statement of confidence, I held up my hand and evoked my terrors. Our enemies—except for Chandra and her grim reaper— struggled under the horrors of their own imagination, some staggering back or crying out. While they floundered, Evianna manipulated the darkness and shattered the four lanterns held by the Sky Legionnaires. The sudden return to darkness only fueled our magic and rendered our opponents blind. Rishan's arcanist mark, along with my own, still glowed with an inner power, betraying the fact we both had true form eldrin.

"Crimthand," Rishan shouted, smiling wide. "Burn this whole tree to the ground!"

The pyre of dragon fire lit the area more than the salamander could ever hope. The flames rushed down the corridor and filled almost every inch of space from the ceiling to the floor. I shadow-stepped in time to escape, but I had to enter the room. A small piece of me worried for Ryker, but I had asked him to stand far away. Hopefully, Crimthand's attack hadn't taken him by surprise.

The temperature of the room rose a couple of degrees.

Evianna emerged near her brother, and I decided to handle the pegasi first.

The four Sky Legionnaires all used their wind evocation at once, creating a powerful gust of wind that caught hold of Crimthand's lingering fire and rushed it around the room like a firestorm. It illuminated the area well enough that the pegasi arcanists spotted me and turned their spears in my direction.

But I didn't care. When they rushed for me, I already knew they had lost. I had the advantage of environment and power—the darkness and my true form abilities. When the Sky Legionnaires came for me, I manipulated the shadows like I had with the salamander. The dragon-shaped shadow rose from a sea of blackness and then tore through my enemies as if I had summoned a creature from the darkness of the abyss itself.

I controlled the dragon enough to crunch through one pegasi and then a second, both torn asunder by the strength of my true form magic.

Unfortunately, Crimthand turned his fire on my creation. The blaze ripped my shadows apart, decimating my manipulation.

But I couldn't let my opponents catch their breath. I slid into the darkness, traveled up the wall and over the ceiling, and then back behind the last two remaining Sky Legionnaires. Retribution was a weapon of anti-magic—the moment I swung and they didn't successfully dodge away, I knew I had won.

I stabbed the first pegasus through an opening in its armor and then cleaved through the rest of the body as though there weren't any resistance. Retribution couldn't cut through the knight's armor, but the flesh itself was already destroyed.

The second Sky Legionnaire rounded on me with a lance and attempted to use wind, but I evoked another round of terrors, hindering all the dastard's fighting. That was when I brought my sword down on the pegasus arcanist and her eldrin, cutting through her leg and decapitating the mystical creature.

For a brief second, the fighting shook me. The knight arcanists weren't plague-ridden or blackhearts—they were just serving a wicked king, carrying out his villainous plans. But then I felt the calming presence of Luthair grip my mind. He kept the horrors of war from penetrating too deep into my thoughts. He kept me sane.

Crimthand roared, frustration in his cry.

With the Sky Legionnaires dealt with, I finally returned my attention to Evianna. She was busy dueling her brother—both of them locked on each other and dealing with no one else. Her cape was burned down one side, but otherwise, neither was damaged. She leapt through the darkness and attempted to slash at him, but his apoch dragon sword was too dangerous. She kept her distance whenever he swung wide, which hindered her ability to run him through.

Not only that, but Rishan's armor held together surprisingly well, even when Evianna used her shadow manipulation to strike at it. Was it magical? No doubt in my mind. He was the king of a large nation—it was probably an artifact.

Despite Rishan's clear advantage in power, he still couldn't see. And Evianna had the luxury of never-ending darkness. It wasn't an even match, but at least Evianna stood a tiny chance.

Crimthand snarled and then belched flame everywhere—circling the room as if determined to catch me no matter what. His fire was so intense, I knew I'd never be able to heal properly if he managed to catch me in the depths of the tree.

I shifted through the darkness, avoiding the attacks as much as possible. I couldn't afford to slip up—my focus was absolute. Each new spot of fire had me on the ropes. I had to turn things around, or else it was only a matter of time before I lost...

"V-Volke!"

Panic flooded my mind, sending ice through my veins.

I hadn't been paying attention to anyone else.

With my heart in my throat, I glanced around the room between bursts of flame.

Evianna and Rishan were still locked in their fight. The dragon fire didn't harm Rishan, and Evianna managed to dodge it like I was. She hadn't been the one to shout my name, however... It had been Ryker.

And I spotted him standing in the mouth of one of the corridors. Demise was behind him, holding the sleeve of his shirt, practically lifting him off the ground.

"Volke!" Ryker shouted a second time.

"Look what I sensed," Demise drawled.

I couldn't allow Ryker to die.

Despite the fact that it would injure me, I stopped dodging to manipulate the shadows. Flames washed across my side—and I used Forfend to block most of it—but I gritted my teeth and dealt with the resulting injuries across my left leg. Then I grabbed Ryker with the darkness and yanked him away from the grim reaper, my thoughts jumbled as I attempted to change my entire fighting tactic.

"My love," Chandra said in a half-taunting, half-sing-song voice. "I think we found the man the Frith Guild is attempting to make the new world serpent arcanist."

Despite the agony across my left leg, I shadow-stepped to Ryker's side. I now had to fight with him in close quarters at all times—I couldn't allow him out of arm's reach.

Crimthand, Demise, and Chandra each turned their attention in my direction, but their lack of sight made it difficult to pinpoint me. I was certain that the grim reaper and his arcanist could sense life enough that they knew my general location, but not what I was doing specifically. Would this work to my advantage? It had to.

"Kill the fool they brought here," Rishan shouted as Evianna leapt back into the darkness. "End them all!"

Anyone who killed a reaper—grim or otherwise—would be affected by the reaper's curse, *the king's revenge*. It was a powerful magic that killed whoever dealt the killing blow, which meant I *couldn't* fight Demise first. I had to focus my attention on Crimthand, and only then could I tackle the grim reaper problem.

With my impromptu tactic set in place, I gritted my teeth and held Forfend high. I pointed at the sovereign dragon and unleashed the rizzel's powerful blast of white disintegrating flame that had been stored within. It lit up the area, but only briefly. Surprise was my ally—all three of my opponents seemed stunned to see the attack, and as long as I kept them guessing, I was in a good place.

The teleporting flames washed over Crimthand. He was too big and bulky to leap out of the way. Bits of his scales, muscles, and horns were teleported around the room, some bits so fine, it was almost a dust. It was his face I had been aiming for, and the small portion that had been damaged included the left eye, which was what I had hoped.

I slipped into the darkness and emerged on his left side, in his blind spot. Retribution usually cut through magic, but the scales of a dragon proved to be a minor inconvenience when we had fought on the docks. I aimed for the portion of his body where the scales had been teleported away—cutting deep and then yanking my blade upward through the beast's shoulder. I hoped I cut through his heart, or at least major arteries. I just needed this monster dead.

"Demise," Chandra snapped. She stomped the heel of her boot. "This is has gone on too long. I won't lose all the prizes I've worked so hard to get."

"Yes, my arcanist," Demise stated with a bow.

In an instant, the grim reaper collapsed as a pile of clothing, devoid of any form. The deadly axe hit the ground as if dropped. Then the executioner's garments flew over to Chandra and wrapped around her, much like how Luthair merged with me. The executioner's cowl covered her head, the belt wrapped around her slender waist twice, the gloves fitted themselves snugly over her hands, and the shirt and pants stitched themselves over her body, covering her robes with a haunting visage of a blood-stained keeper of the gallows.

Then the axe shot from the ground and straight to Chandra's hand. Despite the fact that the axe would weigh too much to swing around like a toy, Chandra managed it anyway, and I suspected it was due to the grim reaper's merged form. Like knightmares, they would live and die as a single being, but being merged increased their magical abilities.

I stabbed at Crimthand a second time, piercing into his chest before he had a chance to recover from my previous blow. He collapsed to the ground, and I hoped it meant he was finished, but I didn't have time to confirm anything.

Chandra wasn't going to allow me to fight uncontested. She swung her deadly weapon wide. If it cut me, even a scratch, it'd spell instant death—I had to take whatever steps necessary to avoid it.

I shadow-stepped away, but when I emerged, Chandra ran in my direction, her speed and power shocking. Her merged form made this difficult, and when I went to swing at her, she "fell" into the blood that had splattered across the ground. Similar to a knightmare's ability to travel through shadows, reapers of any kind could blood-step from one wet puddle to the next.

My heart stopped for a brief moment, but instead of waiting for her to emerge and swing at me, I manipulated all the shadows in the room to stab out in multiple directions. The spines, claws, and teeth I created just thrashed about—some even attacking Rishan and helping Evianna with her duel.

When Chandra did emerge, my shadows stabbed and latched on to her. She grunted, and I spun around with enough time to avoid her attack.

But I couldn't attack back. If I killed her... I would also die due to the king's revenge.

A scream pierced the room.

I whipped around to find Crimthand biting hard on Ryker's right shoulder. The dragon's fangs were deep in Ryker's flesh, crimson blood soaking everything from Crimthand's mouth to Ryker's clothing. The dragon was barely able to move, but somehow, he had caught Ryker and was trying to use the last of his strength to kill him.

Ryker cried louder as Crimthand crunched down harder, the sound of breaking bones echoing throughout the chamber like a symphony of suffering.

King Rishan glanced away from his fight with Evianna to take stock of the situation. I had never seen such a poor tactical decision—Evianna's focus was razor sharp, and instead of just attacking him, she manipulated the shadows to rip his apoch dragon sword from his grasp. She grabbed it for herself, and while he was still reeling, stabbed it through his chest.

The armor... The sword passed right through it. Which meant it had probably been made from magic. A poor defense for the apoch dragon.

The scene was shocking, but I couldn't focus on it. I evoked terrors, which caused Crimthand to screech and drop Ryker. Then I swam through the darkness and emerged with a final strike.

I slashed with all my strength and hate. In one brutal blow, I removed Crimthand's head from his body. The dragon gasped—its final use of breath—and I knew I had won.

Chandra lunged, blood-stepped, and then emerged near me. I grabbed Ryker and narrowly avoided her massive axe before sinking back into the darkness. Her life-sensing abilities would mean none of us could hide...

I would have to kill her.

That truth sank into my gut, twisting my insides. Someone had to do it, and the responsibility fell to me. I'd die from the king's revenge, but then there'd be nothing standing between Ryker and the world serpent. Evianna could handle the rest.

When I leapt out of the shadows, a new fact complicated matters.

Evianna was on the ground, burned from the shoulder to the hip, her knightmare still merged with her, but mostly charred. Rishan was dead, but it was obvious that he had managed one final attack with dragon fire before his eldrin had died.

He had burned Evianna—badly. She wasn't even moving.

"Volke," Ryker said, breathless.

I turned to him as he sank to his knees. He trembled fiercely—blood pouring from the dragon bite on his shoulder. He tried to staunch the flow, but he could barely lift his other arm.

Chandra hefted her axe. "You cur. *I was supposed to be a queen.* And look what you and your *disgusting maggots* have taken from me." Her double-voice with Demise sent a shiver down my spine.

Evianna was dying.

Ryker was bleeding out.

And I still had to deal with the grim reaper.

I tightened my grip on Retribution, my heart hammering so hard, it was the only thing I could hear. Chandra said something more, but I couldn't make it out.

56

A MISTAKE MADE RIGHT

I f I killed Chandra, I would also die.

And then so would Ryker and Evianna.

But if I somehow managed to live, I could take Ryker into the world serpent chamber. He could bond with the god-creature and then he'd gain the ability to heal, like all arcanists. He would make it through this... and then I could focus all my attention on getting Evianna back to the guild. I could still save them.

My arcanist, Luthair spoke. *We could flee. You've decimated the enemy. We could return to the guild, and after we've recuperated, we could finish this mission.*

Was that really an option? No. Rhys was still here. I hadn't managed to cut him down, and he somehow retained the power of teleportation, which meant he would bring the Autarch here the moment he found the world serpent's door.

So many people had sacrificed to get us here. Devlin, Illia, and Zelfree... Everyone fighting on the roots of this giant world tree. If we fled now, I would risk rendering all of that pointless. I had to stay. I had to find a way to deal with this situation.

Chandra stepped into the blood, disappearing from sight.

There was so much gore in the room... Four pegasi, four pegasi arcanists, a dragon, and Rishan himself—so much flesh and blood that Chandra could step out of anywhere.

I tried to warn Mathis the night when he died, Luthair continued. *I failed him. I should've convinced him of the danger. I should've been there when he needed me. I can't do that a second time, Volke Savan. I can't lose another arcanist.*

Chandra leapt out of the gore on the ground and swung hard with her axe. I blocked with Forfend, deflecting the blow, but the force of the strike hurt my arm and reminded me that my leg was throbbing from the dragon fire burns. The intensity of the fight was masking my pain, and I knew I could keep fighting, but if I went much longer, I'd break myself. I had to end this...

I manipulated the shadows—creating chains and hooks—and wrapped Chandra in bindings. My hands shook, my breathing came out ragged, and I could feel my magic slipping. I had been fighting for so long...

But there was no turning back.

Perhaps I could parry the axe with Retribution, breaking the weapon... Then it'd be easier to land a killing blow. But if I missed or if something went *slightly* wrong, that could be the end for me.

I gulped down air and clenched my jaw.

My arcanist... there's no shame in strategic retreat.

No matter what, I couldn't give up. This was my path. I had to get Ryker to the world serpent. I had to get Evianna to someone in the Frith Guild who could heal her. I had to deal with this grim reaper. I couldn't abandon any of these tasks, not for my own safety.

There were times when retreating was necessary, but... I had modeled my life after the arcanists of the vanguard—after the stars in the night sky. Those arcanists, like the stars themselves, were there in the darkest of moments, no hesitation, no wavering. They did their job, bringing light to the darkness, regardless of recognition or fame. I had to do that today. I couldn't falter at the end.

Chandra broke free of my shadowy chains, her strength overpowering mine. She hadn't been fighting for the last hour—she hadn't been injured by dragon fire—so she was still at full fighting force.

And then she hefted her axe and said something else, no doubt a taunt, but I couldn't hear her. It was only Luthair's voice and the cold comfort of his power. I heard nothing else besides my own jumbled thoughts and the buzz of panic when I realized I had no perfect solution to this situation.

What would Gravekeeper William do? How would Master Zelfree handle this?

In the old legends, how would Gregory Ruma escape certain death?

I couldn't think of the answers. Perhaps this was what it meant to write my own destiny—I'd have to find my own solution and become a new legend.

Chandra stepped forward, bracing her weight on one foot for a powerful overhead swing. I could tell. She telegraphed her attacks like a trumpeter telegraphed his location with his music. Chandra fought like someone who hadn't learned the nuances of technical fighting— someone who relied solely on the death-touch of her axe to end her enemies.

So when she came in with the swing, I knew this was my chance. I lifted Forfend, deflected the blow, and when the axe slid off the surface of my shield, I struck at the long hilt with Retribution. Just as I suspected, my black sword sliced clean through the magical weapon— sundering it in two and rendering it useless.

I had half-hoped that she would surrender after my minor victory, but it only seemed to awaken her desperation. Chandra leapt away from me and then waved her hand. The gore in the room answered her summons, crystalizing into scarlet knives. She threw them at me, but my armor protected me from the majority of the injuries, and my shield defended me from the last.

When she realized that was futile, she turned her attention to the injured Ryker and the unconscious Evianna.

In that split second, I knew the plan she was formulating.

And this was my moment. I had to step forward and end her life. After that... I'd have to hope that Ryker had the strength and willpower to make it to the world serpent. If he did, *he* could save Evianna.

But he couldn't even stand... He'd never make it...

When I gritted my teeth, I tasted blood.

I stepped forward, Retribution held tightly. This would be over quickly. I wouldn't feel a thing. And it was the only option. I had to *hope* that Ryker could manage. That was all that was left for me.

My arcanist, fighting by your side gave my life new meaning, and protecting you in your moment of need will be my greatest and most cherished privilege. I will make this right—I won't repeat my past failings.

Before I could respond, or even comprehend what Luthair was saying, he unmerged from me mid-swing.

My breath caught in my throat as Luthair fully separated from my body. He left the star-lined cape on my shoulders, but took Retribution and Forfend as he lunged forward. In one savage slash, he sliced through Chandra's neck and chest—perfect aim to her heart.

She staggered backward and fell to the ground in literal pieces, her blood and body parts adding to the gruesome graveyard all around us.

"L-Luthair," I forced myself to say, almost unable to utter the word.

He stood over Chandra's body and lowered Retribution before turning to face me. "My arcanist—now you can finish what we started. And thank you... for allowing me to serve by your side as you grew into the knight who stands before me today."

As he spoke, his inky armor melted away, pooling into a lake of darkness at his feet. His magic unraveled, and I couldn't find the words. I choked on my own breath, stunned. Luthair had sacrificed himself to suffer the king's revenge without me.

"Future greatness awaits you," Luthair uttered, his tone calm and filled with compassion. "Don't allow this moment to hold you back."

And then...

I knew the moment it happened because my dark-sight failed me. The chamber was suddenly pitch black, devoid of any and all light. I heard Retribution and Forfend clatter to the ground, but the facts barely registered with me.

All his magic... it drained from my body, leaving me unsteady and shaking.

My thoughts, once intertwined with Luthair's, were now quiet.

I glanced around, wanting to say something—to cry out for help— but there was no one. Illia wasn't here. Or William. Or Zelfree. Or even Zaxis, Atty, or the other apprentices. Normally, there would be *someone* who pushed me to continue... Someone who reassured me that the night would eventually come to an end...

But not this time.

I had never felt more alone in my entire life.

Ice gripped my heart and chilled my pulse. After all the fighting I had done, the one enemy that threatened to defeat me was despair. I forced myself to breathe, and then—without much thought—I stepped forward, my boots splashing in the blood.

Groping through the darkness, I bent down and picked up Retribution and Forfend. My leg burned with the agony of dragon fire, and every time my heart beat, I could feel it anew. But that didn't matter. Even if I walked wrong for the rest of my life, I couldn't concern myself with my own injuries. Everyone else was depending on me.

I sheathed Retribution in its scabbard and hooked Forfend on my forearm. Then I carefully turned around and headed for the area where I remembered Evianna had fallen. With slow movements, I made my way to her side and then felt at her mouth and neck. Still breathing.

Although my whole body hurt, I wrapped her in my star cape and then scooped her up. With a grunt, I hefted her over my shoulder. Taking her weight added to the stress on my injured leg, but what else could I do?

Then I hobbled over to Ryker. I could hear him fretting and swallowing air at a fierce rate.

"V-Volke?" Ryker whispered.

"I'm here," I said, my voice rusty, but firm. "Come on. We need to go."

"I tried... tending the injury... but I can't use my right arm." His voice was weak and quavered after every couple of words. "I can barely keep my eyes open..."

"I'm here to help you." I knelt, wrapped an arm around his torso, and then stood, taking him with me. I clenched my jaw and stifled a groan of pain, but I managed it. "We aren't far now. Come."

Ryker didn't have any strength. He tried walking, but his legs buckled with each step, and I imagined he was paler than usual. I kept forgetting he was a year younger than me—and that he had never trained for combat—and I wondered if the stress of this endeavor was too much for him.

But it was over. He just had to stay awake for a few minutes longer. The moment he bonded with the world serpent, he would be okay.

"I'm sorry," Ryker whispered. "I... I'm trying to be strong."

"You're doing fine. You're still here."

"I can't even... walk..."

"But I can," I said. "Don't fret—just conserve your strength. I'll handle this."

"Your eldrin..."

"Conserve your strength."

Ryker went silent, but his breathing evened out as we went. I carried Evianna and Ryker across the bloodied chamber, almost tripping on the corpse of Crimthand, and stopped only once I came to the giant circular door. The jade runestone in Ryker's pocket reacted to the proximity of the door, and it glowed green so brightly it shone through the pocket of his trousers.

"Touch the runestone to the door," I said.

His hand shook, but Ryker did as I asked. He reached into his pocket, withdrew the runestone, and then placed it flat against the door.

And that was when the power of the tree truly revealed itself.

57

THE WORLD SERPENT

The door opened, and bright emerald green light flooded outward, illuminating the room and the corridors behind. It slowly shifted to a soft white glow, and it felt warm against my skin, like a comfortable blanket on a dark and stormy night.

Once my eyes had adjusted to the new light, I took in a sharp gasp. The hallway beyond the massive door wasn't like the rest of the tree. It was a hall straight from a palace or cathedral, with dome ceilings, pillars, and beautiful works of art. The architecture didn't look... human. The pillars themselves appeared otherworldly—all of them shaped like swirling water, trees, and tangled vines. The ivory white of the marble flooring contrasted wonderfully with the gold and silver leaves of the subtle designs in the wall and ceiling. Pictures of animals and war marked every surface, but the pictures were so small and detailed, it required serious attention to really understand their true nature.

But the most shocking aspect of this hallway was the star shards.

Hundreds of them jutted out of the ceiling, and some were on the edges of the walkway, where the wall met the floor. They sparkled with inner power, each golden and twinkling, adding to the majesty of the environment.

The ceiling had to be forty feet high. It made me feel... small. Almost insignificant. Even the pillars were wider than I had ever seen before, as if this place had been designed for giants and not people.

A squeaking emanated from my pocket, and I almost flinched. The mouse... It was still there... And when I glanced down, it was peering out of my pocket, taking in the sights. Did the Mother of Shapeshifters recognize this place? Or was she impressed that I had made it this far into the lair of one of the god-creatures? I couldn't tell.

Ryker took in a ragged breath, but he managed to glance around, examining our surroundings.

"What is this place?" he whispered, his honeyed skin paler than before.

"Conserve your strength," I muttered. "We're almost there."

I was surprised he was still conscious. How much longer could he last?

With Evianna on one shoulder and Ryker held close, I continued my journey into the hall. The burn on my leg threatened to steal my ability to walk, but I refused to allow my body to quit when we had come this far. My father had a limp. Perhaps it was my destiny to have one as well.

Each heavy step I took created a loud *thunk* that haunted the hall as an echo. While the silence of the area might've unnerved me, I was too distracted to let it occupy my thoughts. I kept my attention on the star shards, and then, once I was halfway through the hall, on the far door. We were almost there, and it didn't matter if there was no one else here.

Just like the two previous doors, this one was large and circular, with a carving of the world serpent. The jade runestone glowed as we approached, and Ryker managed to hold it up a second time, despite his shaking arm. He gently pressed it into the stone, and we were engulfed in yet another blast of emerald light.

This mystic tree continued to surprise me. A massive garden stood before us—winding ponds and creeks, pathways lined with flowers, trees bearing fruit, and star shards sprinkled throughout made this the most eldritch of places I had ever been. I took an unsteady step onto the dirt path, surprised by the aroma of fragrant fruits and soil after the first rain. The water in the room glowed a gentle blue, and I couldn't help but admire the swirling shadows cast by the ripples of movement created by tiny fish swimming in the creeks.

This area radiated magic so much, I could feel it in my bones.

I glanced to Ryker, tempted to say something, but his eyes were unfocused. Could he even see?

The pathway led to the edge of the pond in the room, and I held my breath as I went, pushing back the pain and allowing sweat to drip from my chin and onto my shirt.

The fish didn't seem concerned with my presence. Even when I stumbled and got close to the edge of the water, they didn't dart away, like normal creatures. They seemingly watched, as though curious, their eyes glittering in the blue light of the magical water.

Finally—after several deep breaths and moments when I thought I would fall—I made it to the end of the path. I set Ryker down, and he went to his knees, his body weak from loss of blood. Thankfully, he had used his shirt well enough, and his mangled shoulder and arm weren't actively weeping blood, but that didn't mean he had stopped the flow completely. It was only a matter of time before he expired.

I took Evianna to the edge of the water. The burns across her body were severe—I didn't know what to do to help her—but the water radiated magic like I had never felt before. I gently removed her from my shoulder and set her on the shore of the pond, her body mostly submerged in the water, but her head and shoulders on land, so there was no chance of drowning. Her knightmare remained merged, and I hoped their combined strength was enough for them to live through this experience.

The glowing blue water lapped against Evianna's body and my star-lined cape. Would this pond help her recover? I didn't know, but it was the best I could do until I found a way out of the depths of this tree.

The tree rumbled.

My heart caught in my throat as the shaking grew worse. The fish leapt around the creeks and pond, splashing the water as everything shook. Fruit rained down from the trees, and petals fell from the flowers.

"*Volke*," Ryker mumbled, his voice barely above a whisper. "What if…"

What if the tree was about to swallow us whole? It was possible, but without my magic, I couldn't shadow-step to avoid it.

I returned to Ryker's side. If the tree did try to consume us, I'd push

Ryker out of the way and hopefully take his place. It was the last thing I could do. I had nothing more to give.

But the tree didn't open up to swallow us. Instead, the pond swirled and the water crashed on the shores, splashing Evianna more than I had hoped, but she would be okay. Then, much to my shock and awe, something rose out of the water—a massive creature with a serpentine body.

Its scales were jade in color. Its eyes were two separate colors—the right was the purest of scarlet, like a sunset over a desert, and the left was the most radiant of blues, the color stolen from a sapphire. The serpent had the face of a python and the slit irises of a dragon. On its head, instead of a viper hood, it had spines made of crystal, clustered like a mane or crest. The crystals themselves were similar to star shards—glittering with inner power.

The serpent continued to rise out of the pond, heading toward the high ceiling and slithering through the air with a concertina movement like only snakes could manage. It twisted around and then stared down at us with its dichromatic eyes.

The beast was colossal. I had seen a full-grown leviathan before... and this world serpent—supposedly a child, a *hatchling*—was just as large, perhaps more so. And it occurred to me then that the bottom of the pond had actually been the creature's body.

This was the legendary world serpent. The first of the god-creatures to usher humanity into a new age of magic and rulership.

I didn't know what to do with myself. After a deep breath, I knelt on one knee, shaken by the mighty serpent, but also fearful—I had no magic or way to fight it. If the serpent wanted, it could eat us all whole in a single bite. We were at its mercy.

Glowing blue water dripped from the god-creature's face and scales, but it said nothing. It just stared with unblinking eyes, its breath washing over us, each exhale carrying with it the scents of autumn.

"Mighty world serpent," I forced myself to say, though my volume was soft. I cleared my throat and started again. "World serpent—we've c-come to..."

But I wasn't sure what to say. We've come to bond? We've overcome your trial of worth? We've come to ask your aid? Shouldn't Ryker say this?

I motioned to Ryker and kept my gaze to the ground, trying to show deference and respect. "This man, Ryker—" I caught my breath when I realized I had never been given his last name, not once. But I recovered quickly and continued, "—has come seeking to bond with you."

The world serpent pondered my statement, its draconic eyes shifting from me, to Ryker, and then back.

When the world serpent spoke, it did so telepathically, and to everyone at once, its voice so clear and precise, I practically heard it as though spoken aloud.

"**Children of Balaster, you need not fret,**" the serpent said, his voice unmistakably masculine and soaked in magic. "**I witnessed your descent through my lair. I know of your endeavors and hardships. And I know of your purpose here.**"

Children of... Balaster?

I shook the thought from my head and then exhaled. "Thank you, mighty world serpent."

"**The time has come.**" The god-creature lowered his serpentine head, his squared python nose coming within three feet of my location. "**All the world is in peril, and a new warlord must help usher in judgment.**"

He spoke with such confidence and certainty, it was as if the beast was thousands of years old and not a new hatchling.

I pushed myself to stand, and then I gulped down enough air to move. With pained movements, I helped Ryker get to his feet, but it felt like holding a bag of grain and pretending it was a man. His breathing was shallow.

"**No,**" the serpent stated, its telepathic voice forceful and commanding. "**I will bond with one person and one person only. You, Volke Savan. You will be the warlord the world needs.**"

The statement stabbed at my chest. Each word stung more than I had ever thought possible. I shook my head, unable to process everything at once. "Wait—there has to be a mistake. You need to bond with Ryker. *He's* the one we brought."

"Since the moment you set foot in my lair, I knew you were someone I could bond with."

"But that's not right." I took a deep breathing, gathering my thoughts. "The sybil arcanists said the best world serpent arcanist was Ryker. It has to be Ryker."

"He was never a consideration," the serpent said, his voice harsh and deep in my thoughts. "He lacks the qualities needed for judgment. He lacks the determination and willpower. He lacks the essence of a god-arcanist. The only two within my lair who even qualify for my power are you and the Child of Luvi—the kirin arcanist, Orwyn."

What? *Not* Ryker?

No matter how I thought about the situation, my chest continued to hurt. Guildmaster Eventide had been certain. She had gone out of her way to find this answer. If I ignored it... What if I ruined the future the sybil arcanists spoke of?

"What if... I asked you to bond with Ryker in my stead?" I asked, glancing up to meet the god-creature's mighty gaze. "Please. Bond with him. *It has to be him.*"

The gigantic serpent snorted and chuckled, his mirth filling the garden chamber and causing the fish to leap around the creek and pond.

"The Children of Balaster never cease to amuse me," he said, laughter at the edge of his telepathic speech. "You have no desire for my magic? No desire to be a god-arcanist?"

"I don't want it," I said, fighting against my frustration. "I just want what's best for the future. Please—so many people gave their lives for this. So many arcanists fought so hard... I don't want to fail them. I want... I want the world to have the hero the sybil arcanists foretold of."

"Your eldrin perished during your trek here."

I nodded, unable to say Luthair's name.

"Yet you still deny my power? Deny my bonding?"

I held Ryker close, his heartbeat weaker and weaker. "I'd sacrifice anything to fight the darkness sweeping the land," I muttered, my words slow and deliberate. "And if Ryker is the only one who is capable of doing that... I can't be the one to bond with you. I'm sorry."

Again, the god-creature laughed, stirring the fish and shaking the leaves of the tree. I didn't know what it found so funny, but I hoped that meant it would honor my request. We didn't have much time before Evianna and Ryker would be beyond saving...

"**I see and hear everything within this lair, even the darkest and most hidden of thoughts,**" the serpent said, fixing its two-colored eyes on me. "**The prophesy the sybil arcanists spoke did not name a specific individual. They claimed** *a son of the thief, Aarona, would be the world's best hope for peace.* **Nothing more.**"

For a brief and startling moment, I heard and felt nothing.

Aarona was my mother's name.

But... that was impossible. Wasn't it?

No. That would explain Ryker's hesitation from the very beginning. He had never been named specifically. And why he had worried when we had entered the tree—he had known there was a slight possibility it wasn't him.

But that would mean that Ryker was my brother. Why hadn't anyone told me that? Why hadn't *Ryker* told me that?

The next couple of seconds stretched on in silence, but everything came together in my mind.

Ryker didn't know we were brothers. He was younger. He was born without knowing his father, on an island far from Ruma. But Guildmaster Eventide must've known, and she had said nothing. Why? Probably because... she didn't want me to worry. According to the sybil arcanists, either Ryker or I could be the world serpent arcanist, but since I had been bonded with Luthair, it would've implied he had needed to die. And perhaps Eventide had been worried I wouldn't want to risk my brother's life after having just met him.

Ryker was my brother. That fact finally settled hard in my mind. It explained why we looked so much alike...

"**You understand now, Child of Balaster?**" the serpent asked.

"But..." I whispered, still grappling with my thoughts. "Why me?"

The god-creature drew closer. His forked tongue darted out, and I could see the runes and etching on his flesh—every part of him was deeply soaked in magic. "**Precisely because you** *did* **deny my power,**" the serpent said. "**It is a rare and exceptional individual who has such conviction that they would deny personal gain for the betterment of others.**"

Conviction...

It reminded me of the eleventh step of the Pillar. *Conviction. Without it, virtues are just words.* Was that really what the world serpent cared about the most?

"**Those who lead—those who pass judgment—must have conviction in their actions.**" The serpent exhaled hard, rushing his breath over Ryker and me. "**The time is nigh. Bond with me, Terrakona the Second World Serpent, and become an unparalleled warlord of magic.**"

GOD-ARCANIST

I held up an unsteady hand, my fingers outstretched. An inch before I touched the serpent, I hesitated. Thoughts of Ryker and Luthair ate at my confidence. Ryker was on the edge of death, and I had been counting on him becoming an arcanist to heal himself. And I thought of Luthair because... it felt like a betrayal to bond with another creature so soon after he had passed. Luthair had been there for me, and I had yet to grieve for him, yet here I was... moving on.

Terrakona's forked tongue lashed out around me, drawing me back to reality.

"**Your knightmare had wise words at the end,**" he said. "**Heed them.**"

What had been Luthair's last words? *Future greatness awaits you. Don't allow this moment to hold you back.* Even remembering them hurt, but not in a terrible way. It was a bittersweet ache, like even Luthair had known this was what was going to happen.

"**Your brother may yet live.**"

"He's dying," I said as I held Ryker close.

His eyes fluttered open and shut, but he managed to meet my gaze and force a slight smile. Perhaps if I hurried, Gillie would be able to save him.

"Your brother?" a dark, but quiet voice asked.

The mouse in my pocket stared up at me with glowing red eyes, its nose twitching. When it poked its head out, Terrakona darted his tongue out again, spooking the tiny creature. The mouse ducked back into my clothing and only emerged again once the tongue was back inside the serpent's mouth.

"I wasn't aware it was your brother," the mouse said, its voice deeper than a rodent's voice had any right to be. "But now I understand your distress." It squeaked and clawed at my coat. "I apologize I wasn't here to save you or your eldrin, but this small fragment of me is still capable of helping."

"What do you mean?" I asked, my brow furrowed.

"You saved my life, Volke Savan. I owe you a debt. *I* will save your brother."

I reached into my pocket and scooped the mouse out. It was a fragment of the Mother of Shapeshifters, but what did that mean? How was she going to save Ryker?

Did it really matter?

"If you can save him, please do so," I said. "I... I don't want to lose my brother as fast as I discovered I had one."

"As you wish. Consider your self-sacrifice the ultimate completion of my trial of worth."

Her trial of worth?

The mouse leapt from my palm and landed on Ryker's shoulder. Then the mouse poked at his cheek and made squeaks straight into his ear. Ryker managed to open his eyes long enough to stare at the tiny creature, and when the rodent touched his ear, he shuddered.

Then the mouse glowed a bright white. A mark blossomed across Ryker's forehead at the same time—a strange mark that I had never seen before. Most arcanist's marks were seven-pointed stars with a picture of their eldrin in the center, but Ryker's star had *nine* points, and the "creature" woven around it was nebulous—blob-like and covered in tiny eyes.

When the mouse stopped glowing, it squeaked happily and then dove into Ryker's trouser pocket, alongside the jade runestone.

Had he just become a Mother of Shapeshifters arcanist? If he had, he was probably the one and only who had ever done so. She was a unique creature that wasn't like anything else—a semi-abomination born from one of the first god-creatures who had lived thousands of years ago.

Ryker still appeared injured and worn, but the dragon bite on his shoulder had already begun to slowly stitch itself back together. I breathed easier knowing he would likely live.

When my concerns turned to Evianna, I knew the only solution now was to bond with the serpent and get us all out of here.

I lifted my hand and touched the serpent's square python nose. The god-creature snorted, and I waited for a moment, expecting the bonding sensation to fill my body. But it never came. Instead, I just kept my hand on Terrakona, wondering when something would happen.

The serpent chuckled, and in one sudden movement, he scooped me up with his nose, tossing me onto his face. I dropped Ryker, and he fell to the ground, but I suspected he would be okay. Then Terrakona lifted his head, taking me with him.

Unlike most reptiles, who felt cold to the touch, Terrakona was warm—his inner power and magic radiated outward, filling me with a mild amount of extra energy, even though we had yet to bond.

"Where... are we going?" I asked as Terrakona continued up toward the ceiling.

"We can only bond if we can see the sky," he cryptically replied.

"Wait, what?"

The serpent rushed at the ceiling, and I braced myself to be crushed against the tree, but it never happened. Instead, we "hit" the wood and the tree unraveled, separating enough to allow us to continue upward. Faster and faster—Terrakona traveled through the tree like I used to travel through the shadows, moving with such speed that I almost didn't know how far we had gone.

Up the trunk we went, unimpeded by the tree, moving through the darkness with purpose and haste. I held on to Terrakona's head, his scales smooth and luxurious to the touch.

Then we burst out of the tree. Light shone over us, and I had to blink back the brightness. Steady northern winds rushed our way, adding a hint of chill to the experience. The fresh air did me good. I swallowed it down as my eyesight adjusted.

We were... at the top of the tree. Above the canopy of leaves.

I glanced around in all directions. Below me, a sea of rustling green. Above me, an endless ocean of clouds and azure. The afternoon sun shone with such brilliance that I couldn't lift my gaze too high. After just a few seconds, the intense rays baked my skin.

Terrakona practically glittered under the beauty of the sun. His scales glistened, his eyes shone, and the mane of clear crystals on his head sparkled as rays hit them just right.

The air seemed thinner than I was used to, and my head spun, but we were at least where we could see the sun. "Is this right?" I asked, shielding my eyes. "Is this where you meant to take us?"

"Now, as the oldest source of light as our witness, I intend to intertwine our destinies," Terrakona stated, his tone serious, his voice ancient. **"Once a god-arcanist, you can never be anything else. When *I* die, *you* die, and vice versa. When the apoch dragon comes to usher in oblivion, it will be us whom he hungers for. If you can accept these truths—if you can accept these responsibilities—then accept my bonding."**

A strong—almost overwhelming—sense of magic pierced my chest. When Luthair had become true form, I had sensed an edge of infinity. When Terrakona had offered his bonding, I felt it again, but fleeting, almost within my grasp, but not quite. I accepted, and the sensation disappeared as quickly as it had come.

Then the sun disappeared. It melted into the sky, as if it had never existed, and everything was thrown into utter darkness. Much to my surprise, and mild panic, Terrakona glowed a brilliant jade, and a pillar of light rose up from his body and pierced the heavens above. For a long moment, the only thing I could see was the light that was all around me —a pillar of brilliant light so amazing that ships could probably see it for miles around.

It was exactly like when I had seen the rose-pink pillar of light.

Had that been... someone else bonding with a god-creature?

The pillar of jade light disappeared, and the sun returned to its position in the sky, blanketing the world in life-giving warmth.

To my confusion, my forehead didn't burn with a new mark. Instead, my chest flared in agony a second time. I unbuttoned my shirt, my teeth gritted, my heart pounding. A new arcanist mark appeared across my chest, one stranger than Ryker's. Instead of seven or nine points on a star, mine had twelve. It appeared over my heart, etching itself into my skin so deep, a few droplets of blood trickled down my body. And then a serpent appeared intertwined with the points, but the picture of the massive beast wasn't contained by the star. The serpentine mark wrapped around my shoulder and my ribs, and down my hip—so colossal and all-encompassing, I thought it would cover my entire body. Fortunately, it stopped at those locations.

I took in a deep breath, shocked by the strength it seemed to bring with it. I rested back on Terrakona's massive face, my entire body light and filled with energy. The mark over my heart stung for a moment longer, and I somehow knew it was a chain that linked me to the world serpent.

The crystals on the world serpent's head shimmered and shifted. They were once clear, but now they were black and filled with star-like specks. It reminded me of my knightmare cape—the crystals were visions of the night sky. It gave Terrakona a mane of darkness. Why had that happened?

"Evianna," I muttered, my mind consumed by everyone I still needed to help. "She's injured. Terrakona, I need to get her to the Frith Guild."

"**I will transport the knightmare arcanist to the outside of the lair.**"

"And there were others," I said, almost tripping over my words in my haste to speak. "Devlin, Zelfree, and my sister, Illia. Are they... okay? Please tell me you can help them." I gripped the scales on Terrakona's face, so desperate to hear the answer I almost couldn't wait the half a second for him to speak.

"**They live, Warlord, and they will also be released.**"

When I exhaled, my breath took a million worries with it. Now all that mattered was the safety of the Frith Guild. I had to return to them. I had to speak with Guildmaster Eventide.

"**Your guild is under assault by master arcanists,**" Terrakona said.

"Do you know where they are?"

Terrakona turned his massive head, the slits of his draconic eyes tightening into fine lines. "**Events that happen outside my lair are shrouded in a fog. My magic has not yet matured. I can smell the** bloodlust of a king basilisk, and I feel the sensations of master magicweavers, but there is little else I know for certain, Warlord."

A king basilisk?

Akiva.

Of course he was here. *Of course.* He had been traveling with Rhys, which meant he was after Guildmaster Eventide. What if he killed her before I had a chance to speak with her? I couldn't allow that to happen.

"We have to help them," I said as I glanced out over the sea of leaves. "Can we get down there quickly?"

Terrakona chuckled, and then he dove into the branches of his massive tree, taking me with him at lightning speed.

59

THE EDGE OF WAR

W e exploded out of the branches and sailed downward, straight for the ocean waves. I slipped from Terrakona's face and slid into his crystal mane. I thought the jagged tips of the crystals would cut me, but nothing pierced my skin as I reached for handholds. The crystals had a warm and smooth feel to them, like solid silk. Once secured on Terrakona's head, I glanced up just in time to see us impacting the water.

I didn't have enough time to hold my breath. Panic consumed me as we dove *deep* into the frigid depths, though I thanked the good stars in the sky that hitting the water didn't break me in the process. Interestingly, it didn't even hurt... But the slippery currents threatened to steal my grip on Terrakona's mane, and I didn't know what I could do about it. When I had been a knightmare arcanist, I could have manipulated the shadows to help hold me. What could a world serpent arcanist manipulate?

Terrakona arched himself back toward the surface. He swam at an incredible rate, moving through the liquid as though unimpeded, his scales shimmering, even in the dark waters. I imagined this was what a leviathan felt like—a prince of the ocean, free under the surface to move in any direction he deemed interesting.

My lungs burned. Every fiber of my body wanted to inhale.

I feared I'd never make it to the surface, but to my shock, we shattered through the waves and straight into the afternoon air, water gushing up with our arrival, the tides altered by Terrakona's massive serpentine body.

I shook my head, saltwater sloshing from my hair. To my surprise, Gentel wasn't far from us, and I was amused by my height. I had never seen the atlas turtle from above. She seemed... *smaller* than I remembered. And when she turned her head to look at us, I was entertained by how wide her eyes became.

The king basilisk wasn't difficult to find, either. King basilisks were giant dragon-sized reptiles with six legs, giant alligator faces, and four deadly eyes that could turn an individual to stone if they ever met the monster's gaze. Their scales were gray, and their flesh-rending claws were without rival.

Akiva's king basilisk—his name was Nyre—stood on the edge of the massive tree's root, his six legs clinging to the twisted limb, his claws digging in deep. He waited patiently, staring at arcanists fighting near the trunk of the tree. Plague-ridden tengu from the sky and plague-ridden water nymphs from the ocean were clawing their way to the arcanists of the Frith Guild. If any of them glanced in Nyre's direction, they would be killed.

The *Black Throne* and its small team of supporting ships were nearby, each one filled with its crew and carrying more Sky Legionnaires and unicorn arcanists of the Knights Draconic. Some of the ships had their cannons armed and ready, and I could see the blasts in the tree's trunk from the heavy artillery.

The entire time I had been in the tree, fighting my way to the bottom, everyone else had been waging a war against the Second Ascension and the soldiers of the Argo Empire.

I suspected Nyre would've attacked the group outright if the terrain had allowed it, but the tree roots and trunk weren't ideal for a flightless mystical creature. Nyre was too large and heavy—curse the abyssal hells, he was the size of a two-story house!—and he had the mobility of a pregnant hippo.

But that wasn't the case for his arcanist, Akiva.

My heart beat at irregular intervals, which meant Akiva had created his requiem aura. He was gaining speed and strength with each death in the nearby area, be it from an arcanist or a mystical creature. Every plague-ridden monster that fell was just fuel for his destructive powers.

I spotted him at the same time I noticed Guildmaster Eventide. They were locked in a duel, fighting at the edge of a root. Eventide's barriers had a white shimmer when evoked or touched, and the flashes of her magic were enough to draw my eye. Akiva dashed for her, throwing his deadly king basilisk venom in every direction, coating the ground, and fought with a relentless vigor I had come to associate with him.

But before I could join the fray, everyone stopped to stare.

Everyone.

Nyre turned his four eyes toward Terrakona and me. So did the Frith Guild arcanists. So did the Sky Legionnaires and Knights Draconic. Even Guildmaster Eventide and Akiva stopped their death match to give Terrakona their full attention. The silence that followed was only broken by the occasional involuntary laughs of mystical creatures touched by the arcane plague.

"Stop them," I said, motioning to the Argo Empire soldiers. "And... and stop the king basilisk."

I wasn't entirely sure of the world serpent's capabilities. I didn't know what to specifically ask Terrakona to do in this situation—so I just hoped he would have a solution or know his own powers well enough that he could handle this alone.

Terrakona turned toward Nyre. I averted my gaze, fearful I could still be turned to stone if I stared at the king basilisk.

In one brutal swing of his tail, Terrakona smashed the root of the tree and struck Nyre in the side. The basilisk managed to slash at the serpent's tail, and his claws were deadly enough—magically powerful enough—to pierce the world serpent's scales and draw blood, but only barely. Terrakona knocked the massive beast into the ocean, despite his injury, and splinters of wood went everywhere, raining into the waves like a storm of wood.

Nyre yelled as he tumbled into the water, but king basilisks were island-dwelling mystical creatures. He swam through the water with grace and without fear, his crocodile-like face a freight to behold. I kept my attention on his back, rather than his eyes, and I feared Terrakona might not be able to handle a fully grown mystical creature, given that he was still young and immature.

Nyre lunged from the water and snapped at Terrakona. I held on to the serpent's mane as Terrakona lashed around, dodging the attack. With surprising speed, and the movements of a viper, Terrakona snapped back, striking Nyre on the shoulder. The king basilisk had been waiting for it. He whipped his long maw back and bit down on Terrakona, his jaw locking into place.

I didn't know what I could do with my magic. Evocation, manipulation, augmentation—even my natural abilities and auras were all a mystery I couldn't rely on in this dire moment of confrontation. Instead, I pulled Retribution from its scabbard and gulped down a deep breath.

Terrakona thrashed through the ocean and then slammed Nyre against the tree. Both creatures were gigantic, and when they hit things, the *world* felt it. The whole tree shook, the other arcanists had to find their footing, and the rumble from the movement send tremors throughout the area.

The world serpent couldn't seem to dislodge of the king basilisk, and I knew I had to intervene. With my sword in hand, I waited for a moment of relative stillness before leaping off Terrakona's mane and throwing myself toward the basilisk. When I got close, I closed my eyes and then slashed wide. My blade sliced through magic as if air, so when I hit Nyre, I barely felt it. I snuck a peek, saw the blood gushing from Nyre's face, and then tumbled off the massive creatures and into the ocean.

Fortunately, my attack had been enough. Nyre loosened his hold on Terrakona, and that was all my eldrin needed. He whipped his tail around and struck Nyre across two of his four eyes, leaving behind a massive gash. Then Terrakona bit Nyre in the side, his fangs so long and deadly they looked like they went straight into the king basilisk's lungs.

The basilisk slashed with his six claws, injuring Terrakona, though it was a struggle.

I swam through the saltwater, my breathing labored, but I managed to reach my eldrin without much difficulty. Then Rhys appeared on Nyre's back—teleporting with rizzel magic, even though I didn't see a rizzel around. How was he doing that?

With a smirk and a quick twist of his wrist, Rhys and Nyre vanished in a puff of glitter and a pop of air. The giant beast just *disappeared*, and it took me a moment to fully grasp the power of Rhys's teleportation.

Terrakona glanced at me with his blue and red eyes, and then lowered his head so I could climb back to the mane. I positioned myself among the black crystals, thankful he hadn't sustained too many wounds.

"Are you okay?" I asked.

"**Yes, Warlord,**" Terrakona replied. "**That ancient breed of basilisk can be deadly, but we were fortunate he was already weak.**"

King basilisks had the strength of dragons, and since Nyre was full grown, it made sense that his magic would potentially harm a hatchling god-creature. Still—I felt useless, considering I hadn't yet trained with my magic. I should've helped Terrakona more in the battle. I should've been there for him.

Something poked me in the leg, and I glanced down to see *plants* growing out from between Terrakona's scales. They were vines with thorns and other green, leafy vegetation I was unfamiliar with. When I glanced backward and observed most of Terrakona's body, I realized that two trees had sprouted from his back, creating a silhouette of garden-like wings. The weeping-willow-style foliage hung long and brilliant in color.

What was happening?

I watched in awe as the vines from Terrakona slammed into the roots of the tree, connecting him with his birthplace, and then a moment later, the same vines jutted out at different locations from the bark and wood.

The thorny vines lashed out at the nearby enemies, grabbing them, slashing them, and then ultimately pulling them into the tree, just as Devlin and the others had been consumed during our trek. The tree gobbled them up—their screams and laughter were instantly cut off the more the wood twisted around them, locking them away in a cage of magic so powerful, they could never hope to escape.

This was the birthplace of the world serpent—Terrakona had utter dominion over this tree and territory. Anyone fighting him here would surely fail, even if his magic hadn't yet fully matured.

The plague-ridden monsters were easy to draw in. The soldiers of the Argo Empire fought against the restraints but were ultimately no match for the hundreds of vines that pursued them—and finally, when the vines lunged for Akiva, he leapt into the ocean.

"He can't be allowed to escape," I said. *Not this time.*

Terrakona exhaled and then lowered himself into the waters. The currents shifted with his movements, and I wondered if the world serpent had the power to control the oceans themselves. Was he preventing Akiva from getting anywhere? Did the assassin even know what he was up against?

When we swam forward, it was with such grace that the ocean was barely disturbed. The canopy kept the area in a dark gloom, but the world serpent had a glow of magic about him that kept things slightly illuminated. The vines of his body broke away without effort and then Terrakona dove beneath the surface. I held my breath, and in the next instant, he dashed forward and rushed at a tiny dot darting through the depths.

Akiva.

It didn't take long for Terrakona to maneuver his massive body around the king basilisk arcanist. Once surrounded, Akiva tried to fill the water with his venom, but it was too late. Terrakona slammed him with his tail and then wrapped him like a python wraps its prey. I thought Akiva would be squished instantly—Terrakona was so massive—but I had forgotten about Akiva's requiem aura. He had survived, even though he was being crushed by the serpentine muscles of the world serpent, a feat that impressed me, despite my hatred for the man.

Instead of killing Akiva by slowly squeezing the life from him, Terrakona returned to the surface. I gasped for air once above the waves, and I held on to his crystal mane, still in awe of the events. But then Terrakona cried out, his screech both ancient and reptilian. Akiva had slashed Terrakona with an apoch dragon sword, the black sword cutting through the world serpent's scales with relative ease.

Akiva then *threw* the sword at *me*. His strength and accuracy shocked me—the blade was handled with such finesse that it would've gone straight through my skull had I not been paying attention. Fortunately, I brought my own blade up in time to defect the attack, the clang of our weapons mixing with the crash of waves and the chores of giant rustling leaves.

With a curse on his breath, Akiva shot me a glare, but I didn't meet his gaze either. King basilisk arcanists had an arsenal of deadly powers, and I didn't want to risk being turned to stone.

When Terrakona went to hit him with his tail, Rhys appeared again, this time in the water. He teleported himself and Akiva away, his laughter the only thing left behind.

Why? Why couldn't we stop them from escaping? How did Rhys even get out of the tree? My building frustration threatened to steal my rationality.

I shook the thoughts from my head and turned my attention to the Frith Guild.

Guildmaster Eventide surveyed the area with a quick glance and then turned her attention up to me on the world serpent. Her graying hair, pulled back in a braid, fluttered in the ocean winds, but it was her calm and pensive expression that struck me the most. I wondered... had she been stalling for time, just waiting for the world serpent arcanist to arrive and end the conflict?

It occurred to me then—perhaps Eventide had plans that ran deeper than I had ever suspected.

I walked the hall of the guild manor house as though dreaming. My body didn't feel like my own, but I knew I wasn't sleeping. It was the magic from the world serpent. With each hour that had passed since my bonding, I felt different. I had grown—*changed*—and the the more time passed, the more irreversible our bond was becoming. My arcanist mark, the one over my heart, had weight to it. Occasionally, I ran my hand over the etching in my flesh, still surprised by its presence.

The arcanist mark on my forehead was still present, just faint. It would never fully disappear, but I didn't mind. I wanted the reminder— the proof that Luthair and I had once been a team to rival even the most legendary of arcanists—even though it still hurt to think of life without him.

We were on our way back to the city-state of Millatin, but the guildmaster had said we couldn't stay long. The moment the arcanists of the world discovered King Rishan's and Councilor Chandra's death, there would be an uproar... and if anyone figured out it was *me* who had helped kill them, there could be a war on our hands.

The night was settling over the ocean, but twilight refused to fade. The purples and oranges of the sunset created a watercolor painting of color throughout the guild house. I enjoyed it as I strode through the building, my mind still on important issues of grieving, magic, and destiny.

As I neared the infirmary, I spotted Guildmaster Eventide and the Grand Apothecary, Gillie, in the hall. They turned to me with bright smiles, but it was Eventide's who faded first.

Gillie held her arms wide and embraced me. "Oh, I knew you were special, but I never would've guessed something like *this* would happen to you, my darling." She squeezed tightly, and I patted her back, still in a daze.

"Thank you?" I muttered.

When she released me, she continued to smile. "I need to gather some materials for an ointment to help with the dragon fire burns, so don't you go running off and getting injured any time soon, understand me?"

I nodded.

Gillie playfully smacked my shoulder and then hustled down the hall, her yellow robes fluttering behind her and complementing the sunset well.

Once she had gone, it was just me and Guildmaster Eventide. No one else. I met her gaze, curious as to what she would say to me, but for a long while, there was only silence. I crossed my arms, and a slight hint of pain reminded me of the mark on my chest. I pushed it from my thoughts to give Eventide my full attention.

The dying of the sunlight cast harsh shadows.

Although I was no longer a knightmare arcanist, I still welcomed the darkness. It felt comforting. Like an old friend.

"I'm glad you managed to reach the god-creature before the Second Ascension," Eventide stated, her tone reserved. "And I'm sorry about Luthair. It's a tragedy, and we'll show the proper respects for him once we reach the mainland."

"Thank you," I said. But I couldn't bite back all my questions and concerns. Instead of playing coy, I met her gaze straight on. "You knew this was a possibility, though. And you never told me."

She ran a hand over her face, though she never glanced away from me. "I was aware that Ryker was your brother, yes. And that the sybil arcanists could be referring to you rather than him."

"Why keep it from me?"

"I wasn't sure how you'd handle the information, and with so little time on my hands, I couldn't risk disaster." Eventide sighed, and for the first time in a long while, she seemed tired. More so than normal—the type of tired that only comes from a lifetime of adventure and hardship. "I hope you'll forgive me, Volke, but there are certain things I never want to leave to chance. I worried you wouldn't accompany Ryker if you knew there was a possibility that your eldrin would need to die in order for you to bond with the world serpent. I had hoped Ryker would just be the perfect candidate. I had seen you with Luthair, and I knew what he meant to you."

Her words sent a sharp lance of pain through my heart, but it was dulled by memories of Luthair. He wouldn't want me to grieve.

"I hope that, in the future, you'll understand my level of conviction for the cause," I said. "I won't make selfish decisions when it comes to this. I want... a future free of strife more than anything."

"We're on the edge of war," Eventide stated, blunt and cold. "You're not the only god-arcanist. You're not even the first, despite the fact that the world serpent was born before all others."

"I... I know."

The memory of the rose-colored pillar of light stuck out in my mind. Was that the only other god-arcanist or were there more?

"The Autarch specifically wanted the world serpent so that he could unite nations," Eventide said, her tone shifting to something grim. "He made agreements. You've single-handedly foiled those, and the repercussions will cause unrest."

What could I say to that? I simply nodded.

Eventide placed a hand on her hip and sighed a second time, this one filled more with determination and less with fatigue. "Every monarch and ruler will come wanting your power for their own. There might come a time you want to leave the Frith Guild. I hope in those moments, you'll allow me to offer you council."

The way she spoke surprised me. Almost like she was imploring a superior to take certain actions. This wasn't a speech between a guildmaster and a journeyman...

"I want to remain with the Frith Guild," I said.

"It might not be possible," Eventide stated.

"Even if it's what I want?"

She held her breath for a moment and then genuinely smiled. "Well, I guess we'll have to see when the time comes. Perhaps we can pull off what the Autarch couldn't—an alliance between nations. Only instead of *world domination* as a goal, it'll be a defensive alliance against the scourge of the Second Ascension."

"Do you think *they* have the other god-creature?" I asked.

Eventide nodded. "Without a doubt. They're the only others with runestones."

Her blatant statement of facts shook me. They *were* the only other ones with runestones. Which meant... they were going to meet us in battle with their own god-arcanists.

I gripped at my guild pendant, my hand and determination steady. "No matter what," I muttered. "I won't let them win."

Eventide replied with a curt nod. "Then I'm glad you were ultimately the world serpent arcanist, Volke. Because that's the exact attitude we need in these troubled times. It's been centuries since a full-blown war rocked the lands, and I suspect this one coming will put all the legends to shame."

60

MUCH NEEDED REST

I entered the infirmary with a mountain of problems on my mind. But those all disappeared the moment I saw everyone on their cots.

Captain Devlin, Master Zelfree, Illia, Ryker, and Evianna were all awake and turned to face me the moment I entered the room. After all the pain we had been through—both physical and emotional—it almost felt strange to feel a sensation *other* than agony. Relief and elation swelled in me, ending all doubt I'd had just moments prior. I didn't know whom to run to first, so I just stepped farther into the room, my chest tight, my breathing slow.

Adelgis slid from a chair next to one of the beds, making himself known. I snapped my attention to him, both happy and startled by his shadow-like presence.

"Volke," he said, earnest shock in his voice. "I... didn't know you were close."

I walked straight over to him and—probably overwhelmed with emotions—pulled him into a tight embrace. He coughed and let out a weak gasp, but otherwise allowed it to happen. When I let go, he stared at me as though seeing a ghost.

"Are you okay?" I asked. "I was worried. I was worried about everyone."

"I'm... fine," Adelgis replied. "Are *you* okay?"

"Of course. Why wouldn't I be?"

"I can't hear your thoughts."

His statement took me by surprise. Was it because of my new magic? Or was he finally starting to master his abilities? "That's a good thing, right?" I asked.

Adelgis slowly nodded. "I suppose..." But then he swallowed hard and narrowed his eyes. With his telepathy, he said, *"Volke, I'm certain the other god-arcanist—the one who bonded before you—is none other than my father. Please be careful. My father... he's..."*

"I know," I said aloud.

Theasin Venrover wasn't a kind or gentle man. If he really had bonded with a god-creature, he would use his powers however he saw fit, regardless of what it meant for others.

"And he'll have the backing of the Second Ascension. I... I heard their voices and plans when we fought at the tree, Volke. You don't understand what they have planned. I didn't realize whom they had on their side until I spoke with Guildmaster Eventide about the matter."

Which explained why she was so worried about war and the inevitable fallout of my bonding...

I clenched my jaw as the pieces of the puzzle fell into place.

"We can talk about it later," I whispered. Then I forced a smile. "When we have to deal with this mess. Right now, I need to make sure everyone is safe."

Adelgis nodded. "Of course. Whenever you're ready to hear, I'll tell you. I'm with you until the end, Volke Savan."

I patted him on the shoulder and went straight for Captain Devlin. He wore a simple tunic, and his long, wavy hair wasn't held back with a bandana or cap, so it hung disheveled to his shoulders, giving him a vagabond-like appearance. The rest of him was covered by his blanket, but given his restless posture, I figured he was ready to leave.

I didn't care. I went straight to his side and then pulled him into a tight embrace, much to his obvious shock and incredulity.

"What is this, lad?" he barked. "I don't need your pity!"

"I thought you had died," I said, unable to articulate any further feelings on the matter.

It seemed to be enough. Although he remained tense, Devlin didn't fight me. He held his tongue until I broke away and then he frowned. "Is this how all you guild arcanists are? Touchy-feely? Hm?"

I left his side and then went for Zelfree.

His mimic sat on the bed with him, curled into a tight little ball like only a cat could. Her extra-long tail twitched whenever Zelfree shifted around.

He wore a dark button-up shirt and a scarf around his neck. The stubble on his chin looked a few days old, and I wondered if he had decided to grow it out. His expression reminded me of a haggard man on the verge of returning to the drink, but the light in his eyes told me he had been through too much in his life to return to any destructive vices.

When I got close, Zelfree sneered. "*Don't*."

But I ignored him.

"Dammit," Zelfree said through gritted teeth as I held him close. "What's wrong with you? There's nothing to worry about."

I didn't reply. I held him for a long while, thankful I hadn't failed him in that moment of dire need. Zelfree had been my mentor for three years, and I couldn't stand the thought of watching him die on the very first *real* assignment we had undertaken together.

He must have sensed my thoughts on the matter because he exhaled and patted my shoulder. "I sometimes forget you're young. Don't fret so much. Scarier things have come for my life and failed. I wasn't about to let a sentient tree do me in."

"I'll try not to fret," I muttered as I let him go. "I'm just glad we made it through this one."

Zelfree nodded. "Thanks to Vethica, it seems we'll all get through this without the plague, too."

I nodded and then turned my attention to Illia.

She met my gaze with a smile, like she already knew what was coming. She sat at the edge of her bed, dressed in a tunic and trousers, Nicholin in her lap. He stared at me with bright blue eyes, the whiskers on his nose twitching.

I strode over and gave her a hug before either of us could say anything. How many times would I almost lose her? The number felt too high. Too much. But I consoled myself with the fact that no matter how dark it got, we both always made it through. We'd be doing this until we had both seen the world and everything beyond.

"It wasn't *that* scary," Nicholin said. He pawed at me, trying to squeeze between Illia and me—and failing. "The tree just held us in a dark place, that's all. It wasn't like we were in any real danger."

"Still," I muttered into Illia's shoulder. "I was worried."

"So was I," she whispered. "Volke—you're the type of person who would give his life for the mission, and... that's all I could think while I was trapped."

"I came back."

Illia smiled as she broke our embrace. Then she ran a hand over her eye patch, her fingers trembling. "So did I." Before I walked away, she stared at my broken arcanist mark and then frowned. "Don't you... have a mark?"

I unbuttoned my shirt enough to show the spot on my chest—right above the heart—that held my twelve-pointed star. Illia examined it with her one good eye, but then she reached out with a hesitant hand and grazed the lines of the design.

"It's beyond myth," she muttered.

I rebuttoned my shirt, uncertain of what to say.

Illia smirked. "I can't wait to see the look on the faces of the dread pirates who cross our path now, Volke. The seas will never be the same."

I chuckled as I imagined running across Calisto. But at the same time, anger stewed in my system. Last I heard, he had been the one to take Theasin to the god-creature. What if *he* had bonded with a beast? The entire world would suffer at his hands.

"Are you okay?" Illia asked.

I nodded. "Don't worry."

With a smile, she said, "I'll try."

Content that she was okay, I offered a smile before glancing over at my brother, Ryker.

He sat on his bed with pillows propped up against the headboard. His black hair, unruly from root to tip, was a dead giveaway to our relation. How had I not seen it before? He was just as tall, had my same complexion—all the signs were there. I had just never made any connections.

Ryker sat a little straighter as I walked over. His odd arcanist mark intrigued me, even when the only lights in the infirmary were now the six lanterns scattered throughout the infirmary. The Mother of Shapeshifters was a bizarre mystical creature, and I wondered what Ryker would end up doing to learn his newfound magics.

He wore a white button-up shirt and a black bandana around his neck. Sitting on his shoulder, in plain view, was the little mouse that had once lived in my pocket. Its red eyes watched me as I neared, but I ignored it in favor of hugging my brother.

Ryker returned my embrace, his fingers twisting into my shirt as he tightened his grip.

"Volke," he muttered. "I had no idea... we were family."

"It's okay," I said with a chuckle. "Neither did I."

"I should've told you about the exact wording of the sybil arcanists' prediction."

"It doesn't matter now. It's over."

Ryker held me at arm's length, his dark eyes searching mine. "You were so brave at the end. I... I was ready to give up. But you kept going. No matter what."

I rubbed at the back of my neck and shrugged. "It's fine. I'm sure, if you had been in my situation, you would've done the same."

He shook his head, a wary smile on his face. "Well, that makes one of us. I'm not so sure I would've had the fortitude. I'm just... I'm glad you were there, Volke. I'm glad *you* are the world serpent arcanist."

It still felt strange to hear. *I* was the world serpent arcanist? Impossible. But... here we were.

"You should come speak with Mother at some point," Ryker muttered, drawing me back to the present. "I think she'd like to see you."

"And you should probably speak to our father," I said, half-laughing. "He's a lot closer than you think."

Ryker nodded. "I look forward to it."

It was a shame Atty wasn't here, since I wanted to speak with her, but I knew I'd have time in the future to sort everything out. The last person in the infirmary I needed to speak with was the one sitting on a bed near the far window. Evianna watched me with her bluish-purple eyes, her gaze never wavering, her focus on me and me alone. I couldn't help but smile when I saw her, and my breath caught in my throat as I walked over.

Evianna's white hair wasn't braided together. It hung straight and past her shoulders, and I admired the ivory quality. Although it was evening and the sun no longer offered any rays of light through the window, I could see her perfectly. She held out a hand as I neared, and I took it, surprised by her tight grip on my knuckles.

"I have something for you," she said.

Evianna reached under her blanket and withdrew my star-lined cape from the folds of the bed. The liquid-darkness of Luthair's armor shone on one side, while the night sky twinkled on the other. Although it had once been covered in Evianna's blood, it was now clean and pristine, and I wondered if the garment itself had done that.

I took the cape and then slung it over my shoulders. It was wide enough that it fit together in front, like a cloak, and it was also long enough to go all the way to the floor. Luthair had told me that when knightmares died, they left behind the cape—the most powerful piece of their bodies—and I wondered if a small piece of him was still retained in the shadow fabric. I rubbed at the edge, enjoying the cold, silky sensations.

"You could make it into a trinket," Evianna said. "To remember Luthair for all time."

"Or an artifact," I said, my mind wandering. What could world serpent magic create when mixed with a fragment of a knightmare? "I don't want the cape to break to the Second Ascension's decay dust."

She nodded. "Okay." Then she held her blankets tight and stared up at me with a furrowed brow. "Volke... Will you still be my mentor?"

I lifted an eyebrow. "You still want me? Even though I'm basically back to being an apprentice arcanist?"

"You were the only one I know to have a true form knightmare. And I need someone to help me—especially if the Argo Empire is going to get involved in all this fighting."

With my throat tight, I gently pulled Evianna into an embrace. She was different from the others. Our fates seemed more closely intertwined —ever since I had first saved her from the river. I didn't want her to face any problems alone. I didn't want her to ever think I wouldn't be there for her. I didn't want to face any of my hardships without her as well.

"I'll be here for you," I said as I held Evianna close. "As your mentor and more."

She buried her face in my shoulder. "Thank you."

THANK YOU SO MUCH FOR READING!

Please consider leaving a review—any and all feedback is much appreciated!

But what will Volke do as the world serpent arcanist?

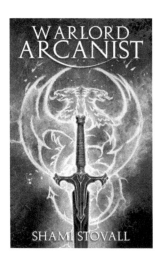

To find out more about Shami Stovall and the Frith Chronicles, take a look at her website:

THANK YOU SO MUCH FOR READING!

https://sastovallauthor.com/newsletter/

ABOUT THE AUTHOR

Shami Stovall is a multi-award-winning author of fantasy and science fiction, with several best-selling novels under her belt. Before that, she taught history and criminal law at the college level, and loved every second. When she's not reading fascinating articles and books about ancient China or the Byzantine Empire, Stovall can be found playing way too many video games, especially RPGs and tactics simulators.

If you want to contact her, you can do so at the following locations:

Website: https://sastovallauthor.com
Twitter: @GameOverStation
Facebook: www.facebook.com/SAStovall
Email: s.adelle.s@gmail.com